The entire class sat in silence, listening to what they knew would happen just like the Ranger Instructor was telling them.

"Rangers, you will become more aware of the need to maintain yourselves and your equipment in top condition during the extended operations you will endure with very limited support. If you get snake bit or hurt, it may be a while before we get to you. Some time back, a Ranger got lost from his patrol. We searched for him for three days."

The RI paused, staring hard at the students. "Then we found him dead in a ravine after having been torn apart by a pack of wild dogs."

The class murmured. A prickly sensation crawled on the back of Christopher's neck. He turned around and saw Grey smiling in the rear.

"Those things happen sometimes. You damn well better watch out for your Ranger buddy. If you thought your piddly two-day patrol back at Benning was tough, wait until you're up in the mountains and you've been out of water for the last twelve hours and haven't had any f   twenty-four. And if the   re not going to snivel   how hungry, tired,   hink you are, you *wil*

"I have one m   fore I turn you over to my instruc   e are people up in these mountains. I don't care if they're backpackers, climbers, hunters, or whatever . . . you stay away from them. Is that clear?"

"Clear, Sergeant!" came the reply.

NIGHT OF THE RANGER

MARK D. HARRELL

LYNX BOOKS
New York

This book is dedicated

*To those who wear the Coveted Black and Gold
but who aren't mere tab wearers
and to those who tried but didn't make it.*

*To those who know what it's like to hump and sweat and
sacrifice
and help out their buddies in times of need
when things were pretty desperate.*

*And finally,
to those who have served and those still driving on
with or without the recognition
they deserve.*

NIGHT OF THE RANGER

ISBN: 1-55802-191-4

First Printing/October 1988

This book is published by Lynx Books, a division of Lynx Communications, Inc., 41 Madison Avenue, New York, New York, 10010. The name "Lynx" together with the logotype consisting of a stylized head of a lynx is a trademark of Lynx Communications, Inc.

Printed in the United States of America

0 9 8 7 6 5 4 3 2 1

Many thanks to the 1st of the 9th club; all the Manchus who wound up together at Bragg in '83 and relived our experiences with me: Rudy, Tom, Mike, Bill, and Dave.

A special thanks to Bob, a highly qualified Special Forces Medic, who helped me get started.

Thank you, Mom, Dad and Billy for setting the example.

Thanks to Mike, Lou, Judy and Naomi for giving it all a chance.

And thanks to Peter Miller, for his energy, faith, and his astounding ability to make things happen.

PROLOGUE

"Lookit the nigger run."

"Ready to sic ol' Rufus and Jeff on 'im?"

The first man who had spoken shifted his wad of Red Man from his left cheek to his right and spat out a stream of tobacco juice in the direction of a fleeing figure who by now had nearly crossed the mountain meadow where the chase had begun.

"Nope."

"C'mon. Jerry. How long you gonna wait?"

"About another minute. Kinda looks like that running nigger target we got back at the base camp, don't he?"

The two men guffawed. Jerry got down on one knee next to two dogs he had tied to an old oak stump and stroked them lovingly.

"Like my dogs, Charley?"

"Shit," Charley snorted. "Ain't never seen no pit bulls track before."

Charley unslung his Mini-14 and sighted his scope

on the running black man who had nearly reached the tree line one hundred meters away. Jerry untethered his dogs, holding their leash tightly with one hand. Then he hefted his twelve-gauge pump in the other hand and stood up. The dogs, yelping mad and snapping in anticipation, strained against their master's grip, begging for the chase.

Jerry smiled gleefully at his partner, revealing a crooked row of nicotine-stained teeth.

"Oh, they can track all right. Let's go."

SweetJesuspleasedon'tleavemenowkeepmegoingpleasegoddon'tletthemgetme. . . .

Second Lieutenant Clayborne Davis dashed through the tree line more scared than he had ever been in his entire life. Luckily, the mountain forests of northern Georgia were not as thick as the woods and swamps back at Fort Benning, so one could at least run if he had to.

He didn't see the tree root sticking several inches above the ground. He fell hard, smacking his face in the dirt, and it stunned him. Getting up, Davis wiped his bloody nose on the sleeve of his jungle fatigues and took off again, this time downhill.

He remembered the positioning of the afternoon sun and the shadows it created on the tree line he had just entered. He decided he was going southeast, and if he could just keep going, he would eventually hit a hardballer, and then he could flag someone down. Just maybe.

Davis rocketed down the mountainside.

Ten hours earlier, at daybreak, Ranger Davis thought he had been lost as hell as he looked for his patrol, and had stumbled upon an encampment that he thought was the objective they were supposed to hit the night before. Two men had burst out from underneath their camouflaged netting and had beaten him senseless.

Davis couldn't remember how long he had been out, but when he woke up, the sun had already climbed high in the sky and he had been hogtied. His pack was gone, along with his M16, compass . . . food and water. His stomach churned and clamored for food, just one C-ration.

He took in his surroundings. There was concertina wire. Civilians in uniform holding M16s and Kalashnikov assault rifles. Machine guns. Claymore mines surrounding the perimeter of a base camp.

He was scared. No. Petrified.

A huge man whom Davis thought resembled one of his instructors back at Benning interrogated him (*Nigger, do you know just where in hell you are? Pick up a pine needle, Ranger, haaa-ha-ha.*). Then he told Jerry and Charley to get rid of him. They'd kicked and punched him a few more times and took him away from their camp to the meadow and told him to beat it. Of course, he *knew* what they planned to do or else they wouldn't have brought their rifles and the dogs.

So he ran, and he ran like hell.

Davis heard the dogs yelping from back up the hill no more than two hundred meters behind him, dead on his scent. He bounded over felled trees and skirted wait-a-minute vines, racing faster downhill. The woods grew dense. He entered a ravine. *Where there is a ravine, there's water*, he thought. *Where there's water, the scent can be lost.*

But the dogs kept getting louder.

Davis tripped again, this time slamming face down

into a sawed-off stump that cut his face and forehead to shreds, making him bleed into his eyes. Disoriented, he staggered to his feet and fell again, this time rolling fifty feet down the steep mountainside and crashing against the broad trunk of a hickory tree. His knee exploded.

He lay there, screaming. His right shinbone protruded through his jungle fatigues, the gleaming white of it grating and cutting through the bloody mess of his leg. The barking grew louder. More menacing. Panicky, Davis crawled downhill, grasping handfuls of the pine straw carpeting the mountainside.

Finally, knowing it was over, Davis turned around, hearing their final predatory growls. Paralyzed in terror, he stared at them through the red sticky haze in his eyes. His lips drew back in a scream.

The dogs lunged for his throat, their huge, powerful jaws opened like pairs of hinged triangles lined with muscles and razors—

CHAPTER

·ONE·

Recognizing that I volunteered as a Ranger, fully knowing the hazards of my chosen profession, I will always endeavor to uphold the prestige, honor, and "esprit de corps" of my Ranger Battalion.

Ranger School's a total bitch.

Sharp white gravel bit into Dan Levy's back and crawled into his shorts as he waved his bare arms and legs back and forth in the air, trying his damnedest to be motivated. *Zero three-thirty in the morning comes pretty fucking early when you don't get to sleep until midnight,* he thought.

"I'm a dying cockroach, I'm a dying cockroach, you prick!" Levy yelled through his cracked, ruined voice. *Two more months until course completion,* he thought. He tried to think of the girl he'd been dating in Columbus throughout the infantry officers basic course, but couldn't even remember what she looked like.

A massive, crew-cutted sergeant swaggered toward Levy, his practiced ears hearing what the Ranger student had shouted through the din created by a whole platoon of volunteers attempting the Army's toughest leadership course. He stood over Levy with his hands on his hips. Levy thought he would smash his face in with his cleated jungle boot.

"What'd you say, Ranger?"

"I'm a dying cockroach, Sergeant Grey!" Levy yelled with more vigor, watching the glower harden on the Ranger instructor's face.

The Ranger instructor—RI for short—kicked a shower of compound gravel on Levy, amused at the squirming student he just knew had to be a Second Lieutenant fresh out of the infantry officers basic course. They all looked the same: young, fresh-faced—straight out of college. This Ranger was no different, maybe a little skinnier than most. Then he noticed something. The Ranger was not wearing a shirt, but that wasn't why the hackles on the back of his neck crawled; the rest of the men in his platoon were only half dressed as well. It was the six-pointed star fastened to a gold chain around Levy's neck.

"I'm a dying cockroach, Sergeant," Levy repeated. "Rangers lead the way!"

"That you are, and they do, Ranger."

The RI bent at the waist and looked closely at Levy, as if he were examining a bug.

"You're an officer, aren't you?" he said, grinning in contempt. They locked eyes, and the grin vanished. "Never mind that, worm-dirt. Hell, you're all the same rank here. Get those toothpick arms and legs up in the air and start waving them around like you got a purpose in life."

"Yes, Sergeant . . . Rangers lead the way!"

"And get rid of the fucking necklace." The RI lumbered off, stalking new game. Minutes dragged on into hours, magnified by the sheer misery of cramps and pulled muscles. Levy knew he had to play the game for an eternity of fifty-eight days, whether humping a seventy-pound rucksack all day and night, and then all day again in the mountains with no rest, or by simply grunting through a humiliating and uncomfortable dying-cockroach position.

The last thing in the world Levy wanted to do was call attention to himself, especially now, when the RIs were busy conducting morning wake-up call. He and the rest of his thirty-five-man platoon of Ranger students had been sound asleep in the old World War II barracks that was to be their home for the next seven days of city phase. Then, just ten lousy minutes ago, the RIs burst their reverie, screaming obscenities and banging on trash cans. They were told they had one minute to get dressed and be outside in the dying-cockroach position, or else there would be hell to pay. Three minutes later, when the last man locked the barracks door and leapt into the company formation, hordes of indignant RIs swooped down on them, meting out the U.S. Army Ranger School's special brand of stress designed to eliminate those who thought they could take it. For now, however, Dan Levy did not care to contemplate philosophies of leadership through stress. He just wanted to get the dying-cockroach business over with.

"Get up and quit sniveling, Rangers. *Move!*"

Levy stumbled to his feet with the rest of the haggard platoon. He knew what was coming next from Sergeant Grey.

"That's not fast enough, Rangers," the RI snarled. "You pukes move like molasses in January. Get down!" Everyone scrambled to assume the push-up position—the front-leaning rest. "Get up! Down . . .

up! Down . . . stay there." Grey strutted back and forth between the prostrate ranks of straining triceps and locomotive lungs, relishing his favorite moment of the day.

"The way you pretty boys move makes me think you don't want to be here," he lectured. "Christ, if my little two-year-old daughter was here, I swear to God she'd tell me you all look like a bunch of Peter Pan fairies."

Levy looked up at Grey, feeling the sweat pour from his forehead into his eyes, burning them. The intimidating RI looked even bigger when he was mad, with two purplish veins sticking out on both sides of his forehead that contrasted sharply with his blond, crew-cut hair. Heavily starched camouflaged fatigues and mirror-polished jump boots accented his weightlifter's physique. On top of his head rested a carefully formed and starched patrolling cap with the highly coveted black-and-gold Ranger tab sewn above his rank.

Any RI over five feet tall looked menacing enough to Ranger students throughout the course, but Sergeant Grey was feared above all else. He made the decisions about who continued through phase one at Fort Benning, phase two in the mountains at Dahlonega, Georgia, and phase three in the swamps of Florida. He was the Ranger class's master and dictator, the head RI. Officially, Grey was the class TAC—training assistance cadre—a duty rotated through all senior RIs assigned to the Ranger department.

After the two and one half months of training, only half of the original students graduated and moved on to their next assignment. The remainder had either quit, broken an arm, back, or leg, or had recycled into the next class, in between phases, for training deficiencies.

And that's the way it had been for the past thirty years of the school's existence.

"You pussies sure you want to be here?" Grey bellowed, legs spread shoulder width, hands on his hips.

"Yes, Sergeant!" the platoon screamed. "Rangers lead the way!"

Grey cupped his hand to his ear.

"*Rangers lead the way!*" The platoon was frantic now, and Levy knew they were in for more harassment.

"That's better. I'll let you off easy this time since I'm such a nice, humane kind of guy. 'Course, if it had been Sergeant Parnell, here," Grey said, jerking his thumb toward one of his frowning assistants, "waking your asses up this morning instead of me, then there's no telling *what* might have happened.

"All right. Take a two-minute-stretch break and get ready for the five miler this morning. Remember: stay alert—stay alive. Fall out."

Thirty-five pairs of lungs exhaled simultaneously, and the men stretched their hamstrings and calves, mindful of the strains they would force themselves to endure in the predawn hours before breakfast. First they drilled through a half-hour-long session of calisthenics, and then commenced the run.

Nobody fell out of the morning run unless he wanted to commit suicide. And some people did just that, or wished they would have before the RIs were finished "developing" the student's capacity for PT back in the worm pit. And that was after he and everyone else had already been drilled in the worm pit.

"Hey, Levy."

Levy looked to his right. It was Keith Christopher, the only black Ranger student in his squad. Christopher was the class stud, the local hulk who combined the broad, muscular chest and shoulders of a linebacker with a marathon runner's endurance to boot. They were the same height—just under six feet—but Christopher's physique made Levy's look almost anorexic.

"You testing Grey this morning or what?" he said, pointing at Levy's Star of David. "That asshole will eat you for lunch."

"Guess I lost my temper a few minutes ago. Do you guys up in the Ranger Battalion actually have NCOs like him?"

"Shit. He's nothing." Christopher made a fist, flexing a massive, very black forearm, and frowned. Levy found himself staring at it, wondering if he should have taken up weight training long before attending the course. "If he ever gets assigned to the battalion, he'd better not fuck with me or I'll give him a permanent appointment with the dentist."

Levy grinned. Nothing could faze Christopher. He was one of the few black Rangers in the course, hailing from the 1/75 Ranger Battalion at Fort Stewart, Georgia. They had drawn each other as Ranger buddies on the first day of the course, and the only thing they discovered they had in common with each other was that they were both Army brats.

Each man in the training company was personally responsible for another man. Where one Ranger went, there went the other. If one knocked out pushups for an infraction, then so did the other. If an

RI caught one man walking around without his Ranger buddy, there would be hell to pay.

"Ready for the run?" Christopher said, changing the subject. "You sucked wind yesterday."

"I may have sucked wind yesterday, but I finished it. *With* the rest of the platoon."

"Yeah, well, I'll be watching you. Pussy out, and I'll kick your ass."

Levy almost believed him. "Don't worry, macho man. I'm no candidate for the Olympics, but I'll hang."

> *Saw an ol' lady walking down the street,*
> *She had a ruck on her back, jump boots on her feet.*
> *I said, "Hey, ol' lady, where you goin' to?"*
> *She said, "U.S. Army Ranger School!"*

The Ranger company resembled an enormous centipede snaking down the Fort Benning access road running from Main Post to the Harmony Church Area, where the Ranger Department was located and on out to the boondocks. Occasionally, a man fell out of the running, chanting formation or lagged behind, bringing much grief to his platoon as an outraged RI would berate them for not hanging together as a team. Of course, at oh-dark-thirty in the morning, with only three or four hours of sleep per man, no one ran well. Even at a seven-and-a-half-minutes-a-mile pace.

Levy sweated. He had never believed he could sweat two gallons' worth in as many hours. He glanced at Christopher, who strode comfortably along beside him.

One, two, three, four . . . Levy counted, concentrating on his pace. It was the fourth mile, and his stomach had cramped at the third. He wanted to puke. But he also wanted to motivate himself to finish the run and quit thinking about why he had come. It was no use. He knew why he had volunteered for Ranger School.

"Mama, why is Dad leaving?" The voice of an eight-year-old, who had known his father for only a cumulative five years during his young life.

A frail, slender woman on the dark side of forty with prematurely gray hair pulled her chair closer to her only child's chair at the breakfast table inside their post duplex. "Oh, Daniel," she murmured, caressing her son's neck, "you know your father is going back overseas. We have both talked to you about it."

The small boy looked up at his mother with huge eyes, deep brown sensitive eyes that accented the delicate features he had inherited from his mother. Down the hall they both could hear his father's occasional curses as he stuffed his equipment and uniforms into two gargantuan duffel bags.

"But Mama, Daddy promised me that we'd go—"

"Your father received orders, Daniel. He has a job to do." Rachel Levy could not keep the bitterness out of her voice.

"You're hurting my neck, Mama."

"My baby—" She moved her hand to his hair, smoothing it down, trying not to cry. "I'm sorry."

"Mama, you're crying."

"Rachel, don't. Not in front of the boy." A looming figure dressed in starched jungle fatigues stood in the kitchen doorway looking down on them. Daniel switched his eyes to his father, a thick, barrel-chested man with bushy eyebrows and coarse black hair.

"Daddy, Tommy next door says you're going to kill gooks—"

"Daniel!" Rachel Levy gripped her son firmly by the chin, forcing him to look at her. *"I told you never to say that word!"*

"And Communists," his father finished for his son. *"Rachel, let me talk to him."*

Rachel Levy got up from the table and walked quickly into the living room, where she turned on the stereo, seeking solace in Rachmaninoff. Then she occupied her couch and tried to read the Sunday paper.

Eli Levy took his son's tiny hand into his callused paw. *"Let us go outside, Daniel. We will go for a walk."* It was a slow, measured voice, a deep, bass voice of a Pole whose mastery of English had come only after many years of hard practice. A Jewish Pole who had immigrated to America with his bride after three years of displaced persons camps after World War II.

Daniel loved his father, but did not know him well. He was always going somewhere with the Army. Tentatively, he took his hand, and as they walked out the door and onto the sidewalk in the junior officers' housing section at Fort Bragg, Daniel was relieved to feel the warm April sun fall on his shoulders. He wanted to play baseball with Tommy next door. He also wanted his father to come play with him.

"Daddy—I mean Dad—why are you going overseas?"

"Son, do you remember when your mother and I told you that I would go?"

"Yes, Dad."

"Do you remember when I told you that a soldier, even if he is a captain, must go where the Army tells him to go? Especially if there is a war?"

"Mama says there is no war, Dad. Mama says it's only a police—a police action. What is that, Daddy?"

"Son, there is a war. I told you where it was."

"Vietnam." Daniel mouthed the word carefully. In 1968, it was a word, even to his young ears, a word that held a certain power to it, a power that made people's eyes open, made them hush their voices—a word for arguments between grown-ups when the evening news came on at night.

"Yes, that is right."

"Mama doesn't want you to go, Daddy. I heard her crying again last night. You—you and Mama were yelling at each other." Daniel hitched in his chest, feeling a thick, painful knot grow in his throat.

Eli Levy squatted down next to his son on the sidewalk and hugged him closely, waiting for the tears. They did not come. Surprised, the big, dark man with the broad forehead and Slavic cheekbones stared at his son's dry face—a face that fortunately had been spared his own peasant features. "I am proud of you, Daniel, for not crying. You must always be strong, my son."

Daniel inhaled deeply and resumed walking around the block with his father. He lifted his chin a little higher. "Dad," he said, "when will you come back?"

"In one year, Daniel."

"Will you really kill gooks?"

"Do not say that word, Daniel. Your mother is right. Do not say that word. It is not nice."

"But will you?"

"I will fight."

They walked on in silence, Eli Levy trying to think of a way to change the subject. Then, "How are your trumpet lessons coming along, Daniel?"

"Mama makes me practice all the time."

"But do you like it?"

"Yes, Dad, I like it."

"Then keep it up. That is something I could never do

when I was your age. It is important that you learn to do something that is beautiful and nice. Something that is not destructive."

"Dad, will I be a soldier someday?"

"Do you want to be a soldier, Daniel?"

Mama told Sally not to go downtown . . .

The greasy fire in Levy's stomach boiled over. He prayed to see the finish line soon.

Too many Rangers runnin' around . . .

"Hey, Ranger!" an RI yelled. "You pukin' in *my* formation? Move it back to the rear of the platoon, *now!*"

Levy shuffled to the rear of the formation, jostling between pumping elbows as he went. Duane Prentiss was back there already, lagging several steps behind the formation. Levy looked at his round face, lathered in snot and sweat, and wondered why the timid loner he had known earlier in the infantry officers basic course had even attempted Ranger school.

As the company turned the last corner, the RIs picked the pace up to a sprint. One hundred meters to go. Fifty. Then they were walking, slowing down, ready to stop. When they finally did stop, steam rose off their naked backs, every man ready to drown and pass out in it, because they realized the worm pit was next.

Daniel Levy ran outside to the mailbox and met the postman there with the late afternoon sun glaring in his eyes.

"Mr. Laughlin, do you have a letter addressed from—" came the voice of a young man due to graduate from the

Fort Devens, Massachusetts, high school with honors the next week.

"Cool it, kiddo. I know what you're looking for. Harvard, right?" The old, paunchy retired sergeant-major now working for the postal delivery liked Lieutenant Colonel Levy's boy. Bright, by Jesus, was he bright. Talented too. Could play that trumpet like no one else. He shared the boy's anticipation.

"Yes, sir, Harvard! School of Music! Anything?"

"Well, now, let me see," the old retired NCO intoned gravely, thumbing through the thick pile of rubber-banded letters and bills. Lieutenant Colonel Levy, Lieutenant Colonel Levy, Lieutenant Colonel and Mrs. Eli Levy, Rachel Levy—boy, you folks sure get a pile of mail; good thing they're not all bills—Rachel Levy. Nope. Nothing for—"

A crushed look. Daniel Levy turned back for his house. "Thanks anyway, Mr. Laughlin."

"Just a minute there, pard."

Dan wheeled around, wide-eyed.

"Well, I'll be darned. Here's something for Mr. Daniel Levy. Got any of those high-falutin' girlfriends there in Harvard, bud?" He handed Daniel a thick, expensive Harvard envelope. •

"Oh, wow! Thanks, Mr. Laughlin!"

"That's sergeant-major to you, kid. And keep up the good work with that trumpet. I heard your solo last month at the concert you kids in school gave."

Dan sprinted back into his house. "Mom! Dad!"

Lieutenant Colonel Eli Levy looked up from his easy chair, his uniform blouse off, Corcoran jump boots on the floor, feet propped up on the ottoman. He had been nursing a beer from a hard day as commander of the 2nd Battalion, 10th Special Forces. Rachel Levy wandered in from the kitchen, the smell of dinner wafting throughout the *house*. The soothing melody of Chopin from the stereo contrasted sharply with Dan Levy's excitement.

Rachel Levy said excitedly, "Did you get it?"

Eli Levy jumped up from the easy chair and huddled around his son with his wife.

"I—I've got something here," Dan replied. "It's been three weeks since I auditioned, and I didn't think that—"

"Open it, Daniel!"

Dan ripped open the letter and read the first line.

"I got the damned scholarship! Harvard School of Music!"

Eli Levy clapped a hairy forearm around his son's shoulders, grinning broadly. Rachel Levy, for once, didn't scold her son for cursing.

Later that evening Lieutenant Colonel Levy retrieved two beers out of the refrigerator, ignored his wife's reproachful look, and took his son by his thin shoulders upstairs to his "war room." It was his den, actually. But hung on the walls were all the old soldier's awards, diplomas, and certificates from his military career. It was his room, the room where he did his writing and after-hours work he brought home. Eli Levy and his son sat in two chairs facing each other. Dan, who had kept his scholarship notification with him the entire time, plopped it down on the coffee table between the two chairs.

"I'm proud of you, Daniel." Eli Levy popped open the two beers and handed one of them to Dan.

"Thanks, Dad." This was one of Dan's best moments. Getting the scholarship was something he had earned entirely on his own.

Eli Levy had read his son's mind. "Do you know why I am proud of you, Daniel?" he said slowly, his Byzantine accent thickening.

"Sure, Pop," Dan replied, wondering what his father was leading up to. It was one of his rhetorical questions.

"Son, I never took the time to really encourage you, or help you with your musical talent. Hell, I was always gone. Not to mention that I know nothing about musical instruments. Your mother is the one who took that time with you."

"You're a soldier, Pop. I understand."

"Yes. But a soldier must often put his family second to his career. I wish I could have spent more time with you when you were young. What I am saying, Daniel, is that there were many things I could not teach you while you were growing up. I could not teach you how to work on a car, or how to make things out of wood. Many times, you learned them on your own."

"You taught me how to shoot, Dad. Remember when you came back from Vietnam, when I was ten?"

"Yes, I taught you how to shoot. And a great many other things, Daniel, I did not teach you. Like how to play your trumpet or appreciate fine music like your mother. I taught you how to shoot. Shooting is not so good, Daniel. Shooting kills. But it is necessary to know how to shoot. And defend yourself, if necessary."

"Dad, I'm leaving for college in another couple of months. I've been thinking about Army ROTC."

Surprised, Eli Levy said nothing. He had never promoted the military with his son; Rachel would have none of it. Likewise, his son had never approached him about it before.

"I mean, I really like music, Dad. But I wonder if maybe I should look at the Army. To be an Army officer, like you."

"Do not do it to please me, Daniel."

"I know that, Dad." Then, quieter, he repeated, "I know that. But I'm curious about it."

"It is hard to be a soldier, son. You know how it is. All the times I could not spend with you and your mother. Son, all I know is how to fight. I have been fighting since I was your age. I have killed. It is not a good thing."

Dan remembered the time two years before, when *"he was finally old enough to understand."* His father had taken him aside in this same war room and told him about his past.

"It is your choice, Daniel," his father continued. *"If you want to know about the Army, and if you want to enroll in ROTC, then do so. But join the Army because you want to be a soldier. A soldier, my son. Be the best. Seek out any and all training that will save your life in combat, should you have to go. But only do so because it is your choice. Not mine, and not your mother's. I will support you in whatever decision you make."*

Levy gasped as he hit the ankle-deep water and low-crawled underneath a maze of barbed wire interlaced inches above the surface. Red-Georgia-clay-stained water gushed into his nose, the wire overhead pricking his scalp and tugging at his fatigues.

The worm pit was an eerie site at dawn, steam rising off the water in the cool June morning. Scores of bald, razor-shorn Rangers waited in columns of ten to take their turn in surviving the worm pit.

It was an obstacle course, one of the many they would negotiate during Ranger School. With a hundred-foot low crawl submerged under water and over a dozen log towers and rope crossings to run, climb, or jump over, it physically depleted all participants; it was a martial ritual the RIs sanctioned daily with the weary bodies of the Ranger students as the sacrifice.

Levy, squirming on his back, rolled his head back

in the mud and saw the upside-down finish line for the low crawl and the log towers ahead. A scornful RI told him to move his ass. He thrashed harder and kicked someone in the head.

"Goddammit, Levy!" It was Christopher.

"Sorry. Didn't know you were there."

"Move it!"

Fuming, Levy struggled through the water and finally made it out, mud caking his entire body. He was tired of putting up with Christopher's impatience.

He sprinted toward the log tower, and Christopher caught up with him.

"What's the matter with you?" said the black Ranger. "You're dragging ass again." He passed Levy and mounted the first rung of logs, immediately reaching for the second rung. Levy followed, angry.

"Mind your own business, Christopher. I can take care of myself."

"Yeah, right. Just keep up with me, Ranger buddy." Christopher was at the top of the twenty-foot tower now, ready to slide down the rope.

Levy watched Christopher as he slid down—a massive, very headstrong man used to having his own way. He outweighed Levy by at least thirty pounds, none of it fat. By comparison, Levy was wiry, with more of a lightweight boxer's physique.

He shook his head and slid down the rope.

Breakfast. They'd had only twenty minutes to shit, shower, and shave after PT, and now they were all in line outside the chow hall standing at parade rest, waiting for their turn to go inside and eat.

Christopher turned around to Levy and gave him a lopsided grin.

"Look. I'm a pretty obnoxious sumbitch sometimes, 'cause I get pretty motivated. It's just that I'm glad to be here, because it's something I've always wanted to do. I mean, I spent three years in the 82nd Airborne Division and a year and a half in the Ranger Battalion before I could come here. *Nothing* is going to keep me from graduating."

Levy studied Christopher's set jaw, and the intensity in his Ranger buddy's eyes told him he had volunteered for more than just the experience.

"You just get too hyper sometimes, man. Slow down. If anyone makes it around here, you will."

Christopher grinned broadly and punched Levy lightly in the shoulder. "You and me both, Ranger buddy."

"Hey! You two jugheads over there," an RI yelled at them, pointing an accusing finger. "No talking in my chow line. Go elevate your feet." He jerked his head toward a tree next to the entrance of the chow hall, and Levy and Christopher double-timed to it. Once there, they assumed the front-leaning rest with their feet angled high up the tree trunk, head and shoulders aiming down toward the ground.

It wasn't two minutes before their arms shook like ancient Singer sewing machines. Both Rangers knew beyond a shadow of a doubt that the RI had forgotten them as soon as he sent them to the tree and had simply resumed monitoring the chow line for more offenders. He finally glanced in their direction.

"Knock 'em out, Rangers," he said, grinning. Painfully, Levy and Christopher cranked out their push-ups, heads drooping close to the ground, arms burning.

Sergeant First Class Frank Wilson Grey felt good this morning, even if he did wake up at zero-three to get ready for another day. His wife simply did not understand why he had volunteered for RI duty at Fort Benning two years ago, let alone why he stuck with it even when the Army said he could move on to another, more comfortable assignment.

He grunted in disgust. She didn't understand. She'd told him so this morning. Again. He could feel his good mood dissipating, thinking about her.

Grey breathed deeply, flaring his nostrils as he looked around at the class from his table. *My class,* he thought. *And some of the finest NCOs in the Army to help me train these nerds and turds. I could really use 'em up north. . . .*

Grey watched them, their bald heads bobbing as they stuffed their faces with morning chow consisting of bacon and eggs, pancakes, grits, and potatoes, knowing they'd have to make every calorie count for the coming day.

"Billy," he said to Parnell, grabbing his coffee mug, "did you see these jokers this morning? They were pukin' their guts up on the run."

"Well, what do you think they're going to do no more than five days into the course?"

"Gotta weed out wimpy, you know."

"Got anybody particular in mind?" Parnell asked.

Grey paused. He had somebody in mind all right. "Naw, you know how it is. We always douche at least a dozen before we move 'em out to Darby." Camp Darby was the field portion of phase one located at an isolated portion of the Fort Benning reservation.

"How many do you think we'll take?"

"Oh, maybe a hundred and ten, hundred and

twenty." Grey glanced at the entrance of the chow hall. "Say, I'm going outside to get this line moving. Why don't you start clearing some of these clowns out of here?" he said, motioning toward a dozen eating Rangers five feet away. They were shoveling chipped beef gravy and toast in their mouths with oversized spoons that resembled the entrenching tools they were issued earlier.

"Sure thing, boss." Parnell stood up and hovered over the Rangers. "You pukes get moving!" he yelled with glee. Grey watched momentarily, almost laughing, but knowing he couldn't in order to maintain proper atmosphere. He rose from the table and walked toward the door.

"Time to move on, kiddies," he said, intercepting two Rangers who had just burst inside. "Mister Rogers has a nice surprise for you in class today. And you can be damned sure I'll have one for you if you're late this morning."

The line shuffled faster. No one dared to look at Sergeant Grey unless he didn't want to eat breakfast. Grey strolled out to the front steps, sipping from his coffee mug.

"Twenty-three, Sergeant! Twenty-four, Sergeant!" two voices croaked in unison.

Grey saw the sagging figures of Levy and Christopher, and his eyes glinted. "The nigger and the Jew," he muttered. He had them picked out from day one.

"Twenty-five, Sergeant!" Levy and Christopher stopped, then bobbed down again. "One for the Great Ranger in the Sky!" Their bellies scraped the ground as they fought to hold on after ten minutes on the tree.

"What'd these two tickturds do, Sergeant Nelson?" Grey asked the line monitor.

Levy kept his eyes averted from Grey. His Star of David had popped out from underneath his T-shirt and was dangling by his nose.

"Just the usual, Sarge. Anybody that talks in my chow line can stay in the front-leaning rest for a while."

Grey felt better now. His mood always picked up when he busied himself. He swaggered toward the two Rangers.

"Talking in the chow line?" he said in mock dismay. "My." The RI squatted next to Levy and spied his Star of David. "Ranger, didn't I chew on your ass this morning for wearing that?"

"Yes, Sergeant." Levy's cheeks flushed, and he felt the bile rise up in his throat.

"You believe in God, Ranger?"

"What?"

"You knocked out only *one* push-up for the Great Ranger in the Sky, dodo-head."

Levy and Christopher took the cue and pumped out five more push-ups for the Great Ranger in the Sky, sounding off until their voices cracked. Grey kept his eye on Levy's Star of David.

"You're keeping a pretty high profile around here with that necklace," he said when they were finished. "Not to mention that I've told you once already to get rid of it." Grey darted an index finger around the delicate gold chain and yanked it off Levy's neck.

Levy jumped up from the tree, wanting to smash his fist into the RI's smug face.

"Get back down, Ranger!" Grey bellowed.

Levy paused, glowering at Grey. Disgusted, he flopped back down into the front-leaning rest.

"You know this is unauthorized." Grey stuffed the Star of David in his pocket. "You can have it back after graduation—that is, *if* you graduate."

You prick, Levy thought, seething. *You bigoted prick. I'll make it through this course if it takes me all year.*

"We'll graduate, Sergeant!" Christopher broke in. "Rangers lead the way!"

"That they do, Ranger," Grey replied, looking at Christopher distastefully. "That they do. And if you and your buddy want to be among them, then you'd better start moving your asses a little faster and doing things right. There's no room here for shiftless, lazy people."

Christopher shot his head up at Grey, eyes flashing. The slur had been intended.

"There's no shiftless or lazy people *here*, Sergeant!"

"We'll see about that up in the mountains, Ranger!" Grey shouted, livid with a sudden uncontrollable rage. "Knock out some more goddamned push-ups. Sergeant Nelson, these two belong at the end of the line for the rest of the week!" Grey spun about and stormed back in the chow hall, furious at himself for losing control.

Levy swore later on that he heard Grey mutter something about kikes and niggers as he slammed the door to the chow hall.

CHAPTER

· TWO ·

Acknowledging the fact that a Ranger is a more elite soldier who arrives at the cutting edge of battle by land, sea, or air . . .

Levy trudged through the thick, damp woods, sweating and tired. Wait-a-minute vines—thorny denizens of the pain-plant kingdom—clawed at his face and ankles, tripping and scratching him. The M16 he carried weighed heavier by the minute, and his rucksack straps cut deeply into his shoulders.

Levy was the last man in the patrol, a snaking line of ten men walking quickly toward their assigned objective three kilometers away. He remembered how glad he and the others had been upon moving out to Camp Darby, only to discover that the RIs there were just as hardassed as the ones in city phase. The difference was less mental harassment but more physical privation in the form of grueling forty-eight-hour patrols. Simply put, Camp Darby was the asshole part of Fort Benning, with miles of dense, tangled forest putrefying in the thick Georgia heat.

The patrol halted and spread out into a security

perimeter—a rough circle, every man five meters apart, on one knee, and holding his weapon at the ready as he scanned the perimeter to his front for possible enemy contact.

I volunteered for all this, Levy thought, panting for breath. He had volunteered for the sweat and exhaustion. The sleep deprivation. The stress. But he had to do it. His old man had told him it would be a bitch, that not to go for it was no shame. But there *would* be, for him anyway. Besides, he'd show the old fart a thing or two. Levy remembered all the moves as a kid, an Army brat. The three times his father had gone to Vietnam. Special Forces. And a Korea vet when he was an enlisted man to boot. Well, Special Forces or not, the old man had never attended Ranger School. Not that he'd ever needed to. Eli Levy had paid his dues as a sixteen-year-old kid fighting the Nazis as a partisan in the Polish Underground.

By sharp contrast, Dan Levy was straight out of college with a music degree. All his life his mother had pushed and propelled him to stick with things cultured, things musical. He had decided to enroll in ROTC against his mother's vehement wishes, but it was *his* scholarship, and if he wanted to be a soldier before starting a career in music, then he'd damn sure do so.

And his father *was* proud of him. And he had remembered his words. *Be the best—seek out and volunteer for any and all the hardest training the Army can offer. It will save your life someday, and those that you lead.* So here he was. No enlisted time, yet he was a twenty-two-year-old second lieutenant who would be assigned to the Second Infantry Division in South Korea as a rifle platoon leader along the DMZ. But only upon graduation from Ranger School. He had to get some hardcore experience somewhere. How, as an infantry officer, could he lead troops without some type of demanding experience? Ranger School was the answer.

Levy glanced at his watch. Already it was 1530. The afternoon sun scorched the back of his neck, and the heat made him sweat through his fatigues until he looked like someone had thrown buckets of water on him. He took a deep breath, removed his patrol cap and wiped his forehead with it, feeling dizzy. He withdrew a canteen from his web gear and took a long pull. Then he noiselessly lowered his pack to the ground, mindful of the big Samoan RI in the center of the perimeter who was watching him. He was their lane grader for the day.

Levy stood up and adjusted the perimeter, making sure every man was in a covered and concealed position behind a tree or a rock, and pointing his weapon out to his front.

"APL!"

Levy rolled his eyes, thinking that if whispers could break glass, Duane Prentiss could do it. Looking toward the twelve o'clock position at the head of the perimeter, he saw Prentiss frantically waving his map case at him.

Levy walked up to the excited Ranger student who had taken command of the patrol three hours before. Prentiss had been calling Levy APL ever since Sergeant Yendall, the lane grader, had made them patrol leader and assistant patrol leader.

"I'm in trouble," Prentiss announced gloomily, sticking his nose back in the map.

Levy squatted beside Prentiss and examined his map. He knew what the problem was already. This had been the fourth halt in as many minutes, and the RI was getting pissed. Prentiss was on the verge of getting the squad's first graded patrol lost because of his own lack of self-confidence in reading a map.

"So what's the problem, Prentiss?" he whispered.

"I'm fucking lost. I'm going to flunk my first patrol." Levy noted that his baby-soft features and wispy brown hair belonged to that of an accountant, not an infantry lieutenant. He had an annoying habit of constantly pushing his glasses up on his nose.

"No, you won't. Besides, even if you do flunk it, you'll still have plenty of chances to do better."

"Jesus, I just don't know. Show me where we are."

Levy picked up a pine needle and examined Prentiss's map, a maze of contour lines, roads, and streams.

"Look here," he said, pointing the pine needle within one of the grid squares, "remember that ridgeline we passed an hour ago? Good. Now, see the stream junction?"

"Yeah."

Levy looked up from the map, pulled his compass out from his shirt pocket, and took a reading. Then he pointed in the direction they had been moving. "We should be about a hundred meters away from it if we keep going downhill. Hit that stream and follow it for about two klicks. It'll take you to the bottom of the hill we're supposed to recon. The objective can't be more than a mile and a half away."

"Klick?"

"Kilometer, then. You know, klick. Six point two tenths of a mile."

Prentiss glanced at the map and back in the direction Levy was pointing, then grinned uncertainly, like he'd just been told a joke but didn't get the punch line.

"Okay. Yeah, I think I see it now. Thanks, APL."

"Prentiss."

"What?"

"The name's Levy. Or Dan. Chill out."

"Sure, Levy. You ready?"

"Let's go."

Levy stood and motioned for everyone to pick up and move out. When he returned to his position, Christopher was waiting there with the machine gun, grinning.

"Numbnuts lost again?"

"Yeah. He seems to have a lot of trouble. You doing okay with that M60? You've been humping it all day."

"No sweat. It's my baby, and no one else carries it." Christopher spun about and joined the rest of the patrol.

Keith Christopher trotted toward the front of the patrol. He felt good, hot and grimy as he was, and the M60 felt reassuringly solid and lethal in his arms. He glanced at Prentiss, who was still clutching his map case and plodding awkwardly along.

"Hey, Prentiss," he whispered, "you know where the hell you're going?"

Dismayed, Prentiss glanced at Christopher and pushed his black Army-issue glasses up his nose. It was a perfect imitation of Clark Kent.

"Yeah, I think so."

"You'd better *know* so, dumbass. Don't get this patrol lost."

Unsure, Prentiss pulled out his map and looked at it, and at the same time the toe of his jungle boot caught a dead log hidden in the pine needles underfoot. He somersaulted, his seventy-pound ruck flipping over his head. The inertia of the heavy ruck carried the rest of his body with it, until he made a complete roll. He lay there, numb with surprise and embarrassment, wondering if his neck was broken.

Christopher blew a thick wad of snot out of his nose, trying to contain his sudden belt of laughter.

"*Fuck,*" Prentiss said loud enough for the RI to hear at the rear of the file. He struggled to his feet and waved for the patrol to form into another security perimeter.

Sides splitting, Christopher kneeled down behind a tree and scanned his front with the machine gun, wondering how the hell someone like Prentiss had even made it through basic. He heard the heavy footsteps of their lane grader approaching them.

"Ranger Prentiss," the RI said with a Hispanic-sounding accent, "show me where we are on the map."

Sighing, Prentiss gazed at his map for the hundredth time. "Well, Sergeant, I think we're . . . here." He jabbed his finger at an area that covered an entire grid square of the one over fifty-thousand map. He looked up at the big RI, hoping he was right.

"Use a pine needle, Ranger."

A pine needle was the best tool nature provided for an expedient map pointer, but many a student, unsure of his location, dreaded using one. It was just too damned specific. Prentiss picked up one from the ground and pointed it somewhere in the grid square his finger had covered moments before.

"Right around here, Sergeant."

"Ranger, that's four klicks off. You're fired." Yendall swung around and looked at Christopher. "What are you so happy about?"

Christopher's grin vanished. "Nothing, Sergeant."

"Good, Ranger, because it's your turn to fuck up now. You've got five minutes to study your map, disseminate the fact that you're the new patrol leader, and get these people moving toward today's objective. Got that?"

"Yes, Sergeant."

"Get busy." The RI walked to the nearest tree and sat down, leaning against the trunk.

Sobered, Christopher jumped to his feet, swapped the M60 he had been carrying for Prentiss's rifle, and trotted to the center of the patrol's security perimeter. Levy met him there.

"Okay," he told him, "I'm the patrol leader now. Pass the word out to the rest of the guys and tell them where we are . . . right here, see?" He pointed at their exact location on his map with a pine needle.

"No sweat. I think everyone knows where we are. They've been looking at their own maps anyway, since Prentiss took charge."

"Okay, okay," Christopher said impatiently. "Get ready to go." He returned to his ruck and shouldered it on. Glancing at his watch, he realized they would have only one more hour to cover the remaining two kilometers to the objective. He turned around and stared at the patrol. Two more minutes and they would move out. He had memorized the route early on, something they'd told him always to do during Pre-Ranger training back at Fort Stewart. He was good at it, like everything else he had learned. *This nigger's gonna make honor grad yet,* he thought.

"Get 'em out of here, Ranger."

His time was up. Christopher looked up and down the perimeter and then waved his arm forward, signaling the patrol to move out. Then he crammed his map case into his trousers cargo pocket, where it was to stay for the rest of the day.

They had made good time. Christopher and another man from the patrol were in a cluster of trees within spitting distance of a mock missile site on top of a small hill. Two privates from the Ranger department support element manned the watch position near the tower's base, munching M&Ms and drinking Cokes.

Pukes, Christopher thought. *Didn't even hear us coming, as dry as the leaves are.* The prone figure next to him sketched the area on a notepad. Christopher glanced at him and exhaled softly.

"Jakes." It was the quietest whisper he could manage. The squat, blond-haired country boy by the name of Corporal Luke Jakes raised his pimply nineteen-year-old face up at Christopher.

"What."

"Get ready to go back. We've got thirty minutes to link up with the rest of the patrol."

"Okay." Jakes put the finishing touch on his sketch and made sure he had everything—the azimuth to the tower, grid location, uniform of the guards, their weapons—it was all there. Looking back up at Christopher, he gave him a nod. Then he gently, ever so carefully, picked himself up and crept down to the base of the hill. When Christopher was satisfied he was out of earshot, he then followed suit.

Linking up with Jakes at the bottom of the hill, they stole down a ravine that led toward the rest of the patrol, two hundred meters away from the target. Sergeant Yendall joined them there. He had been watching them from his vantage point.

"Not bad, Ranger," was all he said.

Christopher knew he had passed his first patrol. He glanced at Jakes, who had been carrying the radio, and grinned.

"Need a hand with that?" he whispered.

"Naw, I'm okay."

They were now well within the ravine, and the RI fell back several paces. Christopher knew what would happen next. It was something easy to forget. He grabbed Jakes's shoulder and put his mouth next to his ear.

"Remember, the number combination is seven."

"Right."

When they were twenty meters away from the security perimeter, they slowed down to a baby step, walking with their toes hitting first, making little noise on the dry leaves and grass.

"Halt." An unseen whisper floated toward them from a bush next to a tree. It was Levy. "Three."

"Four," Jakes replied.

"Come on in."

With an approving nod, Sergeant Yendall followed the students into the perimeter and watched Christopher and Jakes meet in the center with Levy. He plopped down next to a tree to see what they would do next.

Christopher spread his map case on the ground, and everyone kneeled around it. It was now dusk, and the crickets and locusts ushered in the approaching night with their nocturnal hum. Christopher took a deep breath and let it out slowly, gathering his thoughts. Jakes handed him the sketch.

"Okay, we got everything," Christopher said. "Take out your compass and make a reading on the hill . . . two hundred and seventy-three degrees, right?" Levy nodded. "The missile's pointing at an azimuth of ninety-eight degrees." Christopher traced a imaginary line across his map, from the target to the patrol's starting point. "It's aimed at company headquarters back in the rear."

"Looks pretty good," Levy said, impressed. He glanced at Jakes, whose camouflage facepaint had melted down over a mass of peach fuzz and pimples, turning his face into a streaked green hamburger patty with eyes. He had taken out his second can of Copenhagen for the day, and was stuffing his lower lip.

"How 'bout a dip, ol' buddy?" he asked, imitating Jakes's down-home Missouri accent.

"No sweat, GI. Can do easy." Jakes handed him the can. "Didn't know you officers 'n' gentlemen did that sort of thing."

"You two Billy-Joe Jim-Bobs hurry up with that worm dirt and listen up," Christopher said, grimacing as he watched Levy pack the snuff into his lower lip and return the can to Jakes. "Levy, I want you to take a good look at this sketch and then show it to everybody in the patrol. Make sure all the information is disseminated. We've got ten minutes before we move out."

Levy gave him a thumbs-up, picked up his weapon, and walked around the perimeter, stopping at each man and giving him the information Christopher had brought back.

Still leaning by the tree, Sergeant First Class Jonathan Yendall pulled a white pamphlet out of his trousers cargo pocket and wrote Christopher's name down by the reconnaissance patrol checklist. He could barely see it in the fading light.

It wasn't too often a Ranger student passed his first patrol, he thought, checking "go" on all patrol taskings. He remembered when he had attended Ranger school fifteen years before, the first Samoan ever to have attended. That had been back in '67. And he had caught his share of the crap too. The RI suddenly found himself remembering one dark, rainy night with the wind howling through the mountains.

He looked up from the pamphlet and let his gaze fall upon Christopher, who was adjusting the shoulder straps on his rucksack. He studied the Ranger's black countenance, wondering if he would experience the same trouble. The Jewish kid too. What's his name, Levy? He'd already heard about the student who wasn't afraid to knock out push-ups for wearing his Star of David. Maybe he'd better have a talk with both of them. Later.

He let them conduct their business for another five minutes and then climbed to his feet, his forty-year-old joints stiff from the day's walk. He treaded softly to Christopher and squatted down beside him.

"Ranger, you've got another couple of minutes to wrap things up here, and then I want you to establish a good patrol base for the night somewhere in this vicinity." He picked up a pine needle and pointed. Christopher's stomach rumbled at the thought of the patrol base. That's when they were allowed to eat only their daily C-ration and catch some sleep, even though it never lasted more than about an hour and was interrupted at best.

"Roger that, Sergeant. I'll get them ready." Christopher studied his map case, and the RI moved back to his tree. *Seven klicks*, he thought morosely. Then he chuckled at the thought of the way Prentiss would be sniveling with the M60. *Better have him trade it off with one of the other guys*. He looked up, hearing footsteps, and saw Levy return to the center of the perimeter.

"What's up?"

"The RI just told me to move out to the patrol base. Seven klicks."

"Jesus!"

"You swear pretty Christian-like for a Jew, Levy."

"Habit from being around all you gentiles."

"Better get them ready to move out."

"Why, sho 'nuff, boss. 'Rastus be ready *anytime!*"

Before Christopher could say anything, Levy shuffled back to the perimeter to get the patrol on its feet, laughing quietly as he went.

Humping a ruck at two in the morning don't get no easier no matter how long you been doing this shit, thought Sergeant Yendall as he leaned against a tree just out of sight from the rest of the patrol. They were taking ten after the past seven hours of constant movement through swamps and creek bottoms.

The RI lurched to his feet and joined the rest of the patrol, which was spread out in a compact, cigar-shaped security perimeter. Peering at the man five feet in front of him, he barely made out his

Ranger eyes—two inch-long strips of luminous tape on the back of his patrol cap like a section of tiny, upright railroad tracks. He smiled, remembering how one of the students, Prentiss, had broken contact from the rest of the patrol earlier by chasing after fireflies, fooling himself into thinking they were the Ranger eyes on the back of his buddy's cap. Of course, at this time of night anybody could get a little goofy, he thought, silent laughter bubbling up. Who wouldn't? Anybody with only one C-ration a day and no sleep gets weird when the moon rises. Christ, he remembered when he himself had once tried to convince his Ranger buddy that it really *was* Santa Claus sparkling along in the midnight sky with a sled full of machine guns and flamethrowers hooked up to a convoy of deuce-and-a-half trucks, when someone had punched him hard in the shoulder, telling him to *"wake the fuck up, man, you're dronin' . . ."*

"Sergeant Yendall." A hand shook his arm.

"Sergeant Yendall!"

"Get your hand offa me, Ranger," he ordered, popping open his eyes and looking up at Christopher.

"Sergeant Yendall, we're about a hundred meters away from the patrol base. I've got a couple of guys securing the area."

"Okay, Ranger. Move everybody into it when you're ready and conduct patrol base activities."

"Roger that, Sergeant." Christopher walked to the head of the perimeter and launched the patrol toward the patrol base. Levy brought up the rear, making sure no one had gone to sleep during the halt.

The patrol moved clumsily to the designated area,

a damp, low-lying place next to a stream covered with wait-a-minute vines and tall, springy pines. Once there, they formed a circle with five two-man buddy teams spread five meters apart. Levy, Christopher, and Jakes clustered in the middle of the perimeter with the patrol's radio. Relieved, Sergeant Yendall joined them there and parked for the night.

Leaving his ruck, Levy walked the perimeter and placed each position on fifty percent security, meaning that one man guarded his section of the perimeter while the other cleaned his rifle, changed socks, and ate his C-ration. After he was finished, his buddy would do the same.

The RI opened his ruck and retrieved an obscenely large tinfoil package of barbecued chicken his wife had grilled for him the night before. He walked into the tree line away from the patrol base to eat it. No use torturing the students with the smell, he thought mirthfully, leaning back against a tree trunk. Afterward, he pulled out a cigarette from his crumpled pack of Camels and smoked.

He was pleased that the patrol had made good progress on their first time out. With the exception of the first patrol leader, they had done damned good. Rangers Christopher and Levy would indeed do well in the course, barring . . .

Dahlonega. Phase two. He remembered having it out with him when they went through the course together years back as buck sergeants. Of course, it had been racial then, what with that asshole spouting all that bullshit about white supremacy and how they were on *his* turf and so on. Now they were both senior NCOs and instructors in the same course. They had both avoided contact. He wondered how much longer that would last. Standing up, he crumpled the tinfoil and stuffed it into his pocket. Then he walked back into the perimeter of the patrol base. He saw Christopher in the center. Levy was there, too, cleaning his M16 alongside Jakes, who manned the radio.

"I want to talk to you two."

"What's up, Sergeant?" Levy said, wondering if Yendall was going to make them move their patrol base.

"Come with me."

Puzzled, Christopher told Jakes to monitor the perimeter while they were gone, grabbed his rifle, and followed Yendall and Levy out into the woods.

They walked in silence for two minutes up a steep hill. The woods were black and stagnant, as if the day's heat had suffocated it all in fetid, steaming humidity. The RI finally entered a small moonlit clearing and sat on a tree stump in the middle.

"You two did well today. I like patrols that move out quickly and don't get lost. That takes good leadership from both the PL and APL."

Levy exchanged glances with Christopher. *He didn't bring us here to tell us that,* he thought.

Reading his mind, Yendall shot him a piercing look.

"You're Jewish, right?" It sounded like an accusation.

"As a matter of fact, I am. So?"

"And you"—the RI glanced sharply at Christopher—"how many blacks are in your platoon in the Ranger Battalion back at Fort Stewart?"

Christopher's eyes reflected twin flashes of moonlight. "A couple, Sergeant. What are you driving at?"

"I'm Samoan," the RI replied, his accent thickening. "When I came in the Army, a hell of a lot of people didn't even know where the hell Samoa was. Some called me spick, or yellow-butt. . . ." He paused, eyes turning into slits, remembering.

"So what's that got to do with us, Sergeant?" Christopher said abruptly.

"Don't be stupid, Ranger. Forget about Ranger School for the next few minutes and listen to me. And when we're finished with this conversation, you remember it." He paused, staring hard at them. Then he spoke.

"The Army, like anywhere else, has an overabundance of assholes in it. And some of them—not many, but some—happen to be racist assholes. Don't get me wrong, the system's okay and it's been pretty damned good to me. The Army has given me a chance to see and do things I never could have done otherwise. But don't be so naive as to think you're going to do just fine based on some equal opportunity regulation.

"I went to Ranger School in the sixties just before joining my recon team in 'Nam. My Ranger buddy almost killed me during phase two up in the mountains. Think about where that is—you're going to be there in another week. Remember the civil rights movement? You two must have been just children then . . . you probably don't remember how the Ku Klux Klan reorganized and terrorized certain people around those parts." Yendall paused. "Blacks and Jews mostly," he added. "Even a Samoan or two."

The two Ranger students stood in silence, listening. Christopher worked his jaw muscles, the ebony skin along his jawline glinting in the humid moonlight with slow, rhythmic pulses.

"Like I said, my Ranger buddy almost killed me.

He was from Dahlonega, you know, the town a few miles outside Camp Frank D. Merrill. He was born and raised up in the mountains not too far away from the camp. His father was one of the big hitters of the local KKK chapter. I think his title was 'Exalted Cyclops,' or something like that.''

''Sergeant, are you saying that there's some sort of KKK outfit still up there?'' Levy interrupted.

''Shut up and listen.'' Yendall drew a deep breath and exhaled slowly, gathering his thoughts.

Then, ''When you get to phase two, watch yourselves while on patrol. Rednecks are all over those mountains, and they'll follow you. I don't care how good you are. You can be just as quiet and stealthy as hell, but they'll still find you and track you down like a deer. Remember, you're in *their* woods. They'll steal your weapon if they get a chance. Some RIs carry their own piece and some live rounds with them just in case. . . .

''Anyway, we were on our first patrol together as Ranger buddies. It was instant dislike from the start. Once he called me a wetback to my face, so I busted his mouth. I'm from Samoa anyway.'' Yendall chuckled softly, massaging a balled fist. ''The second night out we were pulling security together a hundred meters out from our patrol base up a slope. It was raining like hell, and we were both drenched. Thunder, lightning . . .'' The big man's voice trailed off, and everything was quiet again. He sat silent for what seemed an eternity to Levy and Christopher as his memory relived itself.

''They grabbed me as I was sleeping. It was my turn to rack out for the next thirty minutes, and I remember thinking that my buddy must have been ready to forget our earlier differences, because he was acting friendlier. Anyway, I kicked like a motherfucker, and damned near shook them off me, but one of them knocked me out with a rock. I must have been out for an hour. When I woke up, I had a bandage wrapped around my head and my nose was broken. Had a couple of cracked ribs too. My Ranger buddy was marked up, but not near as bad as me. Both our rifles were stolen, and my Ranger buddy told the RI who was with us on that patrol how they had crept up on us and did it all.''

The RI drew a deep breath and let it out slowly, still massaging his fist. Levy could see five white knuckles standing out in the dark.

''What did the Ranger Department do about it?''

''Nothing they could do about it. Those mountain hicks snuck up on us, fucked us up, and stole our weapons. They were long gone before the rest of our patrol found us.''

Christopher frowned. ''Are you saying that those guys who jumped you back then are still around?''

''Goddammit, Ranger, I'm telling you that it's probably worse, much worse. Haven't you been following the news?'' Yendall was irritated by Christopher's question, but then he realized they had been cut off from civilization during the past three weeks, since they had started the course. ''Okay, so you haven't. It's gearing up again. Last week they discovered a KKK training camp up by the Arkansas-Missouri border, and the FBI flushed them out. There were submachine guns, mortars, and Christ knows what else. Probably some demolitions too. After interrogating the leader of the group, they discovered that members of a neo-Nazi organization had been supplying them with the weapons and training, but they couldn't find any of *them*. But I'll bet you a month's paycheck that there's a large number of these camps all across the United States, training and preparing for the race war they're always talking about. Surely you guys followed the news before you started Ranger School."

Levy had to admit that it was true, although he had taken the stories with a grain of salt. But now it was different. He was in their backyard. He glanced at Christopher, who was still frowning.

"Sergeant Yendall," Christopher said, "you mentioned that your Ranger buddy was a racist too. Did he change his mind after what had happened?"

Several moments passed before Yendall spoke, and Christopher wondered if he was going to answer. Then the RI unlimbered his massive frame from the stump, stood up, and faced them both.

"No," he said softly, "he never changed his mind. I found a note in my ruck the day after they jumped us. It said, 'Nigger-spick, we'll castrate you next time.' He put it there. I could never prove it, but I *know* the bastard put it there. I can still see it in his eyes whenever I see him around the compound."

Levy suddenly grew cold and very alarmed.

"You mean he's still in the Army?"

"Yeah. He's your Class TAC."

CHAPTER

·THREE·

Sergeant First Class Grey bellowed: "Company . . . 'ten-*chun!*"

The Ranger class of now only 109 students out of the original 146 snapped to the position of attention when Grey boomed out the command. Looking at the row upon row of lean, thin-faced men in the company formation, now that his class was back from phase one patrolling, gave Grey a strong sense of fulfillment—he had personally ensured that only the best had so far survived the demanding course curriculum he had programmed for them since day one.

The barracks compound sparkled. The grounds were raked. No cigarette butt dared betray its ruinous existence on the gleaming white gravel of the compound formation area. And every Ranger student to the man quaked in his spit-shined boots while praying to his God that their senior TAC, one Sergeant First Class Frank Wilson Grey, their dictator and boss for the remaining six weeks of the course, would see fit to allow the class its first eight-hour break from the stainless-steel embrace of Ranger School. Every eye stared straight, every back stood erect, every bald razor-shorn head sported a perfectly creased, sweat-stained patrol cap with a Ranger tab ("The Coveted Black and Gold," as the RIs always called it) pinned inside for good luck. Every man hoped beyond hope that Sergeant Grey would turn them loose. Even if it was for only eight hours.

"Stand at . . . *ease*!" Grey paused magnificently, his chest swelling, a carefully rehearsed speech cranking in gear with his mind as every eye strained to see him.

"A hundred and forty-six of you Rangers *started* this course three weeks ago, and now a hundred and nine of you saw fit to use whatever intestinal fortitude the Big Ranger in the Sky gave you to beat phase one. The other thirty-seven dirtballs couldn't take it, and are now either recycling into the next class or transferring their snivelly, ragbag selves to another unit. Every one of you standing before me today is finished—now and forever—with phase one."

A loud, whooping cheer belted from the company. Oh, happy day!

"Men, during these past three weeks you have learned how to break your enemy's back with your hands, slit his throat with your knife, penetrate deep into his territory on patrol, and, most important, you have improved your own leadership skills so that you can teach others to do the same."

The company howled. Grey quieted them down, smiling at them for the first time ever.

"All right, all right . . . now, listen up. In two minutes I am going to dismiss this formation. It is now exactly 1158 hours. You are going to have eight—I repeat, eight—hours, and *only* eight hours, to go into town, clean laundry, fuck mama, and chow down on whatever the hell you want to eat, but remember . . . if any of you pukes show up late or drunk, that's it.

"You all have permission to use your cars while on break. If you get a speeding ticket on your way back and don't make the formation, that's just too damned bad. You *will* be kicked out of this course. Is that clear?"

"Clear, Sergeant!" the chorus of voices replied.

"I said, is that clear?"

"Clear, Sergeant!"

"Good. Next formation is at 2000. My watch now says 1200 on the dot." Grey dropped his wrist and stood erect, hands at his sides.

"Company . . . 'ten-*chun*!"

Bootheels thundered.

"Fall out!'

If, by chance, a civilian happened to observe the melee created just then by a wild mob of bald, skinny, and whooping maniacs as they raced hell-bent for the barracks for their dirty clothes and then to the parking lot, he would have fled for his precious life.

Grey walked through the company area for the next ten minutes after the formation, still amazed at how deserted the place always became within minutes whenever he dismissed students for their eight-hour break. Oh, there were still a few students hanging around, cleaning their own laundry now that there was no struggle for the washing machine, but for the most part, the compound was deserted. After inspecting the last of the old World War II barracks, he decided to walk back to the company headquarters, when suddenly a radio blared out loud music from upstairs.

Nigger music. Can't stand that shit.

He bolted up the stairs and spotted two black students jiving to the music, dressed only in their shorts, fresh out of the shower. Upon seeing him, they froze in place, surprised.

"You two Rangers got anything better to do than listen to that crap?"

One of them leapt for the radio and turned it off, then snapped to attention with his buddy. Neither spoke. Grey didn't bother putting them at ease. He walked toward them, barely concealing the contempt and hatred boiling in his guts.

"You going to answer me, boy?" he said to the Ranger who had turned off the radio. "What's your name?"

"Brown, Sergeant!"

So a-fucking-typical of a nigger's name. Grey glared into the black man's eyes. *Buddy's name is probably Amos.* He wanted to tell them to hand over the radio and get busy on a detail, since they liked it here so much. . . .

"Tell you what, Brown—you and your buddy put up your goddamned boom-box, get dressed, and get your asses outta here. Stick around any longer, and I'll put you to work."

"Yes, Sergeant!" they shouted in unison.

"Get busy."

"Yes, Sergeant!" Grey stomped back to the stairway as the two students scrambled to get their clothes on and the radio secured in the wall locker next to their bunks.

Grey shook his head as he walked back to the company headquarters. *Goddamned coons. Always shucking and jiving. Fucking jungle-bunny music always blaring out of their ghetto-blasters.*

Reaching his office, he remembered a time when things were different. He smiled as he entered. *Things will change. That's for* damned *sure.*

He saw Sergeant Parnell parked at his desk, his feet propped up.

"Get your fucking feet off my desk, Billy," Grey said, scowling.

"Take it easy, boss," Parnell replied, flipping him off as Grey replaced him at the desk, propping his own feet up. "Listen, everybody's cut loose for the day, and only you and me need to be back for tonight's formation. Let's go get a beer."

"Naw, I'm going back to the house in a little bit. The old lady's fixing a late lunch. Besides, I haven't seen too much of her lately."

"Sarah called for you a while ago."

"Yeah?"

"She sounded kind of pissed. Said to tell you that the oven broke down."

"Christ almighty. Guess I'd better bring home some Kentucky Fried or something."

"Yeah, well, guess I'll see you later, then. I'm outta here."

"See you later." Parnell walked out into the heat of the company area.

Grey leaned back in his swivel chair, thinking of his wife and what kind of mood she'd be in when he got home. *Not a very fucking good one*, he thought. The past two years in the Ranger Department had strained their marriage to the breaking point, what with his weeklong absences, three o'clock formations, and the late, late hours when he eventually came home. Sighing, he wondered how much longer it would last. He could transfer to another unit, maybe get a desk job, but then all of the past two years' work would just go down the goddamned drain. Everything. And that wasn't going to happen. *Sarah will have to put up with the bullshit just a little bit longer, or leave me.*

He thought about the past two years and then found himself thinking about the time way before that. How it was growing up . . . the rallies, the midnight raids . . . his father being thrown in jail. How the FBI had come snooping around when he was twelve, his father telling them to get off their property. When he got out of the state pen three years later, his father's klavern had all but disappeared from northern Georgia *(then the goddamned Jews from Channel Six did that horseshit story about him).* He saw it one night while he was a senior in high school and remembered how his father explained it all to him and told him why. How the Jews controlled the media and the banks. Christ, it was pretty fucking obvious, wasn't it? When was the last time they'd gotten a loan? And how the niggers had turned Atlanta into a ghetto, and the goddamned statistics *proved* that most of the crimes committed in Georgia and everywhere else were done by niggers who were too lazy to go out and work for a living like any decent white man. Think about it, son.

It was a proud day when his father gave him his white satin robe and hood. His mother had sewn it all together herself, and gave him a proud kiss when he donned it for the first time. Then he had gone to the small rally his father had organized and swore his solemn oath while a huge burning cross towered over him, blazing in the night air, filling his mind with an overwhelming sense of belonging and worthiness.

He was only seventeen then, but the ceremony of the burning cross was forever etched into his mind. Later, his father had poured a good, solid shot of homemade corn into a paper cup, telling him he was a man now, and that he had to maintain a Grey tradition and honor—that to be a Klansman was an honor above all else. That to defend the Constitution of the

United States and the great white race that created it meant diligently and wholeheartedly to fight against communism—and Zionism—and always and unfalteringly to secure the preservation, protection, and advancement of the great white race.

The descendants of Adam. The *true* wandering tribes of Israel.

He enlisted less than a week out of high school.

His father had told him he was so proud of his son joining the Army. The Paratroopers and Rangers, no less. Rich boys were evading the draft by going to school, and the Jews were running to Canada, all trying to escape Vietnam. Of course, it was good that the niggers were going—as long as gooks and niggers could kill each other, his father reasoned, it made the white man's job that much easier. Be proud, his father told him—to be a soldier in the tradition of the great Confederate General Nathan B. Forrest, who had founded the Klan, was to honor the Klan in the true warrior spirit; to learn the skills of survival and the ways of the guerrilla fighter was to help train the masses of younger, more vigorous white patriots soon to join the great white cause boiling within this country under the banner of the burning cross and the holy preservation of the white race.

Now, after one war and fifteen years of experience in the Army—after airborne training, Ranger training, Special Forces training, by Jesus, any training he could get his hands on—he was ready. His father was an old man but still had a mind as sharp and cunning as ever. He had told him that it was the son's turn to vindicate his father and the race from which he was born. It was time to put guns in hand, to train the young, future leaders of the Klan how to eradicate once and for all the pestilence created by the nigger and the Jew. To *lead* them.

To . . .

It began with a small campout one weekend for the sons and grandsons of his father's friend. Converting semiautomatic and surplus store AR-15s into fully automatic M16 rifles was only a matter of filing the sear lever controlling the hammer. Training young men in self-defense was interesting for them and rewarding for the instructor. He taught them how to plan and execute ambushes and raids. How to establish and maintain a guerrilla base in the woods and keep from being seen for weeks at a time. How to make homemade silencers for their surplus store Ingram MAC-10 and Swedish-K submachine guns. How to use ordinary kitchen supplies and fertilizer in making potent and devastating demolitions. How to create a riot. How to assassinate.

How to terrorize.

His was not the only band of Klansmen to don jungle fatigues. With the public embarrassment of the Carter years and fiascoes abroad in Iran and Lebanon rose the resurgence of white power across the country, the likes of which had never been seen before. Even though Grey and other Klansmen disliked the Fascist and un-American appearance of the neo-Nazis and their fanatical extremes, he nonetheless approved of their policies and actions toward nonwhites, and noted with satisfaction their own chain of training camps across the country. There was a movement in the country, so many splinter groups forming, so many parts of a whole, just waiting for the proper organization and leadership.

It could actually happen. The Great Eradication. And the new order.

Grey's head drooped. Suddenly, he jolted, awake and alert. He had dozed. He was tired and wanted to go home, home to the comfort and solace of a marriage he hoped was still sound. Grey knew the past two years had indeed taken its toll. No time for his wife and little girl, and no time for all of them to be happy, together as a family. But he also knew things would change for the better. He would personally ensure that, and his wife, his father, and the great white race would thank him for it.

Grey pulled his heels away from the desktop, stood up, and looked at his watch. It was already 1300. *Time to get some Colonel's Original Recipe,* he thought tiredly, walking for the door, squaring away his patrol cap in the mirror by it as he went.

The phone rang.

Christ, he thought, moving back to his desk to pick it up. *And after all the time I spent in here just now in silence.*

"Hello?"

"Hello, Frankie." A familiar and warming voice.

"Daddy!"

"Son, I'm over at the Three Sisters Bar and Grill just outside Fort Benning. You know where that is?"

"Sure, Daddy."

"Well, come and see me there as soon as you can. I've got some people I want you to meet."

"Damn, I'd really like to, but I was just on my way home. Can't we just get together later on this week in Dahlonega?"

"Son, this is important. Your wife can wait."

Grey was nonplussed. His father sounded strange.

"I'll be there in fifteen minutes, Daddy."

CHAPTER

· FOUR ·

"Are you crazy? You know we're not supposed to be drinking."

"Relax." Christopher thanked the tall, lithe waitress and paid her a five for a two-fifty pitcher of beer, taking her skimpy body suit off with his eyes as she leaned over them, placing it on their table. "Have a Lite beer from Miller, ol' buddy," he said, smiling broadly.

Levy's earlier resolve not to drink instantly vanished, and he poured the ice-cold beer into a frosty mug.

"Man," he said after taking several huge gulps, "I almost forgot what this stuff tasted like." He belched loudly.

"Not bad. Not bad at all."

They were seated near the entrance by a window that had THREE SISTERS BAR AND GRILL handpainted on it. It was a roomy place with balcony tables and several seating sections set apart on the bottom floor and a bar in the middle. The decor resembled that of a turn-of-the-century hunting lodge: a moose head on the wall, heavy wood furniture, antiques and area rugs all over. Levy slumped back in his chair, holding his mug possessively, trying not to think about going back to the compound later on.

Earlier in the day the two Rangers got their civvies on and Levy's car out of the parking lot ahead of everyone else, and had promptly deposited duffel bags full of filthy towels, underwear, and jungle fatigues at the nearest cheap laundry on the outskirts of Columbus, just off the Fort Benning reservation. It was a ripoff, but the fifteen dollars they paid the proprietor to clean the mess was well worth it. Now, after consuming mass quantities of steak and ice cream, it was time to relax and enjoy their last two hours before returning.

Several moments passed between the two, neither talking much. At first, Levy thought, he hadn't liked Christopher too much—his self-styled macho image, arrogance, pigheadedness—but the more he was around him, especially on patrol, the more he appreciated his Ranger buddy's sense of urgency when it came to getting things done.

He was a good soldier. Bottom line, that's what counted.

"So where did you go to school, Levy?" Christopher asked hesitantly.

Levy paused. "Harvard."

"*Harvard?*"

"Yeah, Harvard."

"Your family into big bucks or something?"

"Nope. I'm an Army brat."

"How the hell did you get into Harvard?"

"I won a music scholarship. 'Course, I worked all

through school, too, since the scholarship didn't pay for everything." Levy tried to think of a way to change the subject.

"Music? Why the hell are you in the Army?"

"My father was a thirty-year man. Special Forces. He was gone so much, I guess I just wanted to see what the Army was really like. You know, the mystique . . . hell, I'm here the same reason you are. You look around you, your friends back home. What are they doing?" He didn't let Christopher answer. "High school football coach, maybe? Mechanic? A businessman locked up in some damned office cashing in on a couple of ulcers for thirty or forty grand a year? That's not for me. And I sure as hell don't plan to work as a band director or play in some symphony without experiencing life to the hilt first. Look, we body-fling ourselves out of airplanes, we go on patrol, we beat ourselves to death—it's all pretty masochistic, huh?"

"That's for damn sure."

"We get paid to do stuff that people back home—civilians, that is—will never have a chance to see or do. We stay in shape. We do all these crazy things like hand-to-hand combat, patrolling, and humping a heavy ruck. Why? Because it's a challenge, man. My old man always told me—'No guts, no glory.' The British SAS have a saying—'Who dares, wins.' Know what I mean? The French commandos say—"

"*Nous Défions,*" Christopher interrupted. "We defy. I've heard all of them. My old man was a Beret too. Two tours in Vietnam. Before that he was in one of the airborne Ranger companies in Korea."

"Mine had three. Matter of fact, he got in SF back in the fifties, when it first started up."

"Must have been one of the originals."

"That's right. We never saw much of each other. He was always deployed somewhere. Broke my mother's heart when I joined ROTC. She was always making a big fuss over me, growing up. Pop let her have her way about Harvard and promised me he'd kick my ass if I didn't keep my grades up."

"I don't want to sound stupid or anything, but . . ." Christopher fidgeted in his chair and decided to pour himself another beer, refilling Levy's mug too.

"So ask your stupid question," Levy said, grinning.

The two Rangers traded obscenities. Then Christopher grew serious again.

"I've never known any Jews in the Army. What made your father decide to come in?"

"Pop," Levy said, and paused, staring at the bottom of the mug as he swirled the dregs. Then, "Pop grew up in World War Two. Literally. He was fourteen when the Nazis invaded Poland, and they wiped out his family. My grandmother was raped by a platoon of Waffen SS after they shot my grandfather. My dad saw it all. He escaped into the countryside somehow and linked up with some partisans." Levy glanced up at Christopher. "That's how he spent World War Two. Taking potshots at Germans."

Christopher was speechless. "No shit," he said finally, under his breath.

"Yeah. No shit. He met Mom at a displaced persons camp after the war, near Auschwitz. That's how she spent the war. In *that* fucking place. They caught the next boat smokin' to the U.S."

"Then your father got in the Army?"

"Not at first. He got his first job as a janitor in

New York, where we had some relatives on my mother's side. After all he'd seen in the big one, I guess he just got bored swabbing out toilets, so he enlisted. Couldn't speak English hardly, but he caught on pretty quick. Guess you could say he had plenty of experience. After Korea—he served there too—Special Forces recruited him, since he had a pretty good combat record and knew how to speak Polish, German, and Russian.''

''Man, I'll say. Here, have another beer.''

''Fill 'er up.'' A warm buzz crept through Levy's ragged body, and he knew he'd better make this his last one. He looked at Christopher as he poured another beer into his not so frosty mug. ''So what's your life story?'' he asked.

''My old man was in Special Forces too. We spent most of our time around Fort Devens, Massachusetts, when he wasn't in Vietnam. Lived a few years in Germany too.''

''You know, our fathers might have even served together at one time or another,'' Levy said.

''Might have.'' Christopher sat back in his chair and fell silent for a moment. ''I wonder if they ever had any problems,'' he said evenly.

''Like what?''

''Like what Yendall was telling us about a few nights ago.''

''Yeah, they probably did. I know my father never took any shit from anybody.'' Levy pulled the six-pointed star out of his collar.

''I thought Grey took that away from you.''

Levy grinned. ''Mom packed me two. This is Pop's Star of David. He was never what you'd call a devout Jew, but when I got my commission, he gave this one to me. He'd worn it all his life. My grandfather gave it to him at his Bar Mitzvah, just before the krauts invaded. Anyway, when he passed it along to me at my Bar Mitzvah, he told me always to remember how the Jews fought the Romans at Masada, how they fought the Nazi SS in the Warsaw ghetto . . . and how they threw the British out of Palestine and destroyed seven Arab armies after declaring the state of Israel. He's always told me never to be ashamed of being a Jew and to kick the living shit out of anybody who ever tries to tell me otherwise.''

The entrance door to the Three Sisters swung open and in walked a tall, lanky, silver-haired old man, followed by another short, cherubic-featured man dressed in a business suit. They were both laughing heartily as if one had just told the other a hilarious joke. The door opened again, and a stocky, blond-haired man with a scarred face joined them. The old man with the silver hair stopped laughing when his gaze fell upon Levy and Christopher sitting by the window, watching him. He stared at them coldly, and they averted their eyes. The hostess arrived, an attractive redhead in her thirties.

''Mr. Grey! How nice to see you again,'' she gushed. ''I believe you called earlier for reservations?''

''Lucy,'' he replied with a smile, ''you're looking prettier every day. I called earlier and reserved one of your private rooms upstairs.'' He leaned toward her and stage-whispered: ''Got to keep away from the coloreds, you know.'' The men around him belly-laughed and glanced at Christopher with jeering eyes.

''Why, Mr. Grey,'' Lucy giggled in mock reproach, "*really* now. If you gentlemen will follow me, please?"

The small group left for the stairs, and Christopher steamed in his chair.

"Fucking rednecks," he muttered. "I think Yendall was right. I'll bet there's Klan all around this part of the country."

Levy was confused. "That old man—didn't she just call him Mr. Grey?"

"Yeah, but—" Christopher gritted his teeth. "C'mon, man, it can't be what you're thinking."

"It wouldn't surprise me any. Like father, like son."

Christopher pushed his chair away from their table. "I gotta take a leak," he announced. "Then we'll go, okay?" He rose from the table and walked toward the men's room, popping his knuckles as he went.

Levy stared at his beer mug and the empty pitcher. Yendall had asked them on that black night if they had been watching the news. Of course he had. He knew there were crazies in the woods, preparing for their self-professed race war. Survivalists. Neo-Nazis. The Klan. All practicing what he had learned in the basic course, and so far in Ranger School. How to sneak up on your enemy and cut his throat . . . snipe at him with a silenced weapon from a thousand meters . . . raid, ambush. *Last week they discovered a KKK training camp by the Tennessee border.* . . .

The entrance door banged open and Levy watched his senior TAC stride into the restaurant.

History, Levy thought. *I'm history.* He crawled underneath the table as if retrieving dropped change and heard Lucy greet Sergeant Grey. She led him to the stairs, saying his father was expecting him and wasn't it so nice to see them all again.

Levy waited until they were out of sight and then darted to the men's room.

"Christopher!"

"Can't you let a guy shit in peace?" He was in one of the stalls.

"Pinch it off. Grey's here." Levy glanced at the door, expecting Grey to walk in at any minute.

Christopher burst out of the stall. "Then let's get out of here before that motherfucker sees us."

Grey opened the door and found his father sitting at the table with two other men—one with a broken nose and blond, short-cropped hair, and a fat one dressed in a constricting business suit who Grey swore looked just like the state representative his father had campaigned for two years back. Jim Beam stood guard at the center of the table next to a bucket of ice, and every man held a glass, laughing.

"Hi, Daddy."

Grey's father smiled broadly at him, throwing a salute. "Have a seat, son. I was just giving these ol' boys some pearls of wisdom."

Grey sat in the chair that had obviously been reserved for him and poured a straight shot of bourbon into his glass. He noticed that Broken Nose was appraising him with cold, calculating green eyes and wasn't laughing at all.

"Like I was saying, why don't nigger mamas let their babies play in the sandbox?" Silas Grey paused, watching the fat man snicker for the punch line. "Because the cat keeps covering them up!"

Jesus, does Daddy ever like telling that one, Grey thought as everyone collapsed in guffaws. He joined in the laughter and gulped a slug of the Jim Beam. *Ol' Daddy.*

Silas Grey stood up and retrieved an off-white handkerchief from his pocket, wiping his eyes as his chest heaved in deep gravelly laughter.

He finally coughed, cleared his throat, and announced: "Gentlemen, I'd like to introduce the finest son ever to come from a man's loins, *my* son, Frank Grey."

Grey stood up and grinned, stupidly feeling like he was eight years old again and his father had just introduced him to one of the hands at the feed mill. The fat man in the business suit immediately rose from the table and flashed Grey a toothy PR smile. Grey felt his lip starting to curl.

"Proud to know you, Frank, though I think we've met before. I'm Vernon Baggins." He extended a fat, moist palm, and when Grey shook it, he remembered the second-rate but rich politician his father had nominated earlier for the representative's seat in Dahlonega's district. He felt the same initial disgust that only a professional soldier can feel toward one whose body has degenerated into a mass of fleshy waste. Especially when the man was no older than he.

"Thought I recognized you, sir." *You out-of-shape lard-ass.* "I understand you're running for state senate this year?"

"That's right, Frank," Baggins replied, pulling his hand quickly out of Grey's and sitting down. "Only this time your father and I have organized a better strategy—*much* better." Baggins threw a quick glance at Silas, as if asking for approval to go on.

Silas Grey cleared his throat and frowned. "We'll go into that later, Vernon." He gestured toward the other man, who had been silent the entire time. "Son, this here's Mr. J. D. Gunther. He's from up north in Montana, and—well, let's say he's from one hell of an organization up there."

Grey locked eyes with the man as he shook his hand and was pleased to feel the iron grip of one who not only had once been in the military (he noticed the Marine bulldog tattoo on his right forearm) but also whose quiet and purposeful demeanor meant that he was a man to be relied upon.

"My pleasure, Mr. Gunther. Marine Corps?"

Piano-wire lips stretched over a row of jagged teeth in a lopsided grin. "Call me J.D. Short for Joe Don, but I prefer J.D. Force recon, Tet 'sixty-eight through 'seventy-two. You?"

"You've got me beat by a couple of years. Spent a tour there with the 173rd Airborne, and another with the 75th Rangers."

"Your father tells me you're still in."

"I'm with the Third Ranger Training Company here at Benning."

"I went through that course when I was in the corps. Damned good one."

"Well, I try to see to it that it stays good," Grey replied, grinning.

A hush fell over the room as a waitress slipped through the door and quietly placed everyone's order in front of them.

"I ordered you a rib eye cooked medium rare," Silas Grey informed his son. He thanked the waitress and gave her a twenty-dollar tip to ensure they wouldn't be disturbed for the next two hours.

Grey pushed away his plate and burped contentedly, his belly full of the Three Sisters' best effort yet. Everyone had eaten in silence, hurrying so as to get on with matters at hand. Grey chunked some ice cubes in his glass and splashed some fresh Jim Beam on them.

He looked at his father. "What's going on, Daddy?"

Silas settled back in his chair. "The time has come, gentlemen, for action. It is time to take matters in hand as our forefathers had during the Revolution. As your great-grandfather did during the Civil War, Frankie. As General Nathan B. Forrest did *after* the Civil War when he founded the Klan. It is time for the white people of this country to get up off their lazy asses and throw the nigger and the Jew out."

He paused, all eyes on him, then snorted, shaking his head. "Of course, we still have much, much more work to do." Silas looked directly at his son. "Frankie—under no circumstances must any of your school patrols be allowed near Camp Forrest."

Grey remembered the time last year when one of his Ranger students had gotten a patrol lost, stumbling dangerously close to their training camp. Fortunately, he had been with that patrol, and after giving the patrol leader a good chewing out, made sure they moved out of the area.

"No problem, Daddy. This time I will personally track each patrol's route prior to their moving out."

"Good, but let me emphasize this: Camp Forrest is gearing up, son. We are getting ready! A dozen of our best men from ten different klaverns in this state will be out there the same time you are. Not to mention about ten more from J.D.'s group."

"*What?*"

"That's right, Frank," Gunther interjected. "Our organization is training with yours this July. Getting to know one another. Your father has been coordinating with my boss—Reverend Samuel Taylor. Ever hear of him?''

''Who the hell hasn't?'' Grey replied, remembering recent *Newsweek* and *Time* articles abounding with stories the past year about robberies, murders, and FBI manhunts for individuals associated with Taylor's group. The Aryan Covenant of True Christ Christians. Its founder and leader was one Samuel Taylor. He had established a commune in the mountains of western Montana, and, like Grey and his father, had organized a paramilitary force whose holy mission it was to prepare for the pending race war.

Grey remembered watching the evening news one night, two months back, delivering a two-part segment on the ''Radical Right'' that had informed its viewers about how an organized group of extremists, dissatisfied with the President's conservative movement, were training in camps like his own for the day when they'd take matters into their own hands. Had his father felt the time had come to organize a cohesive, organized national front? Was it time for them all to become one in the White People's Party? Expectantly, he lifted his eyes to his father's.

''Daddy, you haven't told me about this.''

Silas combed his fingers through his silky white hair and massaged the back of his neck, a habit Grey remembered his father had whenever he was faced with difficult decisions. Then he spoke.

''Son, the only people that know about this are Taylor, his cadre, and the men you see in this room— but yes, the good Reverend and I have come to an agreement. Ain't no way in hell we're ever going to get anything accomplished divided as we are. Next week, a team from our organization will deploy to

Montana to train with the Aryan Covenant. At the same time, one of their teams will train with ours at Camp Forrest. We'll swap ideas, ideology, tactics . . . a trial of cooperation, if you will. The training will last two weeks.

"If all goes well, Taylor will organize his splinter groups, and I'll unite the various factions of the Klan. North and South Carolina. Alabama. Tennessee. Arkansas. Mississippi." He paused. "By September, God willing, we'll *all* be united as one front—*the White People's Party*. Vernon, here," he said, gesturing toward the fat man, "will be our spokesman and party leader, so to speak. And there's not a goddamned thing the FBI can do about it either. Hell, we ain't doing nothing illegal, we're just a bunch of good ol' boys out in the woods doing some shooting and camping."

Silas Grey fell silent, and the only thing heard by each man was his own heartbeat. The old man lifted his chin, his eyes narrowing to slits. "Then, when the time is right—and it's close!—we're going to mobilize, throw those Communist fuckers out of Washington, and get ahold of every Jew and nigger we can find, and see to it that Hitler's job gets finished. It'll be difficult at first, and we'll probably have to go underground, but when the American people see what we're doing, we will have their support."

Grey slouched in his chair. *The old man will see seventy before the year's out,* he thought. *Is it really time?* He leaned over the table and drained the whiskey bottle into his glass. *Daddy. He's always wanted this. I've always wanted it, too, but is it really time?*

"I got out of the Marines two years ago, Frank." Grey shifted his gaze to Gunther. The man appeared to speak only when he had something to say. He liked that.

"Seemed like the more niggers and spicks got in the Corps, the worse the Corps became. I got sick of it, and decided to do something about it." Gunther's cheek suddenly twitched under his left eye. "And any whitey can sit on his fat, lazy ass and complain, but it takes a white man—a strong white man—to do something about it.

"We in the Aryan Covenant are ready." Gunther slowly put his right fist in the palm of his left hand up by his chin and cracked his knuckles, staring at Grey. "Are you?"

Grey knew what he would say.

CHAPTER

· FIVE ·

It was an out*standing* chow hall, as many a Ranger
student had testified—rows of silver milk and juice
urns, the salad counter, the fruit counter, the famous mountain phase blueberry pancakes. It was
the most wonderful place in the world when you
returned from a patrol after eating only three C-
rations in as many days.

Now, five hours before the first bus was to arrive,
a lone figure dressed in immaculately tailored and
starched camouflage fatigues sat at a long table by
the rear of the chow hall. It was a table reserved for
RIs only, and Staff Sergeant Justin MacAlister sat
there, eating his breakfast in cold, seething quiet.

He was a small man, but one used to spending
long, disciplined hours studying the martial arts. He
was tough and lean, a wiry black Bruce Lee. Tiny
scars pitted the skin on the tops of his knuckles, the
result of countless broken boards and bricks. He was
also a black man, so black that his beardline colored

his jaw into the blackest shade of blue. What there was of his hair cast a shadowy oblong pattern on the top of his head. His unusually aquiline features and high cheekbones were inherited from a Portuguese sailor deep within his ancestry and had always made him look much younger that his twenty-seven years, but recently acquired worry lines creased his forehead, and his jaw muscles constantly worked and popped like ripcords, making him seem much older. Before him sat a hefty meal consisting of those famous mountain phase blueberry pancakes, bacon and eggs, and hot, steaming coffee.

Staff Sergeant Justin MacAlister, deep in thought, raised that cup of coffee to his lips and promptly burned the hell out of them.

"Shit!" he exploded, slamming his cup on the cafeteria tray, sloshing coffee on his pancakes. He looked around the chow hall to see if anyone had observed his outburst. The only activity came from behind the serving counter, where he heard Sergeant Harris, the mess steward, yelling at the morning KPs. No one was around—at least none of the other RIs, he concluded. He'd arrived early on purpose, because he had some thinking to do. A lot of it. He stabbed his fork in his pancakes and glared at the offending mug of coffee.

Reflecting on the past two months, Justin Mac-Alister could not remember having been more angry and scared. He should have taken his father's offer.

It had been his first leave in over three years, so he had packed up Lisa and their two sons in their old beat-up Volvo and driven down the Pacific coastline for his parents' house. It was time for it. That much time with the Ranger Battalion at Fort Lewis took its toll.

The next two weeks at his parents' house in San Luis Obispo gave him a chance to relax and catch up on some reading. One night after dinner, his father had told him a position was waiting for him at the fire department whenever he was ready to get out. MacAlister had laughed. He was a careerist. One did not go through eight years of highly specialized training and then trash it before his twenty was up. He was leaving the Ranger Battalion for a new assignment anyway.

The Volvo damned near didn't make the trip. Lisa demanded they stay on the interstate once they were past the Texas border. The country highway north of Gainesville, Georgia, forced the exception. Their Volvo finally limped into Dahlonega with a flat and a hemorrhaged fuel line.

Waiting for repairs at a gas station near the courthouse, MacAlister noticed a gathering of men next to the courthouse lawn dressed in jungle fatigues. At first he thought it was a local Vietnam veterans parade or rally of some sort, but then he saw just how young the participants were. And not a black face in the crowd. After fifteen minutes of milling about, they finally manned a platoon-sized formation, unfurling the Stars and Bars at the head. By then more men had arrived, dressed in what appeared to be police riot gear with black-visored helmets, protective padding, and all were gripping ax handles. When the formation started marching down Main Street, they covered the flanks and the rear, constantly scanning faces in the crowd as if they were the President's secret servicemen.

Some of the crowd chanted slogans with the marching formation—trashy racist slogans. Others in the crowd just stood by, watching it all. Some in the crowd protested against the parade. Soon, fistfights broke out between the racists and the protesters. As he turned back for his car, disgusted, a short, balding man in his forties intercepted him, trying to speak. At first MacAlister tried to shoulder his way past him, but the other man held on, telling him not to judge Dahlonega from the rally he'd just observed. It was the mayor. MacAlister was informed that Dahlonega was a *good* town, but there just wasn't any way he could keep the crazies from doing what they wanted, as long as it was a legal, peaceful march.

MacAlister had appreciated the man's remarks, but pointed out to him that what those "crazies" were doing was anything but peaceful. He walked back to the gas station. His wife and children had stayed in the Volvo the entire time.

MacAlister paid the grinning gas station owner for the new radial and fuel line and swiftly departed for the ranger camp's headquarters fifteen miles up the road with a silent wife and two highly inquisitive boys.

He had found the best house in Dahlonega two hundred dollars a month could rent, which wasn't much, and reported for duty one week later after making the necessary repairs. He had to hand it to Lisa for bearing up as well as she had—the trip, the house, the new environment.

Lieutenant Colonel Cummings, the phase two commander at Camp Merrill, gave MacAlister a welcoming interview two days after he inprocessed the administrative center and signed for his issue. Cummings was a small man, thin and as austere in manner and speech as the Ranger haircut on his head.

"You realize that Benning made a mistake assigning you here," he had said.

"Sir?"

"Sergeant MacAlister, you are the first black RI I have seen assigned here since I took command six months ago. Not only that, but I thought it was policy back at the Ranger Department *not* to send black RIs here."

"That's the first time I've ever heard that, sir." MacAlister felt his cheeks flush.

"Don't get me wrong, Sergeant." Cummings leaned forward in his chair toward his desk and flipped open MacAlister's personnel folder. "I've reviewed your file and I can't think of anyone more qualified to be an RI—basic and advanced infantryman's training honor graduate. *Distinguished* Ranger School honor graduate four years ago, three years as a squad leader with 2nd Battalion at Lewis— you've had an impressive career. You stand a good chance of being promoted ahead of your peer group to sergeant first class next year."

"Yes, sir," he said, shifting in his seat. *What the hell's he driving at?*

"I'll be frank with you, Sergeant." Cummings straightened up in his chair, holding MacAlister's gaze. "You can work anywhere in the Army and do well, but if you work here, you'll have trouble. Serious trouble." Cummings broke eye contact. "You are black."

"I'm well aware of that, sir." *So fuckin' what?*

"Klan activities have increased substantially the past several months," Cummings said quickly. "It's getting ugly, especially around Dahlonega. There're rumors of a Klan base camp up in the mountains."

MacAlister remembered the parade. "Are you requesting my reassignment, sir?"

"That's up to you. I recommend it."

There was a long pause as the men studied each other. MacAlister had never encountered this situation before. The Klan? He had only read about it, seen reports on TV. Fuckit.

"I'll be okay, sir."

"No doubt you will. What about your family?"

MacAlister started to speak, but found he couldn't.

"There will be many times when you'll be out walking a patrol, not knowing your family's safety under these circumstances. Did you see the rally last week?"

"When we drove in." Another long pause.

"Sergeant, I'm not going to order you to move on, though I wish you would submit paperwork to do so." Cummings leaned forward in his chair. "Please understand this: The Klan is powerful in this area. It's not Army regulation, but it will be in your best interest to request reassignment. I say this not as your commanding officer, but man to man."

MacAlister sat in stony silence, listening to Cummings. *Regulations, my ass. Since when does your commanding officer in any unit suggest you do something?*

"There's something else," Cummings added, nodding at three class pictures hanging on the wall behind MacAlister. For every graduating class he had supervised, Cummings had posted a ten-by-twelve graduation picture in his office in chronological order, giving him a total of three so far during his tenure as the camp commander. He stared at the second picture for several moments. It was no different from the others: approximately sixty to seventy Ranger graduates, pinch-faced, bald, and exuberant (dressed in clean fatigues for a change), sitting or standing in six ranks. Cummings knew already that the young black lieutenant he was searching for wasn't there.

"Something else, sir?"

Cummings stood up and walked slowly to the picture. "That was last April's class. Those students were here in March prior to moving out for phase three in Florida. One of those kids—he was just a young second lieutenant fresh out of the basic course—got lost while on patrol in one of the northern lanes. He hadn't been doing so well. Flunked every patrol he led. We were planning to recycle him into the next class. He came from a black university up near Chicago and didn't know shit from shinola about being out in the woods. Scared him, I think. Hell, he'd lived in the city all of his life." Cummings stopped, aware he was rambling. Then, "We mobilized the entire class and searched for him during the next three days. We found him near the entrance of a narrow ravine at the foot of Black Mountain. He'd been torn apart by some kind of animal or group of animals. Probably a pack of wild dogs. Anyway, that's what finally came out on the investigative report."

"Is that what you think it was, sir?"

Cummings returned to his seat before answering and stared at the blotter on his desk. "I'd never heard of wild dogs up in this neck of the woods, and neither had any of the other RIs. I think somebody put those dogs on Ranger Davis's trail and hunted him down." He looked back up at MacAlister. "His body looked like he had been ripped apart by a land mine, like a buddy of mine back in 'Nam.''

MacAlister pushed the breakfast tray away, vaguely aware of the cold pancakes he had scarcely touched. He picked up his coffee mug and drained it, realizing that the cold and bitter liquid now perfectly matched his mood.

He rose from the table and walked to the coffee urn positioned near the rear entrance of the chow hall facing the parking lot outside. As he poured a fresh cup, another RI walked in, and MacAlister, still deep in thought as he turned back for his table, walked into him, splashing the steaming brown liquid on the man's freshly starched jungle fatigues.

''God*damn*, MacAlister,'' he howled, frantically brushing coffee off his uniform.

The man was Larry Quinn, a staff sergeant in his mid-thirties with close-cropped, fuzzy red hair. Jerk *extraordinaire*. He had a slight build and a cocky, abrasive personality that matched it. MacAlister got along fine with the other RIs at Camp Merrill with the exception of Quinn, who like himself was a new-comer.

''Oh, man, I'm really sorry about that,'' Mac-Alister apologized. ''Here, let me help you.'' He reached for the paper napkin holder on a nearby table.

''Forget it,'' Quinn said, brushing by MacAlister for the serving counter, agitated and more self-righteously indignant than the situation warranted.

MacAlister bristled. *Stay cool, just stay cool*, he thought. *Fuckit. Don't like the shitbird anyway*. He returned to his table, angry and pissed at the other RI, who he thought was just as arrogant as some of the townspeople he'd seen on the day he had arrived in Dahlonega.

MacAlister remembered how he had once walked into the instructors' lounge, fresh off a patrol, as Quinn delivered the punch line of a stupid joke. (Know why niggers never go to Denver? Their lips explode at five thousand feet! Haaa-ha-ha.) Real funny. The others in the lounge laughed along with Quinn and then had shut up in embarrassed silence as soon as they saw MacAlister standing behind them in the doorway, trying to ignore it all and let the moment pass, but clenching his fists all the same . . . and trying to keep from pouncing on Quinn like he wanted to do so badly now.

MacAlister suddenly heard the diesel roar of the buses driving into the parking lot outside, and realized the incoming class from Benning was at least two hours ahead of schedule. Leaving his coffee mug, he retrieved his breakfast tray from the table and took it across the chow hall to the KP counter, depositing it there. By the time he returned, the door swung open again, and Sergeant Frank Grey walked in, giving him one of those Christ-is-this-him? stares.

"You Sergeant MacAlister?"

"That's right."

"I'm Sergeant Grey," the hulking RI announced, not offering his hand. He jerked his head toward the door. "I've got the new class up here today a little early."

"So I see." *Pompous bastard.*

"Hey, Frank! What's up?" It was Quinn again, walking toward them, his breakfast tray full to overflowing with grits and pancakes.

"Larry, long time no see," Grey said, smiling. He walked over and slapped Quinn on the back.

MacAlister hung by the door, watching the re-union.

"Listen," Grey said, "let me get my class squared away with MacAlister here, and I'll be right back for some breakfast." He paused, looking the chow hall over. "Man, it's good to be back home. C'mon, MacAlister, let's get these nerds and turds outside situated before they discover there's *real* food in here."

MacAlister snapped his patrol cap on his head, puzzled as he followed Grey out the door. *Must be old home week.*

"See you later, Frank," Quinn garbled through a mouthful of grits. Then he added: "Hey, Mac-Alister—forget about the uniform, man."

MacAlister turned around as Grey walked outside and faced Quinn, wondering if he was trying to apologize. He could still see the twinkling mockery in his eyes.

"No problem," he muttered. He pushed the screen door open harder than he intended and walked out.

Quinn ate his grits, knowing he had them both buffaloed.

CHAPTER

· SIX ·

. . . I accept the fact that as a Ranger, my country expects me to move farther, faster, and fight harder than any other soldier.

"Awright, Rangers, move out, move out, move out!" the class leader screamed as hordes of yelling Rangers burst out of the buses. A student himself, he commanded the Ranger class during all administrative activities, a task the RIs delighted in giving to the most senior officer attending the course. "C'mon, men, move like you got a *purpose* in life!"

"Rangers, fall in on me!" the student first sergeant hollered, dropping two duffel bags and his rucksack at the head of the formation area twenty meters behind the buses.

Utter chaos.

"First platoon over here!"

"Second platoon over here—no, wait—second platoon over *here*!"

"Hey, c'mon, people—"

"Fourth platoon, quit feelin' sorry for yourselves! Over here, ragbags!"

Ranger Knowles, the class leader—Captain

Knowles in the real world—dog-trotted toward the formation, wondering how many push-ups he'd have to knock out for Grey this time. Once there, he threw his equipment to the pavement and double-timed to the front of the formation.

"First Sergeant," he gasped.

"Yo!"

"What'sa status?"

"We're still waiting on third platoon to get their act together." Ranger Clemons—Staff Sergeant Clemons back at Fort Bragg—assumed the awesome burdens of command and yelled toward the culprits: "Hey, third platoon, you got your fuckin' act together yet?"

"We're up!" came the reply from the frustrated student platoon sergeant.

"Okay, sir, we're ready to go." Ranger Clemons turned around and faced the formation. "Company . . . 'ten-*hut*!" He faced about and saluted Knowles. "All present, class leader."

"Post," Knowles replied, returning his first sergeant's salute.

Clemons raced back to the rear of the formation while Knowles about-faced and watched, with great trepidation, Sergeant Grey exit what appeared to be the chow hall with a wiry black RI.

Ranger Knowles froze at the position of attention, sweating through his fatigues. *Man*, he thought, *even here in the mountains, it's hotter than a forty-peckered tomcat.*

Grey walked up to Knowles and stood before him, scowling first at the formed company, then at the smaller man, looking down a good six inches at the top of the Ranger's shaved head.

"All present, Sergeant!" Knowles shrieked into Grey's top shirt button.

"This company moved like a bunch of slugs just now, Ranger Knowles."

"Yes, Sergeant! No excuse!"

"No excuse, my ass, Class Leader! Get on down and knock 'em out."

Grey drilled the company mercilessly with push-ups for the next ten minutes while he chewed them out. When he was finished, he and MacAlister marched the class to a row of ten-man huts lined up against a hillside across the road from the chow hall. Once there, Grey told the student chain of command they had the next thirty minutes to move in and get set up before receiving their inbriefing from the phase two head instructor at the classroom.

"Well, this looks like home for the next couple of weeks," said Dan Levy after they were turned loose from the formation. "C'mon, guys, let's get moving."

Nine Ranger students picked up their duffel bags and rucksacks and followed Levy to their assigned hut. He was their new squad leader, and Christopher and Jakes were the Alpha and Bravo team leaders.

"Looks a hell of a lot better than the barracks back at Benning," Christopher said, unlocking the door. He stepped inside. "All right! Man, this is number one! No floors to mop and buff. Just stash your gear, keep it neat, and deal with it, man."

The rest of the squad moved inside, each man parking his equipment on his assigned bunk bed—Christopher's team on one side, and Jakes's team on the other. Levy, as the squad leader, bunked with

Christopher by the door, so he could be the first man out when called to formations and meetings.

From what he could see during the drive in, Levy decided he liked his new surroundings. Camp Merrill was a small compound consisting of a camp headquarters, mess facility, student huts, chapel, a tiny PX, and a landing strip for helicopters. The camp itself was set on top of a gently sloping hill at the foot of much larger, densely wooded mountains surrounding the area. It was 600 meters across, extending from the small grass runway on one side to the chapel on the other.

Prentiss burst into the hut.

"Formation!" he shouted. "Let's go!" Everybody dropped what they were doing and glared at their new platoon sergeant.

Christopher glanced at his watch. "We've still got another twenty minutes, shit-for-brains."

"Grey moved the time up on us." Prentiss turned and stuck his head out the door. "Well, come on," he said, facing back at them. "The rest of the company's almost formed up."

"Pick it up, fourth squad," Levy said wearily, walking out the door.

"Company . . .'ten-*hut*!" Ranger Knowles faced about and saluted Sergeant Grey. "Sergeant, the company is *formed*!" he yelled.

"They're still too damned slow, Ranger. Knock 'em out."

"Yes, Sergeant!" Knowles flopped to the ground. "*One*, Sergeant! *Two*, Sergeant—"

"No, Ranger. Over there." Grey pointed at the closest hut. Knowles bolted for it and shoved his feet up against the side. Already, he had broken out in a sweat.

"*One*, Sergeant! *Two*, Sergeant—"

"All right, tickturds," Grey lectured the company. "You all definitely disappointed me with the way you looked and acted getting off the buses this morning. You should know by now that you must move quickly. Efficiently. Soldierly. None of you fit those categories."

"*Seven*, Sergeant! *Eight*, Sergeant! *Nine*—"

"And that's why your class leader is knocking out so many push-ups today," he explained, gesturing at Knowles. "You all ain't supporting him. Is that the way you all are gonna support your patrol leader when you're out on patrol?"

"No, Sergeant!" cried a chorus of voices.

"*Twelve*, Sergeant! *One for the Great Ranger in the Sky!*"

"Recover, Ranger Knowles," Grey said disgustedly. Knowles scrambled back to his position in front of the company, which had remained at attention the entire time.

"Tell you what, Rangers," Grey lectured, pacing before the formation. "If you thought phase one was tough, wait till you start humpin' patrols up here in the mountains. You gotta rely on each other. Help each other out. There just ain't no room here for shiftless, lazy people."

Back in the formation, Christopher started. He'd heard that one before.

"Now get this, Rangers"—Christopher swore Grey was looking directly at him—"you all are gonna march up to the classroom in another minute. When you get there, I expect you to bust ass getting inside. I want to hear some motivation. Plenty of it!

You better be sounding off and standing by your desks in less than fifteen seconds after falling out of formation. Is that clear?''

"Clear, Sergeant!" the company cried in unison.

"Damn well better be. Ranger Knowles!"

Knowles popped up before Grey like a marionette. "Yes, Sergeant!"

"Take charge."

Ranger Knowles stood at attention before the head instructor of phase two and saluted.

"Sergeant! One-oh-nine mean, nasty Rangers, present for instruction!"

Master Sergeant Rick Fowlds returned his salute. "Have 'em take seats, Class Leader," he said in a surprisingly low, even voice.

"Take . . . *seats!*"

"Yaaaah-*huah!*" came the reply from the company, and they swiftly sat down. Knowles lunged for his desk, tripping over his feet in the process.

Silence.

Sergeant Fowlds cast a cold eye on the company, appraising their motivation and discipline. He had seen many a Ranger report for duty such as Knowles, as he himself had once done twenty years earlier. He was one of the old-timers who had served with the 75th Rangers in Vietnam—as a mass of scar tissue on his right cheek bore testament. He was thin to the point of emaciation and was as tall as Grey, who was standing at the rear of the class listening to Fowlds's welcoming speech. Like other RIs, his jungle boots were shined to a mirror finish, and his tailored camouflaged fatigues were stiff and boardlike from starch; unlike other RIs, he never raised his voice. He expected people to listen closely to what he had to say—and they always did.

"Think you're gonna kick phase two's ass, Rangers?"

No one spoke.

"Well, answer me." Fowlds's voice cut like a razor-sharp meat cleaver.

"Yes, Sergeant!" the class yelled.

"Okay, I hear you. Only I don't think you can do that, Rangers. You've got to get through *my* RIs first, and they're gonna kick *your* ass.

"Up here you will experience maximum pain, a lot of misery . . . and a lot of learning. These mountains will put you through the test. My RIs will ensure that. Your rucks will be heavier than the ones you humped at Benning, and, more important, this is where your patrols count. You will each receive at least two leadership positions while on patrol here, and you damned well better pass at least one of them. No freebies."

Levy sat riveted in his seat in fascination of this older, intense RI, remembering the patrol he and Christopher had led at Camp Darby, which now seemed a million miles away. They had been two of the few out of the entire class who had passed their first leadership evaluation.

"Here's what you can expect. During the next eighteen days you will divide your time between learning mountaineering techniques and patrolling the wilderness of the Chattahoochee National Forest and the Tennessee Valley Divide. Men, the TVD is a great equalizer. You will become increasingly more proficient in the fundamentals, principles, and techniques of guerrilla warfare against a determined enemy in a mountain environment. In other words,

Rangers, you'll be hashing it out with Ranger-qualified personnel that work for me here, mostly *my* RIs.'' Fowlds paused, letting his last statement sink in for effect.

The entire class sat in silence, listening to what they knew would happen just like the old RI was telling them.

"Rangers, you will become more aware of the need to maintain yourselves and your equipment in top condition during the extended operations you will endure with very limited support. If you get snakebit or hurt, it may be a while before we can get to you. Some time back, a Ranger got lost from his patrol. We searched for him for three days."

The RI paused, staring hard at the students. "Then we found him dead in a ravine after having been torn apart by a pack of wild dogs."

The class murmured. A prickly sensation crawled on the back of Christopher's neck. He turned around and saw Grey smiling in the rear.

"Those things happen sometimes. You damn well better watch out for your Ranger buddy. If you thought your piddly two-day patrol back at Benning was tough, wait until you're up in the mountains and you've been out of water for the past twelve hours and haven't had any food for the past twenty-four. And if the weather turns all to shit, you're not going to snivel out of the mission. I don't care how hungry, tired, wet, cold, hot, or hurt you may think you are, you *will* accomplish your mission.

"I have one more thing to say before I turn you over to my instructors: There are people up in these mountains. I don't care if they're backpackers, climbers, hunters, or whatever . . . you stay away from them. Is that clear?"

"Clear, Sergeant!" came the reply.

"Good. Rangers, in closing, I truly wish you the best. As you probably already know, we have about a twenty to thirty percent washout rate here at phase two. It's up to you, Rangers. Help your buddy, and don't fuck him over by going to sleep or breaking contact with the rest of your patrol. Pull together as a team. Drive-on. Men, you have got to drive-on and push yourself and those around you to make it. Take the challenge, Rangers."

Fowlds paused, looking for the student he saw in every class who was either sleeping or not paying attention. There wasn't any. That pleased him.

"I've said all I have to say. Now I'm gonna give you all a piss break before I turn my instructors loose on you. Good luck. Class Leader!"

The entire class jumped to their feet in unison. Knowles posted himself in front of the RI.

"Take charge."

"Yes, Sergeant!"

Levy walked over to where his Bravo team leader was supporting the side of the classroom; his mouth open, eyes closed, and catching some Zs.

"Hey, Jakes." He prodded Jakes with the toe of his jungle boot, causing him to jump up excitedly, his eyes and mouth open like someone had goosed him in the butt.

"I wasn't sleeping, I wasn't—oh, it's you."

"Who'd you think I was? Gimme a dip."

"Is that an order, good buddy?" Jakes cracked his crooked farm-boy smile as he handed Levy a sweat-stained can of Copenhagen.

"I owe you, pard." Levy grinned back at Jakes and went through the ritual of shaking and thumping the tin can of snuff. The only creature comforts allowed at Ranger School were gum, snuff, and cigarettes. Levy chose snuff, since it kept him awake, toned down the hunger pangs, and gave him a solid nicotine buzz. He wondered how his mother would react seeing him stuff the worm dirt in his lower lip, and almost burst out laughing. He glanced at his watch, a beat-up cheapie he had picked up at Ranger Joe's in Columbus for $19.99. Another minute and it would be time to move back inside the classroom.

Christopher walked up to Levy, punching his arm lightly.

"What do you think?" he asked.

"About what?" Levy handed the can of Copenhagen back to Jakes, who promptly went back to sleep.

"Phase two, so far."

"I think we're gonna suck it up and drive-on like the RI said. Why?" Levy noticed Christopher was even more sour-looking than his usual self.

"I think that scumbag Grey is gonna stick it to us. You know what I mean."

Levy thought about the night before, when they'd seen Grey at the Three Sisters.

"Keep a low profile, Ranger buddy. Just stay away from him."

"I ain't gettin' lost in these damn woods."

"You got that shit right." Levy stared hard at Christopher. "Remember what Yendall said about the rednecks."

"Yeah, man. I coulda swore Grey was smiling back in the rear of the classroom when that RI was telling us about that student they found."

Levy thought about it. None of this was making

any sense. Hell, he'd *seen* a black RI when they first got out of the buses. He had walked to the formation with Grey and then had taken the class to the huts. He grinned at Christopher, who was making fists and popping his knuckles.

"I think we're both getting hyper. Forget Yendall. What he told us about Grey happened fifteen years ago."

Christopher's eyes narrowed to slits. "Then I'll tell you what, Jew-boy. You'd better stick close to *this* nigger on patrol, 'cause I ain't taking any chances."

CHAPTER

· SEVEN ·

"The sniper. A good one is worth as much as a squad of infantry. Back in 'Nam a VC sniper could keep a whole damned battalion pinned down for hours. That's why I became one. A good one. Like you're going to be."

"Shit, city boy. We done grew up with a good ol' Remington thirty-ott-six or a thirty-thirty Winchester. You ain't gonna teach us nothin' about shootin'."

J. D. Gunther gritted his teeth until they hurt. He heard this redneck call him city boy ever since he and his group had arrived a week ago.

The man called Jerry drawled, "Charley, will you for once just shut your mouth and let the man talk? He's trying to teach you something." With that, he spat an amber stream of tobacco juice from his mouth onto the pine needles covering the ground by the firing range.

"Listen, guys," Gunther said to the half-dozen assembled men, "don't get me wrong. I know you've hunted and fished here all your life. I just want to pass on some techniques we learned in El Salvador.''

"Gunther," Jerry replied, "we're all ears. Don't pay no attention to Charley here. He's always been a little off in the head, so don't let him piss you off. Now, what's that you were saying about El Salvador?''

Gunther grinned at Jerry, who seemed to be the de facto leader of the group. No one countered his advice or decisions, whether wanted or not. One couldn't help but like him though—his good ol' boy personality and natural charisma matched perfectly with his bear-like frame and the chew of Red Man constantly lodged in his cheek. The other man, he resolved, was just an ignorant SOB, probably inbred, who tagged along with Jerry constantly. Thin and bald, with ears that looked remarkably like a taxicab with its doors wide open, the dimwit seemed to rely on Jerry's constant approval.

Gunther hefted the M14 rifle in both hands and extended it out so everyone could see. It had an ART-1 scope attached.

"Fellas," he continued, "I've used this weapon ever since my first tour in 'Nam back in 'sixty-eight. I've got thirty-eight kills there, and about eight in El Salvador.''

"How in the *hell* did you get in Ayl Salveedor?'' Charley asked incredulously, his eyebrows popping and arching as he spoke. The rest of the men in the small group murmured, wondering the same.

Gunther lowered the rifle and leaned it against his pack by a huge pine tree, then squatted before the rest of the men, pulling out a pack of Marlboros and lighting up. He took a deep drag, letting it out slowly before talking. "It's not so hard," he said finally. "Matter of fact, it's perfectly legal to fly direct to the capital. Once there—there were only three of us—we went to the embassy and told the military attaché we wanted to help out, that we all had experience.''

''Nothin' like experience, huh, J.D.?'' Jerry said, chuckling.

''That's right. And it'd be a good thing for your group to go too. It won't pay much, but your organization ought to be able to take care of that. 'Course, that's not what we're here for in the first place, right?''

''You got that shit right, good buddy,'' Jerry said, dead serious. ''The goddamned commies in Washington are trying to take our guns away. Next thing you know, this country's gonna be run by an all-nigger police force, and crime's gonna be even worse. Won't even have no guns to protect ourselves with.''

''My sentiments exactly,'' Gunther replied. ''Same thing's happening to the military. Comes to a point where a man's got to make a stand.''

The group nodded in agreement, liking what the blond, hatchet-faced man was saying. Gunther could feel the rapport building between them, total strangers he'd never seen before until last week, when his team had arrived. Already they had made substantial progress in upgrading the Klansmen's skills.

''Well, guys,'' Gunther said, standing up and field-stripping his cigarette, ''I could talk about this weapon all day until I'm blue in the face. Let's fire this mother up.'' He reached inside his ruck and pulled out several large paper photo targets. They were all bull's-eyed pictures of prominent black and Jewish leaders throughout the country.

''I'll help, I'll help,'' Charley said, jumping up. ''Let's go post 'em now.''

''Here,'' Gunther said, passing the targets out. ''There's enough for everyone.'' He led the procession down the firing range, a long, rectangular meadow which was used as a convenient landing strip.

Gunther admitted that the small base camp was *very* satisfactory, which had been a pleasant surprise. It was expertly concealed on a false hilltop deep within the Tennessee Valley Divide. The compound itself consisted of three log cabins twenty-five meters apart in different directions, effecting a triangle. It was surrounded by a sturdy, eight-strand barbed-wire fence with the strands pulled tight. One cabin was the headquarters, and the other was used for the storage of their weapons and ammunition. The last cabin comfortably housed two dozen men, and was the largest cabin, with a kitchen and two bathrooms. Camouflaged netting covered all structures and prevented observation from the air. Five hundred meters south of the compound was the runway, three hundred meters long and just large enough for a light aircraft or helicopter. At the end of the airstrip was another concealed cabin they used as a warehouse for arms and ammunition.

Ten minutes later they had posted targets on the opposite tree line and returned to their firing positions.

Gunther faced the men. They were all in their twenties, with the exception of Jerry and Charley, who were in their mid-thirties. It was a good day for training, he thought. He had always liked being an instructor, a carryover from his days in the Marine Corps. Two men in the group had turned out to be in the National Guard and were already familiar with the basics, and every man present had grown up with a hunting rifle. They were all natural woodsmen, and he enjoyed being with them.

"Let's start shooting," he said enthusiastically. "We'll start with the mayor of Atlanta over there."

Everyone grinned.

CHAPTER

· EIGHT ·

Never shall I fail my comrades.

A solitary candle flickered in fourth squad's hut, a quivering light that danced across Ranger Keith Christopher's brooding face. He had lit it after lights out so he could finish packing his rucksack. An Army ruck not well padded, taped, and tied off felt like stringing yourself against a medieval rack, after having it on all day.

When he was finished, Christopher leaned his ruck against the wall of the hut at the head of his bunk, which was already made up for next morning's inspection. His web gear was draped over it. Both ammo pouches and canteens, his flashlight, knife, and compass were tied off so nothing could fall off and get lost while on patrol.

Christopher scanned the hut, briefly resting his eyes on each sleeping figure. It was no more than ten minutes after lights out, and already people were snoring. He couldn't sleep, and it puzzled him. He had good reason to. The squad had spent the day at the lower mountaineering climbing site, rappeling off the sixty-foot cliff and jumping off the thirty-foot wooden practice wall, while each man's Ranger buddy caught him with a belay. Christopher chuckled softly, remembering the look on Prentiss's face when the RI told him to jump off for the first time. He wound up being suspended upside down and scared stiff, yelling for Jakes to lower him. Fifty push-ups later, the RI made Prentiss jump off ten additional times for practice. It was a good thing Jakes was belaying him—the country boy was short, but as brawny and tough as a badger.

Christopher believed that few things in life were as important as the intestinal fortitude a man had to have. Call it bravery, strength, leadership, or whatever—he had to have guts to accomplish his mission. Couldn't let the heat, cold, rain, distance, and hunger slow you down or make you complain. Going to Ranger School was a test. *His* test. His father had told him that it was the hardest thing he had ever done. Christopher found that hard to believe. How could a man who spent three tours in Vietnam say that?

He loved his father. Command Sergeant-Major Warren Christopher. He had come home from Vietnam for the last time back in '71, and had then retired and moved them all to Colorado when Christopher was in the eighth grade.

Christopher felt for his web gear and removed his sharpening steel from the extra ammo pouch he kept on his pistol belt for his sundries, like water purification tablets, chewing gum, and utility cord. Then he pulled his Ka-Bar from its sheath and stroked it against the steel. It was an old knife; the leather on the handle was worn and stained a deep chocolate brown from sweat and palm grease. The six-inch blade's black anodized finish was almost completely worn off, but the edge was still razor-sharp. The knife had been his brother's. He *hadn't* come back.

Christopher remembered sharing his first drink of cognac with his father at deer camp when he was fifteen. The old sergeant-major had at first laughed and then cried as he reminisced how Christopher's older brother, Rudy, had shot his first buck, and then drunk *his* first cognac later that evening for a celebration. The sergeant-major had then given Christopher the knife. It was the only time Christopher had ever seen his father cry.

As he grew older, Christopher often wondered why his old man had become so close to him—like he'd been with Rudy. It usually seemed that the shadow of a dead son and brother created an impasse between the other son and father in other families. Maybe the sergeant-major saw his dead son in his younger son, and wanted it to be the same all over again, hoping to spend more time with Christopher now that he was retired. There were tae kwon do classes, more hunting trips . . . more talks of the Army.

Christopher enlisted the day after the hostages were taken in Iran, dropping out of his freshman year at the University of Colorado at Boulder. His father tried unsuccessfully to make him remain, but it was something they both knew would not happen. Besides, the younger Christopher had a family tradition to live up to. He would be a paratrooper and Ranger like his older brother and his father. College could wait until later. Even his girlfriend back home could wait until later.

To be a Ranger, to be the best—to be a soldier, a

leader, a noncommissioned officer like his father, maybe even an officer, if he could push his OCS packet through—to do all that would help him become the kind of man his brother once was. His brother had been his idol. Why did Rudy have to die?

Basic, AIT, and Airborne school. Then the 82nd Airborne Division. Christopher spent his first enlistment as a machine-gunner and team leader in the 504th, getting promoted to buck sergeant early, then reenlisting for duty with the Rangers. He remembered reporting in to the orderly room of his new unit at Fort Stewart, Georgia, and how the first sergeant had chewed his ass out for having a high and tight haircut instead of a Ranger *trainee's*—which was no hair at all. He was assigned to the training platoon and enrolled in the Ranger indoctrination program, then Pre-Ranger. By the time those two courses were over, he was in the best physical condition of his life and knew what to expect at Fort Benning.

Now that he was halfway through the course, the training so far seemed anticlimactic compared to the torture he had endured at RIP, but he was prepared for whatever the RIs at Benning dished out. He would deal with anything while making it through the course. Anything. He'd been told before by his girlfriend, his mother, even his father, that he had a compulsive-obsessive personality. That if he got an idea in his head, he damned sure wouldn't rest until he resolved whatever the issue was. The way he looked at it, why the hell not go for all the hard training? Airborne school? Cake. Ranger School? Well, there was a challenge. And he had a family tradition to live up to.

Christopher stroked his dead brother's Ka-Bar against the sharpening steel one final time and then returned it to its sheath. Now he was tired. Tomorrow promised the squad's first patrol in the mountains, and it would last three days. He removed his ruck from the bunk and took out his poncho liner from one of its outside pockets. Then he spread it over the bunk and slipped underneath it, careful not to disturb the others.

He stared hard at the fluttering candle before snuffing it out. Something hitched in his chest.

Dad . . . Rudy . . . I promise I'll make it.

He drifted off to sleep, whispering the Ranger Creed.

Dan Levy hurriedly put the finishing touches on the terrain model he had spent the past hour and a half making. *Like playing in a sandbox*, he thought, and he was right. It was nothing more than a large, shallow wooden box filled with sand. Before moving out, a patrol always developed a detailed plan for the movement and execution of the mission, involving maps, chalkboard sketches depicting contingencies and SOPs, and making a terrain model in the sandbox, illustrating the mountains, streams, and the objective the patrol was to recon, raid, or ambush. Tonight they would execute a raid.

Levy was glad he remembered to put his field jacket liner on earlier in the morning. He'd have to take it off during the hump to their objective later on in the day when the temperature would climb into the nineties, but it was still chilly in the predawn hours, even for July. This morning was particularly overcast, promising rain. He glanced at his watch. 0830. He stepped back from the terrain model and went to the rear of the patrol planning bay. It was a wood and tin overhead shelter, open on three sides, just large enough to accommodate a squad of twelve Rangers—all swarming around, drawing sketches and preparing notes for the operation order that would initiate at 0900.

Levy disappeared into the tree line and relieved himself against a bush, reliving the morning's events. They had been literally bombarded awake at zero-four, with maniacal RIs throwing hand grenade simulators throughout the student barracks area and pounding down the doors of their huts. Within seconds the students had fallen outside with their rucksacks, M16s, and web gear, already dressed. Then they had eaten breakfast. Levy had loved the blueberry pancakes. He was still full. He zipped up his pants and returned to the bay, warmed by the memory. Then a huge drop of rain smacked against the top of his patrol cap.

"Oh, no."

"Please, God, don't let it rain."

"*Fuck!*"

"Okay, guys," Jakes announced, "move all your gear inside the bay. It's gonna pour like hell."

Everyone quickly grabbed their rucksacks and stuffed them underneath the two wooden benches inside the shelter. Some wouldn't fit, so their owners lined the remainder against the corner pole of the shelter. Already a light patter beat against the tin roof, creating a steady din, growing louder and more threatening.

"Hey, Jakes," Levy hollered, tugging at his ruck.

"What?"

"When's the RI 'sposed to get here?"

"Any minute now. You finished with that terrain model?"

"Ready as it's ever going to be."

Jakes walked over to Levy, pulling out his map.

"It's your first patrol, isn't it?" Levy asked him.

"Yeah," Jakes replied nervously, orienting his map with the terrain model.

"Don't be afraid to take charge when people start dragging ass."

"Don't worry, I won't." Jakes turned toward the situation map posted next to the podium at the rear of the shelter. Another Ranger student about Levy's own size was busy tracing the route with grease pencil on the sheet of acetate covering the map.

"Keller, come on over here," Jakes said to him.

Silently, the Ranger stopped what he was doing and walked over to the terrain model. Levy didn't know the man well, except some unusual facts: Juan Keller. He was an ROTC cadet from third squad attending Ranger School in lieu of ROTC advanced camp. He had been attached with the rest of his team to supplement fourth squad for this operation. He didn't talk much and didn't joke and laugh with everyone else. Levy figured he just felt uncomfortable around the others. He'd heard that Keller was from Argentina originally, and had become a U.S. citizen when he entered college at Georgetown. Keller had clear blue eyes that looked into one's own with an arrogant hauteur. What once must have been a stiff, blond head of hair was now a burr of white fuzz over a pinkish scalp covered by his carefully formed and peaked patrol cap that always looked as if it had just been starched. He arrived at the terrain model, appraising its accuracy and detail.

"What do you think?" Jakes asked him.

"I think it will do," Keller said in a barely accented, patronizing voice. He traced the route with his finger slowly. Levy had marked the starting point, where they would infiltrate enemy lines, with a small paper flag mounted on a twig.

"Let me see," Keller continued. "We move by truck to the friendly forward lines ten kilometers from here, dismount, make final coordination with the defensive perimeter, and move through the wire. Then we move from here," he added, pointing from the start of a ridgeline to the top of a mountain, "to here. A distance of three kilometers on a thirty-five-degree azimuth, almost due north. From there we travel seven hundred meters at a thirty-degree azimuth on the opposite ridgeline to establish the objective rallying point, and put surveillance on the target—which is an enemy missile sight with headquarters and approximately six personnel."

Jakes and Levy were astounded. Keller had briefed the entire movement and concept of the operation without mistake. Jakes had put out the information only thirty minutes before.

"Damn, Keller, you got a good memory," Jakes said, clapping the other man on the back. Keller stiffened at the friendly gesture and frowned.

"Of course. We all must know where to go and what to do at all times."

Levy glanced at his watch. "It's time to get started, guys. The RI should have been here by now."

"Keller," Jakes said, "have everyone post the charts and get seated, ready to go for the operations order. Make sure they know the azimuths and distances just like you do." Jakes looked back toward the trail that led back toward the student huts and the chow hall, where the RI would come. He saw a figure with his web gear and walking stick trudging toward them, and knew it had to be their RI. The rain had become a downpour and had engulfed the RI, who was hopping over puddles, his waterproof jacket flapping in the gusts of wind that drove the rain in sheets before him.

Jakes lunged for the podium and shouted, "Listen up! Let's get this patrol off on the right foot with this guy. Don't *nobody* fall asleep during the briefing. He's probably pissed already about the rain, so let's not make it worse with any sniveling or complaining. Let's have a good mission, men."

Christopher, who had been uncharacteristically quiet all morning, stood up by his bench and glared at the other men.

"He's right. I don't want any of you guys from third squad sniveling either. Fourth squad hangs tough." He sat back down by Prentiss, going over the route for the last time with the unsure Ranger.

Levy stood next to the situation map with a stick. He would be the pointer while Jakes delivered the operation order, highlighting the route and objective by pointing at the terrain model and the map.

Everyone waited.

Staff Sergeant Justin MacAlister walked into the shelter, shaking off his web gear and rain parka. He looked at the stocky, pimply-faced Ranger standing before the podium. "You the patrol leader?" he asked gruffly.

"Yes, Sergeant."

"Carry on with the OPORD, and make it quick. The sooner we get out of here, the better off this patrol will be."

* * *

The column of Ranger students moved slowly through the forest toward the ridgeline. A wet, miserable morning had turned into an even more miserable afternoon—wet, slimy, and hot. As soon as the rain had stopped, the temperature climbed to ninety degrees, broiling everyone in an atmospheric sauna.

Levy tripped through the mud at the head of the column, weighted more by his mood than by his ruck. The OPORD had been a glaring failure, and the RI had been super-pissed.

The first thing MacAlister did was make the patrol haul their rucks outside. *"Looks like shit in here, Rangers, clean it up! Get all this crap outside!"* Anyone who had not thoroughly waterproofed his ruck gained an additional ten pounds of rainwater. Then he had caught Prentiss sleeping twice in a row, while Jakes nervously delivered the OPORD. The entire patrol knocked out elevated push-ups in the rain for five minutes to "wake the fuck up."

Fifteen minutes into the operation order, Jakes forgot to cover the alternate route to the objective. MacAlister immediately flunked him, and made Prentiss take his place as the patrol leader. Prentiss kept screwing up, forgetting grid locations of the objective and rallying points. After the first half-hour had passed, MacAlister groaned.

"Stop, stop, stop. Okay, Rangers, this is getting entirely too gross. It's readily apparent to *this* RI that your shit is weak. You're not functioning. Every one of you is severely brain-damaged this morning. Since you don't know what the hell you are doing, I'm going to take you to your starting point and get you moving. Until that time you had best get organized and get to know your mission."

The patrol had climbed aboard a deuce-and-a-half truck and was driven out to the starting point, where Prentiss and Keller made final coordination with friendly elements and moved the patrol through the defensive perimeter into simulated enemy territory. Then they began the long, muddy approach to the ridgeline, which would take them deep into the mountains.

Levy trudged on, placing one foot in front of the other and concentrating on nothing else. He knew it was wrong. He should be concentrating on the route, the objective, anything to do with the mission, but instead he was crawling into his shell, trying to forget how his rucksack straps cut into his shoulders and the new blister forming on his waterlogged left heel would eventually tear open and bleed.

"Levy," a voice whispered behind him.

Levy turned around and saw Christopher. He was dripping wet and hunched under the weight of his ruck. Rain mixed with sweat had caused his green facepaint to streak.

"Yeah?"

"Numbnuts got us lost yet?"

Levy chuckled. Christopher always said that when Prentiss was in charge. His mood lifted.

"Naw. Give him another five hundred meters." They both laughed. MacAlister, who had been trailing the rear of the file, stalked up behind the two Rangers as they talked. "What do you two think is so funny?" he asked.

"Nothing, Sarge," Christopher immediately replied.

"My name's not *Sarge*, Ranger. It's Sergeant. Got that?"

"Yes, Sergeant!"

MacAlister flipped out a small white pamphlet and made two marks in it with his pencil. "That's a major-minus spot report for each of you. In an actual combat situation you'd have endangered the lives of your fellow patrol members by not adhering to strict noise discipline."

Levy's heart flipped, and he exchanged stunned glances with Christopher. A spot report in Ranger School was like a demerit. If you built up so many bad spot reports, you could be recycled into the next class. More than one major-minus made that a likelihood. Angrily, he lowered his head and resumed his slog up the ridgeline.

Christopher gasped as he lunged for the next tree trunk, eyes searching for the next one small enough to get a grip on. *Since when do trees grow sideways*, he thought, grabbing for the next one. He thought of the name of the mountain whose ridgeline they were trying to climb. *Hammerton Mountain? Shit. This mountain's hammering my ass.*

Somehow, the patrol had veered away from the ridgeline and wound up climbing the face. It wasn't rocky—it had plenty of trees and brush to hang on to—but it was steep. So steep that it looked as if the trees did indeed grow sideways out of the mountain. Christopher had never tried to climb anything so steep in his life. Not with an eighty-pound rucksack anyway. They had to take a five-minute break every twenty minutes, each man literally hanging on a tree to keep from rolling and tumbling down the slope, physically spent and dreading the next minute they'd be up and at it again.

* * *

MacAlister worked his rage out on the mountainside, lunging from tree to tree, realizing he was taking his anger from the night before out on the patrol. By the time they reached the top, he would be all right. After the mission was over, he'd be relieved by another RI to walk the patrol and then he would go back down to headquarters and turn in his request for reassignment. It had finally come to that.

MacAlister looked up at the patrol in front of him. He had remained at the rear to ensure no stragglers fell behind and got lost. He was spent himself. It was time for another break. He looked at his watch. 1400. Another thirty minutes and they'd be at the top anyway. They were making good time. He would throw away those spot reports he'd given on those two Rangers earlier. He was just taking it out on them.

"Patrol Leader," he called.

No answer, only the sounds of wheezing gasps and crashing bushes.

"Patrol Leader!"

"Psst. Everyone stop."

"The RI's sayin' somethin."

"Hey! Everyone stop!"

"Goddammit, I want the patrol leader." MacAlister climbed toward the head of the file and met Prentiss in the middle. When he saw him, he almost forgot his bad mood. Prentiss looked so funny. His fatigues were thoroughly soaked through in sweat, his pants were pulled out of his boots, and cuts from wait-a-minute vines had carved scarlet slashes in his face and arms. His glasses were fogged over with sweat and desperately hanging on to the tip of his nose.

"Ranger," MacAlister said, shaking his head, "you need to take better care of yourself."

"Yes, Sergeant." Prentiss mournfully pushed his glasses back up his nose, gasping for breath and supporting himself upright with his M16.

"Go ahead and take ten. No, fifteen. Make sure every man drinks water, I don't care how low he is. You and your APL personally make sure they drain one full canteen, right now. We'll reach a stream tonight so everyone can refill."

"Yes, Sergeant."

"And quit looking so pathetic, Ranger."

MacAlister broke away from the main body and climbed uphill to the head of the file, counting bodies as he went. They totaled thirteen in all, including himself. He climbed another ten meters up front and perched on an oak trunk with a fork in it he could lean his aching back against.

MacAlister grasped at his web gear and withdrew a canteen. Drinking deeply, he thought about the previous night.

It had been a bad one.

He had come home early, around 1500. His wife had been crying. Someone had driven by Justin, Jr., earlier in the day while he was outside riding his tricycle. Whoever it was told the six-year-old that he was a little Oreo nigger who had better not play with any more white children. After calling the child several obscenities, the man had driven off, leaving a frightened little boy running home to his mother.

Three hours later, while they ate dinner, a rock crashed through the living room window. MacAlister yanked the door open in time to hear the squeal of tires as a car raced away into the night, voices screaming: *"Get outta this neighborhood, nig-*

ger, you're not wanted!" Then he saw his front yard.
He thought it was on fire.

It was. A burning cross flamed into the night air.

MacAlister immediately packed his family up in
the Volvo with enough clothes to keep them for the
next two weeks and drove them to the airport in
Atlanta. Once there, he sent them off to San Luis
Obispo back home to his folks. He returned to his
house not caring about the good-sized dent he'd
made in his American Express card. He had the
money saved up anyway. He would finish up with
this patrol in the morning, turn in his request for
reassignment, and get the hell out of Georgia. It just
wasn't worth it for his family to be in danger.

Sighing, MacAlister looked up at the sun. Already
shadows were casting down into the valley below.
It was time to move.

Prentiss huddled in the center of the perimeter
with Keller and five other patrol members, hashing
out the sequence of events for that night's raid on
the missile site. It had been a long hump to the ORP,
the objective rallying point. Here, the patrol would
send out a recon element to fix the objective and
gain last-minute information important for the evening's raid. Prentiss decided he would use Christopher and Levy for the point surveillance team and
told Keller to get them.

"What's up?" Levy asked him when they arrived,
surprised that Prentiss had actually steered the patrol to the ORP on time. He was pleased for him.

"Prentiss—my man!" Christopher added, grinning. "Why ain't you screwed the pooch yet?"

"What?"

"Why ain't you screwed up yet, man? You're actually coming through on this one."

"Okay, okay, guys . . . ease up," Prentiss replied, feeling good. It was the first time he had ever felt that way with the others. "Here's what's going on. Another three hundred meters will bring us to the objective. I'm going on a leader's recon. I'm taking you two, my radioman, and left and right security. When we get there, I'll leave you all in place and return with the RTO. I should have the rest of the patrol up there an hour or two later."

Prentiss paused, looking at every man, trying not to think of MacAlister standing behind him with his grade book. "Any questions? Good. Number sequence is nine, for challenge and password." He glanced at his watch and then looked back up. "Time is now 1730. Keller, make sure the perimeter is tight and that everyone knows the challenge and password and the contingency plan."

"Roger," Keller replied, and he crept back toward the perimeter, drawing it up man by man, and informing each of their situation. MacAlister had listened to Prentiss's briefing and had waited until now, when it was over, to talk to the student before he departed with the recon element.

"Ranger Prentiss," he called softly.

Prentiss looked at the RI, who was leaning against a tree a few feet away.

"Yes, Sergeant," he said, swallowing.

"I'm following you up to the objective. Then I'm going down to the OBJ itself for the next couple of hours to see how your actions on the objective go when you initiate the raid. Understand?"

"Yes, Sergeant."

"Carry on, Ranger."

Levy felt the night come on like a seducing siren out of Homer's *Odyssey*. He wanted so badly to go to sleep. It had been a long day. It was now approaching 2000 and he had been lying in the prone with Christopher in their position seventy-five meters away from the objective for the past hour and a half. The entire time he had dreamed of the food he would eat when he got back home, and had planned no less than a dozen menus in his mind. Mountains of rib-eye steaks and vats of peanut butter (the crunchy kind, of course). Oceans of Coca-Cola. And beer. Yeah, beer, all he could drink.

It kept him awake anyway.

He waited for the sun to disappear behind the mountain to his front. He was pulling surveillance with Christopher at the bottom of the opposite mountainside, surrounded by immense pines and hardwoods. In the valley were two clapboard range shacks, and two instructors stood by them, joking and laughing. Levy recognized the voice of his class TAC, Sergeant Grey. Another RI was with him, a skinny man with fuzzy red hair, whose high-pitched laughter clearly cut through the dusky air. Levy thought it was Sergeant Quinn, a true sadist who had been one of their lower mountaineering instructors when they received their rappeling and belaying classes the day before. He remembered how Quinn was especially hard on Christopher, making him do more push-ups than anyone else and always flunking him on knot-tying when Christopher had the misfortune of drawing him for a knot grader. Christopher was lucky in drawing a different grader for the final knot test, or else he would have been recycled into the next class.

Levy put his hand into his fatigue pants and pulled out a can of Copenhagen. He removed the lid and pinched as much of the snuff as he could hold between his thumb and forefinger and stuffed it in his lower lip. The resultant nicotine buzz surged through his jugulars, making him more alert.

"That fuckin' shit is gross, Levy, *gross*! How can you stand to put that nasty stuff in your mouth?"

"Want some?" Levy handed him the can.

"Fuck no." Christopher replied, curling his upper lip. "Hey, look—that's MacAlister moving out toward the OBJ." Christopher pointed to the cabins.

Levy picked up the binoculars and scanned the site. A few more minutes, and he'd have to use the night vision goggles. They were night light-enhancing binoculars, powered by batteries.

"Yeah, that's him. Man, is he one hard-ass."

"No shit. Motherfucker gave us two spot reports."

"Keep it down."

"All right, all right."

Levy trained his eyes on the RIs below. Grey and Quinn had started a fire in an oil drum and fed it an occasional board. It was chilly in the evening air, about sixty degrees. He shivered, wishing he had remembered to stick his field jacket liner in his trousers cargo pocket prior to leaving the ORP.

MacAlister reached the other RIs. Levy refocused his binoculars, trying to see through the haze of twilight.

"Hello, Sergeant Quinn . . . Sergeant Grey," MacAlister said evenly as he approached the oil drum. He hadn't expected *these* two to be here at the objective.

"Well, hello there, Staff Sergeant MacAlister," Quinn replied mockingly.

Grey said nothing, staring hard at the black RI.

MacAlister looked at the two men in front of him, several feet away. Between them was the oil drum, burning merrily in the night air. He glanced at the doorway of the range shack which was standing ajar, and saw an open bottle of Jack Daniels sitting on the step.

Grey followed MacAlister's gaze toward the bottle.

"Wanna drink?"

Drinking? MacAlister thought. *On duty*?

"No, thank you," he replied stiffly. "I'm waiting for the patrol to come through."

"No thank you, he says," Grey mocked, eyes dancing toward Quinn, standing by his side. "I'll tell ya. I like a nigger with good manners."

MacAlister started. *Keep cool, man. Just let it go. Just let it—*

"Oh, I'm sorry. I meant *nee-grow*."

"Christ almighty!" Levy croaked, refocusing the night vision goggles.

"Whatsa matter?"

"MacAlister just took a swing at Grey. Knocked the shit out of him!"

"What?"

"Now he's stompin' Quinn! Man, he's—he's using his feet. He's all over 'em!"

"No shit? Gimme those things."

Levy handed Christopher the night vision goggles.

"I'll be a son of a bitch! He's beatin' the *fuck* outta those guys!"

CHAPTER
· NINE ·

MacAlister looked down at the two bleeding,
stunned men and rubbed his jaw where Grey had
clipped him immediately before receiving an answering kick in the groin. One of his molars was
chipped. He frisked them and found a .25 on Quinn
and a snub-nosed .38 on Grey. He emptied them of
bullets and threw them out into the woodline. Then
he tossed the pistols into the fire.

Grey stumbled to his feet, shaking his head. He
shoved his hand inside his fatigue shirt.

"It's in the fire," MacAlister told him.

"You goddamned son of a—"

MacAlister clenched his fists, eyes narrowing.
"C'mon. Yeah, c'mon, motherfucker."

Grey hesitated and looked at the prostrate figure
of Quinn, who was still unconscious, then looked
back at MacAlister.

"I didn't want any trouble with you or Quinn. I'm
willing to forget about this."

Grey pondered, then he thought of another way.

"Yeah, sure." Then he added, more emphatically, "I started it, you finished it. I apologize for calling you a nigger."

Quinn came around. They both glanced at him.

"He apologizes too."

MacAlister nodded his head. "Then it's history. My patrol should be running through here in another few minutes, and then I'll be on my way." He turned his back on the two men and faced the direction from which the patrol would come.

Grey dragged Quinn to his feet, who bled profusely from the nose. "Goddamned history all right," he muttered through clenched teeth.

For the next several moments no one spoke. MacAlister eyed Grey and Quinn warily, expecting them to jump him. Then the distant but unmistakable roar of a deuce-and-a-half truck cut through the thick silence.

MacAlister breathed a very controlled sigh of relief. It was the aggressor detail from Camp Merrill. He wondered what had taken them so long. He looked at his watch. It was 2000. The patrol should already be positioned in the assault line, ready to hit the target shortly after the aggressor's arrival.

The truck's engine grew louder. Grey walked to the hut entrance and retrieved the bottle of Jack Daniels. Then he flung it far out into the woodline. He returned to the fire, his face expressionless.

Quinn sat on a log stump by the fire, massaging his jaw with one hand and gingerly holding the bridge of his nose between his thumb and forefinger with the other. Then he jumped up. MacAlister tensed. Quinn hesitated.

"Fuckit!" Quinn hissed. He tossed his head

toward Grey and shifted his eyes at Grey's four-wheeler, a late-model Ford Bronco that had been re-painted into a camouflage pattern. "Let's get the fuck out of here."

Grey reached inside his pockets and took out his keys. "Yeah." He turned toward the Bronco.

Quinn held a steady gaze on MacAlister, eyes brimming with hate.

"You're going to pay for that," he said in a low and even voice.

MacAlister said nothing, but his eyes silently dared the other man to move.

"Shut up, Larry," Grey interjected quickly, stepping between the two men, pulling at Quinn's arm. "Now, c'mon, let's go."

The area suddenly lit up as the truck's headlights illuminated the darkness that had crept upon them. The truck bounced along the dirt road into the clearing, and every man felt relief from the tension of the moment.

"No use in hanging around," Quinn finally said. He stomped toward the Bronco, shrugging off Grey's hand.

Grey stared hard at MacAlister.

"No hard feelings, right?" he apologized sincerely.

"What the hell are you saying, Frank?" Quinn spurted, wheeling around. "Are you apologizing?"

"Shut up, Larry!" Grey exploded, glaring at Quinn. He extended his hand toward the black RI. MacAlister looked at it with contempt.

"Like I said," he slowly replied, "this was just between us three, so forget about it. But it sure as hell don't mean I'm going to shake your god-damned hand."

The truck roared up alongside the three men. The noise was deafening. Grey dropped his hand.

"C'mon," he said to Quinn.

The two RIs walked to the Bronco and climbed in. Then they spun out of the objective site, slinging gravel and dirt everywhere.

The four-man aggressor detail hopped out of the truck, all laughing and joking and clutching bags of Oreos and Doritos. They were dressed in mock Russian uniforms, and carrying Soviet Kalashnikov assault rifles. One of them walked toward MacAlister.

"Hey, you're Sergeant MacAlister, right?" he said cheerfully.

MacAlister recognized Sergeant Pete Childress, the youngest RI at Camp Merrill. His bright, boyish-looking face, accented by a constant smile, easily betrayed his twenty-one years.

"Yeah, what's up?" he asked more gruffly than he intended. "What took you guys so long to get here?"

"We got the damned truck stuck in a rut a few miles back," the younger sergeant replied defensively. "Whatsa matter, there some kind of trouble?"

"Naw, sorry I snapped at you. Got a bitch of a headache."

"No sweat. Is your patrol ready?"

Machine-gun fire erupted from the southern tree line, sixty meters away from the clearing. The two RIs jumped. Even though the patrol was firing only blank cartridges, their stealthy positioning had caught them by surprise. The patrol's assault line at the eastern edge fired in automatic and semi-automatic bursts.

Hand grenade simulators bounced inside the perimeter, exploding deafeningly with the din already created by the hammering machine guns. The aggressor detail sporadically returned fire with their AK-47s and then, one by one, they fell as if hit. One man performed spectacular death throes in the best of Hollywood traditions as he suddenly whirled upright, spraying the air with automatic fire before crumpling to the ground, mortally wounded.

MacAlister had to smile, watching them from his position by the oil drum. He tossed another board into the fire.

A green star-cluster flare whooshed up into the dark sky, casting a greenish glow on the objective. The machine guns belched away their last belts of ammo in continuous fifteen-second bursts. Then a half-dozen screaming shadows leapt out of the tree line, dashing toward MacAlister and the aggressors. As each Ranger ran by an aggressor, he shot him with more blanks and stabbed him with an imaginary bayonet. Then he kicked the aggressor's weapon away, since under real circumstances a wounded enemy soldier could still grab his weapon and shoot. After ten seconds had passed, the patrol had crossed and re-formed on-line at the other side of the clearing, securing it against a simulated enemy counterattack. Every Ranger knelt behind a tree or boulder for cover and concealment.

MacAlister stayed put to see how the patrol conducted their actions on the objective—specific demolitions, intelligence, prisoner, and first aid procedures actuated on every raid or ambush. It was the highlight of the evening.

"Team Leaders, give me an up!" a voice screamed. It was Prentiss. MacAlister recognized him at the center of the assault line calling for a status on ammunition and personnel from each of the assault teams.

"Alpha team, up!"

"Bravo team, we're up!"

"POW/Search team, fall out!" Prentiss yelled.

On cue, two men rushed inside the center and rapidly searched the fallen aggressors, looking for maps and radio frequencies. MacAlister gaped at them as they searched a prostrate Sergeant Childress, realizing that the patrol leader had placed the same two Rangers on point surveillance earlier when . . .

"C'mere, you two," he said to them, just loud enough to be heard.

Levy and Christopher looked up at MacAlister, at each other, and then hustled over to the RI.

MacAlister leaned into their faces and said, "You two were on point surveillance tonight, right?"

The two students nodded and exchanged glances.

"You forget everything you saw. Got that?"

"We understand, Sergeant," Levy replied.

"Yeah, no problem," Christopher added. "Hell, we were glad to see those two get their butts beat."

"It's not your problem," MacAlister said, punctuating each word. He started to say something else but hesitated. Then, "Go on and find the rest of your patrol."

"Roger that, Sergeant," they said in unison, giving the RI a thumbs-up. They ran back to the assault line.

It had been a brief encounter, lasting only seconds. Prentiss ordered the demolitions team into the objective area, and they set a "charge" next to the stacked enemy weapons and equipment. It was a hand grenade simulator. One of the men prepared to pull the fuse.

"Fire in the hole!" he shouted.

"Okay, fall back," Prentiss commanded. "C'mon, quickly—quickly!"

Still on-line, every man jumped up from his position and walked backward to his original assault position, covering his front. Once there, he got under cover.

"Fire in the hole!" the demo man yelled again, jerking the fuse. He raced back to the tree line and vaulted over a stump, covering himself behind it.

The charge blew.

Prentiss leapt to his feet. *"Move out to the ORP!"* The patrol scrambled to their feet and rushed back into the tree line, running uphill to the objective rallying point, where they had left Keller and another man securing their rucksacks. The patrol vanished within seconds, and the objective area grew quiet again.

MacAlister sat on the hut's doorstep, writing notes on his grader's pamphlet, checking tasks accomplished from what he observed on the objective. Ranger Prentiss had passed his first patrol. MacAlister smiled sadly. *At least somebody had a good day,* he thought.

"Okay, guys, saddle up," Childress called out to his aggressor detail, who were huddled together by the burn barrel, swapping jokes. As they climbed aboard the truck, he turned about and walked back to MacAlister, who had stuffed the notepad into his pocket and was ready to rejoin the patrol at the ORP.

"Not bad, Mac."

"Yeah, they did okay."

"You shoulda seen this one kid with glasses."

Childress laughed in his easy way. "Man, he must have tripped and fell three times, running across the clearing."

MacAlister laughed. "That was Prentiss."

"Oh, listen," Childress said, his voice suddenly professional and serious. "I almost forgot to give you this." He pulled a spiral notebook out of his shirt pocket.

"What is it?"

"Bad news, man. You gotta stay out another night."

"Damn! Why?"

"Quinn was supposed to relieve you tomorrow morning at the patrol base, right?"

"Yeah?" MacAlister hadn't known that. Top Fowlds ran the duty roster. "So?"

"So Sergeant Grey called in that Quinn was real sick or something."

"He did?" MacAlister seethed, wondering what was going on. "That's bullshit, man."

"Yeah, well, Top Fowlds wanted me to pass it on to you. Here, I've got the grid coordinates for tomorrow night's ambush. You're supposed to hole up in a patrol base all day and prepare for the ambush later on tomorrow night. Got a map?"

MacAlister pulled the map out of his cargo pocket and spread it across his knee. Then he copied down Childress's notes. He traced the objective with his finger.

"Okay," he said, resigned to another twenty-four hours in the woods. He didn't know what Grey and Quinn were up to, but he'd definitely settle up with them again.

"See you later, Mac," Childress said, departing

for the truck. ''Remember, don't shoot the messengers.''

The truck rumbled off, leaving MacAlister standing by the hut in a cloud of dust and diesel fumes. He started for the tree line. Then he stopped, chilled and uneasy, trying to remember. . . .

He pulled the map from his pocket and flipped his flashlight on, cutting through the dark with its yellowish, tracing beam. He stared at the map, hunting for the following night's objective. Then he found the ambush site Childress showed him. Now he knew why he felt uneasy.

He remembered a conversation with the camp commander months before about a black kid found dead in the woods, torn apart by dogs.

The ambush site was along a dirt road on Black Mountain.

CHAPTER
· TEN ·

The camouflaged Bronco sped down the twisting dirt road leading out of the raid site. Grey sat behind the wheel in silence, staring into the black night in front of him. Quinn sat in the passenger's seat, brooding. Every now and then he touched the bridge of his nose, wondering if it was broken. Neither had spoken since leaving the camp. Quinn turned toward Grey.

"Remember when we was in Vietnam, Frank?"

Grey didn't reply.

"Do you?"

"Of course I do." Grey shifted into second and floored the accelerator as the Bronco climbed a steep hill.

"You know," Quinn continued, "we killed VC together in Vietnam. We fucked whores together in Saigon. We used to beat the livin' shit out of the paper clip commandos downrange together when we had a little R&R, remember?"

"Yeah. So what?"

"So why did you back down from that jive-ass nigger?"

"You'll see."

"Whaddya mean, you'll see?"

The Bronco neared the crest of the hill and Grey searched the tree line with his eyes.

"Whaddya mean, you'll see?" Quinn repeated.

"You're not gonna relieve MacAlister tomorrow morning at his patrol base."

"I'm not?"

"Nope. You're sick."

"Whaddya mean, I'm *sick?*"

"Remember when the deuce drove up and Sergeant Childress was in charge of the aggressor detail?"

"Yeah."

"He had a message from Top Fowlds, tellin' MacAlister to stay out another night with his patrol, since you're sick. I called it in for you before we left to come out here tonight. You've got strep throat."

"No shit? Why?"

Grey smiled. His friend was genuinely surprised, just as he had planned. He knew he would be as receptive when he told him.

They had first met each other on the same inbound plane for Saigon, years back. They were both bound for the same unit—the 173rd Airborne. Once there, they were even assigned to the same battalion and company. A friendship formed.

On patrol they covered each other. Once Quinn prevented Grey from stepping on a booby trap while their patrol crept through the jungle toward a suspected VC base camp. The booby trap had turned out to be a camouflaged 155 mm howitzer shell, rigged up against a tree at waist level. An OD green trip wire was pulled taut an inch above the ground, and the slightest pressure would have set the shell off, killing Grey and half the patrol behind him. Grey still remembered how Quinn had yanked him backward before he stepped on the wire.

There was another time when Grey drug Quinn out of the fire zone of a VC ambush. Quinn had been grazed against the side of his head and shot through the thigh. The bullet had broken the bone, and he had passed out from the pain. Grey had saved his life.

So they covered each other and weathered out the 365 days. The friendship had been formed and cemented through the hell of Vietnam's firefights together. Once back in the States, they parted company. Grey was assigned to Fort Benning, and Quinn got out of the Army. One a careerist, the other just doing his duty.

Then, last March, they met again. Quinn arrived at Camp Merrill as a newly promoted staff sergeant. Grey heard about it and looked him up. When Quinn had gotten out of the Army years earlier, he had joined the National Guard and was also in the police force. He told Grey later on that he had rejoined the Army after his ten-year break in service because he had been dissatisfied with the mandatory racial quotas the police department maintained with their affirmative action program. In fact, a black man had been promoted ahead of him as a result of the affirmative action program, even though Quinn had been more qualified. The National Guard had at least kept him in touch with the Army. He decided to go back on active duty.

Grey rounded the top of the hill and saw a man dart out from the tree line, flagging him down. He slowed to a stop. He looked at Quinn, who still wanted to know what Grey's plan was.

"I'll tell you, my friend," he said, grinning from ear

to ear. "We're going coon hunting tomorrow night. Know what I mean?"

Quinn nodded. "I get you," he said, smiling. "I obviously can't be on patrol if I'm *coon* hunting."

Grey stuck his head out the window as the man approached them. It was Jerry Parson. *Good ol' Jerry*, he thought. *Just as reliable and level-headed as they come.*

"How's it goin', Frank?" Jerry drawled as he approached the Bronco. He leaned against the window of the Bronco toward Grey and spat a thick stream of tobacco juice onto the dirt road, then looked back up at Grey.

"Just fine, Jerry. Where's everybody else?"

"The rest of the boys are about a hundred yards in the tree line over yonder," Jerry said, pointing. "We've got that fella from Montana with us. You met him yet?"

"Yeah, I have."

"Talks kind of funny, but he's all right. Been teachin' us a lot." Jerry peered into the cab toward Quinn. "Who's that you got with you?" he asked guardedly.

"Good friend of mine. Don't worry about him."

"You sure?"

" 'Course I'm sure. Let's get this Bronco hidden."

Grey pulled the Bronco off the road and backed up slowly into the trees. He parked it ten feet inside the tree line and shut off the engine. He leaned over Quinn and opened the glove box.

"Where are we going?" Quinn asked hesitantly.

Grey pulled a .45 Colt automatic out of the glove box and checked the clip, making sure it was full. Then he pulled the receiver back and chambered a round.

"Before we go coon hunting, ol' buddy, we gotta organize our hunting party, right?" Grey replied.

Stuffing the .45 in his belt, he opened the door and stepped out of the Bronco.

Quinn got out and walked over to Grey's side. Jerry joined them.

"Jerry, meet Larry Quinn," Grey said. "Larry and I fought together in Vietnam. He's my best friend, and you can trust him."

Jerry thrust out a hand, and Quinn shook it. "If Frankie Grey says it's okay, then it's okay," he said. "Pleased to meet you."

"Same here," Quinn replied. Then he looked at Grey and said, "You ready, or are we just gonna *talk* about fuckin' that nigger up?"

The three men walked silently through the woods for several minutes and finally stopped twenty feet short of a small circle of prone figures with their weapons facing out. A full moon illuminated the sky, surrounded by billowy clouds. Occasionally, one would blot it out, casting everything in darkness.

"It's me," Jerry whispered. "I've got Frank Grey and a buddy of his."

"Come on in," a voice floated toward them.

Grey walked inside the perimeter, recognizing the voice. He remembered a meeting with his father at the Three Sisters, and a blond scar-faced man, the ex-marine. The neo-Nazi with cruel lips and cold green eyes.

Gunther sat in the center of the perimeter on a stump, with an Uzi submachine gun on his lap. He stood up and met Grey.

"How have you been, Frank?" he said, shaking Grey's hand.

"Just fine, J.D. Meet Larry Quinn, here."

Gunther and Quinn exchanged amenities. Then

they all squatted down in the center of the perimeter. Gunther spoke first.

"We put surveillance on that raid site tonight, like you asked. That nigger punched you two out."

"Yeah, I gotta admit he did," Grey replied, embarrassed. "How was I to know he was some sort of karate expert?"

"Jerry wanted to plug him with his M14. He's got a night site for it, you know. A PVS-4."

Grey whistled softly, impressed. The AN/PVS-4 was a costly telescopic night vision device designed to fit on M16s and M60 machine guns, capable of illuminating and enhancing targets of up to three hundred meters away. "How the hell did you get that?" he asked.

"Same as always," Gunther replied, glancing at Quinn. Grey noticed his discomfort.

"Don't worry about him. He feels the same way about niggers and Jews as we do. I'm recruiting him."

Quinn spoke for the first time. "Hey, I don't know much about what you all are up to, but if it means fuckin' up niggers like that asshole tonight, I'll gladly help out. I've got a score to settle."

Gunther took in a deep breath and let it out slowly, staring at Grey. "Okay. He's with you, and you're running this organization. You got the grid coordinates for that patrol tomorrow night?"

"Yeah," Grey said. "They'll be in the vicinity of Black Mountain."

"What? Why are they going there? It's too close to the base camp."

"That's right. It's also still part of one of the northernmost lanes of Camp Merrill. That's where they're gonna be. I can't bring suspicion on myself back at Camp Merrill by sending patrols outside of the patrolling boundary. Besides, I have an idea."

"What's the grid?" Gunther repeated, pulling out his map and spreading it on the ground.

"Charlie Foxtrot 569475," Grey answered, picking up a pine needle and pointing at the exact location. The patrol's ambush site was along a bend in a dirt road and in between two hilltops, approximately three hundred meters apart.

"I see," Gunther murmured. "That's about six klicks southeast from the base camp. Four miles. I guess that'll be okay. What's your idea?"

"We'll make like we're the aggressors, and then take 'em while they're all bunched up doing their actions on the objective. Get ahold of the nigger RI and rough him up a little, but save something for me. I'll be there with you. Round up the rest of the patrol—there are thirteen of them, including MacAlister—and get their weapons." Grey glanced sharply at Gunther. "Do you have a net established yet?"

"We're still trying to get a couple of more safe houses in between Montana and Ohio. We're fine from here through Kentucky. Once we get the weapons, I'll personally transport them to a safe house we have established across the border in Tennessee. A representative from our group will file off the serial numbers and make sure they're cached somewhere safe. We'll both maintain file copies of the cache report."

"That sounds pretty good. When do you think the net will be open?"

"In about another two weeks. We're working on the farmers pretty heavy out in the Midwest. They're becoming more and more friendly, what with the government and the Jews taking up all the farmland out there. It shouldn't be much longer."

"Great. Have you gone underground yet?"

"Good God, yes. I had to go underground three

years ago, when we were first organizing in Montana.''

"I'm almost ready myself," Grey said bitterly. "My wife's about to leave me, Dad's ready to start a shooting race war . . . hell, I can't keep this camp up much longer and not get found out."

"After we're finished here in Georgia, you might want to do it. We can always use more help up in Montana, and you'd be a damned good liaison between the Klan and the Aryan Covenant."

"I'll think about it," Grey said. He looked at Quinn. "You with me, buddy?"

"You crazy son of a bitch," Quinn replied, grinning. "How I let you rope me into these situations."

"Good enough, then," Grey said, looking back at Gunther. "Tomorrow night. The patrol will be on location at Black Mountain around 2300, with a hit time of 2400. Actually, it's 0100, the way they understand it back at the rear. By the time you're finished with them, they'll all be scattered throughout the mountains, and it'll take the Ranger Department at least forty-eight hours to police all the students back up. That will give us plenty of time to cache the weapons and take care of that nigger."

"Where do you want us to take him?" Gunther asked.

"Blindfold him and take him to the base camp. Leave him tied up, and I'll take it from there."

"Are you going to kill him?"

"I haven't made up my mind yet. I might."

CHAPTER

· ELEVEN ·

"Wake up, Prentiss," Jake whispered. Prentiss jolted awake, trying to locate Jakes. He couldn't. It was black—not dark—it was black. He could barely make out the Ranger eyes on Jake's patrol cap.

"I wasn't sleeping."

"Bullshit. Now, keep awake. It's only another klick to the patrol base."

"Okay."

Jakes stood up and examined his patrol, which had stopped for a five-minute break. They were spread out in a cigar-shaped perimeter on the side of a mountain, which was as steep as the one they had climbed earlier in the day.

Everyone was dogged out. Jakes glanced at Christopher, five feet behind him. He could tell it was Christopher only because he was carrying the radio, and the antennae stuck up in the air. Other than that, in this darkness Christopher was a shapeless, featureless blob with two glowing Ranger eyes on the back of his patrol cap.

Earlier, after the raid, the patrol had scrambled back up the mountain to the ORP, where Keller and another man had secured the patrol's rucksacks and equipment. There, the RI told Prentiss that he'd counsel him in the morning about his performance as the patrol leader, and then he put Jakes in charge. Now they were en route to the patrol base. They had already covered five kilometers, up and down, clawing through heavily vegetated valleys and scrambling up vertical mountainsides. Luckily, enough trees and roots were around so the Rangers could grab hold of something and climb.

The distance covered this night had taken a toll on all. The tall pine trees and hardwoods covering the mountainside with their thick canopy blotted out any illumination from the full moon above. Everyone in the patrol had tied their compasses onto the back of their rucksacks so each man could see the man in front of him.

MacAlister stumbled to the front of the perimeter toward Jakes.

"Ranger," he muttered, "you know where you're at?"

"Yes, Sergeant."

"Then let's get moving."

"Roger that, Sergeant." Jakes turned about to the rest of the patrol, trying to locate them. "Everybody up," he whispered as loud as he could.

No one budged.

"Goddammit, I said everybody up! *Move!*"

Grunting with fatigue, the Rangers began to move around, staggering to their feet under the weight of their seventy- and eighty-pound rucks. Every man grabbed the man in front of him, forming a human chain. At this hour the blind led the blind, and they were all guided by the point man, whose trembling hand held a softly glowing compass.

"Move out, Ranger," a voice cooed in Jakes's ear.

Jakes jumped. MacAlister was still standing next to him. He tugged on the sleeve of the man behind him. It was Prentiss.

"Send up the head count," he told him.

Prentiss in turn whispered the message to the man behind him, and the process was repeated until it reached Keller, the last man in the formation. Once the man in front of him told him to send up the head count, Keller grabbed him by the shoulder and whispered, "One." The man in front of him said "Two" to the next man, and so on.

Prentiss grabbed Jakes by the shoulder. "Thirteen," he said, including MacAlister in the count.

"Let's go," Jakes said, and he stumbled forward, almost tripping over the stump he had sat on for the past five minutes.

"Christopher—that you?"

"Why'd you stop, Christopher?"

" 'Cause we're taking a break, stupid."

"Where're the rest of the guys in front of you?"

"Shut up and go back to sleep. Oh, shit! Hey, guys, wait up!"

"Fuck me to tears, another break in contact."

"Yeah, man, he's dronin'."

"Move it, move it!"

MacAlister stumbled to the front of the creeping formation, wondering why everyone was crawling along on their hands and knees. They didn't have to. They were on top of a ridgeline, and the vegetation wasn't that thick.

He stopped.

Where'd they go?

He slapped a mosquito buzzing around his ear as he rapidly searched the darkness to his front, using his peripheral vision to locate the luminous Ranger eyes. Sweat poured from his forehead.

He heard a movement to his front, twenty feet away. He crept toward the sound. Then he saw the Ranger eyes close to the ground. He grabbed the crawling figure by the back of his fatigue shirt.

"Who's this?"

"Jakes. Who the fuck are you?"

"I'm the *RI*, Ranger. Now tell me what you're doing, crawling on the ground like this."

"You mean we're outta the cave?"

"Oh, Jesus. Stop." MacAlister tried to locate the rest of the patrol. From what he could see, they were all crawling behind Jakes in single file. "Okay, everybody stand up. Go on, stand up." Muffled grunts answered him. MacAlister guessed they were all standing up.

He pulled out his flashlight from the ammo pouch on his web gear and turned it on. He pointed the beam at each man in the patrol until he counted all twelve of them.

"Listen up, Rangers. Gather in close. I want every man where I can touch him . . . do it."

The Rangers shuffled toward MacAlister until they all bunched together in a knot, circling the RI.

"Okay, forget about being tactical for the time being." MacAlister kept his flashlight on, swinging it from face to face.

They all looked the same: gaunt, sunken cheeks,

and eyes barely open, dirty faces streaked with oily, camouflage facepaint, sweat-soaked fatigues, stooped, weary bodies bent double by the weight of their rucks—MacAlister knew the look well. They were all delirious from the lack of food and sleep. Things always got bad between zero-two and zero-five. It was part of the learning process—to drive a man to his limits physically and mentally while expecting him to accomplish the mission at hand: being a leader.

There was a thin line, however, between being hard on the Rangers for their own good and getting into a dangerous situation. Someone could get lost or lose a night site or a weapon. They'd spend the rest of the night looking for someone or something.

"How's everybody feeling? Like shit, right?"

The Rangers in front of MacAlister murmured in agreement. They were past coherent thinking. The RI grinned, remembering his own private hell when he went through the course.

"I want to see everybody take a good swig of water, right now. APL, you make sure they do that."

"Yes, Sergeant," Keller replied. He shuffled from man to man, making sure they drank from their canteens. Some were out of water. "Those of you that are out, bum some off your buddy," MacAlister ordered. "We'll cross a stream before reaching the patrol base. *Everyone* will fill their canteens when we get there."

Someone at MacAlister's right broke out of the group.

"Where you goin', Ranger?" barked the RI, shinning his light on the Ranger student. It was Prentiss.

"Over to the Coke machine. Want one?"

"Get back over here!"

MacAlister slumped against the pine tree in the center of the perimeter. Looking toward the east, he saw the faint glow of sunrise illuminate the horizon. They were halfway up the side of a mountain near the crest of a false hilltop. It was thickly vegetated with small pine trees, and the patrol had established their patrol base within an area where the trees were thickest, escaping observation. They would remain there all day, cleaning weapons and equipment and planning and rehearsing for the ambush later on that night on Black Mountain.

MacAlister chuckled softly, remembering how the patrol had staggered into the patrol base, sounding like a herd of elephants. The country boy he'd picked earlier as the patrol leader had wagon-wheeled the Rangers into a circle, sent out a two-man listening/observation post 150 meters up the side of the mountain, and then had everyone clean their weapons. When that was over, every other man ate a C-ration while his buddy pulled perimeter security. Then they switched. By the time they were all finished, it was 0500.

Then sleep. Ah, glorious sleep. It was every man's dream in Ranger School—sleep. As much as he could get. Each man on patrol averaged thirty minutes a shift, then pulled security while his buddy slept, and so on.

MacAlister pulled his poncho liner tighter around his body. The air had cooled off, especially once they had quit moving. In another hour the sun would crest over the horizon. At that time he would have the students back on fifty percent security, planning that night's ambush.

Black Mountain, he thought. He pulled the map out of his trousers cargo pocket and held it close to his face, searching for the location that was etched in stone in his memory, even though he'd received the mission only hours before at the raid site.

He rubbed the back of his neck, trying to ignore the chill that stole down his spine.

CHAPTER

· TWELVE ·

Silas Grey strolled toward the expensive stone barbecue pit where Vernon Baggins hovered over the grill, mauling steak and ribs with his spatula. People milled about, mostly family members of the guests—some swimming in the pool, some hanging around the barbecue pit, all talking and laughing. It was an afternoon southern cookout done up right. Baggins, the host, wore an apron around his generous middle that looked like a maternity blouse.

"Best damned party you've thrown in a long time, Vernon," Silas said, smiling at the sweating fat man.

"Thank you, Silas," Baggins replied, grinning from ear to ear. "Hope you're showing the Reverend a good time."

"Oh, he's enjoying himself all right. I told him when he got off the plane last night that he'd be eating some of our good southern cookin'. Hell, he's been like a little kid at Christmas today." Silas leaned on his cane toward Baggins and spoke softly.

"Vernon, he ain't goin' by 'Reverend' while he's here. Might arouse suspicion. He's just another guest. Call him Mr. Taylor."

Baggins looked at Silas with a hurt expression, as if he had just been scolded by his mother for peeing in his bed. "I forgot about that, Silas. Whatever you say."

"Why, it's no big thing, Vernon—certainly nothing to get upset over. I just want to keep his identity on wraps while he's down here . . . you know what I mean." Silas winked at Baggins, and the fat man grinned again. "Say, you got any more of that corn here?"

"Ask, and you shall receive," Baggins said, chuckling. He flipped over the last of the steaks and laid down his spatula. Then he opened a large ice chest sitting by his feet and retrieved a Mason jar filled with clear, sparkling liquid. He handed it to Silas. Silas unscrewed the lid and took a small sip, licking his lips after it burned down, and cleared his throat.

"Vernon, I don't know where you get this stuff, and I won't ask—but I damn sure like it. Got any more in the house?" he asked, nodding at Baggins's sprawling two-story Tudor.

"Keep it, Silas. I've got plenty."

"I'll give this to Taylor. Might fire him up a little before he speaks."

"Now, that's an idea."

Silas departed for Taylor, who was talking to a small knot of men by the edge of the pool at a picnic table. It was a picturesque setting that overlooked Dahlonega. Baggins's house was set on the north end of town in the nicest neighborhood.

"Enjoying yourself, Mr. Taylor?" Silas asked a

tall, heavyset man in his late sixties with a kind, grandfatherly countenance. To people who didn't know him, his thick unruly shock of brown hair combed over the back of his head and his pock-marked face made him seem homely, but Samuel Taylor had an air about him—one of charisma and dignity, and a way of putting one at ease that made him easily understood and respected by all who stood in his presence.

"I certainly am," Taylor replied, turning toward Silas, "and please, call me Sam. I must say, this barbecue is fantastic. Baggins is a heck of a cook."

Silas smiled, warming to the large, gentle man. He had a habit of never swearing and always talked in plain, folksy language that people understood and appreciated.

"Vernon would be glad to hear that." Silas nod-ded at the three men who had been talking to Tay-lor, recognizing one of Dahlonega's physicians and another man, a builder who employed more than a few of Dahlonega's younger men for his construc-tion business. Silas didn't know the third man, a young, athletic type who followed Taylor every-where he went. He guessed him to be Taylor's bodyguard.

"We were just discussing the farming situation around these parts before you joined us, Silas," Taylor announced, wrapping a meaty arm around Silas's frail, thin frame. "A truly pitiful situation."

"Silas, I think we've met before. I'm Turner Shockley." The builder extended his hand toward Silas.

"That's right," Silas replied. "Last year, let me see . . . the rally we had at Stone Mountain. We talked a good deal afterward, about getting some of your construction boys involved in our organization."

"Uh-huh, I guess it's been a year. Anyway, I was just telling Mr. Taylor here—"

"Sam," Taylor broke in.

"Right—Sam," Shockley repeated. "I was telling him about how we never do any more work out in the farms anymore. I usually make the rounds every springtime to see what kind of work they need done—backhoe, cow ponds, silos, that sort of thing—and I ain't gettin' nothin'. Hell, I've known most of those ol' boys ever since my daddy introduced 'em to me, and I'll tell you . . . they're running scared."

"They can't afford it, you mean," Silas interjected.

"You're damned right they can't afford it," Shockley said indignantly. "Bills out the ying-yang, fields goin' to shit—broken machinery they can't afford to repair, let alone buy new. Hell, they're going bankrupt."

"I agree," the physician broke in, pursing his lips and holding his chin with a philosopher's thumb and forefinger. "I know they're not seeing me with the frequency they used to. I'm always willing to extend their credit, and I never refuse anybody, but you know these people—they're proud. They won't take what they'd call a handout."

"Gentlemen," Silas said, "what we're looking at here is a classic case of the bankers screwing the farmer with foreclosures. I'm not talking about the little bank here in Dahlonega Gary Soter runs. I'm talking about the big banks in Atlanta. *Jew* banks."

"Wait a minute, Silas," Shockley interrupted. "You mean most of the banks in Atlanta are run by Jews?"

"Hell, yes. Soter doesn't run his own bank here in Dahlonega. He's got to answer to the banks in Atlanta, who subsidize one hell of a lot of his transactions. Now, who do you think controls the banks in Atlanta?"

"New York?"

"Yes! Ever been up there? Jews *run* those banks. They run the diamond market there. Christ, some of the richest Jews in the world own that city. The place is crawling with Jews. Goddammit, I know I'm getting off on a tangent, but these Jews are stealing the farmer's land and calling it *their* promised land. Lord God, it's happening all over the country." Silas had built his last statement into a crescendo of fury.

Taylor smiled at Silas, squeezing his shoulder with his hand.

"Mr. Shockley," he said, gently interrupting Silas, "all during the seventies the Jews offered, through their proxy state banks throughout the country, and ultimately through the local banks such as here in Dahlonega, incentives for the farmer to take out loans for new equipment, land, livestock, and so on. Our country's farmers were much more productive than they estimated. Several years down the road, the world grain market was flooded with U.S. exports, and the prices were driven drastically down. That meant no more profit for the farmers, and no more interest for the Jew bankers. That meant that every farmer who took a risk—to become better, bigger, what have you—was forced to pay on his loan regardless of the profit he made that year."

Shockley pondered the explanation. He himself didn't like taking out loans, but it was a way of life for the farmer. Reading his mind, Silas said, "That's right, Turner. I don't like taking out more loans than I need, and neither do you. But you have a quantifiable business. You sell machines. Hell, I'm just a foreman at a feed mill. We don't depend on the earth to earn our living. The farmer does. And if he has a good year, he's screwed, because he can't get the price he deserves on his crop. If he has a bad year, he's still screwed, because the Jew bankers still expect him to pay on his note. It never used to be this way until the past five years. Why? Because they're greedy, that's why. And because they're un-American.''

"I must admit," Taylor said gently, "that the situation has gotten entirely out of hand. As a matter of fact, it's one of the topics I came here tonight to discuss."

It was a small but happy gathering at Vernon Baggins's place late that afternoon, full of barbecue and good fellowship—clappings on the back between friends, the swapping of discreetly narrated dirty jokes in the women and children's absence, the omnipresent six-pack of Coors in sweating coolers beading in the heat. And it had been a nice party. Laid back. Good-ol'-boy time. Most of the women had packed up the kids and gone home after wringing out promises from their husbands that they'd dutifully be back before much longer.

With that out of the way they had haphazardly placed lawn chairs around the north end of the pool in a semicircle. The location and view as late afternoon slipped into early evening offered the perfect auditorium, basking in the golden glow of midsummer sunset, reflecting brilliant rays off the pool and glinting beer cans. And they all, every handpicked one of them—the builder, the physician, the welder, the trucker, the farmer, and the realtor—had come at Grey's and Baggins's request to listen to what the Reverend from the North had to say.

Samuel Taylor, Reverend for the Church of True Christ Christians of the Aryan Covenant and leader of the most dangerous domestic terrorist organization in North America, faced the leaders and lieutenants of the Confederate Knights of the Ku Klux Klan and spoke.

"My friends and colleagues—today we are faced with a question of survival. Yes—survival of the white Aryan race." Taylor's chest swelled as he stood fully erect, concentrating his steady, hypnotic gaze on the dozen men sitting before him. Two flags flanked him on each side, and all were furled and covered with sheaths. His bodyguard stood on his right and slightly behind him, eyeing the gathering with a wary vigil.

"And I ask you today," he continued in a louder voice, "are you prepared to defend yourself? Are you prepared to strike at the Zionist government that has infiltrated the halls of Capitol Hill and the White House?

"*Are you?*" Taylor shouted, pointing his finger at Baggins, who shivered slightly in his chair. Gone was Taylor's genial, grandfatherly manner.

"Our Constitution, our Declaration of Independence—the very documents and maps of this great country's birth and existence—have been betrayed! Bastardized! *Corrupted!*

"When our founding fathers wrote of 'one nation,' did they refer to crime? Greed? Zionist bureaucracy? *No!*

"They wrote our most hallowed documents for a

just and Christian people! Not the niggers who sodomize our culture! Not the Jews who skim the fat from our earnings! Not the homosexuals who pervert our morals!

"One nation of Christian people! Under God! Indivisible!"

"You tell 'em, Sam!" a voice cried.

"Damn right, Reverend!" said another. "We're with you, by gawd."

A murmur arose from the gathering and then broke into a round of applause. It was an aggressive sound, a sound as tense and as taut as the pull on a hunter's bowstring before his razor-tipped arrow finds its mark.

Taylor's chest heaved in emotion, and he pulled a handkerchief from his pocket, mopping his forehead as the men before him clapped with approving cheers. He reached for a glass of iced tea sitting on a picnic table beside him and drank deeply from it. Then he set it back down, cleared his throat, and focused his steady gaze upon all before him until it was quiet again.

Then it was quiet. Deathly quiet. No one moved or spoke. All sat spellbound before the Reverend from the North. The sun had set, and shadows from the mountains stalked slowly downhill, casting a dark, dewy hue around the gathering.

Taylor spoke again.

"Your children implore your action for their future. Their immediate future.

"They ask that they *not* be forcibly bused to different, far-off neighborhoods for their schooling, where they must mingle with blacks, Jews, thugs, rapists, and hoodlums.

"They ask that they *not* be forced to pay huge

sums of taxes to sustain the cannibalistic and greedy Zionist occupational government in Washington.

"They ask that they *not* be raped, mugged, murdered, and cheated by the mobs of Negroes, Jews, Mexicans, and Asiatics that abound in this country and who slowly but surely mingle their impure blood with the blood of our own.

"They *do* ask to keep their deer rifles and shotguns, their handguns for self-defense, rather than giving them up to the state!

"Your children *do* ask for religious freedom! Freedom from state-funded and -condoned abortion! *Moral dignity!*" Taylor's voice had risen to a crescendo of righteous fury. "They ask for the truth—not that Christ was a Jew! He was an Aryan! They must be told that the wandering tribes of Israel were the true Aryans; that they settled Europe; that they later on immigrated to the United States; and that therefore, only the *United States* can be the promised land! Not Palestine!"

Taylor paused dramatically as every man present craned his neck toward him, transfixed.

"Today you must realize that the extermination of the white race is the goal of our adversaries. For your sake, and for your children's sake, you must come forth and do battle with your enemies."

On cue, Taylor's bodyguard removed the sheath from the first flag on Taylor's right. Taylor gestured his trembling, open hand toward it and held his other toward the gathering in supplication.

"The Stars and Stripes," he lectured. "Our flag. Our countrymen's flag. Oh, how many people—white Christian people, mind you—have shed their blood for it! This flag represents all that is good about this great country—as our founding fathers had intended it to be—but it has been betrayed by the Zionist occupational government in Washington."

The bodyguard removed the sheath from the next flag, and Taylor pointed toward it.

"The Stars and Bars. The flag of the South. This flag represents how the good Christian people of the South fought for Christian ideals and independence. The South . . . is this country's moral keystone."

The bodyguard walked to the other side of Taylor and unfurled the flag on his left. Several of the older men in the group started.

"Yes—the Nazi swastika. I know that some of you or your fathers fought the Nazis in World War Two. So did I. But let me also remind you that this flag represented a group of men who exterminated the Jews from their own country. A group of men who had the courage and conviction to do so. A group of men such as us."

The bodyguard lifted the sheath from the remaining flag. Then he came to the position of attention, clicked his heels and saluted it, arm held straight out, hand stiff with the palm down, his head sternly bowed.

It was a large flag with gold tassels fringing the edges. The Stars and Bars crisscrossed a black border, and emblazoned at the center was a baby-blue shield with a flame-embroidered white cross in the center.

A swastika occupied the cross's intersection.

Taylor did not speak for several moments, searching the faces of the men before him. They were expectant—anticipating. The bodyguard dropped his salute smartly and stood at parade rest behind and to the left of Taylor.

"And now . . . the last flag. A flag of hope. A flag

that someday soon will rally the masses of this country's white patriots. A flag that combines the best of the others before you. The Flag of the Aryan Covenant!

"This flag . . . this *flag* represents the white Christians of this country that for so long have been force-fed abuses and Communist control by our government of Jews. I ask you today, gentlemen . . . how much longer will you tolerate it? *How long?*"

"No longer, by God!" a voice yelled stridently. It was Turner Shockley, who had jumped up from his seat in martial passion.

"Are you men," Turner continued in a voice climbing to a shrieking pitch, "who will allow a system that sponsors . . . rape and murder?"

"No," came the loud, chorused reply, a frenzy of vigor and hate.

"Gun control?"

"No!"

"Niggers and Jews!"

"NO!"

"Zionist government control!"

"NO! NO! NO!"

"I think you won them over," Silas told Taylor. They both sat at the picnic table by the pool, drinking Baggins's moonshine. The rest of the gathering had gone home for the evening, and Silas had sent Baggins on an errand for more of the home-stilled liquor Taylor had taken a liking to.

"Won them over," Taylor mused, swirling the dregs of his whiskey in the mason jar Silas had given him. He slouched in a lawn chair, his long legs crossed at the ankles. "For the past thirty years I've tried to win them over." Taylor cocked his head at

Silas. "I guess we've *both* tried to win them over now for quite a while."

Grey blinked. "I think you came down here this weekend to do more than make a speech."

Taylor fished for a pipe lodged deep in his left trouser pocket and went through the smoker's ritual of filling and lighting it. Then he lit it, sucking thick blue smoke in brisk puffs before answering.

"Baggins is your financier?" he said finally. It was more a statement than a question.

"Yes."

"How long have you known him?"

"Hell, we grew up together. I own stock in his feed business. Run a few of his mills."

"Where does he get his money?"

"Inherited—well, mostly. Believe it or not, ol' Vernon *does* run a pretty good feed business. He owns over fifteen mills scattered throughout this part of Georgia." Silas eyed the big man sitting before him. He wasn't used to being the one answering all the questions, and it unsettled him. "How 'bout you?" he countered.

"Well." Another slow grin enveloped Taylor's face, causing his generous nose to droop toward his upper lip. "A couple of different ways. Take it and make it. Won't be more specific than that."

"I figure the boys you sent down here are pretty capable of doing that."

"Fine group of young men, aren't they?"

"Not bad for a bunch of damn Yankees."

They both laughed. The uncertainty and wariness of their first serious talk alone together since they had last met vanished.

"You know," Taylor said, "that group you sent me taught us a few things. I'm talking about the basics, you know, the *very* basics. Things like stealth. Basic marksmanship. Woodsmanship."

"Yep," Silas replied. "They're all country boys, every last one of 'em. I wanted to send my son up to you on that exchange team, but he was needed down here. He couldn't break away from his job."

"He's the one in the Army?"

"That's right," Grey replied proudly. "That young man joined up right after high school. Did his duty in Vietnam and stayed in. He's with the Rangers down in Fort Benning and is the best advisor I've got for our organization."

"Most of our cadre is prior service," Taylor offered.

"Like Gunther, eh? I like that man."

"He's our best. Knows how to handle a job too."

Silas straightened in his chair and arched a snow-white eyebrow at Taylor. "What kind of job?" he asked.

Taylor pulled a pipe nail from his shirt pocket and tamped down the ashes in his pipe bowl, and then went through the conveniently time-consuming habit of relighting it.

"Every now and then," he finally said, "we take out someone. Like this one Jew who was a newscaster back in Montana. He was always bitching about something or another controversial on his nightly commentaries. He was a Communist. Not in the literal sense, mind you," Taylor added, looking closely at Silas, "but all the same, a Communist. Always taking up for women's rights, black rights, busing, welfare—always sniveling for some liberal cause. Then he started talking about us. At first we enjoyed the publicity. Then he became a nuisance. We took care of him."

"We've done that a time or two ourselves."

"So I've heard. The Greensboro shootout?" Taylor queried, chuckling softly.

"Christ almighty, that was a mess," Silas replied, embarrassed. He opened the cooler next to his feet, pulled out a Coors, and popped the lid. "Yep. But there have also been a few other things we've done without all the media hoopla *that* fiasco got." Silas took a deep swig from his beer, burped, then wiped his mouth with his shirt sleeve. "Hell, normally we love it when the media comes snoopin' around. You know, rallies, cross burnings, that sort of thing. The Jew-boys at the TV station blow it up real big, bigger than it actually is, and before you know it, we got a dozen or more country boys breaking the door down trying to join up."

Silas Grey's eyes grew slightly out of focus as he took another swig from his beer. "We do have a little action committee," he continued softly. "Took care of this one nigger who was living with a white woman. Broke into his house, beat his ass up, and then we whipped that woman and her half-breed brats with a belt right in front of him." Silas snorted and shook his head self-righteously. "White slut. We tolerate a few coloreds as long as they know their place, but not often. There was this one that raped a woman—a good, decent, white woman in Gainesville. We hung him."

"I think you're my kind of man, Grey." Taylor was smiling broadly. "I did a thing or two like that back in my day."

"You ain't gettin' any younger, Reverend," Silas said point-blank.

Taylor's smile vanished. He took a long drink from

the mason jar and then wiped his mouth with a trembling hand.

"I'd say you aren't either."

"Reckon that makes two of us, then. Let's cut the shit and get down to brass tacks."

Silence.

"Look, Reverend," Silas continued, "I've a pretty fair notion as to why you're down here, and it's not just to check up on your boys and make speeches."

Taylor went through another ritual of knocking out the ashes from his pipe with the heel of his hand, lost in thought. Silas countered by pulling out a crumpled pouch of Red Man and stuffing his right cheek with what appeared to Taylor to be most of the leafy contents of the package. He was prepared to wait for his answer.

"The mood is almost right." Taylor searched Silas's eyes to see if the Grand Dragon understood. He did.

The Reverend from the North continued.

"All across the country white people are realizing that it's eventually going to come to a head. Problem is, there's no organization. No united front. As far as I know, we've been the only two major organizations out of over fifteen hundred splinter groups in this country that have managed to talk seriously about any kind of coordinated action."

Silas nodded his head in agreement. "We've damned sure had our share of problems," he said, remembering how disorganized and fractional the United Klans had become years before.

"But tonight," Taylor said, "I could feel the discontent. The farming situation—well, it's the same all across the country. The administration has ruined them by not controlling the bankers' monopoly in New York. Over the last two years I've recruited sixty different families scattered from North Dakota all the way to Missouri. They've bought assault rifles and plenty of ammunition. Every once in a while I'll send a team—no more than three or four men like Gunther—out to them for basic instruction. They help us out by letting us set up caches on their property and sometimes providing us a safe house."

"I understand my son to say you and me now have a chain of those safe houses established in every state between here and Montana," Silas interrupted.

"I hope he didn't say that over the phone."

"Give us a little more credit than that, Reverend. We talked last night at a little restaurant here in town."

"I thought he was at Fort Benning," Taylor said, surprised.

"Nope. He's up at the Ranger camp about fifteen miles from here for the next few weeks."

"Well. That's interesting. Very interesting."

They both remained quiet for several moments, each waiting for the other to talk next. Then Taylor spoke again.

"The NAACP is sponsoring their annual black mayors' convention in Atlanta next week. Black actors, comedians, and other prominent blacks will be there. Other political figures."

A knowing grin spread across Silas's face. "I know," he said.

"Then you also know who's going to be there."

"Well, you got those niggers from Chicago, L.A., and of course, Atlanta. Even heard that little kike from New York will be there."

Taylor bent forward in his seat toward Silas and

spoke quietly. "A good chain of riots should get the ball rolling. Hit all those mayors at once, coordinated with a hit on a few selected *white* targets . . . in Washington . . . and watch the sparks fly." Taylor leaned back in his seat and smiled. "My people are ready," he added drolly.

Silas grinned hugely from ear to ear as he reached over and clapped Taylor on the back.

"Welcome to Dahlonega, Reverend."

"She left me, Daddy. She called me just after dinner. Sarah, my little girl—they're both gone. She fuckin' left me!"

"Settle down, son."

"Christ, why did she have to do that?"

"Son!"

Grey sighed deeply into the phone. He knew he had to get a grip on himself. The fifth of Jim Beam he'd consumed in the past thirty minutes hadn't helped any.

"Okay, Daddy," he said, the lump in his throat growing hard.

"Do you think you can go on as planned?"

"I've got everything set up."

"Call me again tomorrow night after you've taken the Rangers."

"Sure, Daddy. I'll—I'll do you proud."

"I know you will, son."

"Good night, Daddy."

"Good night, Frankie."

Grey hung up the phone.

CHAPTER

· THIRTEEN ·

Miserable, Dan Levy looked up at the slate-gray sky and guessed that the sun had already set. Throughout the day a steady drizzle had enveloped the patrol base, its searching fingers soaking the Rangers through their poncho liners and fatigues. The approaching night would bring temperatures in the fifties with accompanying short tempers and petty bickering.

"It's gonna get colder'n a bitch tonight," Christopher moaned, having just woken up from a restless catnap at Levy's right. They were pulling security out on the listening/observation post a hundred and fifty meters away from the camp up on the crest of a ridgeline.

Levy looked at Christopher in shock. "I don't believe it."

"What?"

"Ranger John Wayne Christopher, sniveling."

"Fuck off and die."

"Think I might do that. My pussy's been hurting all day." Levy, still grinning, braced his cheek on the stock of his M16 as if watching the perimeter and closed his eyes.

Christopher laughed and pulled his patrol cap over his face, muffling the sound. Finally, he said, "Yeah, guess mine has too. Go ahead and rack out for a while. I can't."

Levy's eyes popped back open.

"What's the matter?"

"I've got better things to do than sleep."

"Oh, really?" Christopher asked sarcastically. "Like what?"

Levy scooted up to the huge oak in front of their position and rummaged through the ruck he had leaned against it. Everything inside was soggy—clothes in a definitely nonwaterproof bag, multitudes of soaked rifle ammunition blanks (complete with disintegrated cardboard boxes and loose rounds everywhere), the night-sight he'd used the night before, a fifteen-pound roll of DR-8 communications wire (seldom used), soppy poncho liner—a total mess that weighed a dozen pounds more when wet. He finally fished out his prize: an issue wool sock that he had stuffed with C-ration cans.

"You eating again, man?"

"Yeah."

"What?"

"Peanut butter." Levy shook out a small, OD green disk of a can from the sock and opened it with his Swiss Army knife.

Christopher's eyes lit up like a five-year-old's at his birthday party.

With deliberate slowness Levy stuck a grimy index finger with accumulated filth and dirt into the

opening and mashed down on the oil that had
formed in the center, mixing it up with the rest of
the coarse, government-issue peanut butter. He noticed Christopher examining his every move, as he
knew he would. He always did, when it came to
chow.

"What are you looking at, dog-breath?"

"Nothing."

Levy scooped up a large glob of peanut butter with
his finger and stuck it in his mouth.

"Levy, can I—"

"No."

"Aw, c'mon, man—"

"How many Cs did *you* bring?"

"Five."

"That's one more than *I* brought."

"Buddyfucker." Indignant, Christopher returned
his attention to their front. Chuckling, Levy continued eating, until the peanut butter was almost gone.

"Levy?"

"What."

"Can I have the can when you're finished?"

"Here, I saved the last bite just for you. Don't cut
yourself licking the can like you did last time."

"Wow, thanks!" Christopher greedily snatched
the can from his grinning Ranger buddy. "First thing
I'm gonna do on our next break is buy me a whole
fucking jar of Peter Pan. The crunchy kind."

Levy shook with laughter, trying to keep it quiet.
"Chowhound."

Someone approached them from behind. Christopher stuffed the can in his shirt, thinking it was
the RI.

"Levy—Christopher," a voice called out softly.

The two Rangers turned around and saw Jakes looking for them about ten meters to the rear.

"Over here," Levy replied.

Jakes treaded softly toward them. Prentiss trailed behind him, forlorn and disoriented. The day before had sapped all of his energy.

"What's up?" Levy asked when they arrived.

"Merry Christmas," Jakes said, squatting down next to Levy. "You're APL and Christopher's the PL for the ambush tonight. Sergeant MacAlister sent me and Prentiss out here to relieve you. Better report to him ASAP."

MacAlister sneezed and realized he was coming down with a cold. Fumbling through the dark, he opened his pack and retrieved his field jacket liner. Weather in the mountains was fickle even during the summer months. One night it would be steaming hot, like the night before, and the next would be so cool that you had to wear a jacket to keep warm.

The RI sat against a tree in the patrol base's center watching the students go over their operations order. Actually, they were all huddled next to him underneath a poncho shielding a red-lensed flashlight, looking at the map, and making last-minute adjustments to the plan that had been prepared by the patrol the past afternoon. He knew he should stick his head underneath the poncho to hear what they were saying but had put it off, hoping they would finish the operations order and get moving.

No such luck. He glanced at his watch. It was close to 2100. If they didn't move out by that time, they would be behind schedule for the midnight ambush, over four klicks away.

MacAlister stood up slowly, feeling the muscles in

the backs of his thighs ache and cramp from the damp and the chill. He walked over to them.

"Levy," Christopher said, his breath steaming underneath the poncho, "you and Prentiss will stay at the ORP a hundred and fifty meters away from the objective. That's pretty close, since it's near the top of the hill next to the ambush site."

"Why so close?"

"So that the patrol doesn't piddly-ass around and get lost trying to get back to it. We're leaving our rucks there. When the assault and security teams move out, line all the rucks together by team. When you hear us initiate the ambush, wait ten minutes and then shine your flashlight in our direction every minute on the minute—three long flashes, about five seconds each—then wait for the next minute and repeat. Keep doing it until you hear us get close, then guide us on in. It's gonna be dark as hell with all this cloud cover, so keep your ears in tune and don't go to sleep."

"No sweat."

"Who do you want to stay behind with you?"

"Make it Prentiss. He's too dogged out to be of any help to you anyway."

"Okay, fine. Just make sure he doesn't go to sleep."

MacAlister drew a deep breath, held it, and stuck his head through the poncho hood. An incredibly foul stench punched through his nostrils from the unwashed bodies of the three Rangers inside. It was like the ripe smell of a possum on the side of a country road that had been dead for three days.

"You Rangers about ready?" he croaked, not daring to inhale.

"Yes, Sergeant," Christopher replied. "Give us another minute, and we'll be ready to move out."

"Hurry up."

"Roger that, Sergeant." Christopher looked at Keller, who was his security team leader. "Remember, you and another man will pull security about a hundred meters north of the objective on the road leading into the ambush site. Once we hit 'em, make sure you fire up anybody coming or going from the kill zone. Make sure the security team on the south side understands that too."

"You've already gone over that," Keller replied condescendingly.

"I don't give a shit how many times I go over it. You just do what I tell you to do."

"I don't have to take that."

Christopher grabbed Keller by the shirt and shook him furiously. "Listen, fuck-face, I've had enough of your prima donna attitude."

"Let go of me!"

"Then do what I say, and don't give me any lip about it."

"Break it up!" MacAlister interrupted. "Now, quit screwing around and get moving. You people better learn how to cooperate and grad—*Jesus!*"

MacAlister yanked his head out from the poncho, gasping for breath. He didn't mind so much one Ranger "persuading" another to go along with a plan, as long as he was in a leadership position. He just couldn't stand smelling dirty Rangers underneath a poncho. Besides, there was something else that needed to be done. Soon.

The flashlight switched off, and the poncho was thrown clear of the small group of figures underneath. Keller shuffled back to his position like a kicked peacock, and Levy walked the perimeter, gathering the patrol together and sending them in to the center. Christopher remained in the center with MacAlister, waiting.

An awkward silence. It had been the first time MacAlister had been alone with Christopher since the night before, when the black RI had decked the Ranger's class TAC.

"Are you ready for this patrol, Ranger?"

"Yes, Sergeant."

MacAlister took of his field jacket liner and stuffed it into his ruck. He wouldn't need it for the movement to the objective. He pulled something else out. Christopher busied himself by repainting his face with his cammie stick.

"Be on your toes tonight."

"I don't think we'll have any problems, Sergeant."

"That's not what I'm talking about."

Christopher looked up at the RI.

MacAlister stared hard at Christopher. "If something should happen tonight . . . like last night . . ."

"I didn't see *anything* last night, Sergeant."

"I know, I know. Give me your hand."

"What?"

"I said give me your hand."

Christopher stuck his hand out, hearing the edge in the RI's voice. MacAlister shoved a cardboard ammo box into it, only this one wasn't disintegrated with the wet and the rain. Cartridges rattled inside. Christopher looked at it in disbelief.

"I just violated a lot of areas covered by the Uniform Code of Military Justice by doing that. Enough to send me to Fort Leavenworth. Do you understand that?"

"Y-yes."

"Your buddy is staying behind at the ORP, right?"

"Yes, Sergeant."

"Then you'd best split those with him."

"Why are you doing this?"

"Don't be stupid, Ranger. Now, you listen to me, and listen good. Like last night, this never happened. In all likelihood, nothing *will* happen. I'll collect those rounds back from you when this patrol is over. Do you understand now, or do I have to spell it out for you?"

Christopher stared at MacAlister for a long time. The other patrol members were arriving in from the perimeter. He shoved the box deep inside his trousers pocket and nodded.

"I understand."

CHAPTER
· FOURTEEN ·

"Just like old times, huh?"

Jakes threw an extended middle finger in front of Christopher's face. "This radio is kicking my ass, and you know it. Why do you always want me to carry it?"

"Because you're so good at it, my man." Christopher looked at Levy, who squatted next to him, almost hidden in the dark. "We'll be gone for the next half hour conducting the leader's recon," he whispered. "If we're not back by that time, give us another half hour. By then we ought to be back. I'm taking Jakes with me, along with Keller. We'll pinpoint the objective and then come back and move the rest of the patrol up to the site."

"Better hurry," Levy said, looking at his watch. "It's already 2200."

"That's why we busted ass getting to the ORP. Don't let anybody go to sleep while we're gone. We'll make it back in plenty of time."

Christopher looked around for MacAlister, who was crashed out against a tree ten feet away. The rest of the patrol was in a small perimeter. It was a good ORP, established in a thick growth of pine saplings near the top of the hill. He grabbed Jakes by the shoulder.

"Go ahead and link up with Keller and the rest of his security team. I'll be with you in a minute."

"What am I, some sort of pack mule?" Grunting, Jakes stood up and stumbled to the next most convenient tree several feet away and flopped down next to Keller, who had passed out next to it. "Wake up," he groaned.

Christopher leaned close to Levy's ear and gripped him tightly on the shoulder.

"Here, take these," he whispered, shoving a magazine into Levy's hand.

"I've already got enough blanks for the whole goddamned patrol."

"Those aren't blanks. Feel the tip of the cartridge."

"What the—?"

"Don't say anything, just *trust* me." He squeezed Levy's shoulder and then let go. "I've got the other half out of a box of twenty. Don't ask me any questions. I'll get the rounds back from you after the patrol. I'll explain it to you later."

"No shit, Sherlock. We can get in a lot of trouble for having these."

"We could get in a lot of trouble for *not* having them too."

"Whatever." Levy stuck the magazine in his trousers pocket, not wanting to confuse it with the blanks he kept in his web gear.

"We'll be back soon." Christopher rose, buckling

his web gear together after making sure he had everything. Levy noticed that the blank firing adapter was missing from his buddy's M16.

"Hey, what's going on? Where's your firing adapter?"

"Like I said, don't ask questions. Take yours off too." Christopher grabbed Levy's weapon and shoved the muzzle in front of his face. "I mean it," he added.

"Okay, okay." Levy unscrewed the firing adapter and looked at Christopher. "I want a thorough debriefing later on."

"Take care of yourself, buddy. We'll be back ASAP."

"Jerry—hey, Jerry, I think I see something."

"That's about the fifth time you've said that in the past half hour."

"No, really! Look!"

"Keep your voice down. Here, give me your binoculars."

Excitedly, Charley handed his friend the binoculars he had been so proud to carry all night. He felt they had given him status in front of the others.

"I'll be damned," Jerry whispered, focusing the binoculars. "You're right." He clapped Charley on the back. "You done good, pard. You're talking about that fella movin' around down by the bridge, right?"

"Yeah," Charley replied happily. He had been vindicated. *And after all that time they said I was always gettin' in the way*, he thought. *Good ol' Jerry.*

"Looks like a nigger too." Jerry swung his binoculars in a slow arc around the area where a figure moved in the tree line next to the bridge. "There's someone else there with him. Looks like he's carrying a radio.''

''Let's get 'em!''

''Not yet. J.D. says to wait until they ambush the truck we're sending through. We'll fake 'em out and catch them while they're all together.''

''What about those guys?''

''They're probably some sort of scout party.''

''Oh.''

''Got any questions?'' Christopher asked Levy, who had rearranged all the rucks in the center of the perimeter while he had been out on the leader's recon. The rest of the patrol members had drawn up in a small perimeter around the rucks, faces blackened, caps pulled down low over their foreheads, weapons at the ready and pointed out. Jakes, worn out from carrying the radio, had collapsed in the center with Christopher and Levy.

''Nope.''

''Okay. We've got another forty minutes before the ambush. The site's not far away at all. Look . . . see that ravine over there?'' Christopher pointed toward the direction where he and Jakes had returned from the recon.

''Yeah,'' Levy replied, eyes squinting.

''The objective is five minutes away, down that ravine. That's where we're gonna return after we hit it. Have the flashlight ready.''

''Right. You hit the objective, and then we link up and move out of the AO ASAP, just like every other patrol we've been on. Now, you wanna tell me what's going on with this one?''

''Just keep what I gave you handy in case you need it.''

"Thanks for the explanation."

"We're off." Christopher helped a protesting Jakes to his feet and led the patrol down the ravine. MacAlister trailed behind them.

Levy watched them as they left and wondered what in hell was going on. Then he checked the rucks over again and found Prentiss sleeping against one of them. He nudged him in the butt with the toe of his jungle boot.

"Wake up, Prentiss. It's going to be a long night."

"I wasn't sleeping, I wasn't—where are we?"

"J.D., is that you?" A shadowy figure crept up close.

"Yeah. Have you seen them yet?"

"Over by the bridge." J. D. Gunther raised his night vision goggles to his eyes and scanned the bridge, thirty feet below. Then he saw movement at the base of the hill next to the bridge, opposite their position.

"Good work, Jerry. I see the patrol moving into position now." He handed him the goggles for confirmation.

"I see 'em too." Jerry handed the goggles back to Gunther. "You'd better warn the others."

Christopher scanned his left and his right. He thought he had a good plan. The patrol flanked the dirt road, thirty meters from where it met the bridge, and all six men of the assault team were spread alongside it, five meters apart. Two-man security teams were positioned 150 meters outside the left and right limits of the kill zone, equipped with small hand-held PRC-68 radios. There they could see a greater distance beyond than the rest of the patrol and give the assault team advance notice, should the aggressor detail or its reinforcements come from either direction.

They waited. 2400 came and went. Christopher's eyelids grew heavy. He could already hear the snores of the Rangers around him. The chill set back in, only temporarily warded off by the movement of the past three hours. The drizzle that had soaked the entire day and night now picked up in tempo and intensity, creating a light rain that would surely increase to a steady downpour by morning. 0025. Still no truck. MacAlister sidled up next to Christopher.

"If no one shows up by zero-one, we'll move out and set up another patrol base," he told the sleepy Ranger.

"Believe you me, Sergeant, that's no problem." MacAlister faded back into the tree line, checking other Rangers.

A noise.

Suddenly, every nerve tingled in Christopher's body. It was the far-off but unmistakable grind and roar of a deuce-and-a-half's diesel engine.

Christopher's PRC-68 burst to life.

"Alpha-Tango, this is Romeo-Sierra, over," Keller's voice crackled through the tiny speaker.

"This is Alpha-Tango," Christopher replied nervously.

"Aggressors coming your way in about two mikes, over."

"Roger, out."

Christopher flipped the safety off his M16, wondering if he should have locked and loaded with the rounds MacAlister had given him.

* * *

Gunther tapped the shoulders of the two men flanking him. They were hiding next to the bridge abutment barely twenty meters across from the Ranger patrol. He heard the truck moving inexorably toward the raid site.

He whispered into the ears of one man and then the other, "Anytime now. Keep control. Don't jump up till I give the word. Wait until our guys get out of the truck and are playing dead. Pass it on." And so the message was passed from man to man, until all ten of them, armed and ready, knew what to do.

Dan Levy heard the rumble of the truck as it approached. He didn't feel good about what Christopher had told him earlier, and about the live rounds he had been given. Something was going on. At least that was what the tingling sensation on the back of his neck had told him for the past hour, ever since Christopher had moved everyone out of the ORP.

He kicked Prentiss in the butt.

"I wasn't—goddammit, Levy, quit kicking me in the butt!"

"Get up. We're linking up with the rest of the patrol."

Grey sat erect in the cab of the deuce-and-a-half he was driving. He saw the bridge fifty meters away and knew everyone was in place. Every muscle was tensed and his adrenaline flowed, secreted in huge amounts throughout his body. Small beads of sweat popped out on his forehead, running into the green facepaint covering his face. His camouflage uniform was sterile, his web gear taped and equipped for the coming action.

He would have to go underground for this.

Christopher waited. The truck got closer. Closer. Its headlights beamed through the dark, silhouetting the raindrops that grew heavier and more aggressive as the early morning hours ran their course. Two aggressors with Kalashnikov assault rifles walked out in front of the truck, chattering in make-believe Russian and dressed in mock Soviet uniforms.

He felt relieved. Nothing would happen, if anything was *going* to happen in the first place. These aggressors were just like the others he had ambushed or raided throughout Ranger School. Everything would be okay.

The deuce-and-a-half rumbled by his immediate front.

He squeezed the shoulder of the M60 gunner lying prone next to him and threw his first hand grenade simulator at the truck.

· FIFTEEN ·

I will always keep myself mentally alert, physically strong, and morally straight . . .

BANG!

The first hand grenade simulator exploded just beneath the cab of the truck. Christopher pulled the fuse of another and threw it. The M60 belched noisily from his right, showering the ground beside it with expended shell casings and blasting a din that rattled Christopher's teeth. The assault team fired their M16s in automatic bursts for fifteen long seconds.

The two aggressors in front of the truck dropped to the ground. Five more aggressors leapt out of the bed of the deuce-and-a-half, sprayed the tree line with automatic blank fire, then fell.

The driver slumped at the wheel.

"Assault!" Christopher yelled.

The assault team scrambled across the dirt road, yelling and screaming, executing their much-rehearsed and school-reinforced way of assaulting an ambush site: Run, shoot, stab, kick away the bad guy's weapon, and seek cover on the other side of the objective on-line with the rest of the patrol.

MacAlister emerged from the tree line and slowly walked toward the road, watching Christopher command the patrol, ticking off a mental checklist of his actions and leadership. He scanned the fallen "bodies" of the aggressors for familiar faces, hoping to find his replacement among them. Finding none, he then walked toward Christopher to find out what was taking so long in getting the demolitions and POW/search teams out on the site. Then he turned around, puzzled. He retraced his steps.

An aggressor was sprawled on his back by the truck's front wheels with his weapon clenched tightly across his chest. He did not look like any of the other aggressors from Camp Merrill. The uniform was right, and so was the web gear, but MacAlister noticed his hair was way too long—halfway down his ears.

Damned sure looks *like a civilian*, MacAlister thought. After being in the Army for over seven years, he could tell. *The weapon he's got . . . since when does anybody use a Mini-14 on these drills?*

"Hey, buddy."

No answer. MacAlister squatted down next to the man's head and assumed his best drill sergeant's accent.

"My name's Staff Sergeant MacAlister; I'm the lane walker for this patrol. What are you doing with that unauthorized weapon? Hey, I'm talking to you!"

The aggressor bolted up and slammed the butt of his Mini-14 into MacAlister's face.

"Now!"

Jerry and Charley scrambled out of the bushes they had been hiding in. The patrol had secured the far side of the ambush kill zone twenty feet directly below them. The two men held their Uzis at waist level, fingers at the trigger as they padded quietly downslope to take the Rangers.

"Freeze!" Charley yelled when they reached them. The six-man assault team looked upslope in surprise at the two civilians with Uzi submachine guns aimed at them.

"Throw your weapons out in the road," Jerry commanded. *"Now!"*

The Rangers exchanged glances of bewilderment, all looking at Christopher for approval, as if he were still in charge no matter what had happened.

"Who the hell are you?" Christopher bellowed at Jerry, holding his M16 at the ready. His eyes were riveted on the nine-millimeter hole aimed at him and the tobacco-chewing civilian dressed in cammies holding it.

"Nigger, throw your gawd-damned weapon in the road before I blow your tar-baby ass away! That goes for all of you!"

Seething, Christopher tossed his weapon in the road, wishing now that he *had* locked and loaded the rounds MacAlister had given him. The others did the same.

"Hold your hands on top of your head, and walk out to the truck," Jerry ordered, swinging the Uzi in a wide arc. "You—" he added, glancing back at Christopher, "you keep your fuckin' mouth shut."

Christopher glared at Jerry and slowly clasped his hands on top of his head. Then he looked at Jakes. Tired as he was from the weight of the radio, the country boy managed to wink and nod. The assault team backed out of the tree line onto the road.

Christopher saw MacAlister lying prostrate on the

dirt road in front of the truck, groaning and semiconscious. The aggressors they had just ambushed were now on their feet and pointing their weapons at them, waving them toward the back of the truck. Another aggressor in camouflage fatigues guarded MacAlister with what appeared to be a smaller version of an M14 rifle.

The Ranger instructor's face was a bloody mess. A deep gash ran from the middle of his forehead, across the bridge of his nose, and down his left cheek. The bleeding had already splattered the front of MacAlister's shirt and the ground beside him. Shaking his head, he tried to sit up. The guard kicked him in the ribs. MacAlister grunted and went back down, writhing in pain and clutching his chest.

"What the hell do you people think you're doing?" Christopher yelled at Jerry.

Charley stepped forward and clubbed Christopher in the gut with his Uzi.

"Shut up, nigger," he said as the Ranger doubled over. Jerry kicked him in the back of his knee and Christopher sprawled on the dirt road. Jakes rushed over and grabbed him under the armpits, helping him back to his feet. Christopher's eye flashed at the two men as he limped about.

"Boy," Jerry drawled, "I'm tellin' you for the last time to keep your fuckin' mouth shut."

Levy and Prentiss made good time running down the ravine. Once the fireworks started, noise hadn't been a factor. When the assault quieted, they slowed down to a stealthy creep.

Levy didn't like it. It was too quiet. No commands for the POW/search team. No situation reports on ammo and casualties. Nothing. He searched for the site, the dark and the rain of the moonless night casting a misty veil over his eyes.

Then he heard someone yell. In pain. Muffled voices, different from the familiar sounds of his own patrol. He grabbed Prentiss by the shoulder and pulled him down behind a tree growing from the side of the ravine. "Listen," he whispered.

"What?"

"Something's not right."

Levy removed the magazine from his M16, replacing it with the one Christopher had given him. It made a small click as he locked it in the magazine well of his weapon. He gently pulled the charging handle back and then slid the first bullet into the chamber with help from the weapon's forward assist instead of releasing it, which would have rammed the bolt carrier noisily against the chamber.

Prentiss pulled at Levy's shoulder, alarmed at seeing the live rounds. "What's going on?"

"Man, can't you *hear* what's going on? Nothing, except a few muffled voices, right?"

"Yeah. So what?"

"So it's not right, that's what. During actions on the objective, everyone's screaming at the top of their lungs. Look over there." Levy pointed the muzzle of his weapon at a boulder the size of a small car twenty meters to their front. It was surrounded by bushes and small pine trees. "That place ought to be pretty close to the road. We can probably see the ambush site from there. We're gonna low-crawl to it."

"Low-crawl? C'mon, Levy, nothing's going on."

"Bullshit. Get on down."

Levy pulled Prentiss down to the ground next to him, and they crawled on their elbows and knees to the boulder. The pine straw that covered the ground muffled their movement, and soon they were there. Levy climbed up to the top of the boulder and saw that he was over the road, where the rock had formed a wall of granite next to it. He also saw the headlights of a deuce-and-a-half truck fifty meters to his left and ducked back down. Then he cautiously poked his head back up and gazed at the ambush site for several moments.

"What do you see?" Prentiss called softly.

Levy didn't answer. He was transfixed.

Suddenly, from the right, a pickup truck blasted down the road toward the ambush sight, slinging mud and gravel everywhere.

Levy ducked, praying he hadn't been seen. When he looked back up, the pickup had stopped before the deuce-and-a-half, its occupants getting out with rifles. The guard who had been riding in the bed kicked out two people who were handcuffed together. It was Keller and another man from his security team. A second pickup roared up to the ambush site from the opposite direction and offloaded two more handcuffed Rangers. They were kicked and shoved toward the main group standing by the rear of the deuce-and-a-half with their hands on top of their heads. MacAlister sat leaning against the front wheel of the deuce-and-a-half, bleeding from the nose and mouth.

Levy slithered down the boulder and rejoined Prentiss. "The aggressors . . . they've got the patrol," he said.

"That's all we need," Prentiss snorted, "a bunch of RIs running us through some POW routine."

"No way. Somebody beat the shit out of Mac-Alister."

"What?"

"You heard me. This ain't no fun and games. The

rest of the patrol is rounded up by the rear of the deuce-and-a-half that came through the ambush. It's some sort of setup.''

''Oh, my God! What are we going to do?''

''Calm down, Prentiss. They're probably looking for us, too, so don't spaz out on me.'' Levy glanced at the tree line leading up to the ambush site and crept toward it.

''Where are you going?'' Prentiss whined.

''To get a better look.''

''You wanna be a fucking hero? Let's get out of here, man.''

Levy grabbed Prentiss by the back of the neck and squeezed hard, pulling his face down close to his own. ''Those are our *friends* down there. What would *you* do, leave them?''

''No,'' Prentiss said, shrinking back. Then he added, ''Of course not.''

''Then you stick close to me, and don't make a sound. We may be all they have left.''

The two Rangers slipped into the tree line.

J. D. Gunther looked at his watch. It had taken only five minutes from the time the Rangers initiated their ambush to the time they had been corraled together behind the truck. He walked to the cab of the deuce-and-a-half and opened the door.

''Are you going to stay in there all night, or what?'' he asked the occupant.

''I'm waiting until you get them all in the truck bed, blindfolded, and covered up,'' Grey replied. ''I've still got some unfinished business back at Camp Merrill.''

''What about the nigger?''

''Get everybody handcuffed and in the truck first.''

''No sweat.'' Gunther closed the door and walked

to the rear of the deuce-and-a-half, where he spotted Jerry and Charley. They were joking around with Hood Dietrick, one of the men he had brought with him from Montana. He was a tall, redheaded man in his thirties, thin to the point of emaciation. Dietrick was guarding MacAlister, who stared up at them from the rear wheel of the truck, where he sat, numb from pain. Gunther swaggered up next to Dietrick and slapped him on the back.

"How's it going, Hood?" he said, glancing at MacAlister. The black RI stared back at him levelly. "You keeping a good eye on Sambo?"

"I'm about ready to plug him if he doesn't settle down. I've had to kick him twice already, since I first bashed his face."

"Keep a good eye on him."

"No problem, boss."

Gunther walked toward the group of Rangers kneeling on the ground behind the truck with their hands on top of their heads.

"Jerry," he said to their guard, "why don't you and Charley get the handcuffs out of the back of the truck. It's time to cuff these pretty boys and get the hell out of here." Gunther walked back to the newly arrived pickup truck to talk to the driver, another one of his crew from Montana.

"C'mon, Charley," Jerry said. "Give me a hand."

The two mountain men lumbered over to the back of the truck, kicking a couple of Rangers out of the way before they climbed in. They came out a moment later, each carrying a wooden crate. Metal rattled inside.

They set both boxes down on the dirt road several feet in front of MacAlister. The RI studied their every move, desperately trying to clear his mind and evaluate his situation.

MacAlister wondered how he could have been so stupid about the whole thing. First, his family's harassment two nights before, then last night's fight with Grey and Quinn, and now tonight. He should have seen it coming. God knew what Grey and his people were trying to do. Or start. Where was Grey now? He decided the best thing to do was sit tight—act like he was hurt more than he actually was—and wait for the right time to move.

"Good idea, bringing them handcuffs along," Charley said, looking at Jerry for approval. He retrieved a set of chrome handcuffs from the wooden box and held them up against the truck's headlights.

Jerry squinted at the group of Ranger students. "Charley, bring me that mouthy nigger we busted a few minutes ago. We'll cuff him first."

Charley checked the safety on his Uzi and walked over to Christopher.

"Get up," he said, ramming the muzzle into Christopher's ribs.

Christopher stood up, his hands on top of his head. He wanted to wrap his fingers around the apparent halfwit's throat and strangle the life out of him. He walked slowly toward the other man who seemed to do all the talking.

"Move it, nigger," Charley taunted, walking behind him. "Tar-baby-Sambo, move it!"

Christopher stiffened, straining for self-control. Charley hit him between the shoulder blades with the butt of his Uzi, staggering him toward Jerry.

Standing before Jerry, Christopher realized he had acquired a blazing headache, which made everything worse. He wished there were something he could do.

He couldn't just stand there and take the abuse. He glanced at MacAlister, who suddenly seemed not quite as bad off as before. The RI was watching him. His eyes kept moving back and forth between the guard's Mini-14 and Charley's Uzi like a signal. *Like a . . .*

Charley moved up next to Jerry, so he could lock the cuffs on Christopher's wrists. Christopher saw that Jerry's Uzi was slung around his back. Charley still held his, but it was pointed toward the ground—he wasn't thinking. Christopher stole another glance at MacAlister. Their eyes locked, as if saying *"Whenever you're ready . . ."*

Dietrick swung his Mini-14 toward Christopher.

"What are you looking at, nigger?"

Suddenly, MacAlister lunged up at Dietrick and drove his elbow deep into his groin, making the guard howl in pain. Christopher, on cue, lodged a solid kick into Charley's gut, knocking him down and sending the Uzi flying. Then he slammed his fist with all of his might into Jerry's face.

MacAlister wrestled the Mini-14 away from Dietrick's grip and hit him in the head with the butt. Dietrick collapsed, splaying in the mud of the road.

Fire opened up from the tree line, fifteen meters away!

The other "aggressors" guarding the rest of the patrol ducked behind the truck, yanking the Rangers along with them. Gunther joined them, flying out of his pickup.

One man remained in sight, returning automatic fire with an AK-47. A three-round burst erupted from the tree line, and he was blown backward, falling flat on his back, a neat hole oozing blood from the center of his forehead. The exit hole made the back of his head mush like a flattened tomato, staining the dirt road beneath it with blood and gray matter.

Christopher pounded Jerry's face again and pulled the Uzi away from him. MacAlister leapt over him for Charley, who was scrambling for his Uzi a few feet away by the road. He caught up with him and smacked him in the back of the head with Dietrick's Mini-14, stunning him.

Suddenly, Jerry wrapped arms around Christopher's legs, tripping him. Christopher hit the ground, and Jerry hit him square in the face. Christopher felt his nose break in stunning, excruciating pain. Blood erupted from his nostrils and his eyes streaked tears. He was on the verge of blacking out. With the agility of an alley cat, Jerry straddled Christopher's chest and hit him again. The Ranger's head flopped on the road, explosions crushing his brain behind his eyes. Pinned, Christopher felt helpless and numb, as he watched Jerry pull a long Gerber Mark II survival knife from his boot.

Jerry raised it up, ready to drive its serrated blade through Christopher's larynx. Christopher passed out.

MacAlister raised the Mini-14, aiming a shot at Jerry before he could kill Christopher.

Another burst of fire from the tree line. Jerry flipped off Christopher and jolted on the ground, dead. Three rounds had burst open his chest, the crimson blood misting the cool mountain air.

Levy lowered his rifle in disgust, his magazine empty. There was nothing more he could do. For one wild moment he considered going in with his knife, but knew the others behind the truck would kill him before he could even cross the road. Already they were returning heavy fire in his direction. He grabbed Prentiss by the arm and tore out through the forest, running and tripping through the vines and trees.

Charley ran up behind MacAlister and wrapped his arms around the black RI, choking him and knocking him off balance. MacAlister dropped the Mini-14 and flipped Charley over his head, trying to break the other man's powerful grip.

Grey poked his head through the window of the truck. He quickly surveyed the damage, thinking that the sniper from the tree line—probably a student with a few bullets he had snuck on the patrol—hadn't fired more than a dozen rounds at the most and had fled already.

He took a chance and jumped out of the truck, yanking out the .45 he had stuffed into his belt earlier. Crouching, he glanced up and down the road. Jerry was dead, half his chest gone. Grey did not allow himself the luxury of grieving for him. The nigger Ranger student was either dead or passed out on the road. The rest of his crew had taken cover behind the truck where they held the rest of the students, firing into the tree line.

Then he saw Charley and MacAlister thrashing in the middle of the road, thirty feet away. MacAlister had chopped Charley in the throat and was choking him. He was going to kill him. Grey sprinted toward them, chambering a round in his .45.

MacAlister hammered his bony fist into Charley's face and chest one last time and lunged for the Mini-14. He grabbed it and was about to finish Charley off, when he heard heavy footsteps running at him from behind. He swung around, but it was too late.

Grey stood before him ten feet away, green, huge, and ugly, aiming his .45 at him, legs spread apart and both hands on the grip in a shooter's stance. Mac-Alister tried to swing the Mini-14 up and squeeze the trigger, knowing he wouldn't have time.

Grey fired first.

In the last millisecond of his life, MacAlister thought only of his family, safe with his parents back in California, and then the huge bullet from Grey's .45 shattered his teeth and plowed through his skull.

He flew backward, arms shooting straight out, and crashed to the ground.

''Oh, Jesus, Levy. OhChristalmightyHailMaryfull-of . . .''

''Shut up and keep moving.''

''We gotta stop!''

''Move your ass, Prentiss!''

Prentiss tripped suddenly and fell downslope, rolling and crashing through the trees and wait-a-minute vines. He jerked to an abrupt halt fifteen feet below, his body bent double around a pine sapling. Levy scrambled down to him.

It was almost two-thirty in the morning, and they had been running nonstop for the past hour. Levy could see the fear and panic etched on Prentiss's face, cut and dirty green like his own. He had to do his damnedest to keep from panicking, too. Then the thought penetrated his mind again, like a broken record playing it for the umpteenth time.

He had killed two men tonight.

He helped Prentiss to his feet.

''You okay?''

''Y-yeah, I think so,'' Prentiss said, shaking. He had broken his glasses in the middle and each half dangled around his ears, held only by the retaining strap. In another time, another situation, it would have been funny.

''Let's get moving, then. They're coming after us.''

CHAPTER

· SIXTEEN ·

A hand tugged on Staff Sergeant Larry Quinn's shoulder as he lay sleeping on the cot.

"Sergeant Quinn . . . Sarge! Wake up."

"Wha-what?" Quinn bolted upright, blinking at the light that had just been turned on. His eyes focused on the tall, skinny figure of Corporal Hastinger, his duty driver for the night.

"Someone's on the phone for you, Sarge."

"Shit." Quinn stood up, yawning. "What time is it?"

"Zero-four."

"Fuck me to tears. Okay, tell 'em I'm coming."

Hastinger left the room. Quinn blinked his eyes and rubbed them, trying to wake up. He was pulling radio watch and security that night at camp headquarters. Every hour on the hour all twelve patrols from the training company called in their situation reports, and Quinn's duty was to monitor the traffic and watch the arms room. He'd had Hastinger doing it for the past hour since things had quieted down.

Quinn walked into the orderly room and picked up the phone.

"Camp Frank D. Merrill, Staff Duty NCO Staff Sergeant Quinn, sir."

"Larry."

Quinn jolted wide awake. It was Grey. "Where the hell are you?" He glanced around for Hastinger and was relieved to see that he had taken the opportunity to steal Quinn's cot back in the other room. "Top Fowlds has been asking for you ever since we broke contact with that patrol a few hours ago."

"I'm in Dahlonega. What did you tell Fowlds?"

"That you were spending the night in Dahlonega, trying to patch things up with Sarah."

"Good . . . good."

Silence.

"You still there, Frank?"

"Yeah." Grey sighed. "That bitch left me, you know."

"Are you all right?"

"Yeah, I'm okay. Can you talk?"

"Hang on." Quinn glanced back at the door leading into the other room. It was ajar, and the light was still on. He guessed that Hastinger was reading his endless supply of *Playboy*s and was waiting for him to get off the phone.

"Hastinger!"

"Yo!"

"Go ahead and rack out. I'll man the radios for the rest of the night."

"Thanks, Sarge." The light flicked off, and the door was shut. Quinn then heard the cot creak as Hastinger lay down.

"Go ahead, Frank," he said quietly into the phone. He sat down by the duty desk, staring at the bank of radios on the side counter, wondering what had happened.

"Has the camp been alerted yet?"

"No. Fowlds thinks it's just a bad radio."

"Good. That'll give us until at least zero-eight or zero-nine until they start looking for the patrol."

"Are things going as planned?"

Another pause.

"Frank—you still with me?"

"I took care of that bastard tonight."

"MacAlister? What do you mean?"

"What do you think?"

"What—what about the rest of the patrol?"

"Do you really want to know?"

"I'm in. You know I'm in."

"We've got 'em in a secure place."

"Where?"

"I'll tell you tomorrow. Meanwhile, tell Top Fowlds that you got ahold of me tonight, and that I'm coming in at 1000 in the morning."

"He's going to ask you about the patrol. He's ready to alert the entire camp. He doesn't want a repeat like what happened to that nigger lieutenant a few months back."

"I know, I know. Look, things are kind of screwed up."

"How's that?"

"One of the patrol members staying back at the ORP got ahold of some live rounds somehow and snuck up on us while we were taking the main body. He fired some of my people up."

"Anybody hurt?"

"Jerry Casey and one of the guys from Gunther's

group. They're both dead. Charley was beat up pretty bad."

"Who did it?"

"Levy—he had to be the guy with the weapon. He's the Jew I was telling you about. Apparently, he was securing the ORP with another man, then got curious. I checked the patrol roster before going out tonight. There's another guy with him—Prentiss, I think. They're still out in the woods."

"Aren't you looking for them?"

"Hell, yes. My dad's got most of the klavern hunting for them right now. I've also got some of my people from the base camp looking for them. They're not going anywhere."

"What's next?"

"Things are going to be smokin' for the next twenty-four hours, Larry. I'll need your help."

"You got it."

"Levy and his buddy are trying to make it back to Camp Merrill. I want you to keep an eye out for them."

"How far out are they?"

"The patrol was about twenty klicks out from Camp Merrill. About twelve or thirteen miles as the crow flies. They should be back in your AO sometime after dark tonight. Depends on how fast they move. Hopefully we'll intercept them before you do."

"I'll be ready. Fowlds put me on light duty for the next couple of days since I came down with that case of strep throat you told him about."

"Good. Now, listen to me real close. I'll be back in the camp in a few hours for breakfast. No one knows what's really going on, right?"

"Like I said, you're still down at Dahlonega as far as Fowlds is concerned."

"Then meet me in the chow hall at zero-seven. We need to talk." Grey's voice trailed off.

"Frank?"

"Yeah, I'm still here. Larry, I need you to help pull my ass out of the fire, like old times."

"You got it buddy."

"This is it, man. This is *really* it."

Grey hung up the phone and faced Gunther.

"Sure you can trust him?" Gunther asked.

"With my life."

The two men walked up to the front of the tiny country store with a couple of Cokes and plopped some change on a dirty, stained counter. A skinny old man leaning back in a rocking chair nodded at them as they went out the door and walked back to Grey's Bronco.

They had stopped to gas up after driving throughout the night in Grey's Bronco. They had searched all along Black Mountain since the raid for the two students still on the loose and had come up with nothing. Gunther's men had taken the rest of the patrol back to the base camp, along with MacAlister's body and the other two corpses. Now they were twenty miles out of Dahlonega near Turner's Corner. A dirt road split off from the highway five miles farther up the road that led to the base camp.

Grey looked at his watch. It was a quarter to five in the morning.

"Dietrick ought to be here pretty quick," Gunther said, reading Grey's thoughts. He stretched back in his seat and pulled his bush hat low over his eyes.

"Dietrick?" Grey said, remembering the ambush. "Seems like a good man. Prior service?"

"He was in Special Forces. Got out last year when

his unit found out about his political leanings, and what he'd been up to. He was only a buck sergeant. Demolitions specialist. He was on a mobile training team down in Central America and was siphoning plastic explosives and nitro from his team's ammo supply point. Somehow or other his unit found out about it and court-martialed him. Damned near spent some time in Fort Leavenworth."

"I'm surprised he didn't."

"They got him for only one offense. Luckily, the investigators didn't find out about all the other demo he'd stashed. After we recruited him, he gladly dug up all his caches and gave them to us. He turned out to be an outstanding asset. Last time I went to El Salvador he went along as my guide and interpreter. He is a good man, but *goddamn* is he goofy sometimes."

"What do you mean?"

"Let it suffice to say he's got a strange personality. He's not a homo or anything like that, but he's got a real mean streak in him. Kind of twisted sometimes. You wouldn't want to get on his bad side. 'Course, he's completely loyal to me and the Covenant. You tell him to do something, and he'll do it right."

"Think he'll be okay? I mean his head, where that nigger slugged him last night."

Gunther snorted and laughed. "Why, hell, yes. Hood's got a head harder than a whole barrel full of woodpecker lips."

Grey couldn't laugh with Gunther. Jerry had been killed by the kid out in the tree line. Jerry, of all people. *Damn!*

He remembered how Jerry had taken him under his wing after the FBI had locked up his old man. Grey was only thirteen. Jerry had been the older brother he'd never had. Deer hunting, patient answers to em-

barrassing questions, his first real drink . . . how they
both had laughed till they cried once, watching Charley piss all over himself when that barmaid he'd prop-
ositioned none too discreetly grabbed him by the
crotch at the Lucky Spade Tavern—

Grey swallowed hard and stared out the mist-
covered window. Gunther poked an eye out from
underneath his bush hat.

"Kind of long in the face. Jerry a good friend of
yours?"

"The best. Known him all my life."

"I'm real sorry, Frank," Gunther said, pulling out
a pack of Marlboros and lighting up. He offered one
to Grey, who accepted with a trembling hand. "I liked
him a lot too. He seemed to be the leader in your absence. I promise you, we'll get the bastard that shot
him."

Grey pulled deeply at the cigarette and nodded at
the ex-Marine. He cleared his throat and managed a
grin.

"Yeah, we'll get him all right. Did your boss talk to
you last night?" he said, changing the subject.

"Yes, he did. I assume your father reached you
too."

"Yeah. What do you think?"

"I don't think we have any more than a fifty-fifty
chance with the equipment we've got. The best we can
do right now is to sneak into the civic center with concealed MAC-10s and some CS grenades for crowd dis-
persion. Maybe a sniper's position up in the rafters for
backup and support."

"I've got a better idea," Grey said slowly, pulling
out his .45 and removing the magazine. He pulled the
slide back, ejecting a round from the chamber.

"Lay it on me."

"A week ago Fort Benning shipped two dozen LAWs up to Camp Merrill for a patrol live-fire exercise we run each class through. They screwed up and sent us actual 66-millimeter rockets instead of the scaled-down training version."

Gunther's eyes lit up. He had used the light anti-tank weapon in Vietnam on a multitude of occasions. Not only was the expendable, shoulder-fired rocket system good for busting tanks, but it also destroyed bunkers and machine-gun nests with devastating efficiency. One rocket would easily wipe out the entire section of an auditorium where the guests of honor and main speakers would be seated.

"No kidding?"

"Yep. All I've got to do is get inside the arms room. Colonel Cummings shit all over himself when he found out they'd been shipped to Camp Merrill."

"Who's he?"

"The camp commander. Covers his ass like you wouldn't believe. Sees no evil, hears no evil, speaks no evil. Just another careerist type."

"I know what you mean. We had 'em in the Corps too."

"Anyway, the dumbass ordered them to be stored in the arms room until we can get them back down to Fort Benning, using *their* transportation. Some regulation says you can't transport them in anything other than an ordnance vehicle."

"If you can get them, taking out that conference would be a piece of cake. Just secure the entrance, go in heavy with plenty of tear gas and submachine guns, and blow the fuckers away with the LAWs. We can use some of the patrol members we caught to cover our tracks. Hell, make it look like *they* did it and start a riot. Drug them, walk them into the auditorium with us, and then leave them after we blow the niggers away." A wide grin spread across Gunther's face. "Savvy?" he added.

Grey nodded his head slowly. "Make sure one of them is Ranger Christopher. And when I catch his buddy Levy, we'll use him too. I can get the LAWs."

"When?"

"Tonight. No one back at Camp Merrill suspects me yet. I'd like to take your man Dietrick with me for security."

"No problem."

"Quinn will be on duty. It'll go down quiet and neat."

"I'll notify our safe house and alert the rest of the net. Are you ready to go underground?"

"I'll have to. I was ready when I pulled the trigger on MacAlister." Grey rolled down the cab window and tossed out his cigarette butt. Headlights cut through the early morning dark and mist, and Grey recognized the silhouette of a pickup heading toward them.

"I think your ride is here. Remember, we've got to find those two punks out in the woods. If we don't, the whole damned plan is blown."

The pickup pulled up alongside Grey's Bronco with a screech. Gunther got out of the Bronco and climbed into the pickup, clapping Dietrick on the back and joshing him good-naturedly. Then he rolled down the window and leaned out, facing Grey.

"Dietrick will be ready by 1500. He'll be at the base camp with two vans to transport everything in."

"I'll be there," Grey said. "Hopefully, I'll have those two little cocksuckers with me. You keep a sharp lookout too."

"Happy hunting," Gunther replied. "I have a feeling that Hood here might beat us both to the punch."

Laughing, Gunther rolled up his window, and the pickup sped off toward the mountains. Grey turned his engine over and picked up the .45, which had been lying on his lap the whole time. He opened the glove compartment and retrieved a box of rounds. He filled the empty magazine and stuffed it back into the .45, then pulled the slide back and chambered a round, remembering how he had emptied all seven rounds the night before into MacAlister's jerking, twitching body.

Then, washing over him like a tidal wave, he remembered how he had gone back to Jerry's corpse and had seen his friend who was more like a brother to him lying on his back, spread-eagled with his mouth open, raindrops spattering on lifeless, glassy eyes opened toward the clouds, and how the body had almost come apart when he picked him up and held him close. . . .

Grey slammed the glove compartment shut. Gunning his engine, he tore out of the parking lot onto the road, heading south toward Dahlonega, ripping down the highway at ninety miles an hour.

"Jew-boy's gonna pay," he muttered to himself. "Little bastard's gonna pay. . . ."

CHAPTER

· SEVENTEEN ·

*. . . and I will shoulder more than my share of the
task, whatever it may be.*

The black of the night slowly gave way to the darkest
shades of gray. Levy and Prentiss slipped down a
hillside covered with pines growing progressively
steeper as they went. An hour before, the rain had
turned into a dense, swirling mist, and now a thick
and muffled quiet enveloped them. The only sound
was their jungle boots padding and slipping on the
soggy pine needles underfoot.

The two Rangers scrambled to the bottom of the
hill and entered a gully where a stream gargled at
the center. For the tenth—or was it the hundredth?—time that night, Levy tripped on something and fell. This time it was a moss-covered rock,
and when he fell, he cracked his knee against the
boulder next to it. Prentiss followed suit.

"Owww!"

"Shut up, Prentiss," Levy groaned. "C'mon, get
up. Gotta keep moving down this gully." Levy
stumbled to his feet, pulling Prentiss up with him.

"We—we've got to stop, Dan." Prentiss yanked his arm away and sat down heavily on the boulder, drooping his head between his knees. "Can't you see? We're dead tired . . . dead . . ."

Levy swayed back and forth on his feet, staring at Prentiss. How long had they been running? Four hours since the ambush? He stared at his watch for several long seconds. Five. It was now officially 0530. 05 . . . 05 what? 30. Okay . . . time to go to . . . to sleep . . .

Levy's head popped up, and he realized he was hallucinating.

Again.

They had gotten snatches of sleep only in the patrol base the day before, and before that had been the hellish night movement. Neither of them had actually slept for the past forty-eight hours they'd been away from Camp Merrill. Most of the time had been spent on the move.

Levy plopped down next to Prentiss. He pulled his canteen out from his web gear and swished the water around. It was only half full. His other one was empty. He drained the canteen and then looked at Prentiss, who was sleeping like a stone statue.

"Wake up, wild man." Levy punched his arm. Prentiss fell of the rock and sprawled in the sand of the stream.

"What the fuck!" he sputtered, jumping up. "Did I go to sleep?"

"When are you *not* sleeping?" Levy crawled off the rock and pushed his canteen underneath the water. "Better fill up your canteens. It's going to be a long day."

Prentiss squinted at Levy, dejected. "I don't have any water purification tablets."

Levy fished a tiny bottle out of his shirt pocket and handed it to Prentiss. "Here. What happened to yours?"

"They're back in my ruck." Prentiss sighed as he opened his canteens and dropped one iodine tablet each into both of them. "Along with everything else," he added.

Levy stuffed both his canteens back into their pouches on his web gear and stood up, looking at the sky. Already the sun was burning the mist off. It was light enough now to look at his watch without holding it up to his nose. *Zero-six-ten*, he thought. *It'll take ten, maybe fifteen more hours of humping before we reach Camp Merrill.*

Levy breathed deeply, stretching his arms high above his head, wincing when the magazine well of his M16 dug into his back where he had the weapon strapped muzzle down to keep the rain out. He pulled the assault rifle off and examined it closely. It was dirty. Carbon had built up in the chamber. He pulled the charging handle back and forth, feeling the rough vibration of the movement, indicating too much dirt and grit and not enough oil along the bolt. He carefully laid it against the boulder. Prentiss studied him curiously. He, too, had his M16 strapped across his back.

"Why are we still carrying these, Dan? You don't have any more ammo."

"What do you mean, why are we still carrying them, stupid? What do you *propose* we do with them?"

"I don't know. Leave them here, I guess."

"You really surprise me sometimes, Prentiss. I swear to God, I really wonder about you."

Prentiss jumped up, yanking off his weapon.

"Well, what good are they gonna do us now?" he yelled. He threw it down in the sand and stood before a very surprised Levy, hands clenched into shaking fists, his eyes gleaming with defiance.

"What goddamned good are they gonna do us? You bastard! You got us into this! You shot one— no, *two* of those people last night!"

"Take it easy, Duane."

"Don't tell *me* to take it easy!" Prentiss ranted. He swung at Levy and missed, slipping on the wet sand.

"Stop it!"

Prentiss swung at him again, this time landing a glancing blow on Levy's jaw. Enraged, Levy grabbed Prentiss by the shirt and threw him over his hip into the sand, then crammed his knee on the squirming Ranger's chest. He slapped him hard against the face.

"I'll knock the shit out of you if you don't stop it!"

"Get offa me!" Prentiss sputtered, kicking. Levy stayed on top of him and cocked his fist back.

"I'm warning you . . ."

Prentiss went limp all at once. His head rolled over to one side, and tears erupted from his eyes. He cried softly, making pitiful moaning noises. Levy stood up, disgusted.

"What's the matter with you, Duane? What the hell do you want to fight *me* for? We've got enough problems as it is."

Sniffling, Prentiss sat up in the wet sand and wiped his nose with his sleeve, leaving a trail of mucus-glued sand on his dirty face. "Why—why are we running like this?" he said. "Why are we being chased by those people?"

Levy picked up Prentiss's weapon and knocked off some of the sand. He handed it back to Prentiss. "I don't know. I think it's got something to do with the Ku Klux Klan. Yendall told us it could happen—"

"Yendall? Sergeant Yendall from phase one?"

"Yeah."

"What did he say? I never heard anything."

"Remember our first patrol, back at Camp Darby?" Prentiss nodded. "He told Christopher and me that up here in the mountains, something like this could happen . . . like what happened to him years before."

"We need to get back and tell someone. Sergeant Grey—he'd know what to do."

"He'd know what to do all right," Levy snorted. "Duane, he's responsible for this whole mess. I can feel it in my gut. He had something to do with that ambush last night."

"C'mon, Levy, our class TAC?"

"Damned right. Night before last Christopher and I were pulling point surveillance on that raid we conducted. You were the patrol leader, remember?"

"Yeah. So?"

"When you went back to the objective rallying point to move the rest of the patrol up to the assault line, MacAlister went to the fake missile site so he could watch your actions on the objective. Grey and Quinn were there, too."

"Sergeant Quinn," Prentiss interrupted. "He's that asshole that tried to flunk everybody on the knot test a week ago, right?"

"That's the one. He and Grey are buddies. Anyway, they were giving MacAlister a hard time. I couldn't tell what it was they were saying, but MacAlister beat the hell out of them both."

"How did he do that?"

"Karate. He knocked them both on their asses. Later he told Christopher and me not to say anything about it, that nothing would come of it. Christopher gave me those live rounds I fired last night. MacAlister had to have given them to him."

"So last night must have been payback."

Levy buckled his web gear together and grabbed his M16. "And then some," he replied, slinging his weapon across his back. He extended his hand to his Ranger buddy and helped him to his feet. "So let's see if we can't get ourselves out of this situation without messing each other up."

Prentiss brushed the sand off his uniform and slung his weapon across his back like Levy's. He averted Levy's gaze and hung his head.

"I'm sorry I acted like an asshole. I'm tired."

"So am I. Scared too."

Prentiss jerked his head up, eyes glinting. "That damned sure makes two of us."

"Forget about it and let's just drive-on, man. You watch my ass—I'll watch yours. It's the only way we're gonna get out of this mess. Still have your Ranger handbook?"

Prentiss nodded and pulled a tiny manual the size of a pocket notepad out of his back pocket. He had wrapped it in a plastic bag to keep it waterproof. Every student in Ranger School carried one. It was a quick and handy reference guide for patrolling techniques and tactics. Since a billfold was not part of his uniform, every Ranger carried a ten- or twenty-dollar bill taped in the back cover, behind their military identification card.

"Good," Levy said, patting his own back pocket to make sure his was still there. "How much money did you bring?"

"Twenty bucks."

"Same here. That'll give us forty if we need it."

"How much longer do you think we'll be moving?"

"All day. Probably through the night too. You can be damned sure somebody will be looking for us, so we've got to be careful."

"Know where we are on the map?"

Levy pulled out an acetate-covered map from his right trousers cargo pocket, squatted, and spread it across his knee. Prentiss knelt down next to him. Levy pulled out his sheath knife and pointed the tip within one of the grid squares.

"Right here—PJ061259." He glanced up and took in the surrounding terrain for confirmation. "See the stream we're by? If we follow it for another three klicks, we'll come to a major highway. There's got to be a filling station or a store along the road that'll have a phone. Then we can get help."

"Three more klicks," Prentiss said, heaving a sigh of relief. "And food too."

Levy's stomach automatically rumbled at the mention of food. "Yeah," he said, nodding solemnly. "Food."

"You look like hell," Quinn told Grey.

"I feel like it," Grey mumbled through a mouthful of pancakes. Grey picked up a glass of milk and drained it, then looked around to see who all was left in the chow hall. They were the only two there.

When he had stumbled into Camp Merrill twenty minutes earlier, Grey looked no different from the rest of the dirty, camouflaged, facepainted Rangers and RIs who had just come in from the other patrolling lanes that morning. No one asked him any questions about where he had been.

"First sergeant told me this morning they were definitely going to mobilize the camp to search for that missing patrol," Quinn announced.

"When?"

"Around 1300, if they don't come in by then. He's out now, looking around for them."

Grey snorted. "Old Fowlds. He'll get his ol' buzzard ass shot off if he stumbles into the wrong hunting party."

"From what you've told me, you'd better find that Jew and his buddy before Fowlds does," Quinn muttered.

"I'll find 'em before 1300. I've got their location narrowed down to within ten grid squares. Dad and Gunther have hunting parties scattered all across the countryside. I'm going back out myself in another few minutes."

"So soon?"

"Yeah, pard." Grey got up and retrieved two mugs from the serving counter and came back to Quinn with hot coffee. He sat down and locked eyes with his friend. "Let's talk about this afternoon, like around 1600."

"Everybody will be out searching," Quinn said, wondering what Grey was leading up to.

"You'll be back in the TOC manning the radios again, right?"

"That's right."

"Do you have access to the arms room keys?"

"As always," Quinn replied, his eyes lighting up.

"Good." Grey smiled broadly. "Ol' buddy, I'd

like to put in an order for about a dozen LAWs. Not to mention some machine guns, rifles, and night vision devices.''

The two men roared with laughter.

Levy crawled down the heavily forested mountainside on his hands and knees with the grace of a cat. Fifty meters back up the ridgeline, Prentiss covered his rear.

A sound.

Levy froze and listened. There it was again. The unmistakable sound of a car as it whooshed on down the highway, immediately followed by the thunder of an eighteen-wheeler. Levy crawled farther. Then the dense scrub oak covering the lower slopes of the mountain thinned, revealing the highway they had been seeking for the past two hours. He saw a road embankment thirty meters away. He crawled to it and stayed there for the next fifteen minutes watching the highway. Then he crawled back up the mountain for Prentiss.

''See anything?'' Prentiss asked.

''Came right up on a store!'' Levy answered excitedly. ''It's just a hundred meters from where we are right now.''

''Great!'' Prentiss said, standing up. ''Let's go.'' Levy yanked him back down.

''Not so fast. There could be people down there looking for us.''

''So what do you want to do, stay up here all day and take notes?''

''No.'' Levy massaged his temples in thought. ''All right, look. We'll go on in. I'll go first. Stay about five meters behind me and watch my rear. We'll have to leave our M16s in the bushes by the road so we won't freak out any of the locals down there." Levy glanced up at Prentiss, whose eyes had glazed over from lack of food and sleep. "Got it?" he said, shaking Prentiss's arm gently, waking him up.

"Yeah, yeah. Let's go."

Levy stood up and crept back down the mountain, Prentiss following suit. They reached the embankment five minutes later.

"Check it out, man." Levy pointed to an old paint-peeled country store that had two pumps out front and a rusty Gulf sign nailed to a telephone pole. A '56 Ford pickup was parked out front. Levy guessed it was the owner's.

"Doesn't look like much," Prentiss said. "But beggars can't be choosers. Let's go get a Coke and some munchies."

"Remember," Levy said, "watch my rear."

"Gotcha."

The two Rangers hid their weapons and then slid down the embankment and ran across the road. They walked across the tiny pot-holed parking lot and up to the entrance. Levy opened the door, and a clanging bell which had been fastened to the top announced their entrance to the skinny old man half-asleep in his rocker behind the counter.

The old man took one look at Levy and Prentiss as they stood before the counter and jumped up, wide awake.

"What do you want, soldier boy?" he said in a shaky tenor with hairy white eyebrows popping and arching over rheumy eyes. "You're a sight!"

Levy stepped back, overwhelmed by the alcohol and tobacco vapor escaping from the old man's mouth. He guessed that the only other smell that could possibly be worse was the old man's body odor ventilating out of his greasy overalls.

"Sir, do you have a phone we could use?" Levy asked politely, trying not to burst out laughing. Here he was, talking to the first civilian he had seen since his last eight-hour break, and he smelled worse than a dirty Ranger fresh off patrol.

"Why, hell yes, I got a phone," the old man answered with his thumbs hooked through the shoulder straps of his overalls. He stood fully erect and rocked back and forth on his heels. "What you boys need it for?"

"Well, sir," Levy stammered, looking around for Prentiss—*Dammit, there he is, already sucking up a Coke by the cooler*—"we need to get back to Camp Merrill, over by Dahlonega. We're with the Army there. Right now we're lost. Or we were until we found this place."

The old man stared at Levy for several moments, as if he didn't believe him. "Well now," he drawled reluctantly, "I reckon it won't hurt none. Long as you buy somethin'." He jerked his head toward a pay phone at the back of the store.

"Yes, sir, thank you very much."

The old man sat back down in his rocker, opened up a jar of H&H snuff—Levy was amazed, he'd never seen snuff in a jar before—pulled out his lower lip, and poured half of it in, packing the powdered tobacco down with his tongue over decayed, useless teeth impacted in brown gums.

Levy turned around, looking for Prentiss. He spotted him back in the bread section, snatching Twinkies. Already he had his arms full of Doritos and soda pop, greedily picked off the shelves.

"Prentiss!"

"What?" came a petulant, you-said-it-was all-right reply.

Levy sighed. *What's the fuckin' use?* "Get a sack and pick me up a basic load of whatever it is you're getting too."

"Hokay!"

Levy turned back around to the phone and dialed the operator. *Finally . . . finally.*

A car pulled up outside, a brown Ford LTD that stopped with the passenger side facing the screen door ten feet away from it. Levy shifted his eyes in its direction, ready for anything. Then, relieved, he saw the gold and silver county sheriff's markings on the car door and the red strobe light on top of the roof.

"Operator, sir."

Levy jolted, forgetting all about calling for the police. "What?"

"Operator, sir, what is the number you're dialing?"

"Uh, it's okay now, ma'am. Thank you." Levy hung up the phone and turned toward the door. A tall, big-gutted deputy got out of the LTD and walked in, taking off his Stetson and revealing a bald head fringed with shaggy black hair around his ears and collar. He stopped when he saw Levy and Prentiss.

"Sir," Levy said, walking toward him, "are we glad to see you."

The deputy peered at the two Rangers over his mirror-tinted sunglasses.

"Forgive our appearance, Officer," Levy apologized. "We're with the Rangers out at Camp Merrill."

"No kidding," the deputy replied in a soft, low

voice. "Every now and then I *do* see one of you Rangers come stumbling out of the woods. You boys get lost?"

"Yes, sir, we sure as hell did. We've been wandering around all night, hoping to find a place where we could make a call. Now that you're here, everything's all right."

"I reckon so. You all need a ride back to Dahlonega?"

"Yes, sir."

"Go ahead and pay for your soda pop, and I'll be glad to give you one." The deputy walked outside and leaned through the window on the passenger side of the patrol car, talking to his partner.

The two Rangers paid for their things and walked toward the door. Prentiss carried a huge sack loaded with Mars Bars, Doritos, Cokes, and anything else he had seen in the space of the past three minutes.

The deputy stood by the front hood of the LTD with his hands on his hips, facing the two Rangers as they came out. His right hand rested on the butt of his .357, and Levy noticed that the hammer-retaining strap on the holster was loosened.

Levy hesitated. Prentiss walked past him and opened the screen door. Levy peered outside. The deputy wasn't alone. Facing the door was the passenger side of the car. Half in and half out of the car sat an immense, hairy man dressed in camouflage, who looked to be in his early thirties. A two-day-old beard showed the lack of sleep on his haggard face. As soon as he saw Levy standing in the doorway, his eyes flashed as if he had found something—or someone. Then he broke eye contact and flipped the cigarette he had been smoking onto the ground, snuffing it out with a muddy jungle boot.

"Any time you're ready, bud," the deputy called to Levy, opening the door for Prentiss on the driver's side of the car.

Levy's stomach hurt. He moved forward, concentrating on every movement the man in the car made. *Friend of the deputy's? No . . .*

Definitely not.

Prentiss shifted the overflowing sack of candy bars and chips to his other arm and started to climb into the back seat. "C'mon, Dan," he mumbled through a mouthful of Mars Bar. "These people are waiting."

Levy slowly opened the screen door. The deputy watched him, smiling broadly. "Let's go," he said. Levy noted that the smile was gone from his eyes, which were now suddenly black and hard.

He glanced back at the civilian, who had picked something up from the car seat. Levy saw the glint of gunmetal. *Oh, Christ . . .*

Prentiss clumsily dropped his groceries on the other side of the car as he was getting in. He'd had Coke bottles inside, and they broke with a crash.

Surprised, the civilian wheeled around, revealing a huge .357 revolver with a six-inch barrel.

Levy leapt out of the door's entrance and slammed his foot against the car door, snapping the man's leg halfway between the knee and ankle. He screamed in surprise and pain. Levy screamed back at him, surprised himself at what he'd just done. Frantically, he yanked the door back open and grabbed the civilian's gun, twisting his wrist at the same time. A round from the .357 exploded through the roof of the police car, sending fragments of the strobe light high up in the air. They struggled. Levy punched the man in the throat and felt his grip on the gun relax. Ripping it from his fingers, he fell back out of the car, rolled, and took cover behind the front fender. He aimed the heavy revolver with both hands at the deputy.

"Don't even think about it," the deputy muttered, holding his own .357 against Prentiss's temple. He held the squirming Ranger in a choke hold with a thick forearm that threatened to crush Prentiss's larynx.

"D-Dan," Prentiss moaned. "This guy's gonna fuckin' *shoot* me."

Levy slowly straightened up, aiming the massive revolver at the deputy. The old man burst out of the store.

"What in hell's going on?" he ranted.

"Go back inside, Mr. Jacobs," the deputy ordered. "Get down behind the counter."

"I said what's going on?"

"Get inside, goddammit!"

The old man scurried back into the store, slamming the door behind him.

"Let him go," Dan said evenly, fighting to steady his hands.

"Put the gun down, Jew-boy." The deputy shoved the muzzle of his .357 hard against Prentiss's skull. Prentiss squealed in pain.

"I'll shoot you."

"No, you won't, you little pussy. Put the gun down."

Levy shifted his eyes toward the civilian. Moaning from pain, he rolled out of the car and fell into a mud puddle, clamping his leg with both hands. Blood spurted out from the open wound his shinbone had made. He defecated and passed out. The pungent odor made Levy sick to his stomach. He glanced back up at the deputy.

"Let my friend go," Levy repeated.

"I'm tired of fucking with you, you little kike. Now, put the goddamn gun down."

They locked eyes. The scant five feet between them was unbearably magnified as Levy stared at the bore of the deputy's gun. Levy swallowed as the deputy pulled the hammer back into the full cock position. Prentiss was a 140-grain hollow point away from death. Levy did the same, aiming the front sight post on the bridge of the deputy's nose.

Then he fired.

Prentiss screamed as the blast shattered the deputy's face and caused his own pistol to go off. Luckily, the bullet only grazed Prentiss's scalp. The deputy crashed to the wet, pot-holed asphalt of the parking lot. His face was an oozing mass of bleeding tissue, shards of cartilage and bone surrounding the wound like broken plastic.

Prentiss screamed again and suddenly bent double, throwing up. He fell to his hands and knees, choking and gagging.

"Let's go now, Duane," Levy said, amazed at the calm he heard in his voice. He grabbed Prentiss by the shoulders and propelled him into the car. Then he ran around to the other side and jumped behind the wheel. His fingers searched the ignition for the keys. There were none. Levy jumped back out of the car and walked over to the prostrate deputy. With cold-blooded efficiency he rifled through his pockets and heard a jangle. He yanked out a bundle of keys. A piece of paper came out with them.

Snatching it up, he saw several sets of numbers and letters. One set was his own social security number and blood type. Below that was another social security number and blood type. Levy felt for his dog tags hanging around his neck, and realized that someone had given the deputy his and Prentiss's description and personal data. It could be easily backed up by their ID cards for confirmation, which they all carried in their Ranger handbooks, taped over their emergency cash.

There was another number. Two letters, followed by eight digits. A map location. Levy slapped the cargo pocket against his right leg and felt for his map. Reassured, he stood up and stuffed the paper into his pocket, knowing he wouldn't have time to look at the map location now. It would have to wait. He started to get back in the car, when an idea came to him. There were other things to do. Like ammunition.

"Prentiss!"

No answer. Only sobbing and sniffing. Levy reached back into the car and shook him.

"Prentiss!" he repeated. "Listen to me!"

"What?"

"Hang tight, man. We'll make it."

"I'm bleeding." Prentiss gingerly touched the right side of his head.

"You've got a scalp wound. You're okay. Listen to me now: I want you to run back to the tree line and get our weapons."

"Why? What's the use?"

Levy resisted the temptation to smack him and patiently answered, "Because I'm going back into the store to get some ammo. We're going to need it."

"Okay."

Levy pulled Prentiss back out of the car. "Come on, buddy. Get moving."

Prentiss sidestepped the dead deputy, not daring to look at him, and shuffled across the street.

Levy ran inside the store. The old man cowered behind the counter.

"What are you going to do to me?" he said in a hushed, quavering voice."

"I'm not going to do anything to you." Dan breathed deeply, calming himself. "Don't be scared. Those people were trying to kill us. There are more out there."

"Then what do you want with me?" The old man straightened up, hesitant, holding his hands to keep them from shaking.

"Do you have any .223 ammo?"

"What?"

"Two-twenty-three rounds. You know—the bullets you use with a Mini-14." Levy realized he was still holding the .357. He stuffed it in his pants.

"How many do you want?"

"*Goddamn*, mister, as many as you've got!"

Five twenty-round boxes magically appeared on the counter. Levy scooped them up and shoved them into his cargo pockets.

"Sorry I can't pay you."

The old man didn't reply. Levy looked out the window and saw Prentiss running back to the patrol car with their weapons. He started for the door, then turned back around.

"Where's your phone?"

"Over there," the old man said, pointing at the pay phone. "You just used it."

Levy leaned over the counter, looking hard into a pair of frightened, rheumy eyes.

"Your *other* phone."

The old man whipped out a phone from underneath the counter, immediately followed by a tattered phone book. Levy cut the cord with his sheath knife.

"Sorry." He went to the pay phone and did the same. Then he walked back to the front door, pausing before he went outside. "I really *am* sorry, mister."

Then he ran outside and got into the car. Prentiss was already inside cradling the M16s in his arms and staring at the bugs glued on the windshield. Levy twisted the keys in the ignition, and the engine roared to life. He pulled the car out of the parking lot and onto the highway. Then he punched the accelerator and soon they were doing the speed limit down the winding road leading into Dahlonega. Levy almost smiled as he realized how pleasurable it was to ride in a car again, after having gone for the past month without even seeing one.

"Dan?"

Levy faced Prentiss. He looked very pale. He still cradled their M16s in his arms.

"Yeah?"

"What are we going to do?"

"Well, for starters," Levy replied, pulling ammunition boxes from his pockets, "you can load those weapons up."

CHAPTER

· EIGHTEEN ·

One hundred percent and then some.

Christopher stirred and felt damp pine needles crushed against his face. He strained for wakefulness, realizing that he had been sleeping facedown on the ground for quite some time. With great effort he pried opened his crust-covered eyes and winced at the onrush of pain that greeted his nose, which had ballooned overnight. His right arm had gone to sleep, and he couldn't feel it. He blinked and focused on Jakes, who was handcuffed next to him on a chain encircling a tree. He struggled to sit up, tugging heavily on Jakes's wrists.

"Take it easy," Jakes said softly, shifting closer to the tree.

Christopher recoiled at the sound as pitchforks stabbed the backs of his eyes. He finally sat up, contorting in pain as his back muscles cramped up.

"Where are we?" he croaked, discovering the handcuffs binding his wrists to the chain. To his surprise, he saw that he still had his watch on. *0835*, he thought. *How long—?*

"Hell if I know. We're in some sort of camp. There're a couple of cabins up on the ridgeline."

Christopher looked around for the rest of the patrol. They were all within spitting distance, paired and bound around trees with handcuffs like himself and Jakes.

He suddenly remembered the night before, how he and . . .

"Sergeant MacAlister—"

"Dead."

"What?"

"Grey shot him."

"Oh, no. Not . . ." Christopher hung his head and shook it slowly. "Who else?"

"No one else."

"What about Levy? Is he here too?"

"No. He and Prentiss got away."

Christopher raised his head and looked at Jakes, who had been speaking in a monotone the entire time, and noticed a furious new rash of acne blistering his forehead. His fatigues were mere tatters, drenched in mud and sweat.

"Are you okay?"

"I'm so fucking tired," Jakes said.

"Me too, buddy. How long was I out?"

"You've been kind of off and on all night, mostly hallucinating like everybody else."

"Get any sleep?"

Jakes snorted. "No. It's weird. After they brought us here a few hours ago, everybody crashed. Not me. I stayed awake."

Christopher saw the dark circles formed under Jakes's eyes. He looked around and saw the others—

still shadows in the early morning mist—stirring about, groaning, and mumbling to each other.

"So Levy got away, then."

"And Prentiss. You don't remember much from last night, I guess."

"The last thing I remember was that motherfucker sitting on top of me with a knife ready to cram it down my throat."

"Levy shot him from the tree line. Good thing he snuck some rounds on patrol, or else you'd be dead."

Christopher nodded grimly, silently thanking MacAlister.

"Your knife."

"What?"

"Your Swiss Army knife—still got it?"

"Yeah. Sure."

Christopher glanced to his rear, and then faced Jakes again. "See if you can't dig it out of your pocket."

"What for?"

"I'm gonna get us out of here." Christopher scooted closer to the tree and extended his arms toward Jakes. "Okay. That ought to give you enough slack."

Jakes awkwardly pulled a red pocketknife out of his pocket with a white cross emblazoned on it and a zillion tools folded in between the handles. He handed it to Christopher. "I don't think that'll help much."

"It's worth a try," Christopher said, pulling his handcuffs together and bringing Jakes close to the tree.

"Christopher, what the hell are you doing?"

Christopher looked to the tree on his left. It was Keller.

"What do you think I'm doing?"

"You'd better stop."

Christopher glared at the blond, slim Ranger with the angular features and weird, almost European accent.

"Who the fuck are you to tell me to stop what I'm doing?"

"What if we get caught?"

"What if we get caught?" Christopher mimicked. "Dumbass! We're already caught! What do you think they're gonna do with us? Put us on a Greyhound and bus us back to Dahlonega?" Turning his attention back to the handcuffs, he opened the screwdriver blade of the knife and pried at the key hole.

Jakes kicked him.

"They're coming! Put it up!"

Without looking up, Christopher immediately shoved the knife into his front pocket. Then he turned around.

Two men approached, the upper halves of their bodies concealed by the rising ground mist. Then Christopher recognized them, and he froze, staring at the same two men he and MacAlister had beaten the night before. The hammer inside his head pounded pitchforks behind his eyes with a vengeance.

Charley and Dietrick stopped before Christopher, glaring at him, each carrying Mini-14s and dressed in cammies.

Christopher turned and ducked just in time to keep Charley's boot from kicking him square on his broken nose. Instead, the heel glanced off his right ear, slamming his face into the tree trunk. He screamed.

"I'll do it again if you don't quit lookin' at me," Charley said like a sixth-grader winning his first fist-fight. "I don't wanna see your nasty black face lookin' at me again."

Dietrick swaggered to the center of the group of Rangers. "I want everybody's undivided attention, except yours, nigger," he said, glancing at Christopher. "You keep your face pressed up against that pine, unless you want Charley's boot on it some more."

Christopher bit down on his lip, feeling blood running down the bridge of his nose where he had been cut by the tree bark.

"Any Jews here?"

Silence.

"I said, are there any Jews here?" The grin vanished, replaced by a scowl of pure hatred. He ran from tree to tree, yanking each Ranger upward by the shirt and looking at the name tag. "Any Steins? Goldmans? Fischers?" He walked back to the center. "How about Levy? Where's Levy?"

No one spoke.

"Where is he, goddamn you!"

"He's not here," came a feeble response.

Everyone looked at Keller. Dietrick walked over to him, squatted, and put his arm around his shoulder. "Tell me about it, son."

"Shut up, Keller!" Jakes yelled. Charley struck him between the shoulder blades with his Mini-14. Jakes grunted and fell silent.

Dietrick smiled at Jakes as he squatted next to Keller, his arm still around Keller's shoulder. "What's your name?" he said in a patronizing singsong.

"Jakes," the squat Ranger muttered.

"Press your face against the tree, like your nigger buddy. Or I'll sic ol' Charley on your ass." Dietrick turned back to Keller. "Now, tell me, hmm, let me see . . . Keller?" he said, looking at Keller's name tag. "Is that your name?"

"Yes. Yes, sir."

"Now, I like that," Dietrick said expansively, beaming at the rest of the Rangers. "A man who knows when to say 'yes, sir.' You'll go far in your military career, son."

Keller trembled under Dietrick's grip, plainly scared.

"Tell me where Levy is."

"I don't know."

Keller recoiled instantly, trying to avoid Dietrick's open-palmed slap, but the hand found his face with such cruel force that it left fingermarks on his cheek where the blood had been slammed away. Dietrick raised his hand again.

"O-ORP, ORP!" Keller yelled.

Dietrick smiled broadly and put his arm back around Keller's shoulder.

"Tell me more," he cooed.

"He was back at the objective rallying point with Prentiss when you people captured us last night!"

"Tell me something I don't already know, dammit!" Dietrick raised his hand again.

"I swear to *God* I don't know anything else, mister!"

Dietrick's scowl softened into another smile. He hugged Keller around the shoulder again.

"Okay, son. All right. Don't be afraid. I believe you, I really do. I'll find out where the Jew-boy is. And his buddy." He stood up, facing the rest of the group. "You see, two of our people were killed last night by your friend Levy. I lost a friend. And Charley lost a friend. Right, Charley?"

Everyone looked at the hulking dimwit, whose lower lip trembled in deep-seated hurt.

"You guys had best cooperate with us. I personally don't know how long you all will enjoy your stay with us, because that hasn't been decided yet. But you're about to find out."

Dietrick wheeled about and walked back up the ridgeline, while Charley stood in the center watching the Rangers. Five minutes later Dietrick returned with another scowling man, a blond, crew-cutted man with a scarred face and murdering green eyes.

"It's time for your first class," J. D. Gunther said. "Pay close attention," he added as every eye riveted on the ex-Marine. "You white boys need to know the truth about your race and the nigger race. After I talk, some of you may want to join us. The rest of you can figure things out for yourselves."

He glared at his audience. They were filthy, rips in their fatigues exhibiting elbows and cracks, knees and backs. Their gaunt faces and hollowed-out eyes betrayed their hunger and fear.

"Uncuff that nigger, Charley," he ordered, jerking his head in Christopher's direction. "Stand him up here in the center, where we can all see him."

Charley pulled a massive key ring from his pocket and fumbled with Christopher's handcuffs, trying to find the right key. While he muttered and fought with them, Gunther swung his attention back to the group.

"There are certain racial differences in our society that are so damned self-evident, most people—most *white* people—have forgotten them. Well, your first class will dispel any myths the Jew media has brainwashed you people into believing over the years.'' He glanced at Dietrick. ''You got a recommendation?''

''Yes, sir.''

''Stand him up, then. Next to the nigger. Where *is* the nigger? Charley!''

''Can't f-find the right key!''

''Hurry up!''

Charley reached into his other pocket, and his eyes lit up.

''I found it!'' He pulled out a single key and unlocked Christopher's handcuffs. Christopher sullenly let himself be yanked up from the ground, noticing that Charley left the key in the cuffs. Then he was shoved toward the center of the group next to Gunther.

''Watch him close, Charley,'' Gunther said. ''Don't let him pull any shit on us like he did last night. He moves, you shoot him.''

''Okay, okay.'' Charley tossed the key ring to Dietrick and then shoved the muzzle of his Mini-14 into Christopher's back.

Dietrick swiftly unlocked Keller's handcuffs and led him into the center. Gunther stood him up next to Christopher. Then he looked at his audience.

''First class: Racial Superiority. Now, look,'' he said, pointing one hand at Keller and the other at Christopher, ''do you people see the differences between this nigger and this white man? The fundamental differences?''

Gunther picked up a stick from the ground and peeled off the smaller twigs from it, making it into a pointer as he strutted in front of the handcuffed

Rangers. Then he pointed the stick at Christopher's face, much as an anatomy professor would in pointing out the various bones of a skeleton.

"Let's start with the head. It's a well-known fact that the average IQ of a nigger is below that of the white man's."

What the fuck, Christopher thought. *This guy has really gone off the deep end. Didn't even notice how that home-fry moron left the key in the handcuffs—*

An idea exploded in his mind.

He cautiously peered at Jakes out of the corner of his eye.

"Take the size of his head, for example. See how small it is? He's got the brain of a gorilla." Gunther pointed the stick at Keller's head. "This white man's got a much bigger brain. More ounces in the gray matter.

"More examples?" he said, waving his pointer around Christopher's face. "Look at his bigger jaw, his widespread eyes, his lips, his nose—again, the smaller skull . . ." Gunther broke into a huge smile. "It's self-evident."

Christopher simmered but fought to keep his cool. He knew that the professor with the can-of-Spam face wanted him to make a move. He peered again toward Jakes, who still seemed to be in a zombielike trance. *C'mon, Jakes, look at me. . . .*

"What is my point, you ask?" Gunther said, pausing grandly. The assembly of handcuffed Rangers stared back, disbelieving the neo-Nazi's spew of diatribe. "My point is that an American nigger is exactly the same as the primitive African niggers who are more like their gorilla and headhunter ancestors, regardless of whether he's gotten some bullshit college degree or knows how to speak like a white man.

"Gentlemen, if you get anything from this lecture, I want you to remember one thing, and forget what the Jews on TV have told you since you were five years old: The nigger can't be equal to a white man, and he never will be. He has a smaller brain."

Gunther paused for several long moments, as if he expected a thunderous applause, smiling, quite pleased with himself in a detached, neurotic way. The Rangers looked at one another with disbelieving stares, their eyes asking each other: *Who* is *this guy?*

Dietrick walked out in front of Gunther, glaring at the Rangers.

"Well?" he thundered.

No response.

"Clap, damn your hides!"

No one applauded. Gunther's smile downturned into a sullen scowl.

"I said clap!"

Jakes jerked his head up and shot the maniac a cold stare of contempt.

Then the solitary sound of flesh beating upon flesh thumped out a steady rhythm. It was Keller. Keller clapped. It was a catalyst for the other Rangers, and the rest of them hesitantly applauded the neo-Nazi's pretzel logic. Each realized the game had to be played. Each felt totally ridiculous as they clapped their hands, since they were still bound by handcuffs around their respective trees. Then it stopped.

Gunther scowled at them, and then his furrowed brow relaxed. He turned around and faced Keller.

"What's his name, Hood?"

"Keller, sir," Dietrick replied. "Hey, boy, what's your first name?"

Keller shifted his gaze from Dietrick to Gunther, massaging his wrists from where the rusty steel of the handcuffs had bitten into them. "Juan, Sir."

Gunther's face fell. "You're a spick?"

"No, sir!"

"I didn't think so." Gunther grinned at the trembling Ranger. "Where are you from?"

Keller paused. "Georgetown University, sir," he finally said. "I'm a cadet attending Ranger School in lieu of ROTC advanced camp."

"Georgetown, huh? Daddy must be into big bucks. Now, tell me where you're *from*. How you picked up a moniker like Juan."

"I'm from . . . Argentina."

"Argentina!"

"Yes, sir. My family moved there shortly after the war. From Germany."

"Well, I'll be. So you're German. Hardly noticed your accent."

Jakes listened to the interchange in disgust as Keller told the two neo-Nazis about his grandfather being an SS colonel. He wondered how much more that blabbermouth Keller was going to tell their captors about himself, Levy, Christopher—any of them.

He had never trusted the cadet. Especially since that night on their first patrol back at Camp Darby, when he had caught Keller pulling a C-ration out of his rucksack. Cadet or not, he had the skinny Ranger by the scruff of his neck, ready to smear his face on the closest tree. But Keller had whined so hard about making a mistake that Jakes had let him go, not wanting to waste his effort on such a douchebag.

It always seemed he had an answer for everything. Or an excuse. He remembered how Keller had played "spotlight leader" while he was the APL a few nights ago, always acting energetic and assertive when the RI was around, and then slacking off when the RI wasn't nearby.

Jakes suddenly felt the flesh-crawling sensation of someone staring at him and looked up. It was Christopher. Christopher blinked his eyes rapidly. The three men in the center holding him and Keller were talking to the cadet and not watching the black Ranger.

Why is he blinking so fast, Jakes wondered. Then Jakes noticed Christopher locking his eyes again with him, blinking rapidly, and then shifting his gaze back to the ground. *What the . . .*

Lock eyes. Blink blink, pause, blink, pause, blink shift to the ground.

Morse code!

Jakes winked solemnly and nodded at Christopher. The two neo-Nazis and the dummy hadn't noticed Christopher. He spelled out the message—dit-dah-dit, dah-dah-dit—H-A-N-D-C-U—*Handcuffs!* He looked at Christopher's handcuffs.

The goddamned key's in them!

He looked back up at Christopher. He was blinking again. *Get . . . key. I'll . . . distract.*

Jakes glanced at the handcuffs lying next to the base of the tree. Even though he was bound, he still had enough reach left to get to them. He nodded at Christopher again and swallowed, a thousand butterflies flapping in his knotted stomach.

Christopher turned his attention back to Keller and Gunther.

"You mean your grandfather was awarded the Knights Order of the Iron Cross by Hitler himself?" Gunther asked a perspiring Keller.

"Yes, sir. For actions in the Ukraine." Keller swallowed, wondering how much more he should tell them. Judging from where their interests lay, he decided to tell them what he knew they'd want to hear. The truth.

"What actions, Juan?" Dietrick interjected suddenly, his eyes gleaming.

"He—he was in a special unit. *Einsatzkommando.*"

"Jew killers!" Dietrick cried happily. "Hunter-killer teams!"

"Yes." Keller glanced at the rest of the Rangers in his patrol, who stared back at him in contempt.

Although Christopher's concentration had been on the key in the handcuffs and getting the message across to Jakes, the conversation unfolding between Keller and the men holding them sickened and outraged him. So far Keller had revealed the fact that his grandfather had been a Nazi—something he had never previously mentioned, let alone bragged about—and that his family was affluent enough from their vineyards in Argentina to send him to America for a first-rate education at Georgetown. What really bothered him was how Keller was sucking up to their captors, playing on their racist beliefs.

Christopher slowly turned around just enough to catch a look at the moron behind him, whose mouth hung open as he listened to his boss talk about the *Einsatzkommando* with Keller—*if Levy was here, he'd beat his ass good*—but the glazed look in his eyes revealed that not much was really soaking into his thick skull. *Bottom line*, Christopher thought: *The idiot's not paying attention right now. And that's good.*

He stole another quick glance at Jakes, who nodded back at him furiously. *Christopher allowed himself the luxury of a small grin. He's about ready to pee all over himself.*

Then he wondered how many more beatings he could take.

"Hey, Keller!"

All talking stopped as Dietrick and Gunther glared at Christopher, amazed that he had broken in on their conversation.

"Shut up, nigger!" Charley said, jabbing Christopher in the back with his Mini-14. Christopher stiffened and braced himself for the worst.

"Keller, these guys you're talking to are nothing more than a couple of shitbird-racist-wanna-be-krauts who have nothing better to do than to talk to an abortion like you!"

Screaming obscenities, Dietrick and Charley rained blow after blow upon Christopher. The black Ranger fell to the ground and curled up into a ball, shielding his face. Gunther watched with one eye and kept the other on Keller.

Jakes snatched the key from the handcuffs.

Hours later Christopher woke up for the second time that day, the sun broiling him in humidity. His face was wet, and his fatigues were soaked through in sweat. He tried to sit up but was forced gently back down by Jakes. His body was racked in pain.

Jakes poured more water from his canteen onto his drive-on rag and wiped it across Christopher's face again, daubing away at the caked blood and mucus. Both of Christopher's eyes were nearly swollen shut, and he had another gash on his forehead. Jakes wondered if his buddy had a skull fracture, thinking he had a couple of broken ribs for sure.

"Jakes," Christopher croaked.

"Yeah."

"What happened?"

"You took a nap, courtesy of that asshole's boot."

"Where are they?"

"I don't know, but they left the retard back here to watch us. He's not doing a very good job. He's sleeping over by that tree."

Christopher grimaced and raised his head just high enough to look over the toes of his boots. Charley was leaning against a tree fifteen meters away. His head kept drooping and bobbing. The rest of the patrol were still handcuffed to the trees together in pairs. Most of them were sleeping.

"Did you get the key?"

"Yeah."

"Where is it?"

"Don't worry about it; you don't have a need to know in case they find out it's missing. They'd just wail on you until you told them."

"All right. Good thinking. God, my head hurts."

"Lay back down, and take it easy on yourself. Your nose looked like a damned football. Your lips look like a—"

"Enough with the flattery," Christopher muttered. "I'll be all right. They don't even know it's gone?"

"Nope. That guy over there that unlocked you don't exactly have it all packed in one duffel bag, you know?"

Christopher grinned. "No, I guess not. What time is it?"

"Almost noon."

Christopher looked up at the sky. The clouds were gone, and a steady breeze blew.

"What's the illumination tonight, my man?"

"Full moon. It'll be pretty bright."

"Then what do you say we sky out of this place?"

"I kind of had that in mind myself."

The two Rangers said nothing for a moment. Then, reflexively, they both turned around and saw Keller staring at them.

CHAPTER

· NINETEEN ·

*Gallantly will I show the world that I am a spe-
cially selected and well-trained soldier.*

The deputy's patrol car trolled on down the road at an
even fifty-five. Levy kept his ear glued to the squad
radio, listening to its traffic.

"Duane, I just realized something."

"What?" Prentiss shifted both M16s in between him
and Levy, having finished lubricating them with gun
oil and loading all their magazines. They had a hundred rounds in all.

"The dispatcher keeps asking for a radio check. I'm
pretty sure it's for us."

"Think they know something's up?"

Levy glanced at his Ranger buddy and marveled at
how quickly he had calmed down from his panicky
state of just five minutes before. Levy was relieved
that he had taken care of the weapons and ammunition so soon. It meant that Prentiss was finally getting
a grip on things.

"Yeah. I think we'd better get rid of the car."

"But we're only fifteen miles out from Dahlonega. We've got to tell somebody—do something."

"Tell them what? Here we are, two hungry, bloody Rangers, armed with automatic weapons. There's a dead man and one seriously hurt back there at that gas station."

Prentiss slumped back against the seat and sighed. "So what are we going to do?"

Levy pulled the map and piece of paper out of his pocket and gave them to Prentiss.

"Here. Locate Camp Merrill on the map. Okay, now see the grid coordinates on the paper?"

Prentiss fumbled with the paper and glanced back and forth between it and the map. He wasn't the best map reader in the world, but he found the location. "Yeah . . . yeah, I've got it," he said. "It's about twenty klicks north by northeast of Camp Merrill. Hey," he added, raising his voice, "these grid coordinates are pretty close to where we had the ambush last night."

"No shit. I took that piece of paper off the *deputy*, Duane."

Prentiss said nothing.

"Think about it. Why would that deputy have a military map with a grid location by our ambush site? I'm thinking it might be a camp, some sort of place they've got in the woods. That's where those people might have taken Christopher and Jakes and all the rest."

"Levy, we gotta get help." Prentiss displayed a sudden interest in the cleanliness of the weapons between them and picked one up, checking the bolt action.

"Where? If we go in town, we're dead men. No

· 227 ·

telling who's who around this place. We've got to get back to Camp Merrill and notify the camp commander.''

They passed a highway sign, indicating that the Camp Frank D. Merrill access road was seven more miles away.

"Take the road, Dan. We're almost there.''

"That's what I'm afraid of. If we—''

The radio burst to life and squawked: "Charlie-Boy One, Charlie-Boy One, this is Charlie-Boy Three; units two, four, and five are in place. Ready to execute, over.''

"Oh, shit. Hear that? I've been listening to the radio, man. I think they've got some sort of roadblock up ahead.'' Levy searched for a dirt road turnoff and located one three hundred meters up the highway to the right. It was the closest one before reaching the crest of the hill looming ahead. Past that would be the roadblock. The dirt road paralleled a ridgeline that ran up into the mountains.

"Duane,'' he said, punching the accelerator to the floor, "we gotta un-ass this car ASAP.''

Prentiss searched the backseat and found a Savage twelve-gauge pump on the floor, fully loaded. He picked it up and checked the safety, then nestled it between his legs while he readied their M16s between himself and Levy for quick recovery if they had to get out fast.

Levy checked the .357 he'd liberated from the civilian. It was securely fastened to his web gear next to his ammo pouch, where he usually kept his flashlight. The dirt road was dead ahead. "One more thing, Duane.''

"Yo.''

"That sack of groceries you dropped. Did you save the candy bars?"

Prentiss grinned and whipped out a Payday.

Levy scanned the highway 600 meters away from a rock outcropping jutting out from the game trail he and Prentiss had followed. They'd left the patrol car halfway back down the mountain, where the dirt road had petered out to four-wheeler country. There they had pushed it off into a ravine.

Levy watched another patrol car crest the top of the hill before their turnoff, go down the highway for a mile, turn around, and slowly scan the side roads. He knew it would be just a matter of time before it would find the right one. He turned around and faced the rest of the mountain before him, realizing they still had another kilometer to go before reaching the top of the ridgeline. When he looked back at the highway below, the patrol car stopped by their access road, and three tiny figures popped out. Then, several more patrol cars drove over from the opposite side of the hill, joining the one that had stopped. More men got out. Levy counted them. There were twelve in all, dressed in orange hunting vests. All carried rifles.

He figured it out. *Open season for Jews and miscellaneous Rangers, courtesy of the "national association for the advancement of white people" and your friendly neighborhood KKK.*

Another vehicle pulled up, this time a pickup with dogs in it. Two more men hopped out and each tethered the dogs together, two to a leash. Levy pulled out his map and oriented it to the terrain around him, spreading it flat against the rock. Then he retrieved a pencil from his shirt pocket along with his compass. He took a compass reading from his location to a water tower six kilometers to his left, back toward the gas station from which they had come, and then made another reading at the patrol cars below, where the dirt road bisected the highway. He copied down the degree readings and drew the back azimuths on his map until the two lines intersected. The X he made marked his location. He measured the distance to Camp Merrill. Then he jumped to his feet, stuffed the map back into his pocket, and walked back to the game trail, where Prentiss lay slumped against a gnarled pine tree.

"Get up, Duane. Time to get out of here."

"Whatsamatter?"

"They found the road where we turned off. There are twelve hunters looking for us with dogs."

"Jesus!" Prentiss leapt to his feet, cradling the twelve-gauge in his arms. He had strapped his M16 across his back. "Did you make the resection?"

"Yeah. We've got another twelve klicks to go before we reach Camp Merrill."

"Christ, Levy, that's another eight miies moving through this shit!" He looked at his watch. "Hell, we won't get there till 17—almost 1800."

"Nobody said it was easy. C'mon, let's shag ass."

The two Rangers started the long climb uphill.

Ring!

"Camp Frank D. Merrill, Staff Duty NCO Staff Sergeant Quinn, sir."

"You ready?"

"Of course I'm ready. When are you getting here?"

"How's the camp?"

"Deserted."

"Me and Dietrick will be there in another hour."

"Roger that. I'll be at the arms room."

"Out here."

"Out here."

Quinn hung up the phone and glanced at the wall clock. It was 1630.

Levy and Prentiss slogged up the mountainside, bent double by the angle of the climb, grasping at tree branches to haul themselves up. Even with no rucks it had been hard going. Levy stopped, gasping for breath.

"Take a breather?" Prentiss wheezed.

"Yeah." Levy took a slug of water from his canteen and passed it to Prentiss.

They had made good time and were almost there. Levy, who had been breaking trail, knew he was on the last ridgeline before reaching camp. Another few hundred meters and they would be home free.

"C'mon, Duane. Let's go."

Prentiss handed the canteen back to Levy, and they started climbing back up the mountain. Plodding. Sweating. Hurting. No sleep, and no food. No real, honest-to-God Mother's home-cooked chicken-fried steak lately.

One foot in front of the other. Just . . . keep . . . going.

Then they were on top. Levy knew it as soon as the ground leveled off even though he had been staring at his feet the whole time, plopping one dusty jungle boot in front of the other, like he'd been climbing a ladder. The ground had leveled off, and a cool breeze hit him on his head. He looked up and felt the breeze caress his face. Then he focused his eyes on Camp Merrill below, no more than 700 meters away. He turned around.

"Hey, we're there, man! We're—" Levy woke up

suddenly, adrenaline pumping. "Prentiss!" *Where is he?*

He limped back down the mountain for ten meters and was about to call out again, when he saw him, prostrate on the trail where they had been climbing. Levy ran over to him and dragged him into the shade. He got out his canteen and shook it. There was precious little water left. He forced the mouth of the canteen past Prentiss's lips and tilted it all the way up. Prentiss gagged and coughed.

"Hey, you okay? You gonna make it?"

"I'm . . . dizzy, man, real dizzy. How'd we get here?"

"You passed out. Why didn't you tell me you were getting dizzy?"

"You might think . . . I dunno. Pussy or something."

"Here, drink some more water. All of it. Man, you could die of heat stroke. You should have said something."

Levy gave Prentiss the rest of the water and then put the canteen back on his web gear. He took off his patrol cap and wiped his forehead with it, looking up at the sky. The sun was falling. They couldn't afford to spend another night out with no food or water.

"Duane, get up. You can make it." He helped Prentiss to his feet.

Prentiss swayed and finally steadied. Levy pointed him toward the ridgeline.

"Look. We're almost there. This is the last hill. If you can make it this far, you can make it the rest of the way in. Goddammit, Duane, don't pass out on me!"

Prentiss took a step forward. "All right," he said.

"I'm okay now." He started walking. Levy took the other Ranger's M16 and the shotgun.

They made it to the top. They made it halfway down the mountain. Then they were almost there.

The late afternoon sun cast its shadow over all of Camp Merrill.

Staff Sergeant Larry Quinn rocked back and forth on his heels, looking at the access road that led into the tiny camp. He stood outside in the formation area and parking lot in front of the camp's headquarters, glancing at his watch, wondering how much longer Grey was going to dick around before showing up for the weapons. They were already on a tight schedule, and everybody would be back soon after looking all day for the missing Rangers.

He heard the sound of a vehicle approaching. He darted his eyes to the right, shielding them from the rays of the setting sun with his right hand. A black '79 Chevy van approached him with another one following close behind.

Grey!

Quinn ran back inside the headquarters and opened up the arms room, where there lay ten cases of M72A2 LAWs, 174 M16 rifles, 82 .45-caliber pistols, 25 AN/PVS-5 night vision goggles, and 24 M60 machine guns, among other things. Quinn heard the vans park outside the door.

The door swung open and Grey walked in, followed by Dietrick. Quinn stuck his head out the arms room vault entrance.

"It's about time you guys got here," he said. "Another fifteen minutes and it'll be 1800. First sergeant told me everybody'd be back no later than 1900."

"Save it," said Grey. "Let's get busy." He walked

inside the arms room, looking at the racks of assault rifles, machine guns, and grenade launchers. He spotted what he was looking for. The LAWs. Then he saw something else and started. Beside the LAW packing crates were two 60mm mortars.

"When did the mortars come in, Larry?"

Quinn's eyes lit up. "I called down to Benning the other day and had 'em delivered special. Said we were running mortar classes for garrison training."

"Shells too?"

"Out back in the ammo shed. Before we leave we'll stop by and pick up some rounds. There are Claymores too."

"Goddamn, Larry," Grey said happily. "You've been thinking." It was turning out better than he'd hoped. *Claymores*. The compact, electrically detonated mine harnessed the power of twenty shotgun blasts going off at once, all firing buckshot. Anything caught in its kill zone of sixty-five meters was dead or wished it was.

"What about the guard?" Dietrick said without humor. He walked in the arms room and picked up a set of night vision goggles. "What about the guard at the ammo shed?" He turned toward Quinn and locked eyes with him.

"No need in taking him out, if that's what you mean," Quinn replied. "I'll relieve him of duty and send him to the chow hall. I've already talked to him."

"Okay, then let's get busy." Grey lifted the locking gate of a rack loaded with M16s and gathered six of them together in his powerful arms, galvanizing the other two men into action. Within the next fifteen minutes they had loaded one of the vans to bursting capacity.

Grey surveyed the arms room once more, nodding

his head with satisfaction. They had taken all the grenade launchers and the M60s, not to mention all of the night sights and the two 60mm mortars. Only three racks of M16s were left, but they had no more room for them. They'd need the other van for mortar shells, the LAWs, and the Claymores. Then he thought of something else.

"Dietrick."

"Yeah?"

"Across the street is the commo shack. Get the keys from Quinn and get some radios. About a half dozen PRC-77s, and as many PRC-68s you can lay your hands on. You may as well take the van that's already loaded. We'll meet you by the ammo supply point with the other."

Dietrick took the keys and left the room.

"Don't you think that's pushing it, Frank?" Quinn asked, looking at his watch. "We don't have much time left."

"We'll make it. I want to clean up the arms room and lock it," Grey said, glancing at the huge industrial lock that secured it. "We'll take the keys with us. By the time they get back, they won't even realize it's empty."

"And by the time they do, we'll already be at the base camp."

"You got it, Ranger buddy."

Levy trudged down the last gently sloping ridgeline to the clearing that led to the road in front of the camp's headquarters, tired and weak. His throat felt like cotton, and it hurt to breathe. Every time he tried to swallow, he felt his tongue stick to the caked tissue lining the back of his throat.

Prentiss followed close behind, barely hanging on.

Levy heard another crash as Prentiss tripped and fell. He stopped and helped him back to his feet. "Okay, buddy, hang on," he said. "Just hang on. We're almost there." They *were* almost there. But the camp was dead. The only noise came from the cooks out in back of the chow hall he could barely see through the screen of trees to his front.

That bothered him.

Levy had had the camp in view the whole way down from the ridgeline where Prentiss had passed out. No trucks or deuces incoming or outgoing, no screams or chants from formation—no hungry Rangers lined up before the chow hall. He guessed at first he wasn't quite ready to come back into the sudden scheme of things after all he and Prentiss and the others—*wherever the hell they were*—had been through. But it was more than that. It was *too* quiet. So he was wary.

"How much . . . how much farther?" Prentiss croaked.

"Just a little more, Duane. Look, the chow hall's only another couple hundred meters away."

Prentiss tried to scramble past Levy. "I want some water now."

Levy held him back. "Take it easy, buddy. Soon enough. Listen, you stay here and I'll go get some."

"Why don't we just walk right the fuck on in?"

"Not yet," Levy replied more harshly than he intended. Then, "Hell, I don't know. Just stay here so I can scout around a little bit. Look, see that spigot behind the classroom?" Levy pointed to the classroom on their side across the street from the camp's headquarters. "I'll get us some good ol' H_2O and be back in a minute."

"But—"

"Sit down," Levy snarled. Prentiss shrank back.

"Trust me. After what all's gone on, we're *not* gonna get fucked again."

Prentiss sat down quietly.

"Get down behind that tree and cover me."

"Okay."

Looking both ways, Levy snuck out of the tree line, trying to stay in the shadows as much as possible. By the time he made it to the small classroom, automatically associating it with the stench of unwashed bodies and the claustrophobic need for sleep, he wondered if he wasn't taking things too seriously. *Probably out looking for us. Why* not *shut the whole damn post down and use every available body? The camp commander's ass is on the line as it should be. Still . . .*

Levy poked his head around the corner of the classroom and looked at the headquarters complex across the street. It was a horseshoe-shaped affair with a parking lot/formation area in the middle. The two legs of the horseshoe faced the street. The headquarters and arms room was on the left side. A lone black van was parked out front. Levy thought it was the duty sergeant's and made up his mind to get Prentiss and take the dehydrated Ranger to him. He desperately needed to rehydrate him or else he would succumb to heat stroke. He walked back to the center rear of the building and filled his canteens up at the water spigot. Then he trotted back to Prentiss.

"Drink this," he said, handing Prentiss the canteen.

Prentiss seized it, drinking huge gulps of water that overflowed and went up his nose and down his shirt. He coughed and snorted and drank more, then handed it to Levy, who drank just as deeply. Then Levy put it away in his canteen pouch. He put his hand on Prentiss's shoulder, and pointed with the other to the classroom and the headquarters complex.

"The camp's almost deserted," he told him. "They're probably out searching for us and the other guys. But I don't want to go in there fat, dumb, and happy, know what I mean?"

"Yeah, I guess so."

"We'll go up behind the classroom, where I got the water. From there I'll move across the street to the left side of the headquarters complex. That's when I'll wave you on across. You cover me the whole time. Got it?"

Prentiss nodded his head.

"After we link up, you'll cover me as I walk in the headquarters front door. It's easy to spot, because a van is parked outside in front. Stick to my rear, keep your eyes open, and keep that shotgun at the ready."

"Sounds a little gung-ho to me," Prentiss said, grinning weakly.

Levy smiled back and clapped Prentiss on the shoulder. "Well, we may look like fools to the duty sergeant, but better safe than sorry."

Prentiss's face turned somber. "Yeah."

"Check out the twelve-gauge and make sure it's fully loaded. Take it off of safe, but don't blow my ass away as you're walking behind me."

As Prentiss inspected the shotgun, Levy pulled the .357 from his web gear and broke open the drum, making sure a round was in every chamber. He snapped it shut and and set it gently on the ground. Then he unstrapped his M16 from his back and gently worked the bolt back and forth, checking the action. After lengthening his sling and turning the selector switch on automatic, he draped it on his right shoulder, keeping hold of the M16's pistol grip with his right hand and his index finger brushing the trigger. He picked the .357 up with his left hand and turned toward Prentiss.

"Ready?"

"Whenever you are."

Levy took Prentiss out of the tree line, creeping back down the slope to the clearing, then across the clearing to the classroom. Then they treaded softly to the corner of the building, where Levy had reconned the headquarters complex moments before.

Levy jerked his head in the direction of the headquarters building. "See it?"

"See what?"

"The black van. That's where I'm going. It's parked right outside the front door."

"Okay."

"Remember—as soon as I get across the street, I'll wave you across. Then we make our way to the front door. Cover me."

"Okay, okay."

Levy sprinted around the classroom and across the street, where he stopped behind the left side of the horseshoe. He inched over to the corner and peered around where he could see the van. Then he turned back toward the classroom and waved at Prentiss. Prentiss shuffled across the road and joined Levy.

Levy saw that Prentiss had already broken into a furious sweat from the exertion. "You okay?" he whispered.

"Of course not. Drive-on."

"Okay, follow me."

Levy tiptoed his way around the corner of the building and walked a few meters left to the entrance. Prentiss followed close behind.

Levy counted the steps, his heart hammering. He couldn't help it. He and Prentiss were both on edge.

A little closer. Ten more feet. Five. He glanced back at Prentiss, whose eyes were wide with apprehension and shifted nervously in all directions. They were there.

Levy motioned at Prentiss to open the door while he readied the .357 and the M16. Prentiss reached out with his left hand and touched the doorknob, holding the shotgun in his right. Then he yanked the door open and Levy burst inside.

Grey! Quinn!

"Freeze!" he shouted, leveling both weapons at the two men. They were as surprised as he was.

"What the hell are you doing, Ranger?" Grey yelled in his best authoritarian manner. "Put those guns down!"

"No way, shitbird. You're behind all this. Prentiss. *Prentiss!"*

"Behind you!"

"Cover me, man. Watch the rear!"

Grey's cold eyes cut at Levy as he stepped forward. "I don't know what the hell you're talking about, Ranger. Now, give me that goddamned gun!"

"Make another move, Sergeant Grey, you racist pig! I'd love to blow your ass away!" *Easy, boy, easy. Don't blow it.* "It was *you* that set us up last night at the ambush, wasn't it? *Wasn't it!"*

Quinn stretched out his hands, imploring Levy to calm down. "Ranger, put the gun down. Nobody's out to get you. Hell, the camp's mobilized just looking for you and the rest of your patrol."

"No shit!" Levy snapped. "And you just so happen to be the duty sergeant. My ass! I saw what happened between you two and MacAlister the other night. You guys set us up."

Grey glanced nervously at the arms room door. It

was still ajar, as he hadn't locked it yet. Levy followed his eyes.

"What *are* you doing here, Sergeant Grey?" Levy's eyes narrowed. "Open that arms room door. *Do it!*"

Grey walked across the room to the arms room and opened it all the way.

"Now move away!" Grey backed off.

Still training his weapons on the RIs, Levy edged to the door and looked in. One glance told him everything. He moved back over to Grey and Quinn.

"What did you do with the weapons?"

Grey and Quinn exchanged glances.

"I want some answers!"

A crash and a scream!

Levy wheeled about, pulling the hammer back. Another man was on top of Prentiss just outside the doorway, beating him. Prentiss's shotgun lay three feet away on the sidewalk. The man jumped off to the side as Levy yelled and fired his .357. He missed, the round striking the doorjamb an inch away from the man's head, gouging concrete cinderblock and wood splinters away with the force of the .357's blast. He squeezed the trigger of the M16, and blasted another hole on the doorframe, but then the weapon jammed.

Quinn leapt out and clubbed Levy on the side of the head with a devastating roundhouse.

Levy sank to the concrete floor. Everything turned black.

CHAPTER

· TWENTY ·

My courtesy to superior officers, my neatness of dress, and care of my equipment shall set the example for others to follow.

Voices faded in from far away.

". . . then take 'em out in the woods on the way back and kill 'em."

"Or take them back to camp. More fodder for the riots. What do you think, Frank?"

"What the fuck are you saying, Larry? Listen to you! I said I wanted these two dead. *Dead!* Are you trying to weasel out on—"

"Easy, man, you're getting too wound up. Calm down. I was just thinking—"

"Goddammit, Larry! You just make it happen!"

Levy's eyes focused on a fire ant on the concrete floor crawling toward his nose. His right ear felt numb, and the rest of his head was blazing. He came to.

Grey stomped over to the two prostrate bodies. Dietrick had dragged Prentiss in as soon as he had dodged Levy's bullet, clipping him once more behind the ear to keep him out. Grey stood over Levy and kicked him in the shoulder hard enough to roll the Ranger over on his back. Levy's arms flopped around and bashed against the floor. His eyes fluttered, still numb from Quinn's blow moments before.

"The kike's starting to wake up," Grey announced. "Fuckin' douchebag." He knelt down and pinned Levy's chest with his knee. He reached inside the Ranger's collar. "Thought I told you to get rid of your jewelry, Jew-boy," he said, ripping off Levy's Star of David and sticking it in his pocket.

"Let's move it," Dietrick said brusquely. "The whole damned camp will be back any moment."

"I'll decide when we 'move it'! In case you've forgotten whose in charge—"

"You know I didn't mean it that way. The *time* . . ." Dietrick pointed at the wall clock. Already it was 1910.

"This bastard killed a friend of mine last night—and what I heard about Leroy Dennis was true."

"Who's that?" Quinn asked.

"One of the deputies in town, who was working for my father. He's dead, over by Turner's Corner. There was another man with him, one of *my* men. That's his .357 this kike had. These two ambushed them earlier in the day." Grey reached down and squeezed Levy's cheeks together. "You're history, Jew." Then he stood up, digging his knee hard into Levy's chest as he got to his feet. "Tie them up and throw them in the van."

Quinn walked over to Levy and kicked him hard in the ribs. "Get up," he growled. *"Get up!"* Levy crawled to his feet, holding his side and glaring at his tormentor. He could barely stand straight. "Fuckin' sheenie greaseball," Quinn muttered. "You're gonna wish this day never came before I get finished with you." Quinn reached into his desk drawer and retrieved a two-inch-thick roll of OD green Army duct tape and a shoeshine rag. He quickly taped Levy's hands behind his back with the hundred-mile-an-hour tape. Tearing the blackened rag apart, he stuffed one half in Levy's mouth and secured it in place with four wraps of tape around his head.

Within moments Quinn had bound Prentiss the same way. He shoved them both outside and threw them in the rear of the van, where he taped their ankles together. Meanwhile Dietrick departed to collect the radios he had left in the communications shed, where he had first spotted Prentiss standing outside by the headquarters entrance. He told Grey later that he'd gotten suspicious after hearing the yelling back in the arms room, and had climbed to the roof of the building, walked over to where Prentiss was standing, and jumped him from the roof. Grey cleaned up the headquarters and locked the arms room.

Then everything was ready. Dietrick drove the other van up. Grey and Quinn walked outside and locked the door.

"We're running out of time," Grey said to Quinn. "I'll handle the ammo supply point myself. Hastinger is pulling guard duty there, right?"

"I told him I was coming," Quinn replied.

"No sweat. And I agree that there should be no bloodshed here. I'll send Hastinger on down to the chow hall, like I'm relieving him. He'll believe me since he used to work for me back at Benning. Besides, I want to personally pick out the rounds we'll need for the next mission . . . the ones I was telling you about."

"That's cutting it pretty close."

"I want only the Claymores and some grenades if they have any, so it won't take long."

"What about those two?" asked Quinn, jerking his head toward the van.

"You and Dietrick take the weapons back to camp

ASAP. Kill them on the way and fix it so they won't be found.''

The van lurched along a bumpy dirt road in its endless, sidewinding journey to the base camp. It was slow going up the steep mountain road, a trip best made with a four-wheeler or a pickup. Dietrick drove. That made it worse. It was all Quinn could do, putting up with the neo-Nazi's arrogant abrasive personality.

"Dietrick, why don't you slow this thing down a little? You'll break the shocks the way you're going."

Dietrick smiled. "Won't hurt a thing. I know this route. Hell, we've got only another ten miles to go."

Quinn looked to his rear at Levy and Prentiss, who lay squirming on the floor of the van. Every time the van hit a bump, one of them would bounce against a machine gun or an M16 and a muffled yell would penetrate his gag. "When do you want to take care of 'em?"

"It doesn't matter. We can do it now, if you want. Hey, it'll give me a chance to show you what I was talking about—"

"You mean with the ice pick?" Quinn interrupted, unfastening his seat belt. "Yeah, I want to see that. Pull over."

Dietrick drove on a little farther until he found a small clearing just big enough to drive the van off the road. He pulled the van off the road and cut the engine.

Quinn looked up at the sky as he climbed out of the passenger side. Already a bloody orange full moon hung low over the horizon, promising maximum illumination during the night.

Dietrick opened the van's rear door. "Ride's over, kiddies," he announced, giggling. He took out his knife and cut the tape off Levy's ankles, then leveled a .45 automatic at him that he pulled from his shoulder holster.

He yanked Levy out of the van, letting him fall face-down in the dirt. Quinn did the same to Prentiss. They shoved the two Rangers downslope through the thick-est patches of vines and trees, searching in the oncoming darkness for an inconspicuous cut in the ridge filled with dense vegetation. They found one fifty meters inside the tree line.

Quinn jerked Prentiss down next to a tree, making him sit with his back against the trunk. "This place is as good as any," he said to Dietrick. "Sit the Jew next to him and tape them together." Quinn threw him the same roll of hundred-mile-an-hour tape he had used earlier in the arms room.

Levy suddenly stomped Dietrick on the foot. The neo-Nazi shrieked in pain, and Levy tried to break away from his grasp. Dietrick held on and punched Levy a paralyzing blow to his gut. Levy doubled over, snot blowing out of his nose. His airtight gag smoth-ered him as he fought for air, and he sank to his knees, wanting to vomit.

"*Fucking kike bastard!*" Dietrick screamed, hopping around on one foot. He kicked Levy in the stomach, knocking him against Prentiss.

"I'll cover the son of a bitch," Quinn said, aiming his .45 at Levy. "Tape them up now before he gets any more ideas."

"Yeah," Dietrick replied, shoving his .45 back into his shoulder holster. He grabbed the tape and began wrapping Prentiss's and Levy's wrists together, back to back. "I've got big plans for you two. Might even give you another circumcision, Jew-boy. Might even . . ."

"You can stop what you're doing now, and put your hands on top of your head." A calm, even voice.

Dietrick looked up and found himself staring at the bore of Quinn's .45, less than a foot away from his nose. His jaw dropped. In Quinn's left hand was a badge.

"FBI. You're under arrest." Quinn deftly shoved the badge back into his front trousers pocket and then steadied his .45 with both hands.

"You're shitting me." Dietrick's eye shifted to the right, farther downslope.

"Make a move, and I'll plug your ass. You have the right to remain silent . . ."

Dietrick lunged to his right, clawing at his shoulder holster. Quinn belted the other man's chin with the heel of his right boot, putting him out cold.

Levy and Prentiss couldn't believe it.

Later.

Levy rubbed his mouth with the back of his hand and swore. "You sure as hell had me convinced, Sergeant Quinn. Wait a minute—what's your *real* name?"

"You got it right. Larry Quinn. Sorry about all the rough stuff back at the arms room. Couldn't blow my cover."

Prentiss was guzzling another canteen of water. Levy watched him. "You doing okay?"

"Better now," Prentiss replied. He choked suddenly.

"Take it easy on that stuff. You'll puke your guts out if you don't watch it."

Prentiss took the cue and promptly blew chunks, turning his head to avoid hitting Levy and Quinn. He did manage to douse a groggy Dietrick, who squirmed and yelled through his gag of shoeshine rag and hundred-mile-an-hour tape. He was splattered, since he was securely tied and taped against the tree Levy and Prentiss were to be executed on earlier.

Levy turned back to Quinn, laughing. Then he grew serious. "Why the hell are we in this situation?" he asked the agent.

"It's a very long story," Quinn replied. "But I guess you deserve an explanation. It all goes back to when Frank Grey and I served in 'Nam together."

"Go on."

"We don't really have the time, but I'll tell you this: We once were friends. Once. No longer."

Quinn took a deep breath and exhaled it slowly, craning his neck back to stare at the rising moon. "A long time ago we were the best buddies in the world. He stayed in the Army after we got back, and I got out. My cover story says I was in a local police unit for several years and that I stayed active in the National Guard; that I came back on active duty to get back into soldiering after being disgusted with equal opportunity this and affirmative action that within the police department, et cetera, et cetera. Fact: I joined the FBI. Lost all contact with Grey. They assigned me to this case six months ago, after a black lieutenant was killed under mysterious circumstances up here during his mountain phase of Ranger School. FBI headquarters checked into it and tied the situation up with their suspicions of a paramilitary outfit the KKK was training in a base camp north of Dahlonega, not too far away from the Tennessee border. They also had reason to believe Grey was running it, since his old man was a Grand Dragon."

"And you volunteered for the infiltration," Levy interjected.

Quinn paused a moment before answering. "No,"

he finally said, "I didn't. They volunteered me after a computer scan showed that Grey and I once served together in the same unit. After a briefing session with them, headquarters told me to pack my bags, put on a uniform, and show up at Camp Merrill." Quinn paused again and shook his head.

"Frank Grey used to be my friend. When we were in 'Nam, I knew he was a racist. Gotta admit, there was no love lost between me and the blacks in our platoon either, but—" Quinn fell silent for a moment, seeming to be lost in thought. Then, "But I didn't know how far he was into it. I never used to let it bother me—we all depended on each other out in the jungle. . . ." A dark look suddenly clouded Quinn's eyes. "We all . . . we all depended on each other," he finally said. His voice had gone flat. "Besides, Frank could never afford to fuck with any of the blacks in our platoon there. They would have fragged him." Quinn clammed up again, saying nothing more, as if he wanted to say more but couldn't.

"And now—" Levy prompted.

"And now," Quinn continued, "Grey's actually formed up his own terror squad that's gearing up to go to war. I mean they're really getting ready. Scary as hell."

Quinn looked at his watch. "Okay, enough jaw-jacking. We're in a bad situation. I didn't expect you two to show up the way you did." He glanced over at Dietrick, who squirmed against the tree, frustrated with Quinn's taping method. He wasn't going any-where. The gag kept him quiet.

"I want you two to stay here with him," he said.

"You're still going to the base camp?" Levy asked, incredulous.

"That's right. I told Grey I'd get the weapons up there, and I can't blow my cover."

"What about him?" Levy said, glancing back at Dietrick.

"That'll be the hard part. But I can stall Grey long enough."

"What about the rest of our patrol? They've got to be there. We've got to free them somehow. We can sneak into the camp and set up a diversion or something."

"You're not making any sense, and you haven't the foggiest idea of what my headquarters has set up. You and Prentiss stay here."

Levy's eyes narrowed. "You said you could stall Grey long enough. Long enough for what? What's going on?"

Quinn stared hard at Levy. "Tonight," he said. "Tonight we're raiding the camp."

"You're crazy."

Quinn shrugged and stood up. "Just stay here and watch him," he said. He turned back to where the van was parked farther uphill and started walking. Levy sprang forward and pulled on Quinn's shoulder, yanking him around.

"Wait," he said. "I mean, you're crazy to just go in there by yourself, reinforcements or not. Why not take me and Prentiss to—nearby the camp. Or something. We can . . . we can . . . I dunno, infiltrate the perimeter and take out security guards or—"

"Give me a goddamned break, boy scout," Quinn exploded, yanking his arm away from Levy. "What the hell do you think this is? Another graded patrol? Frank Grey is a goddamned murderer! You think you're just gonna sneak in and pop a few caps and expect to get away with it? Don't give me that hero shit."

"But Grey will know something's going on when you show up without this neo-Nazi, or whatever the hell he is."

"Gee, that thought hadn't occurred to me," Quinn mocked. "How long do you think I've been in this game, stud? Now, you listen to me: They've already got Claymore mines set up around their perimeter. Machine-gun positions. Snipers. We've traced at least three different armory rip-offs around the country to the same network that Grey and his crew have set up. That's how they got all that stuff. We've got good reason to believe that Grey himself organized and actually participated in a burglary against an armory in Tennessee several months ago. Unfortunately, we didn't find out about where all this shit was located until I infiltrated Grey's organization and saw it first-hand. First-fucking-hand!"

Quinn paused, staring Levy down. Then his eyes mellowed, and he reached out and clapped Levy gently on the shoulder. "All that stuff's for real, man. The only way we're gonna take their little fort down is with an assault team. Tonight. And only if I'm inside, messing things up for the bad guys. Yeah, I know my shit's weak. I knew that from day one."

Levy's stomach developed a bad case of adrenaline rush. "What about the rest of my patrol?" he said. "What will happen to them when your high-speed rescue team hits the camp?"

Quinn looked away from Levy. "They'll be taken care of," he said quietly. "I've already told the team about the students being held there. My men will know what to do."

Levy had detected a dull, alien look in the agent's eyes. A look of resignation. Fate. He didn't like it.

He decided to tell Quinn what he knew he wanted to hear. "Please get them out. Safe."

Relieved, Quinn gave Levy another squeeze on the shoulder. "Don't sweat it. Our guys were trained by a Special Forces unit at Fort Bragg. They know what to do."

That look again, Levy thought. *Yeah, right.* "Well—I guess Prentiss and I would screw things up if we got in the way." Levy glanced to the rear searching for Prentiss's silhouette through the darkness that had stolen upon them.

Quinn nodded his head. "I'm glad you understand," he said. "It's the only way."

"You'd better give us something to guard that asshole with. How about some chow too?"

"Come on up to the van."

Prentiss joined Levy by the road several minutes later, as Quinn pulled away. He noticed his Ranger buddy staring vacuously at the van as it bumped and ground its way up the mountain. He held two M16s, their web gear, and several boxes of ammunition. A set of night vision goggles hung around his neck, and next to his feet were two C-rations and a five-gallon water can.

"C's!"

"Yeah."

"Water!"

"Yeah. Water."

"What are you staring at?"

"Here's your weapon," Levy said, thrusting one of the M16s at Prentiss. "Take some of this ammo and load your magazines. Here's your web gear too."

"What's going on?"

Levy picked up the water can and lugged it down-hill. Prentiss followed close behind. When they reached Dietrick, Levy pulled his flashlight out from his web gear and turned it on, inspecting the Nazi's tape job. It was bombproof.

Dietrick glared at Levy, working his eyebrows furiously and tugging against the tape. Levy glared back, flipping the flashlight off and hooking it on his web gear.

"Recircumcize me, huh?" he said. "You sick puppy."

Dietrick quit thrashing when he saw Levy take his Swiss Army knife out of his pants pocket and flip out the scissors blade.

"What are you doing, Dan?" Prentiss asked. Levy ignored him and tapped the flat side of the scissors blade on Dietrick's nose. "Do you really get a kick out of doing things like that?" Tap. "What if somebody ever did that to you?" Tap, tap. Suddenly, Levy snipped the scissors rapidly in front of Dietrick's nose.

Dietrick moaned behind his shoeshine-rag gag.

"C'mon, Levy. Cut it out."

"Wouldn't be too fun *then*, now, would it?"

Dietrick emphatically shook his head no.

"That's right, shitbird." Levy jabbed the scissors underneath the tape binding the Nazi's gag and cut it, pricking Dietrick's scalp. Levy saw his eyes roll and thought the man would pass out. Part of the tape peeled slowly away from the back of Dietrick's head, where he had cut it.

"Take it easy," Levy chuckled. "I don't do strange things like that, you pervert. Like you wanted to do to me, that is. I'm not like you, remember? I'm just a Jew.

Kike. Sheenie. You know." He grabbed his canteen and twisted off the cap. "Want some water?"

Dietrick swallowed, and nodded his head.

Levy grabbed the tape where he had cut it and yanked the gag off Dietrick's face. It was a pretty hard yank.

Dietrick screamed. In the tape's place was raw, bleeding flesh.

"Drink this whole canteen," Levy said, sticking it in the neo-Nazi's mouth none too gently. "It'll be the last you'll get for a while."

Dietrick coughed and started swallowing. Water flowed over his cheeks, up his nose, down his fatigues. As soon as he drained the canteen, Levy refilled it from the water can and put it back in his web gear.

"What are you going to do to me?" Dietrick sputtered, gasping for breath.

Levy noticed how his voice, so arrogant and cocksure before, now sounded whiny, like a dog gone bad kicked hard in the gut.

"Tape your ass back up," he replied, grabbing the roll of tape and binding the rag back in Dietrick's mouth. When he was done, he turned around and faced Prentiss, who was eating his C-ration. Prentiss offered him the other C-ration. Levy looked at it closely in the glow of the moon which had risen.

"Ham and eggs," he said, shaking his head. "What did you get?"

"Beans and baby dicks."

Levy cursed softly. Beans and frankfurters was the best C-ration. That was the one that had the cinnamon nut roll in it.

Afterward Levy stood up and stretched, gazing at the moon. He burped contentedly, and felt his eyelids droop. He was tired. No doubt about it. How long had he been up? Two days straight? He wanted to go to sleep more than anything else in the world.

But he had something to do. Or did he? Was it not the best thing to do, to just sit tight and guard the neo-Nazi as Quinn had ordered? Then again, what about the look in the agent's eyes, the hesitation in his voice? *Oh, I've already told them about the students being held there. The assault team will know what to do.*

Or will they, Levy thought, *with Claymores and machine guns and assault rifles from three different armories being fired at them?*

He glanced at Prentiss, who leaned against a tree, dozing. He reached down for the five-gallon water can and twisted off the cap. Then he held it above his head and let the water cascade over his head and shoulders. He gasped at the impact, instantly awake. The temperature had already dropped down into the mid-sixties, and Levy knew it would plummet to the fifties later on that night. That would keep him awake.

He kicked Prentiss lightly in the behind, jolting him awake. Prentiss jerked his head up and almost rocketed off the ground.

"What! What!"

"Settle down, Duane. You were asleep."

"Then why'd you wake me up, buddyfucker? And quit kicking me in the butt!"

Levy smiled and patted his pockets for his can of Copenhagen. He found it in his right breast pocket, amazed that it hadn't burst open from the beating he'd received earlier. "We've got another mission, ol' buddy," he said. He opened the tin of snuff and stuffed a wad in his lower lip, grimacing from the pungent smell of ammonia the mildewed tobacco exuded. Seconds later he felt a powerful surge of nicotine plow through the arteries in his lower jaw and throat. He grinned thickly at Prentiss and offered him the can.

"No way. That stuff makes me puke."

"Whatever." Levy carefully put the can back into his pocket. "Got that ammo loaded yet?"

"Another mission, huh?" Prentiss said, shaking his head. "Guess I should have known." He started to get up.

"Relax, hero. You're not going this time."

Prentiss shot up his head. "What?"

"You're weak. Dehydrated." Levy nodded toward Dietrick. "Why don't you just stay here and watch that asshole?"

"Well . . ."

Levy saw the guilt and embarrassment on Prentiss's face and felt sorry for him. He wished he and the others earlier on in the course hadn't ridden him so hard. With the support rather than the ridicule from his comrades, Prentiss might have done a lot better. He had a lot of heart. The bottom line though: another cross-country movement would do him in. Heat stroke was easily fatal.

"Duane, it's for the best. Face it, man, you're smoked."

"And you don't want me around screwing things up like I usually do," Prentiss replied bitterly, turning away. "I know what you guys think of me. I'm the patrol's fuckup."

"That's not true. You've been going it on guts alone for the past forty-eight hours. I admire the hell out of you for that, Duane."

Prentiss cleared his throat, his chest hitching. "You'd better get moving." He staggered up from the tree and attempted to smile. "I'll watch Dietrick." He reached into his pockets and pulled out the boxes of ammunition he had brought down from the road. ''Here. I'll need only one box. Let's load it now.''

Five minutes later Levy counted six magazines between them, fully loaded. He shoved one in the magazine well of his M16 and charged his weapon. Then he stuck four more into the ammo pouches on both sides of his web gear. He held the last one out to Prentiss.

''Here. You'll need this.''

Prentiss took the magazine from Levy and put it into his M16. He charged his weapon and flipped on the safety.

''Watch that guy close.''

''Yeah.''

''Don't go to sleep.''

''No sweat.''

''Duane.''

''Yeah?''

''You're not a fuckup, man. I mean that.'' Levy held out his hand. Prentiss stiffened, looking at it. Then he shook it, swallowing the lump in his throat and feeling his eyes grow hot and salty.

''Thanks, Dan,'' he choked. ''You'd better go now. It's already 2030.''

Levy looked at the moon, which had by now become very large and very bright.

Then he left.

CHAPTER

· TWENTY-ONE ·

Quinn crawled the van along the steep mountain road for the next half hour after leaving Levy and Prentiss behind with Dietrick. It was slow going. He estimated it would take another fifteen, twenty minutes to reach the base camp, and that was good.

That meant he was close to his cache site.

He had to get to a radio. His stomach told him so. For the past month, when things with Grey had developed far beyond what he had expected for this mission, his ulcer had acted up. Even now, bumping and lurching along a seldom-traveled road, each jolt reminded him how this particular onslaught just might be the one to burn right through the lining of his solar plexus. When he thought of what lay ahead at the camp, and what he would have to do later on that night, each pulsating throb in his gut felt like a battery-acid Alka-Seltzer gone haywire.

He had developed his first round of ulcers immediately after returning from Vietnam by remembering. Remembering things like what he had told Ranger Levy about Grey earlier, things that had stirred deep within the bowels of his cerebrum, remembering things he had done his damnedest to forget. He was not successful, especially during the entirety of this mission.

He could not have refused this mission. It was his penance.

Quinn tried to forget about the ulcer burning a hole in his gut; he tried to reject the lush green image on the van's windshield suddenly forming before him.

And he was unsuccessful.

Ka-wham! Shreds of ferns from the triple canopy jungle and blood mist and viscera whirled through the air.

Ambush, Vietnam-style, early 1969. PFC Larry Quinn screamed. He'd just seen the first four men of his patrol in front of him torn up beyond recognition from the daisy-chain of stolen Claymores the VC had rigged up beside the trail.

"Larry!" Corporal Frank Grey screamed behind him. "Get down!"

Numbed, nineteen-year-old Larry Quinn leapt from one side of the trail to the other, unsure of the ambush's location. AK rounds popped all around him, kicking up the trail dust, popping beside his ears.

"Larry!"

A bullet smacked into Quinn's thigh, ripping through the fleshy part. It felt to him as if he'd just been tackled by the biggest noseguard he'd ever faced in high school football. He somersaulted from the force of the round and was thrown down violently on his side. Then, all at once, raw nerve endings registered a crimson-seared belt of pain exploding in his upper leg. He shrieked. "Frankie!"

Rounds socking the dirt trail all around him, more explosions, excruciating pain. Then a rushing figure, huge and strong, grabbed him by the web gear and dragged him off the trail. "Medic! Mediiiic!" The big presence left him. Quinn stared at his leg and watched jets of blood pumping out of his femoral artery. He heard shots firing nearby, the empty shell casings flipping out from an M16's chamber and landing on his chest. One rolled inside his collar, searing the flesh on his neck. He screamed again.

Another presence appeared before him, looming dark and sweating in front of his face. Quinn smelled his body odor and recognized Donaldson, the platoon medic, hovering over him, the clenched fist sign the black soldier wore around his neck bumping against his nose.

The husky medic hauled Quinn by his web gear deeper into the jungle, away from the firefight. Quinn fought to keep his fist pressed against his leg, where gouts of blood kept pumping out. He grew dizzy, his breathing shallow, knowing he was going into shock. Then he felt a belt being pulled tight around his right thigh, close to his groin, cinching the blood flow. Donaldson rolled up the sleeve on his right arm. Suddenly, there was a prick inside the hollow of his arm, and then numbness surging throughout his body as the morphine took effect . . . the pain in his leg subsided. He drifted. He passed out.

He woke up in the hospital in Nha Trang. Six weeks of recuperation. No broken femur from the wound, just flesh healing. Soon he was well enough to go back to his unit. The whole time he had spent in the hospital, he'd thought about how close to death he had come. If it hadn't been for Frankie Grey, he'd be dead. But no, he wasn't the only one—Donaldson had saved him too. Donaldson, yeah, that's right, Donaldson the medic. That jive-ass coon—no, the black guy. He could have left him there to bleed to death, but he didn't. He would have bled to death otherwise. He thought about how ironic it was that the two men who hated each other more than the enemy had teamed up to save his life. Two men who had actually sworn to kill each other through nothing more than racial hatred, Black Panther against Klansman, white against black, two men fistfighting in the base camp one day until the first sergeant had broken it up—they had both saved his life. Quinn had amends to make, whether his best friend had sworn to kill Donaldson or not.

Quinn limped back into base headquarters and met Grey there.

"How ya feeling, limp-dick?"

"Up yours," Quinn replied, clapping Grey in a bear hug. As they turned to go to their squad hut, they passed Donaldson, walking in the opposite direction. Grey averted his gaze, trying to control his temper. Quinn turned toward Donaldson, hand extended.

"Hey, Donald—"

"Fuck off, whitey." Donaldson kept on walking.

Grey pulled his friend along. "You don't owe that shit anything."

"But—"

Soon he fell back into the comfortable routine of hating blacks, coons, and niggers along with his friend Frankie Grey, and he took solace in the rejected offer of friendship to a man who had saved his life by reviving the old hate and the old bigotries. His offer had been spurned, and he hated Donaldson for it.

And then they were out in the boonies again. Back on fucking patrol. Quinn had only one month left in-country, Grey only two weeks. It was an ambush that night. They reached their assigned ambush point and set up, stringing Claymores along the trail. Quinn's leg still throbbed, and *the healed bullet wound reminded him what havoc daisy-chained Claymores could wreak against mere flesh encased in cotton jungle fatigues. His eyes searched for and found Donaldson, who occupied a position five meters to their left. He felt the same wasted emotion—useless hate—suddenly rise up in him. And then he tossed the feeling out of his mind.*

Later that night the enemy came through, ten of them in all, padding quietly through the jungle. Quinn glanced to his right side, seeing Grey's intense stare welcoming them into the kill zone—a stare that occasionally switched to his left and focused on Donaldson.

Ka-wham!

Quinn emptied his M16 on full auto into the torn VC bodies caught inside the kill zone, relishing in his vengeance from the time before. Several VC had reached cover on the other side of the trail and were returning fire. Rounds popped overhead, and Quinn ducked. Then the assault line picked up after the initial thirty-second burst of fire and swept through the kill zone, chasing after the VC who had broken contact, escaping into the forest. Quinn leapt up to run across, but tripped over Grey's extended jungle boot. Sprawling, he looked up in time to see Grey sight his M16 on a running figure and fire. And Donaldson's head popped violently toward his chest, his forehead disintegrating from the exit wound. He pitched forward against the trunk of a mahogany tree and sprawled on the ground.

Shocked, Quinn let Grey haul him to his feet and run on across the trail into the jungle beyond. After linking up with their patrol minutes later, he was too exhausted, bewildered, and hurt from his still-throbbing leg to say or do anything. As they were humping back to the base camp, he stared at the back of Grey's patrol cap in front of him, wondering if he had truly witnessed a murder that night.

Larry Quinn never said anything. Donaldson had just been another casualty, shot by those VC who had survived the initial ambush. Besides, they were going home within the month. Grey never mentioned that night to Quinn later on. And Quinn could never develop the inner courage to confront Grey with it. He kept quiet. He kept the peace. And he tried to forget.

For many years afterward he had tried to forget.

Until this past year. To forget—or at least try to forgive oneself for the past's shameful cowardice—was impossible. He had joined the police force. He had been a good cop. Then it was the FBI. He found his marriage taking second place to a force deep within him that begged absolution for a murder—yes a murder—he had participated in through condoning a friend's hate. Special Agent Quinn turned out to be an overachiever, a volunteer for the most dangerous assignments. Drug missions, Mafia missions—and then this infiltration mission. A mission offered to him when headquarters started questioning him about an old liaison with one Frank Wilson Grey, son of a KKK Grand Dragon. The computer age had arrived, and his military experience had matched perfectly with Grey's. He was offered the mission strictly on a volunteer basis—to infiltrate Grey's organization, find the weapons he had stolen, and expose his conspiracy.

Would he do it?

He had to volunteer. For once in his life he needed to look in the mirror without remembering.

He found much more to the conspiracy than he had bargained for. Extremists armed with Uzis and modified Mini-14s. A race war in the making and a dead RI on his hands. Captured Rangers in the hands of madmen.

And God help them if the Federal Bureau of Investigation was not prepared to deal with hostages when they took down the camp.

***

The radio. Were they ready? Quinn slowed the van to a stop at the top of a ridgeline and turned off the headlights. Then he closed his eyes. One minute later he opened them and stepped out of the van, taking in the horizon.

He remembered that his cache was near the top of the second to last ridgeline before turning left to access the runway road five hundred meters away from the camp. He walked out to the front of the van and leaned against the hood, the heat of the engine warming him through his jungle fatigues. He searched the valley below with his night vision, constantly shifting his eyes so his vision wouldn't blur. He was glad the rain had finally stopped. The moon and the stars promised almost eighty-five percent illumination by 2400, when the moon was at its highest.

He found what he was looking for—a set of three east/west ridgelines leading up to a vertex aimed at a higher mountaintop no more than a thousand meters to his front. At the top of that mountain was another ridgeline that led down the opposite direction from the three toward the runway road. It was another fifteen minutes to the cache.

Quinn hopped back into the van and drove on. When he reached the top of the next mountain, he stuck a flashlight out the window and shined it to the left of the road. Ten seconds later he found a dead oak tree, slashed in two by lightning, twenty meters off the road. He pulled the van over and killed the engine. Then he reached underneath his seat and retrieved an entrenching tool and got out. He walked to the oak tree and took a compass out of his pocket. Then he took a bearing of 360 degrees and walked five meter-long steps. He dug one foot into the ground and hit wood. Then he dug all around the wood until he could pick the foot-square board up and reach inside the hole.

One minute later he had a type-87 sonics radio out and hissing on a frequency he knew would be monitored precisely at 2100. He looked at his watch and grunted with satisfaction. It was 2059.

Quinn readjusted the six-foot antenna, making sure it was aimed toward the east, and broke the squelch by squeezing the button on the hand mike. It was ready. He glanced at his watch. There would be a twenty-second window, starting on the hour.

The second hand swept past the 12. He squeezed the mike.

"Falcon-Sweep One, this is Court-Jester, over." Quinn said in a hushed monotone, shaking his head, thinking that every government agency whether Army, CIA, or FBI had used some sort of heroic-sounding bullshit for whatever the operation. "Falcon-Sweep One, this is Court-Jester, over," he repeated.

"Go ahead, Jester," came a crackling reply.

"Situation report for the One . . . new input . . . confirmed, I say again, *confirmed* ten Ranger students being held at Falcon-Nest . . . how copy, over?"

"I copy new sit-rep with ten students at Falcon-Nest. Roger that, over."

"Scarecrow en route to that location," Quinn said, thinking about Grey somewhere in the woods close by with the ammunition he'd stayed behind to get. "I rendezvous in thirty minutes. Chickenhawk is already there with the rest of their personnel, over." He thought of Gunther and the rest of Grey's hit squad. *How many will there be tonight? Two, maybe three dozen?*

"Good copy, Court-Jester. Be advised time-on-target has been moved up three hours, over. TOT is now 0200, over."

"Negative, repeat, *negative*—move TOT back to 2400. My cover is blown. I don't know how long I can stall them."

The mike stared back at Larry Quinn in silence. His gut throbbed.

"Falcon-Sweep One says stick with the new TOT. Falcon-Sweep HRT won't be in place until 0100."

"That you, Bentley?" Quinn snarled. "Turn me over to Whisenhunt, *now*!"

The mike fell silent for several long seconds. Then, another voice.

"Stick to proper radio procedure, Court-Jester. What seems to be the prob—"

"Goddammit, Whisenhunt," Quinn swore into the mike, breaking his supervisor off, "you'd better fuckin' *listen* to me! My cover is blown. Or it will be if you guys don't move the schedule back to 2400. I don't know how long I can keep it up. You copy that?"

"Uh . . . roger, Jester," came the reply. "Give us your sit-rep since the last twenty-four hours, over."

"Okay." Quinn cooled down. "I've got the weapons Grey wanted. I'm en route with them now to the base camp. The firing pins are all filed down just in case, so they're inoperable. Here's the problem: Two Ranger students from the abducted patrol stumbled in on Grey, Dietrick, and me this evening while we were getting the weapons. Me and Dietrick were to dispose of them. Grey is supposed to meet us back at the base camp around midnight. I had to take out Dietrick in order to save the two students. Dietrick and the two students guarding him are five miles down the road toward Camp Merrill from my present location now. How copy, over?''

"Good copy, Jester. Go ahead.''

"I have confirmed from Grey that the remainder of the patrol is at the base camp—Falcon-Nest, or whatever the hell it is. I repeat earlier message: ten students. Can you handle that?''

"Stand by, Court-Jester.''

Heart thumping in rage, Quinn glared back at the silent mike, wondering if headquarters would pull their heads out and approach the assault in a way that wouldn't get all the students killed. . . .

"Court-Jester, this is Falcon-One, over.''

"Go ahead, One.''

"Roger TOT at 2400. Be advised that HRT elements will be in place on the north side of the camp at 2300 to 2330, no later than. When you go in, stall them as long as you can.''

Quinn breathed a sigh of relief, knowing that there were at least some good men running the hostage rescue team. As long as they were in place, things would work out. He glanced at his watch, knowing he had to move on. He squeezed the mike.

"Good copy, One. Remember when you go in that the students are all skinny, bald, wearing OD jungle fatigues. Don't confuse them with the bad guys. I don't know where they are located, but they're there.''

"Roger, Court-Jester. Be sure you're wearing your mike, over.''

Quinn reached down into the cache site and pulled out a box that held a tiny transmitter and wire mike no larger than a hearing aid. His life would depend on it later on.

"Wilco, One. Anything else for me? Over.''

"Negative, Jester. Proceed with mission, over."

"Roger that. Remember, ten students on site. Watch for them. Out."

Quinn turned off the switch to the radio and put it back into the hole. Then he replaced the wooden top and covered it back up, scattering dirt and brush on top to camouflage the area. He walked back to the van, rubbing his solar plexus where an all-too-familiar throbbing pain had intensified.

A sudden weariness fell upon him as he opened the door and sat behind the wheel—a sort of sleight-of-hand lethargy. His stomach hadn't quieted at all. It burned. Quinn wondered if his pain was due to nerves or if it was a bad omen. Or still, the memory. He turned the engine over and lurched back onto the road, heading for the turnoff that would take him into the camp.

It had been a long mission, one that had taken a toll. First the ulcer flared up, then his marriage had gone to pot only a month ago—*that was the last anniversary* he'd *miss*—the mind games he had to keep playing along with his cover, the long-awaited acceptance into Grey's inner circle . . . all in all, he'd done one hell of a job, or so Whisenhunt had told him on occasion. They were on the verge of cracking the most dangerous reactionary movement in the United States. A movement—if left unchecked—that would rock the nation into racial violence and destruction. He wondered if the FBI's assault team could take down the neo-Nazis and Klansmen on the initial attempt, what with all the weaponry at Grey's base camp.

He also wondered if headquarters was taking the ten Ranger students seriously enough.

CHAPTER

· TWENTY-TWO ·

"Look at him," Jakes whispered to Christopher. "Think he's asleep yet?"

Christopher straightened his back, trying to stretch out the cramps that had plagued him all day, and peered through the darkness at Charley's position thirty feet up the ridge from them.

"It's hard to tell. From the way he's slouching, he might be. Then again . . ."

"It's been dark for at least half an hour. If we're going to bust out of here, now's the time to do it."

"Not so fast. They've got dogs out here. Remember when they brought us those Cs a while ago?"

Jakes shuddered, remembering the pit bulls two men from the camp brought down when whoever was keeping them finally decided to feed them. There had been one man with an assault shotgun strapped across his back who held the leashes of the two pit bulls. Another man carried a case of Cs.

Every one of the Rangers had looked at the dogs in

awe. They had huge triangular heads with muscles that literally bulged out of their jaws. The dog handler had joked about how one of them had bitten the air out of his four-wheeler's front tire one day. The dogs weren't that big in size, like a Doberman or Shepherd. But what they lacked in size they made up for in sheer muscle-bound weight, strength, and a notable lack of fear. Even more frightening, they had been trained as man-killers.

"Yeah, I remember. I used to have a pit bull back at our farm in Missouri. Used to go in the woods for days and kill wild hogs. He'd drag 'em to our back porch, like he was helpin' us out. He'd eat 'em whole—bones, guts, and all."

"You don't have to draw me a picture. Seems like they use them as guard dogs here."

"I reckon so. But we can't let them keep us from getting out of here."

"No, but I can recon this AO beforehand. Won't take any longer than an hour."

"What?"

"You heard me. I'll slip out of these cuffs once we're sure dummy over there's asleep and make a recon."

"You're crazy!"

"Shhh—lower your voice."

Juan Keller woke up from his slumber five feet away and propped up on one elbow, looking at Christopher and Jakes.

"Man, those dogs will get you," Jakes said more quietly. He knew that Christopher had already made up his mind.

"It's a chance I'll have to take. Look at that guy Charley again. Think he's asleep?"

"Where are you going?"

Christopher and Jakes turned around and faced Keller, surprised that he had spoken. He had been quiet all day since the "lecture."

"We're getting out of here, Keller," Christopher replied calmly. Something more than mutual dislike bothered him about Keller. Especially since his performance earlier in the day. He seemed to have enjoyed the attention he had gotten from their captors and their racist conversation.

"I agree with Jakes. You're crazy."

"Don't worry about it. It's my ass, not yours."

"Sure, and first chance you get, you'll skip out on us. You see, I know you got that key. You had those guys faked out pretty good, but I saw what happened. So far I haven't said anything."

Christopher stared at the cadet Ranger, speechless. He simply couldn't comprehend that Keller might say something about their only chance for escape. Suddenly, his eyes flashed and every muscle in his worn-out body tensed.

"And you *won't* say anything either, motherfucker, 'cause if you do—"

"I'll personally kick your yellow-striped ass," Jakes finished for him, glaring at Keller. "You won't say a goddamned thing while he's gone."

Christopher turned his attention to Jakes. "So you're with me."

"Of course, stupid." Jakes chuckled softly. "You think I'm a buddyfucker like him?" Jakes glanced uphill, where Charley lay slouched against his tree, his Mini-14 laid across his lap and his chin resting on his chest. In the quiet of the woods, the only sound was his heavy breathing, broken every so often by a choking gurgle that passed for a snore. "He's gotta be asleep again. He did the same thing after he ate lunch, right about the time you woke up. Which reminds me—you look like hell. Are you up to it?''

Christopher gingerly touched his broken face, wincing. His ribs felt no better. "I'm alert, aren't I?''

"You're going to skip out on us, Christopher. Why don't you just admit it?''

Christopher boiled, wanting to smash Keller's face into a bloody mess. Then he forced himself to cool down, realizing that to get angry now and do some thing to the arrogant asshole next to him would wake Charley up and spoil everything.

"Keller, I'm telling you once more," Jakes muttered, massaging his wrists where the handcuffs bit into them, "you say anything, and somehow—some way—I'll fix you good.''

Keller shrunk back, intimidated by Jakes's intensity. He laid his head on the ground and closed his eyes.

"Go for it," Jakes told Christopher. "Make the recon and get back here ASAP.''

"Okay. There's no need to tell the others what's going on. If anybody wakes up and sees that I'm gone, try to keep a lid on things.''

"Gotcha.''

"It's . . . 2135," Christopher said, glancing at his watch. "I'll be back before 2300.''

"That's too long.''

"2245, then. It'll take at least that long to find out where everything's located—guards, dogs . . . perimeter security. They've got to have people out on security.''

"Make it 2245, then. What if they find out you're gone?''

"Man, I don't know. Just keep it quiet here, and there shouldn't be a problem. If they do find out—well, I'll try to do something." Christopher locked eyes with Jakes. "I gotta get moving. Where's the key?"

Jakes lifted a rock by the trunk of their tree and scooped up a handful of dirt. He picked the key out of the shallow hole and gave it to Christopher.

"Real imaginative hiding place."

"What'd you expect? They couldn't beat the living shit out of you forever."

"Sure felt like they did," Christopher said, unlocking his handcuffs. He looked uphill at Charley, barely seeing him in the twilight. "Scoot around in front of me so you're in his line of sight if he wakes up."

Jakes moved in front of Christopher as quietly as he could, rustling the pine straw underneath as he moved. Then Christopher stood up, crouching.

"Be careful," Jakes told him, looking up. Christopher nodded solemnly, wondering if this would be his last recon ever.

Then he quietly slipped into the shadows and was gone.

Levy felt lighter, more free than he had been in several days, moving by himself. He didn't regret leaving Prentiss behind with the neo-Nazi. Given the mountain he was humping now, Prentiss wouldn't have lasted long.

He had been clawing his way up what his map showed to be the last ridgeline en route to the base camp where the others were being held. Or at least whatever location it was according to the coordinates written on the deputy's slip of paper.

Levy pulled out his canteen and guzzled a deep slug of water. Before leaving, he had drunk as much as he could from the five-gallon water can, thoroughly hydrating himself. He would need the reserve for later on when he found the others. He hoped he was going to the right place. Levy looked up the mountain and decided that another hundred meters would take him to the top of the ridgeline. He started climbing again.

Finally, he made it. He crested fifty meters to the right of the broad summit, crouching so he wouldn't expose his silhouette if anyone was observing from the opposite side. He was satisfied that he had chosen a good route to follow during his map recon before moving out. The top was sparsely vegetated and he had an unobstructed line of sight across the valley below. What he saw across the valley and on the next ridgeline across from him no more than another klick away was a high mountaintop rising to the left. Below that, and connected by the same ridgeline to the mountaintop's right, was a false hilltop with a small clearing next to it where a long gradually sloping finger ran down the rest of the mountain. Parallel to it was a gash in the trees, like a clearing made for power lines.

Levy's stomach growled. He picked out a rock to sit on by a clump of trees and walked over to it. Once there, he opened the can of cinnamon nut roll he had managed to pry out of Prentiss's clutches and started to eat it.

Flipping on the power switch of the night vision goggles he had brought along, he scanned the ridgeline to his front.

Levy twisted the lenses of the goggles, focusing them. They weren't that good at far range since they were made for maximum scanning distances of only a few hundred meters, but they were better than nothing. He was glad he'd been able to swipe them out of Quinn's van earlier. He scanned his front, from the top of the mountain and then to the right. He stopped when he reached the false hilltop to the peak's right, barely making out three dark, blurry objects forming a triangle. His heartbeat picked up, and he twisted the focusing knobs again. Suddenly, a flare lit up inside his goggles, blacking the area out. Levy ripped the goggles off his face and stared across the valley. A tiny flame had erupted, which was quickly snuffed out.

A match! He strapped the goggles back on and saw the glowing dot tracing a cigarette trail in his line of sight. It had to be the camp.

He ate the remaining chunk of cinnamon nut roll and drank again from his canteen. Then he stood up and turned the selector switch of his M16 to the semi-automatic fire mode. He was going to find that cigarette's owner.

Then Levy heard something soft and low up in the air. He looked up. Nothing. The noise faded away. He shrugged his shoulders and started walking down the mountain.

He heard it again, this time louder, with a barely perceptible whine and a humming, steady purr. Levy turned around and walked a few steps back to the summit. The noise faded. Then it came in again, quieter than the past two times, like the noise a lawn mower makes three blocks down from your house. Levy peered over the crest and saw three pairs of red and white lights moving in the darkness far away, over ten kilometers south of his position.

Helicopters!

Levy watched the Blackhawk for the next fifteen seconds as one landed after the other at a location masked from Levy's view. Their whirring rotors differed from the "thumpa-thumpa-thumpa" of the Hueys Levy had ridden in the past.

Why else would they be in the AO unless they're the FBI's?

Levy turned his night vision goggles on again and scanned the mountain he had looked at earlier, this time searching around the spot where he had seen the cigarette. He saw nothing more than the same dark objects in the tiny clearing on the false hilltop where he had first seen that match light up. Suddenly, a bright green dot appeared near the summit of the mountain on the side opposite to the clearing. He scrambled down the mountain to the most convenient bush, turning the goggles off, realizing the green dot was another night vision device that had been turned on the infrared mode. If whoever it was looked in Levy's direction, he'd have seen the same thing.

Levy got up from his bush and low-crawled through a patch of weeds to a denser area of the tree line. When he was certain he was better concealed, he got back to his feet again. As he scrambled down the mountain, Levy thought about the helicopters and the other night vision device he'd seen, and concluded it had to be part of the raiding party Quinn told him about earlier.

He thought about it. What if they saw him? For this type of operation they might shoot before asking questions, thinking he was part of the KKK outfit holding his friends. He made a mental picture of the mountain with the false hilltop and the clearing where he'd seen the cigarette.

That had to be it—the encampment. The long gash in the tree line? It couldn't have been a powerline firebreak. He'd seen no poles or wires when he scanned the area with the goggles. Besides, it paralleled the ridgeline, rather than crossing it, and couldn't have been more than 300 meters long. Then he knew what it was. A landing field for a small aircraft.

Levy congratulated his logic. Of course! The tiny airstrip was there for light aircraft coming and going to the camp for arms smuggling, emergency transportation, taking visitors and Klan trainees there blindfolded so that they would never know the route—there were many possibilities.

A sobering thought hit him. The FBI would use it to their advantage with the Blackhawks. So he had to steer clear of *two* groups of desperate men tonight, the neo-Nazi/Klan faction, and the FBI assault team. With all the fireworks the night's events promised, he had to get to the patrol before anything happened. Firing would be indiscriminate, and judging from the look he'd seen in Quinn's eyes earlier, the assault team wasn't placing any priority on saving the Rangers before taking the bad guys. Levy quickened his pace.

A trail materialized to his front. He wondered if he should risk being seen on it, versus making much better time by following it out to the valley below.

He decided to take it. His best security lay in speed. Holding his M16 at the ready, he loped down the trail gracefully, careful not to make too much noise, the glow from the moon high above him picking out the rocks and boulders standing in his way.

Prentiss jerked his head up and blinked rapidly, aware that he had nodded off again. He looked at Dietrick no more than six feet away from him. He was still. Asleep. Relieved, Prentiss took a deep breath and felt his eyelids droop again. He fought to keep them open.

That guy spooks me, he thought. *Hasn't moved an inch since Levy left.*

He listened closely as Dietrick's even breathing hissed in and out of his nostrils. Then his eyes lost their focus as he listened to Dietrick's smooth, unbroken breathing. He shivered and thought of when he could get back to civilization and be warm and eat his mother's shrimp scampi and drink a root beer without someone chasing him.

Five minutes later Dietrick popped his eyes open, listening to Prentiss's breathing go back to a steady rhythm as the Ranger slumbered off. The gag choked him, and the tape cut off his circulation long ago. He fidgeted with the tape again, his fingers and forearms immediately cramping. Just before Prentiss had woken up, he'd had a good grip on the running end of the tape, and had worked the first wrap loose by rubbing it against the tree trunk he was tied against. With a little more time he'd get loose, and then he would close his fingers around the sleeping kid's throat.

Dietrick fought the tape for the next half hour. His fingers contorted around each strand, slowly peeling it from his wrists, torturing his forearms in endless series of cramps. Each time a spasm hit him, he clenched his jaws together, forcing his mind to control the pain and keep from crying out. Sweat popped out on his forehead and flowed from his armpits and down the sides of his rib cage. The muscles inside his thighs cramped as well, since his ankles were still bound together. His whole body cramped from the effort. His head pounded from the headache Quinn had given him. He squirmed. Agonized. He moaned softly, then bit down hard on the rag in his mouth. Mucus whistled in and out of his nostrils as he fought for breath. Each time he fought the bindings, he thought he would suffocate from the effort it took. He focused his rage on the sleeping Ranger student next to him, concentrating on loosening his wrists, and thinking about throttling him. Just when he felt he couldn't take anymore, the cramps would peter out, and he could feel the tape break apart, bit by bit.

It was progress. He did it all over again.

Finally. He drew in his breath, filling his lungs to bursting capacity, and pulled his wrists apart. Veins popped out of his head and arms. A low animal growl surged through his gag. The tape snapped apart like a small firecracker.

Prentiss opened his eyes just in time to see Dietrick lunge for him, his right fist cocked back. He yelled and tried to duck.

Dietrick struck Prentiss hard against the forehead and fell heavily against him, his ankles still taped together.

Prentiss kicked and screamed as he clawed the ground with his M16, holding it in a death grip. He scrambled out from underneath the Nazi and smashed the stock of his weapon into Dietrick's face. Dietrick yelled and swung wildly at Prentiss with his fists, still trying to use the surprise of the moment to his advantage. Prentiss kicked clear of him and almost fainted when he got to his feet, dizzy and disoriented from Dietrick's blow. He stuck the muzzle of his M16 into the neo-Nazi's face. Dietrick froze, staring at the bore.

Prentiss pulled the trigger.

Nothing happened. It was still on safety.

With a triumphant yell Dietrick grabbed the muzzle and ripped the weapon away. He immediately smashed the stock into the Ranger's gut.

Prentiss fell back, retching from the blow, and scrambled for the tree line on his hands and knees.

Dietrick aimed the weapon at him from five feet away. This time Prentiss knew that the M16 would be on full auto.

He threw himself into a patch of bushes downslope

as a three-round burst stitched the trees before him. Prentiss hit the ground rolling, wait-a-minute vines tearing at his face. He crawled away on his hands and knees until more trees stood in between him and Dietrick. Then, crouching, he sprang to his feet and flew down the ridgeline, bullets cracking into the trees all around him. Then one grazed his hip and spun him around, making him crash against a thick, sap-covered pine. He pulled away from the sticky bark and tumbled down the ridgeline in blind panic, clutching at his hip, blood oozing through his fingers.

Dietrick checked his firing, realizing he had expended over half the magazine. He listened closely to the diminishing crashes and yells as Prentiss ran down the ridgeline. Then he clawed at the tape around his ankles, adrenaline coursing through his arteries.

His face stretched into a sudden neurotic grin. He remembered the time when he and Gunther had chased a woman down in the jungles of El Salvador. They had been interrogating local peasants about the Sandanistas during a raid on a village considered to be under the enemy's influence, and had caught a young guerrilla—a female guerrilla still in her teens—trying to escape. They had taken her out into the jungle to rape her before turning her into the government forces, but the woman had broken loose from them with surprising strength.

They had chased her for the better part of an hour before finding her cowering behind a tree near a stream, her ankle broken by a sudden fall in the rocks.

Dietrick remembered. It had been a good chase, full of excitement. Anticipation. It had made it better.

His loins ached from the memory. He tore off the final strip of tape and got to his feet.

It was time for another chase.

Dan Levy saw the sudden glare of headlights to his left and leapt back into the tree line. He had reached the bottom of the trail, where it crisscrossed a dirt road in the valley next to the mountain where the base camp was located.

He waited. A minute later a black van bumped along the road to his front and abruptly halted twenty feet past him. Levy wondered how he could ever have beaten Quinn to the base camp on foot, even though he had been moving cross-country.

The driver got out, leaving the engine idling, and stood before the hood. He unzipped his pants and urinated in the road, looking all around as if he thought he was being followed.

Grey.

Levy almost laughed out loud. *And after all this shit I've been through because of him. Now I can put a bullet in his head just as easy as you please, while he's got his pants down . . .*

Levy raised his M16, wanting to shoot the RI, wanting to call out his name and see him wheel around in blind panic before spinning a .223 round through his brain, opening the top of his head like a can opener.

Then he lowered the weapon, wondering if Grey had a passenger with him. If he did, there was at least a fifty-fifty chance he'd get away before Levy could shoot him. Levy strained to see through the passenger window for a silhouette.

Grey zipped up his pants and climbed back into the van, ruining any chance Levy might have had for a decent shot. The van started forward, driving on for another few feet, and then it turned left, rattling and bumping up a barely discernible turnoff Levy hadn't seen.

Levy jumped up and shot across the dirt road, running without concern for the noise he made while the sound of Grey's engine was still within earshot. He followed the van's headlights with his eyes parallel to the road, running as long and hard as he could, until the steep angle of the new mountain defeated him, forcing him to stop and catch his breath.

Levy took off the rolled-up poncho he had tied to the back of his web gear and draped it over his head, and then he sat on the ground near a clump of bushes. He pulled out his map and laid it on the ground, shining his red-lensed flashlight upon it with his hand covering the beam so the light wouldn't penetrate the thin nylon covering of the poncho. According to what he'd seen on top of the mountain and from interpreting the map, he decided he couldn't be more than a few hundred meters away from the camp. The road he was following had to be the access road, or Grey wouldn't have taken it. He brought the map close to his eyes, closely examining the false hilltop where he guessed the camp was located.

The road Grey had taken wasn't on the map. Neither was the trail he had been following from the other mountain. That told him they must have been made fairly recently, since the map itself had been made in 1979, according to the legend. Levy stared at the map for several moments. Then he stuffed it back into his trousers pocket, realizing he could stare at it for an hour and still come up with the same conclusion. He had to forget about the map and concentrate on climbing uphill as silently as he could without calling attention to himself from either Grey's people or the FBI.

Levy heard another vehicle approaching. He looked downhill, searching for headlights. He found none. He turned on his night vision goggles and peered through them. He saw a camouflaged four-wheeler approach from the same direction Grey had come, twenty meters below just before the turnoff. The driver wore the same kind of goggles. In the four-wheeler were three other men, all dressed in camouflage and carrying M16s. Levy switched the power off and took off his goggles so that the driver wouldn't spot his infrared signal.

More FBI. He remembered how Grey had looked all around when he got out of the van earlier, as if he knew he was being followed.

He listened intently. The driver reversed the four-wheeler into the tree line for a quick exit if necessary, and then cut off his engine. The others with him dismounted and formed a security perimeter around the vehicle.

Levy rolled up the poncho, fastened it back on his web gear, and stuck his flashlight back in the grenade strap next to his ammo pouch. Then, for the next fifteen minutes, he crept farther up the mountain. Finally he was out of earshot. He quickened his pace.

Son of a bitch!

Wincing, Christopher raised his hands to his neck and gingerly picked at the wait-a-minute vine trying to strangle him. Its thorns were deeply embedded around his throat, and he felt blood forming in tiny drops around the punctures. He pulled the vine away from his Adam's apple. This was no ordinary vine. Most of the time, Christopher had called them wait-a-minute vines, or Himalayan death vines if they were particularly thorny. This one was a son of a bitch in every sense of the word. It had draped his head and shoulders with a sticky mass of spider webs.

Christopher shuddered. He hated spiders. He imagined dozens of them swarming all over his body as he crept through the impenetrable black of the night. Swallowing, he shifted his eyes to the left and then to the right, trying to see if anyone from the camp would suddenly appear to investigate the tiny yelp he had made. Hearing nothing, he swiped his hands across his face in frantic, jerky movements, clawing at the sticky, finely spun strands tangled in his hair, his eyebrows, and across his face.

He calmed down, forcing himself to quit thinking about tarantulas crawling between his shoulder blades. Kneeling, he peered through the darkness at the top of the hill, reorienting himself. Since he had left Jakes and the rest of the patrol in the contonement area ten minutes before, he had contoured a gently curving ridgeline twenty meters from the crest. Judging from the terrain he had covered and the position of the moon, he was located along the southern approach to a hilltop.

Christopher decided to climb farther uphill and see what was on the other side of the crest. He stepped out silently on tiptoe, every move premeditated, this time holding his right hand in front of his face to keep from walking into another unseen wait-a-minute vine.

Moments later he crouched near the top of the ridgeline. He saw an orange glow in the distance and slowly walked toward it. The glow turned into a flicker. It was a campfire. Christopher hesitated, his heart thumping.

He cupped his ear, craning it forward. He thought he heard voices. A group of men were talking around the fire, the sound of their voices blending in with the constant chirping of night crickets and a ringing in his ears he had noticed when he first woke up that morning. He moved closer, painfully aware of the leaves crunching underneath his feet each time he took a step.

The trees thinned out as he went. The fire grew brighter, and he heard the crack of a pine knot as it exploded in the embers, showering the crisp mountain air with orange sparks. He melted noiselessly to the ground, placing his hands down with the grace of a cat, then one knee at a time. He stared at the fire, leaning forward, trying to hear the men he knew would be around it. Something brushed across the tip of his nose.

He froze, and a bead of sweat trickled down between his eyes, to the bridge of his nose, and onto a wire stretching before him, a wire as tight as a piano string. He hadn't seen it. Christopher said a silent prayer of thanks that he hadn't detonated the booby trap. More than likely it was an early warning device—a small explosive with a tripwire stretched tight in order to go off when brushed against or cut. Then again, he realized, it could just as easily have been a phosphorous flare that would have blinded him in a flash of light and heat. He would easily have been captured had he tripped it.

Christopher looked back at the campfire. Shadows danced on the face of a man whose features he couldn't quite make out. He was alone now. The others must have gone away. He saw a building behind the remaining man. It was a log cabin straight out of a Currier and Ives Christmas card.

He didn't know if he could get any closer. He squinted his eyes trying to get a better look, but it was no good. He wasn't getting anywhere. He peered at his watch. Already he had been gone for twenty minutes. He decided to get moving and scout around the other side of the cabin he had seen.

The Ranger backed off from the wire. When he had backtracked twenty feet to where he had first seen the glow, he crawled to the top of the ridge, intending to go to the opposite crest and cloverleaf around to the other side of the camp.

On top, he found a trail large enough for a vehicle. He paused before crossing it, looking in both directions and listening for any security positions his captors may have posted. He couldn't afford to get sloppy. He knew that if the Klan and neo-Nazis were good enough to have hidden booby traps around the perimeter, they were good enough to have manned security positions surrounding the area. Just before he started across, he heard the sound of a gunning engine. He ducked back into the tree line. Seconds later a black van rattled down the road to his front, slowly grinding its way to the camp. Christopher waited until it passed him, and then he ran across the road, crouching low. Once across, he slipped on a rock and twisted his ankle. He crashed into a pile of leaves.

He stifled a cry of pain as something raked across his side, scraping his already tender ribs. His body tensed into rigidity, and he gritted his teeth together hard. The pain subsided. He felt along his side to see what he had fallen against. His hand closed around plastic. He picked the object up for an inspection. Then his eyes bulged when he saw what it was.

Seven hundred lead pellets of death encased in a pound and a half of C4 explosive stared back at him. He was holding a Claymore mine.

A break in the maple tree branches forty feet above his head allowed enough moonlight to gleam on the Claymore's concave face, which read: FRONT TOWARD ENEMY. Two black wires dangled from the top where the blasting cap was screwed in, and two pairs of forks stuck out from the bottom of its OD green plastic case, where it had been stuck into the damp earth facing the road and covered with leaves. Christopher set it back down on the ground, wondering why he hadn't been blown up. He should have been, if whoever held the electronic detonating clacker had squeezed it.

Breathing easier, he knew he had found one of the security posts. More than likely, the wires traveled fifteen meters back to a position where the man pulling security was sleeping. Christopher said his second prayer of the night, thanking his maker that the Claymore's owner hadn't heard his fall after sprinting across the road. He repositioned the mine, facing it back toward the security position. The man on guard duty would get a nasty surprise if he ever decided to use it.

Christopher backed off from the pile of leaves and walked farther down the face of the ridge. Minutes later he turned left, walking toward the glow still visible in the treetops. The trees thinned out again, and he knew he was nearing the campsite. Soon the campfire and the man—no, now there were two men—were back in view. The black van he'd seen earlier was parked next to the cabin. He glanced up at the sky. The moon shone brilliantly from above, unimpeded by the now-sparse forest canopy. He edged forward, hiding in the shadows of the trees.

He saw another cabin he hadn't seen earlier thirty meters to his right, surrounded by concertina wire. Just enough trees covered the area to keep the cabins from being seen from above. Camouflaged netting had been pitched above their roofs for insurance. Christopher had to admire the setup. It was a professional job. He wondered how many more cabins were in the area. More important, how many people were there in the camp? Was there an arms room? Perhaps un-secured M16s or Mini-14s lying around? He decided to risk a closer look.

Christopher inhaled deeply and let it out. Then he got back on his hands and knees and crept closer, this time gently waving his hands in front of his face, feeling the air for more of the deadly tripwires. He stalked from shadow to shadow, weaving a clandestine path through the tree line running up to the camp. He moved in closer, not daring to breathe. The voices and laughter grew louder. He spotted several boulders surrounded by bushes not forty feet from the campfire. The tree line he had been following led right up to them.

He knew that was as close as he could possibly get. Minutes later he emerged from the tree line and low-crawled through the bushes. Then he crawled inside the nest of rocks, hidden completely from view. It was good cover.

He now plainly heard the men talking by the fire. He got down on his belly and pressed his face into the dirt so he could peer around the boulder to his front without being seen.

He saw their faces. He recognized them now.

Levy climbed up the mountain in a swelter of pitch-black darkness. It was like any other mountain he had climbed throughout phase two of Ranger School—steep, never-ending, and cluttererd with trees and wait-a-minute vines. Finally, imperceptibly, the sharp degree of the slope eased up. Levy knew he was getting close. When the trees started to thin out, he slowed his pace.

Levy stopped, strapping the night vision goggles back on his head and scanning his front. Through the enhanced starlight he saw a glow arc over the horizon toward the false hilltop he had been moving toward. It could have been anything—a lantern, a small campfire—but in any case, it was the camp, and it was only a couple of hundred meters away.

Levy hung the goggles around his neck and rubbed his eyes. He had been relying too much on the goggles. If he used them much more, his natural night vision would peter out for the rest of the night. Already it was all he could do to catalog the shadows filling the dark in front of him into trees, rocks, and deadfall. He shook his head and moved out.

He was back on tiptoe, walking like the South Korean Rangers Christopher had once told him about. They approached their objectives in the worst kinds of weather—preferably when it was raining to beat all hell—by raising their feet high, toes pointed downward, and putting them back down gently, toes touching the ground first before shifting their weight in order to feel for sticks that might crack underneath their feet. Levy's mind wandered as he walked, and he hallucinated about a very large, very cold pitcher of iced tea with near-frozen beads of condensation slowly dripping down its glass side.

He stumbled into something and fell, crashing on his face. A deep, growling voice cursed softly in the darkness.

"Goddamn. Goddamn! That you, Pritchard? *Goddamn!* When are you gonna learn to quit sneakin' up on me like that?"

Mortified, Levy sprang to his feet, trembling from surprise and fear. Looking down, he saw a prone figure get up on one knee, rubbing his mouth and cursing with an endless supply of "goddamns."

"Can't find your ass with both hands, you know

that, Pritchard? You go out in the fucking tree line to take a fucking shit, and then you come back and trip over me because you can't find your fucking ass with both hands. *Goddamn!*"

Levy stared disbelievingly as the shadowy figure stood up to an amazing six and a half feet tall, dusting himself off and cursing with indignation. What to do? He certainly couldn't shoot him.

He put down his M16 and edged away, pulling out his knife from its sheath.

"Well, why don't you speak up, shit-for-brains?" the giant muttered. "Pritchard? Hey, where are you going now?"

Levy crouched into a knife-fighting stance and tried to see through the darkness. The frightening size of the lumbering figure to his front reminded him of a linebacker in college who had been in the ROTC program with him. They called him what anybody that size would have been called—"Mongo."

"Talk to me, Pritchard. This some kind of game?" The giant lumbered toward Levy, his head hunched between his shoulders, trying to find Levy.

Levy knew what he had to do. And it had to be done as silently as possible. He hefted the knife in his right hand, blade up. Moonlight glinted off its razor edge.

"Hey. Hey, now, goddammit! You're not Pritchard," Mongo said, louder this time. "Who the fuck are you? Answer me!"

Levy lunged forward with the knife.

Mongo met him halfway with a hamlike fist that slammed into Levy's chest. Simultaneously, Levy sunk his Ka-Bar into the giant's gut to the hilt. Levy's breath exploded from his chest cavity at the force of the other man's blow, and he nearly passed out.

The huge man expelled a wheezing grunt and bellowed out in pain. He wrapped his hands around Levy's throat, instantly cutting off the Ranger's air and blood supply to his brain.

Levy knew he would be out in a matter of seconds. He crammed his knee deep into the man's groin. The giant screamed and squeezed Levy's throat harder. Levy withdrew the knife and plunged it deep into the man's lower stomach, just above the pelvic bones, twisting the knife blade, searching for the kidneys.

Mongo's grip relaxed, and he made nauseating, gurgling sounds deep in his throat. Levy pulled the bloody knife out again and this time slashed it across the other man's jugular and trachea, cutting off any more sounds he might have made. A shower of blood sprayed Levy's face, and Mongo sank to his knees. Levy tore away from his grip and kicked the big man square in the head. He crashed to the earth, a twitching Goliath.

Gasping for breath, Levy fell to the ground on his hands and knees, wiping the other man's blood away from his face and eyes. He was amazed that it had taken so long for the big man to go down, and that he had maintained the grip on his throat for so long. Another second, and he would have been just as dead.

Levy fought to clear his head and struggled to keep from coughing. The big guy had called him Pritchard. That meant someone else was around. He got to his feet and dragged Mongo to a sitting position against a tree. Then he hid behind another tree ten feet away, pressed up against the trunk. He held his knife with a bloody right hand, ready for the next round.

A series of breaking twigs greeted his ears from the right, opposite from the body against the tree. Levy cursed silently. The other man—Pritchard—would certainly see him before he could get right on him.

Levy waited. The noise of breaking brush grew louder, and soon another man materialized out of the darkness.

"Drew!" a voice called. "Drew, what's going on? I heard you hollerin' up here, and you know what J.D. says about—" The man walked up to his dead buddy. "Drew? I heard something up here, like you was . . ."

Levy saw the man stop and bend down, looking closely at his friend's face. The man reached out and touched the pool of blood that had formed on his chest.

Levy tensed as he prepared to leap out from behind the tree, gripping his knife so hard that the veins popped out on his forearm. The full moon above shone brightly on his white-tipped knuckles.

"Oh, sweet Jesus . . . Drew . . ."

Levy jumped out and rammed his foot into Pritchard's side, knocking him off balance. The twelve-gauge automatic the other man had been carrying flew from his hands and clattered to the ground. Levy pounced on him, sticking the Ka-Bar in him again and again.

The man died quickly. Long before Levy quit stabbing him.

When he was through, he searched the area for the nearest thick clump of bushes. He didn't have to look for long. He dragged the bodies into them and covered them up with more brush. He knew it was half-assed, but it was the best he could do. He had to get to the others.

Levy examined the area for any other signs of the carnage. Other than blood everywhere, there was nothing left. He had thrown their weapons in the brush with the dead security team, except for the twelve-gauge automatic he had kept, which he had strapped across his back.

Just as he was ready to go, Levy suddenly felt an overwhelming wave of vertigo and thought he would black out. He slumped against a rock, holding his hands out before him. They shook violently and were covered with dried blood and gore. He gazed up at the immense, bright yellow moon above, tears streaming down his cheeks in fear and rage and hate.

Then he bent forward at the waist and heaved his guts dry.

CHAPTER

· TWENTY-THREE ·

Energetically will I meet the enemies of my country.

"You got *how* much?"

"A whole fucking van full," Grey said. The campfire in front of him felt good, and its hypnotic effect had calmed his ragged nerves from the day. "Quinn and Dietrick are on their way with a lot more. They should have been here by now."

"Jesus." Gunther scratched the back of his head and stared into the fire, thinking about what Grey had just told him. He whistled softly. "How many 60s?"

"A dozen," Grey replied, smiling broadly. "You name it, I got it."

"LAWs, like what we were talking about? Claymores?"

"Yep."

"Jesus," Gunther repeated. "That ought to funnel enough weapons into the net to arm at least five more hit squads on the West Coast." He got up from his folding chair and walked toward Grey's van. He opened the back door and peered inside. Then he pulled out a wooden case of M16 ammunition and set it before the campfire. He looked at Grey curiously.

"I know. The only stuff I brought was a couple cases of 5.56 ammo for the M16s. I didn't have time to get anything else, because the cadre was returning to the camp. I had to beat it."

"They know about you yet?" Gunther asked, returning to his folding chair.

"They will soon enough. They've probably figured out it was me already. Like I told you, me and Quinn cleaned the arms room out."

"When will Quinn and Dietrick get back?"

Grey clasped his hands behind his head and stretched his back, rocking back and forth on his heels before the fire. "As soon as they get rid of the two students we caught. Hell, I don't know. I figured they'd be here by now."

Behind the rocks Christopher clenched his teeth hard and forced himself to keep calm, realizing that Grey was talking about Levy and Prentiss. Rage consumed him, compounded by a feeling of helplessness. If he were to jump them now, not only would he get shot trying—they both wore holstered .45s—but the others would surely die as well.

He knew he had to keep still. Be patient. Wait and listen.

Christ, but you're gonna pay, you bastards!

"I'm just glad you found them," Gunther said. "Those two on the loose were our weakest link so far."

"So, getting back to the hit tomorrow—what do you think? Any changes?"

"Not unless they decide to call the convention off," Gunther replied, staring into the fire. "But that won't happen. This thing has blown up into a full-scale minority leftist Communist party. You got *all* those damn mayors there, all of them. Not to mention nigger celebrities. There'll be more of 'em there than you can shake a stick at."

"Ready?"

"Shit," Gunther snorted. "What do you think we've been practicing for the past two weeks?"

"Nothing like a good rehearsal for actions on the objective."

Just then something whistled off to the right, sparkling like a huge bottle rocket, and smacked off the door of the cabin not ten feet away from them. An accompanying report followed it from the tree line up the mountain. Automatic small-arms fire opened up from the same area. Knocking his folding chair over, Grey fell prostrate to the ground, fumbling with his .45.

"Relax, relax," Gunther said, laughing and slapping his hand against his knee.

Grey twisted around in the dirt and shot Gunther an evil look. Tears streamed down the neo-Nazi's face.

"What's going on?" Grey demanded.

"Your rehearsal," Gunther choked, gasping for breath. "Your actions on the objective. Man, you couldn't have said that at a better time. That incoming rocket was a training LAW one of your National Guardsmen stole from his armory."

Christopher had jumped and almost yelled when he'd heard the LAW rocket hit the cabin by the campfire. He hugged the ground even closer and prayed that Grey and Gunther hadn't heard him. Seconds later he lifted his eyes and watched as shadowy figures with camouflaged faces assaulted the campsite from the tree line, firing M16s at Grey and Gunther. Christopher realized that they were rehearsing a raid with blank ammunition, just as he and the rest of his patrol had been doing in Ranger School.

Judging from what he'd heard the Klansman and the neo-Nazi talking about moments before, they weren't doing all this just for shits and grins.

Christopher's spine tingled. He and the others in his patrol were being held hostage for something big. Something that would demand their deaths.

A cold sweat popped out on his forehead and the back of his neck.

Something *really* big.

Grey watched the assault line race across the camp. Three-man teams each secured the two cabins, and the remainder of the twelve-man force swept across the area and secured the opposite side, each man expending two full magazines in the process. He noticed that each of them carried a cardboard tube strapped across his back. Every other man fired submachine guns, a mixture of Ingram MAC-10s and Uzis. Two men fired M60s. He pulled on Gunther's sleeve.

"Why the tubes and the 60s?" he yelled above the din.

"Those are the other LAWs—simulated, of course." Gunther's face broke into a maniacal grin. "That first training LAW you heard . . . well, when we do this thing for real tomorrow, multiply that LAW times twelve. *Real* LAWs. All we have to do is drive the vans to the front of the convention center, get out, and take aim at the lobby. After firing the LAWs, we run inside, and then gun down every nigger we see still standing with the submachine guns and the 60s. We use the Ranger students we took last night as decoys, making it look like they did it. They'll be drugged, of course. It'll create max confusion, and give the police something to shoot back at while we take off. During the same time-on-target, we'll have smaller, compartmented teams up in D.C. assassinating selected targets. White targets.''

Christopher had almost freaked when one of the raiders plopped down to the prone in front of his boulder, firing his machine gun. Making himself keep absolutely still while the man fired his M60 in perfect nine-round bursts was the hardest thing he had ever done. Staring in terror to his left, he watched the snout of the machine gun jolt up and down in rapid concussions as it fired into the tree line behind him, the noise hammering his eardrums mercilessly. The firing finally stopped when the gun jammed, but it was replaced by a high-pitched ringing in his ears. He buried his face in the dirt.

''Fall in,'' Gunther barked, hands on his hips.

With professional discipline the twelve-man hit squad jumped up from their firing positions around the camp's perimeter and ran to the center, assembling in two ranks before Gunther. Grey stood next to the neo-Nazi.

''Relax, men, you looked good tonight.'' Gunther smiled expansively at them and swept his hand before Grey. ''As a matter of fact, you did so well, you made our fearless leader shit his pants when you attacked.''

The assembly broke into laughter as Grey stood before them, grinning at the jibe. Gunther walked off to the side, and Grey moved to the front, his face growing serious. Everyone quieted down. Then Grey spoke.

''Half of you men are from my group, and, if you'll remember, it wasn't too long ago when none of you could tell me how to set in a Claymore mine. How to fire the M60 machine guns you used so well tonight. Sniping at five hundred meters with an M14, as well as house clearing with shotguns and .45s. You men make me very proud. The other half of you from up north, well, let me tell you that I have the utmost appreciation and respect for your help and talent. It was about time the Klan and Aryan Covenant linked up to fulfill our common goals. Our *destiny*.

''As you all know by now, my father and Mr. Taylor have brought our forces together for the same reason you have been honing your skills together out here at this base camp. It's all very simple, men. Tomorrow we will be the white patriots this country needs. Tomorrow we attack.''

The two ranks of men broke into cheers and loud, hooting rebel yells.

''I've got the actual LAWs you're going to use tomorrow on the way up here,'' Grey continued, raising his voice. ''Quinn and Dietrick are bringing them up from the Camp Merrill armory with a shitpot-full load of other weapons. They should be here in about another half hour. Meanwhile, go ahead and rack out until zero-three. That'll give you at least four hours of sleep tonight. At that time we'll conduct our final inspection and load up in the vans.''

Then Grey lowered his voice into an intense, determined growl. ''By 1430 hours tomorrow, there's gonna be a lot of nigger orphans in Atlanta.''

Christopher let himself breathe again when the M60 gunner left his position by the boulder and went back to the campfire. Then he had heard Grey talk with his men, and his suspicions were now confirmed.

Even though the cool mountain air kept the mercury below sixty degrees, sweat poured from Christopher's armpits. He'd already been gone from Jakes well over the hour he told him he'd be away. By now the patrol would be fidgety. At least Jakes and Keller would. Keller was probably mouthing off about how he had run out on them.

If not worse.

He listened as Grey droned on about his race war until finally the Klansman quieted, saying something inaudible. Then he heard the raid element whoop and holler, then break up and walk in a column toward his nest of boulders. Christopher ducked, trying to control his sphincter muscle. They walked on by, no more than five meters away from his position. They were so close he could hear them swapping jokes and insults, reminding him of how his own patrol acted after a successful training mission. As the last man trudged by, he heard him say something to his partner about a cabin down the ridgeline toward the airstrip, and then something or other about an arms room.

Airstrip? Arms room?

Cautiously, Christopher peered around the boulder and searched his front for Grey and his neo-Nazi buddy. He saw them walk into the cabin the LAW training rocket had hit earlier. No one else was in the area. He decided to follow the column.

He waited until the last man was just within ear-shot, and then boldly stood up and followed the sound of their footsteps. He was careful to stay in the shadows and out of the splashes of moonlight that turned the pine-needle-carpeted ground into a black and white mosaic. The hair on the back of his neck crawled as he wondered if anybody could see or hear him. Then he remembered how one of the RIs earlier in the course had told him to take maxi-mum advantage of noise in the woods when moving at night. If you heard a vehicle approaching or an aircraft flying overhead, take advantage of the noise and move out fast. Christopher supposed the same applied to a moving patrol—even an enemy patrol—and picked up his pace until he regained sight of the last man in the column.

Five minutes later they veered left toward the dirt road he'd found earlier that led back into the camp. Since leaving the camp, they had paralleled it the entire time. They stopped and formed a security pe-rimeter, and then crossed the road one by one. Christopher froze against a tree for an eternity of fifteen seconds, until he was sure no one had seen him. He waited until all of them but the last man were across, then made his way to the crossing point. The last man walked across, looking all around him, pulling rear security.

Christopher watched him disappear into the thickest part of the tree line across the dirt road. Any illumination from the moon above ended right there. It was the proverbial Black Hole of Calcutta in there.

Christopher looked at his watch. He'd been gone now for an hour and fifteen minutes. If he were to break off his recon now, it would take him only another ten minutes to make it back to the rest of his patrol at the contonement area. He would watch the area first to make sure everything was as before, sneak up behind the idiot guard, conk him over the head, get the keys, free everybody, and scram. But where to? Camp Merrill was the only safe place. Any civilian location was probably sympathetic to the Klan. Camp Merrill was still at least a day's hump away, probably two. The camp would be alerted within the hour of their escape, and then they'd be hunted down. They wouldn't have any weapons other than the guard's. They'd be wasted.

But if he followed the hit squad to their arms room, there *would* be weapons. Maybe they'd have a chance, then. Maybe . . .

Christopher took the risk and stole across the road, melted into the bushes on the far side. He heard voices. He stood up just enough to see, and cupped his hands next to his ears. He heard the voices again. They came from deep within the tree line. He crept toward them. As he tiptoed toward the sound, the trees thinned out. Moonlight broke through the canopy.

And then he saw the airstrip. It was a gash in the trees, much like a power line brush break, only not as wide. Christopher snuck up to the tree line. It was no more than fifty meters across and three hundred long; he was close to the end of it. He heard the voices again, and this time he jumped, hearing every word. He squatted behind a tree.

"Open the goddamned door, Hainey."

"Friggin' lock's rusty. Get off my ass."

Christopher swallowed as he turned around. He could barely make out a knot of men, clustered together about fifteen, maybe twenty feet to his left. He had almost walked right into them. They had congregated in the densest part of the woods at the far end of the airstrip. Christopher squinted his eyes so hard to see what they were doing that he could feel the beginning of another headache coming on. He barely made out the cabin they were trying to open. It was like the others he'd seen earlier at the camp—camouflaged netting pitched over the top and pulled taut, sloping to the ground rather than simply draped around the cabin walls. It broke up the cabin's silhouette well, and even Christopher could barely see it at night from only twenty feet away. He heard a metallic rasp.

"There," said the same voice as before. "It's open. Gimme your flashlight."

A glaring beam of light punched through the black, and Christopher shielded his eyes to protect his night vision. The beam danced around the tree line and then steadied into the cabin's entrance. Uncovering his eyes, Christopher saw the glint of metal inside.

It *was* an arms room.

For the next ten minutes Christopher watched them as they lighted up a Coleman lantern and cleaned their weapons. Then they brought out some wooden crates full of ammunition and reloaded their magazines. The machine gunners each set out three one-hundred-round bandoliers of 7.62 millimeter belt ammo by their weapons. A case of grenades was brought out. Each man got four apiece.

Christopher mentally counted each round. Two hundred ten rounds of M16 ammo for each man.

Five hundred rounds of M60 ammo for the two machine gunners. Four grenades per man. A grand total of 2500 rounds M16, 1000 rounds M60, and 48 grenades. And that didn't even include the LAWs.

"Wrap it up, guys."

Christopher slunk to the ground even lower as he heard the voice belonging to Hainey. Christopher supposed he was the honcho of the raiding element. He watched them as they gathered up their loose rounds and stuffed magazines into the ammo pouches of their web gear. Then they put their cleaning equipment and excess ammunition back into the cabin. Again Christopher saw the glint of metal inside. He knew there had to be more weapons.

That, he decided, was good information.

When they were finished, the man called Hainey turned off the Coleman lantern and put it back into the arms room. Then he locked the door and faced his men.

"Okay," he said, looking at his watch, "we've got another couple of hours to kill. Anyone have any more questions about the raid?"

"How much longer till we get the LAWs?" another voice said.

"You heard Grey. Anytime. Depends on how soon Quinn gets here."

Silence for a moment. Christopher broke out into another sweat. His uniform was drenched already.

"No more questions, then? Okay, like I said, we've got another couple of hours yet before we move out. We'll go back to the main camp. Wiley, you stay here and watch the arms room. Raynor's been here all night."

"All right," came a resigned reply.

Christopher's ears perked up. He hadn't figured on them leaving a guard. That would definitely create problems.

"Don't take it so hard, Wiley. We'll be back for you later after the LAWs get here. The rest of you all—let's go on back to the camp."

Christopher watched the raiding party fade into the tree line. One man remained behind, sitting down on a wooden chair next to the cabin. He lighted up a cigarette. The match flared into the night.

Dumbass, Christopher thought, automatically keying on the guard's lack of concern for light discipline. *I'll be back for you.* He quietly got up from his position and crept into the tree line until he was out of earshot.

He started walking back to the road. The trees grew dense again, and soon he couldn't even see his hand out in front of his face. Moments later he reached the road, pausing before crossing, looking to his left and to his right. On up to the right he could still hear the rest of the raiding party as they walked back toward the base camp.

Christopher waited until they were out of earshot. Then he ran across the road. He took a knee behind a large tree trunk and visualized where his position was. He decided to parallel the road for fifty meters, and then he would veer off to the left and go downslope for another thirty. By contouring the mountainside for another fifty to seventy-five meters, he would find Jakes and the rest.

Reoriented, Christopher got to his feet and followed the tree line next to the road, counting his pace and staying in the shadows as always. Fifty meters. He turned to the left to go downhill. What he saw turned his bowels into water.

Ten feet away, silhouetted in the moonlight, crouched another man, his knife drawn.

Christopher gulped and stared at him. His heart pounded, his breathing picked up. It was a standoff. He didn't have a knife. The Klan had taken his Ka-Bar when he had been captured. All he had was the Swiss Army knife Jakes had given him earlier. That was useless against the gleaming knife waving back and forth before him now. There was only one thing to do.

Christopher turned his side to the man and flexed his knees with his right foot out. His hands closed into fists, his arms bent at the elbows. He took a step forward.

The other man circled around Christopher, his knife out with the blade turned up. He lunged forward. The blade tore into Christopher's fatigue shirt and scratched his side. Another few inches to the left, and the knife would have ripped into his gut.

Catching him off balance, Christopher stepped in, grabbed the other man by the wrist with both hands, and cruelly wrenched it to the left, backward and down, flopping his opponent to the ground across his right leg. The man grunted in pain, and he released his grip on the knife. Pinning his knife hand to the ground, Christopher dug his knee into the other man's chest. He cocked his fist, ready to drive it deep into the man's throat.

Moonlight splashed across his features. Christopher pulled his fist in mid-strike.

"Levy?" he croaked.

The other man stared back. Then he nodded his head slowly and started shaking. His breathing picked up with disturbing rapidity. "Yeah," Levy gasped.

Christopher got up and pulled his Ranger buddy to his feet. Levy bent double, his chest heaving, his lungs billowing in and out.

Christopher dragged him to a tree and leaned him against the trunk. He pulled off his patrol cap and placed it over Levy's mouth, helping him get the carbon dioxide he needed.

"Take it easy, man. Don't breathe so fast. You're hyperventilating."

Levy gasped in and out spasmodically for several moments. Then he slowed down. Christopher looked at his eyes, which had glazed over. He didn't like what he saw. He realized that his friend must have been on the run ever since the night before. Levy's breathing finally steadied.

"You okay?" Christopher whispered, rubbing the back of Levy's neck.

"Y-yeah," Levy said, still shaken. Christopher could feel him shuddering like an overloaded washing machine. Something was wrong.

"Can you talk?"

"Yeah."

"Man, you're shaking like a leaf."

"No—no shit."

"You really look bad."

"So do you. Help me to my feet, you big son of a bitch."

Christopher grabbed Levy by the armpits and hauled him up. Levy's knees buckled, and Christopher lowered him gently back to the ground.

"Give me another minute," Levy whispered.

Christopher looked at him, still amazed that he and Levy had found each other, and thankful that they hadn't killed each other in the confusion of the dark. He picked up Levy's knife and put it back into its sheath. Then, bending over, Christopher grabbed Levy by the wrist and pulled him over on his back, picking him up in a shoulder carry.

"What are you doing?" Levy protested.

"Relax. We're getting out of here." Christopher shuffled downslope through the forest, knowing someone might have heard their scuffle. He didn't want either of them to be around in case that someone wanted to investigate, and Levy was in no condition for the time being to travel on his own.

Minutes later Christopher figured they were getting close to the contonement area. He slowed and hunted for the best place to turn off from the main ridgeline and contour the mountain. He put Levy down and leaned him up against a tree, sighing with relief. Levy had relaxed some, and his breathing was back to normal. He also wasn't shaking as much. Christopher sat next to him.

"So how are you feeling now?" he whispered.

"Better. Where is everybody?"

Christopher clamped his hand against Levy's mouth. "Keep it down," he whispered, withdrawing his hand slowly. "They're all handcuffed to trees about seventy-five meters from here. I got loose and was doing a recon of the AO when we found each other. We're busting out of here."

"Anybody hurt?"

"They—they hit us around some," Christopher replied, touching his broken nose. "They killed MacAlister . . . shortly after you opened up with the rounds I gave you last night."

Levy paused before answering and nodded his

head slowly. Then, "Prentiss was with me. After the rounds were gone, we *had* to scram."

"Where is Prentiss?"

Levy looked at Christopher for several long seconds.

"Man, it's a long story."

Levy told Christopher about how he and Prentiss had run from the Klan all night, catching only snatches of sleep in a cave they had found. How he had blown away the deputy with a list of their names, and the map and grid coordinates he'd found in the deputy's pocket identifying the base camp. He told him about how they had been caught hours later at Camp Merrill by Grey and Quinn. How Grey was behind a master plan to start a race war by instigating riots and assassinations in Atlanta, and how he had taken hostages from his own Ranger class to disperse the cadre of Camp Merrill on a false manhunt while he looted the arms room. And how he would use them as bargaining chips or decoys in case things went wrong.

Christopher shook his head in disgust. "Yeah, I kind of figured that's what the motherfucker was up to." He went on to tell Levy about Grey's and the neo-Nazi Gunther's plans when he had snuck up on them earlier in their base camp. Then he stopped, cocking an eyebrow at Levy. "How did you and Prentiss get away if you got caught?"

"Remember Quinn? The other night when MacAlister beat the shit out of both him and Grey?"

"Yeah. He's that redheaded asshole that flunked me on my knot test."

"He's an FBI agent, Keith."

"What?"

"He's got Grey faked out all the way. Grey told

him and another neo-Nazi to waste me and Prentiss right after we got caught at Camp Merrill. I gotta admit he played the part. Beat the hell out of me in front of Grey and then taped us both up with hundred-mile-an-hour tape and threw us in the back of a van. When they took us out in the woods, I thought we were goners for sure. Then he turned on the other guy, knocked him out, and taped him up to a tree. Talk about the pucker factor, man, it was way up.''

"So where is he now? What about Prentiss?''

"Prentiss is guarding the other guy a few miles away from here, back toward Camp Merrill. He was in no shape to come with me. Quinn's on his way to this place, if he's not here already.'' Levy stopped suddenly and grabbed Christopher by the arm. "Listen—on my way up here, this whole area was crawling with FBI. They're gonna raid the base camp at any time.''

"Then we're home free,'' Christopher said.

Levy's face clouded. "I don't think so.''

"Why not? What's to keep us from just busting out of here with the rest of the patrol and linking up with the FBI? Hell, why are *you* here, man? You should have stayed back where it was safe.''

"Keith, I don't think the FBI is too concerned about us.''

"What do you mean?''

"Call it a gut feeling more than anything else, but when I talked to Quinn, it seemed that we interrupted the FBI's overall game plan when we got captured. They're planning to raid this place, but they didn't know about us until the last minute, when Quinn found out about us early this morning.''

"So?''

"So this thing is *bigger* than we are. We're just not that fucking *important.* These radicals have a hit squad that's supposed to raid some black mayors' conference in Atlanta tomorrow. They may even have a network in Washington, D.C. Keith—we've gotta look out for ourselves, you know?"

Christopher felt his eyes mist over and clamped his arm around Levy's shoulders, squeezing him hard. He couldn't have had a better goddamned Ranger buddy in the world. "I heard Grey say something about that when I reconned the camp a while ago. I also watched their rehearsal and followed them to their arms room."

"So you know exactly where the camp's located?"

"Yeah," Christopher replied. "And their arms room. You wouldn't *believe* all the shit they've got."

"You see now why we just can't blindly haul ass? I mean, we've got to get out of here but . . . I don't think we can expect the FBI to be too picky about saving us. They might even think *we're* part of the Klan. We're gonna have to make it on our own."

"So we hit the arms room first, and load up for bear. I was planning to do that anyway. I wanna waste some of these motherfuckers if it comes down to it."

Levy didn't reply. Christopher looked at him closely.

"What's that all over your face?"

"Blood."

Christopher started. "Yours?" he said.

Levy stood up and pulled his knife out of his sheath, examining it as if he were looking at it for the first time. Christopher stood up slowly, staring at his Ranger buddy. He was uneasy at Levy's abrupt mood shift.

"No," Levy said, a tremor in his voice. "But I killed a couple of assholes tonight with this." He put the knife back in its sheath and took in a deep breath.

Christopher helped Levy to his feet. "C'mon, man. Let's go get the rest of the patrol."

Levy looked back at Christopher. Christopher saw that his friend had that glazed look in his eyes again.

"I just want to take a fucking bath and get some sleep," Levy told him, his voice breaking. "You know what I mean?"

CHAPTER
· TWENTY-FOUR ·

I shall defeat them on the field of battle, for I am
better trained and will fight with all my might.

"He's not coming."

Jakes twisted around and glared at Keller, wanting very badly to rip his handcuffs away from the tree and smash them into the other Ranger's mouth. For the past thirty minutes Keller had kept making comments about Christopher's absence. Up until the past quarter hour Jakes hadn't said anything, but now . . . well, Christopher should have been here by now.

"You don't see it, do you? Christopher said he'd be gone for an hour—"

"An hour and ten minutes," Jakes said.

"An hour and ten minutes, then. What difference does it make? Look at your watch. It's not broken. What does it say?"

Jakes said nothing.

"He's been gone for two hours. It's a quarter till midnight."

"So?"

"So he took off. Ran away. Left us hanging. Just like a—" Keller mumbled something that Jakes couldn't hear.

Jakes leaned toward Keller, peering at him through the darkness. Keller squirmed uncomfortably.

"What did you say?" he asked the cadet. "Go on. Tell me what you said."

"I said—I said, just like a nigger."

"Would you say that to Christopher's face, Keller? Just what's your definition of a nigger?"

"You know what a nigger is," the cadet retorted. "The way they walk. The way they talk. They're always jiving around, scratching their nuts and listening to that stupid jungle-bunny music."

"So Christopher walks and talks funny and scratches his nuts, huh?"

"Well, not—"

"I thought you said he was a nigger."

"He is!"

"Why? Because you know he despises you just like the rest of this patrol? Because you can't pull your own weight like the rest of us? Is that it?"

"Fuck you," Keller said. "I don't have to listen to this."

"You don't like him because you're afraid of him, Keller. You're afraid he's gonna make you do something you don't want to do. And do you know why? Because he's a leader and you're not. You're nothing but a complaining shitbird."

"Shut up!"

Jakes started and looked up the hill where their guard, Charley, leaned against his tree trunk, sleeping. Jakes could still hear him snoring. He turned back to Keller.

"Keep your voice down," he said.

"He's a nigger, and you're one of these liberal types who'll buddy up to any nigger you see, so you can justify your liberal views."

Jakes chuckled. "Now, wait a minute, buddy. Let's backtrack. Let me get this straight. *I'm* a liberal and I take it you're not?"

"That's right."

"You're the one that's in college, pretty-boy. Georgetown at that. And you have to be pretty rich if your kraut family is able to send you to Georgetown from Argentina to go to college. I'm nothing but a redneck from Missouri who dips Copenhagen and raises pigs. *I'm* a liberal?"

Keller said nothing.

"I think you actually believe the shit those guys up on the hill told us today, don't you?" Jakes didn't wait for an answer. "It's convenient, isn't it, Keller, to believe things like that?

"Oh, I know what a nigger is, Keller. I saw niggers at college the semester I had to drop out because I couldn't afford the tuition anymore, who drove around in Daddy's Porsche and joined Daddy's fraternity and partied all week on Daddy's money, and then flunked out. You fit that description, pretty-boy. As a matter of fact, I know as well as you do that niggers are shiftless, lazy people. You fit that description too. Ever since we've been together as a patrol, you were always the one that played spotlight leader whenever you were put in charge. But whenever one of us was patrol leader, you kicked back and did nothing but whine and complain."

"Fuck you," Keller repeated.

"You know something, Keller? You're nothing but a goddamned nigger."

Keller made a strangled sound in his throat, and spat at Jakes. "I'm *not* a nigger," he yelled. "You are, and so is Christopher!"

"Quiet!" Jakes hissed.

"Hey, what's going on?" A cracked voice, broken from sleep. Charley got up from his tree trunk and walked slowly toward the Rangers, rubbing his eyes. "What's going on?" he repeated, turning on a flashlight and holding his Mini-14 in his left hand. The beam of light found Jakes's face. He squinted at the glare and tried unsuccessfully to shield his eyes with his hands to keep from losing his night vision. Charley's footsteps thudded toward them. Everyone in the patrol was awake, and all eyes focused on Jakes. Jakes was relieved that if anyone had noticed Christopher's absence, they didn't say anything.

"That you talkin', boy?"

"No—I mean yes," Jakes replied.

Charley towered over Jakes. All Jakes could see of him were his knees, which he knew could easily smash into his face at any given moment, and there wasn't a damned thing he could do about it.

Charley held the grip and trigger housing of his Mini-14 with one hand and the flashlight with the other. He shoved the muzzle of the weapon under Jakes's chin, lifting it. Above Charley's shoulders was the beam of glaring light, and it blinded him. His peripheral vision was shot. Jakes felt the cold, metallic muzzle of the Mini-14 gouge into his throat. He swallowed, his Adam's apple nudging the muzzle. Jakes heard a click as Charley flicked his weapon off safety. A bead of sweat trickled down between the Ranger's shoulder blades.

"What you jabberin' about, boy?" Charley muttered slowly.

Jakes exhaled softly. "We were just talking, sir." *Why doesn't he see that Christopher's gone?* Jakes's eyes darted toward Keller, who had faded back against his own tree.

Charley jabbed the Mini-14 harder into Jakes's throat, rocking the Ranger's head back until it thumped against the tree. "Talkin' about what? Charley maybe? You all talkin' about me, boy?"

"Oh, no, sir, we weren't talking about you."

"Maybe you were talkin' about my . . . my, uh, friend who was killed," Charley stuttered, searching for the right words. "One of *you* guys . . . killed him last night."

Charley was on the verge of tears. It upset him to remember how Jerry had been blown away by the person in the tree line when they had taken the patrol the night before. He had tried to forget it all day, but Jerry was the only one who ever really paid attention to him . . . the only one who was his *friend.* Now he was alone. No one at the camp gave him anything important to do. They just told him to guard the patrol all day, while the others practiced for something *important.* Earlier, he had heard them practice without him. He had woken up, hearing the rockets and blank rounds firing, and then went back to sleep later feeling very sad. He didn't know exactly what all the firing was for, but it was for something *important.* If Jerry was around, he'd explain it all to him.

Now he was dead. Someone out of this patrol— one of their friends—had killed him.

His only friend.

"You . . . make me very mad," he said to the

Ranger, jabbing the Mini-14 harder into Jakes's throat. "Your friends make me very, *very* mad."

Jakes winced from the pain and coughed.

"Does that hurt?" Charley said, jabbing him again.

"Of course it does, you idiot," Jakes snarled, pissed off. Then he shrank back, terrified. *Oh, God, I'm the idiot!*

"Idiot? Idiot? You called me an idiot!"

Christ Jesus!

Charley slammed his foot into Jakes's side. Jakes smacked against the tree and slumped over on his hurt side, grunting from the pain. He was sure he had a cracked rib. Charley kicked him again, this time sinking his foot deep into the Ranger's gut. Spittle flew from the Ranger's mouth, and he vomited on the ground.

Charley stepped back, shining his flashlight on Jakes, watching him throw up. Something wasn't right. He didn't know what, but something just wasn't right. He was all mixed up in the dark, and that made things worse. He shined the light on the man next to Jakes, who sat very still against the next tree.

"You!"

Keller winced as his eyes caught the full glare of the light. He stared back in horror, his lips trembling.

"What were you talking about!"

"Nothing, sir. Nothing!"

Charley knew that something was wrong. He decided that he had better count heads. After all, he had been asleep. He felt bad—very, *very* bad. He ran from Ranger to Ranger, counting them. In his excitement he lost count, so he ran back to Jakes and started over. By the time he was finished, he had counted only nine people.

He was supposed to have ten. He *knew* how to count to ten. He wasn't *that* damned stupid.

Charley ran back to Jakes, who had managed to sit back up against the tree trunk. Puke covered the front of his shirt. Tears streamed from his eyes from throwing up, and bloody mucus poured from his nostrils. Bits of pine needles and dirt stuck to the sticky mess. Charley stuck the muzzle of his Mini-14 in the hollow beneath the Ranger's Adam's apple. Jakes tensed, ready for more abuse. Defiant, he raised his head and glared at his tormentor.

"*One man's gone!*"

"No shit, Sherlock."

Enraged, Charley slapped his flashlight across Jakes's face. Jakes's head spun, blood spurting from his mouth. He ran his tongue across the bloody craters two of his molars once occupied. He looked back up at Charley, seeing two of him.

"Tell me where he is! Tell me where he is!"

"I know where he is," another voice said.

Charley wheeled around just in time to see Christopher's gnarled black fist smash into his mouth. He sank to his knees like a shot bull moose. The last thing he felt was the stock of Levy's twelve-gauge slamming into the back of his skull.

"Son of a *bitch!*" Christopher grunted, standing over Charley. "I think I broke my fucking hand!"

"Quit worrying about your hand and get his keys," Levy ordered. "I'll cover you." Levy ran uphill where Charley had pulled guard and selected a good field of fire in case the neo-Nazis and Klansmen in the base camp had heard them.

"You guys don't know how glad I am to see you,"

Jakes moaned, spitting out more blood. "Hurry up with the keys."

As Christopher searched Charley's pockets for the handcuff keys, the other Rangers mumbled excitedly, just now realizing that Christopher had come back with—amazingly enough—Levy. And with weapons at that.

"Everybody shut up!" Christopher ordered. "Keep it down."

Silence again filled the night. The only sound was the jangle of keys as Christopher pulled out a key ring from Charley's front pocket. He freed Jakes and gave him the keys to set the others loose. Then he bent over Charley and pried open his eyelids. All he could see were the whites. Satisfied, Christopher pulled off the big man's web gear and set it down next to the Mini-14. Then he dragged him fifty feet downhill until he found a cut in the ridgeline filled with bushes. He threw him into the small ravine and then rejoined the others.

All eleven of them clustered together in a small perimeter, each man facing out. Jakes and Levy squatted in the center. Reaching them, Christopher flashed Levy a thumbs-up and buckled on Charley's web gear. Grabbing the Mini-14, he checked the magazine for ammunition and then put it on safe, not wanting to give away their position with an accidental discharge.

Levy motioned for the others to stand up, and Christopher led them in a staggered column downhill in the same direction he had taken before. Jakes joined Christopher at the head of the file while Levy brought up the rear. After a minute's walk through the pitch-black forest, Jakes felt a hand grab him by the shoulder and someone whispered—"Nine"—in his ear. It was the head count. Jakes trotted up to Christopher and clapped his hand on his shoulder.

"Ten," Jakes whispered to Christopher as they shuffled through the dark, dodging wait-a-minute vines. "You make eleven, so we're all accounted for. Now, what gives? Where'd Levy come from?"

"Long story, man," Christopher muttered. "Wait till we get to the ORP, and I'll tell you."

"Objective rallying point?" Jakes asked, slowing down. "Why are we setting up an ORP? Man, we gotta get the fuck outta here."

Christopher reached back and grabbed Jakes by the collar. "Keep moving," he said, pulling Jakes up with him. "We ain't got much time. We're gonna take their arms room."

Fifteen minutes later they had retraced Christopher's earlier route and were now assembled in a security perimeter twenty meters away from the dirt road where Levy and Christopher had nearly killed each other. Across the dirt road and down the opposite side of the ridgeline was the arms room he'd discovered. It was no more than a hundred meters away. They were that close.

Levy knelt in the middle of the security perimeter with Christopher and Jakes. They had decided since Christopher knew the area best, he would be the patrol leader, and Levy the assistant patrol leader. Jakes was the assault team leader. It took them five minutes to hash out a tenable plan.

"So we move on across the road one by one with flank security and reconsolidate in another Ranger file?" Jakes asked.

Christopher nodded. "Yeah, then we move to within twenty meters of the arms room. We get any closer than that, and the guard will hear us. Make sure everybody's quiet."

"I'll move up front with Christopher at that time," Levy said, looking at Jakes. "Jakes, you hold the fort down with the rest of the patrol. And keep that loudmouth Keller shut up. Me and Christopher will take out the guard. I'll come back and get you. You bring up the patrol, and we'll get what we can out of the arms room."

"Quietly," Christopher added. "Very quiet. I want as much ground as possible between us and those rednecks before they find out we took their guns."

"Who are you callin' a redneck?" Jakes grumbled.

"You, fuckhead," Christopher replied, grinning.

"Watch out for the FBI," Levy solemnly added. "They're crawling all around this place."

"Prentiss would shit his pants," Jakes said, grinning through his puffed-up lips. "I think I already have. Wait a minute—where *is* Prentiss?"

"Oh, he's in a safe place," Levy replied. "C'mon, let's get moving."

Prentiss yelled through clenched teeth as another vine raked its thorns across his face, ripping open his cheek. He had been running blindly for the past fifteen minutes down the ridgeline without any earthly idea of where he was going. Every so often he would stop and listen, only to hear the sound of crashing bushes and breaking limbs from up above, and that meant that Dietrick was still chasing him.

Limping heavily, Prentiss wondered how much blood he had lost. He knew he had been shot in the hip by Dietrick's last burst from the M16, but he didn't know how bad. Whenever he put his hand down on the wound, he still felt the blood oozing. It wasn't bleeding profusely, but it bled nevertheless.

And after all he'd been through, things were definitely not looking good.

Prentiss ran harder, tripping and stumbling over roots, rocks, and more vines. Then he saw that the trees were thinning out, and the slope downhill was not as steep as before. He was finally getting close to the bottom. He prayed to see a road. Maybe there would be a house nearby or a passing car. Anything.

The trees parted, and Prentiss saw the yellow-orange glow of the setting moon as it sunk toward the horizon. Below that, a cow pasture stretched out at the bottom of the valley, no more than another fifty meters away. Prentiss raced downhill toward the pasture.

He got close. The trees parted again, and—there it was. A dirt road. He would run down the road paralleling the tree line and then flag down the first vehicle he saw.

Right.

He wouldn't have a chance. He'd still get blown away, running down the road in the open like a damned fool.

Panicking, he slipped into a cut in the ridgeline that led straight down to the road. It was littered with small boulders and gravel. Slipping to the bottom of the ravine, he tripped on one of the rocks and twisted his ankle. Prentiss yelled out in pain, and then clamped his hand over his mouth, realizing he had just given his position away. He listened. Nothing.

He scrambled to his feet, limping on the other leg

now. Then he heard something. He stopped again, looking back over his shoulder at the mountain.

"I heard that!" Strange, giggling laughter followed. Dietrick couldn't have been more than thirty meters away. He was stalking him as he would a gut-shot deer. Wincing, Prentiss limped toward the road. The ground got steeper. He plunged toward a stand of thickly clumped oak and pine trees next to the roadside. Unable to stop himself, he ran headlong into them, slipping on the pine needles underfoot. Shadows loomed in front of his face.

And then tree bark bit into his forehead with the force of a baseball bat as a limb caught his head and knocked him to the ground.

Prentiss squirmed on the ground, lights flashing behind his eyes. He was dizzy. He wanted to stop. To lie still. To sleep it all off. Forget about the whole mess and just *die*.

Get up, a voice deep inside told him. *Quit feeling sorry for yourself and get the fuck up!*

Prentiss crawled to his feet, pulling on the tree trunk with bloody, torn hands, and grabbed at his web gear, searching for his knife. Then he remembered he had lost that a long time ago.

He spotted a rock on the ground twice as large as his fist, and he bent over, snatching it. When he straightened back up, he banged his head on the same tree limb that had sent him sprawling moments earlier. He lost his composure and swore breathlessly, mere whispers piercing through his dehydrated, cracked lips.

You stupid son of a bitch. You ignorant—
Wait . . .

Prentiss held the rock in one hand and grabbed the tree limb with the other. Then he pulled himself up on the tree limb and climbed up to a fork in the tree eight feet off the ground.

The noise from the breaking brush grew louder. Looking back from where he'd come, Prentiss saw a rifle-carrying silhouette rushing down the ravine. Dietrick would be on him any minute now.

Prentiss prayed and held on to his rock, readying himself.

Dietrick spotted the road and whooped. He ran downhill and then slipped on the pine needles as Prentiss had done. He lost control for a moment and then was back on his feet, running faster. He got close to the road. To the tree. To Prentiss.

He hit the same tree limb, and it knocked him flat.

Prentiss leapt on the neo-Nazi. The rock flew from his hands. Desperate, he struck at Dietrick, glancing wild blows on his face. Dietrick hit him back with the butt of the M16, and kicked Prentiss away.

They both jumped to their feet. With a triumphant yell Dietrick raised his weapon at the same time Prentiss ran screaming toward him and kicked him in the balls.

The M16 belched out fire and noise, drowning out the neo-Nazi's wide-eyed shriek as he sprayed the air and the trees with a full twenty-round burst. Prentiss held the muzzle of the gun away from him, feeling the barrel burn a groove into the palm of his hand, searing it with pain.

Yelling in terror, Prentiss rammed his knee into Dietrick's gut and ripped the M16 away from him. Dietrick doubled over, cupping his testicles with both hands. Prentiss stepped back and punt-kicked him in the face. The neo-Nazi flopped down, writhing on the ground.

Prentiss straddled Dietrick and pushed the M16

down against his throat, trying to crush it. He didn't hear the sound of a gunning four-wheeler approach him from the road and crash into the tree line. A spotlight penetrated the dark with glaring intrusion and landed on Prentiss. A megaphone squealed, a voice following it.

"Freeze!"

Prentiss froze, his eyes huge, his heart hammering his brain apart.

"Stay right where you are," the megaphone squawked, *"and don't make a move. Keep your hands above your head."*

Prentiss swallowed and looked down at Dietrick. He was out. Blood leaked from his nostrils and ears. Prentiss breathed a little easier. He heard the tread of footsteps as they approached him. A rifle muzzle prodded him in the back.

"Get up."

Prentiss stood up, favoring his sprained ankle, and limped away from Dietrick. His tongue felt thick and numb, and he grew faint. Forceful hands yanked his wrists behind his back and handcuffed them together. He was spun around and immediately blinded by a huge spotlight beaming from a vehicle that had come out of nowhere. Then he was shoved down the rest of the slope to the road. He walked quickly, too numb and confused to speak. Two men followed him. Two more had remained behind to take care of Dietrick.

One man held him by the neck, steering him toward a Chevy Blazer that had been repainted in a camouflage pattern. Prentiss felt flushed. Hot. His eyes watered. Then his knees buckled, and he went totally numb. He passed out.

A voice cut through the night.

"Sporillo! Turn the damned light off!"

The driver of the camouflaged Blazer flipped a switch to turn off the spotlight that had blinded Prentiss. The man who had spoken bent over the prostrate Ranger and picked him up over his shoulder in a fireman's carry. He carried him in a half trot to the Blazer and tossed him unceremoniously into the back. The two men behind him threw Dietrick in the rear next to Prentiss, then ran around to the front of the vehicle and unslung their M16s and took a knee, pulling security.

The man who had carried Prentiss pulled a small penlight out of his breast pocket and shined it on the Ranger's face. Then he turned it off and searched Prentiss's back pocket, finding his Ranger handbook with his military ID taped in the back. After confirming Prentiss's identification, he closed the back door of the Blazer and ran to the front, where he hopped into the passenger's seat.

"Move out, pronto!"

The driver shifted the Blazer into reverse and exited the tree line. When he reached the shoulder of the road, he faced the four-wheeler in the southbound direction, and the other two men pulling security out front climbed in the rear, keeping an eye on Prentiss and Dietrick. The Blazer took off into the darkness without its headlights.

After they had gone a mile, the driver veered off the road next to a stream crossing, and parked within the trees that lined the bank. A radio screwed underneath the glove compartment broke squelch and filled the cab with static. The man sitting in the passenger's seat grabbed the mike.

"Falcon-One, this is Falcon-Sweep. Be advised we have two, repeat, two rabbits in our possession who entered our sector. One of them is from the hostage group, over.''

''Roger, Falcon-Sweep,'' came a hesitant reply. ''Stand by for Falcon-Scratch.''

The two men exchanged glances. They had just been told to stand by for raid initiation. It wasn't the answer they had expected.

''What about the two rabbits?''

''Intel's on the way to debrief you at your location. Repeat, stand by for Falcon-Scratch.''

''Roger. Out.''

The driver looked at the man in the passenger's seat.

''What's up, Lieutenant? Why don't we take 'em to the rear now?''

''Don't ask so many questions, Sporillo.''

''I heard a rumor about hostages.'' Sporillo looked in the back, where the other two men guarded Prentiss and Dietrick. ''What gives, Lieutenant?''

Before the lieutenant could reply, a black '79 Chevy van lumbered down the road to their front. In reflex, both men hunkered down in their seats as it passed by, even though they were well camouflaged from view. Then the lieutenant sat back up and sighed.

''That was Quinn,'' he said. ''Party time's gonna start real quick.''

CHAPTER

· TWENTY-FIVE ·

Surrender is not a Ranger word.

Quinn shifted into second and ground his gears up the last steep ridgeline leading into the base camp. He'd be there in another ten minutes.

It had been a long, bumpy ride, a ride that had given him time to think about the events to come—and reflections of memories long past but not forgiven. He didn't enjoy thinking about how he would have to shoot Grey if he had to.

Quinn dropped his right hand from the steering wheel so he could scratch under his left armpit where the wire was taped—the wire that led to the battery box and microcassette taped beneath his solar plexus and the small, wafer-thin mike threaded through his collar.

He hated being wired. Once, during a drug raid in Atlanta, he had almost blown his cover when he had sweated so much that the transmitter assembly shorted out and burned his chest prior to the roundup. It had been all he could do to keep his mind in control while he excused himself so he could go to the bathroom and rip it off. Fortunately, the backup team actuated the bust before the dealer discovered what was going on.

This time would be trickier, and he didn't want another repeat of the earlier fiasco with the wires and batteries. The plan he had worked out with his higher headquarters was a simple one: Go in the camp, wait for the most opportune tactical moment when things were the most disorganized, and then squeeze the transmitter button he kept in his front trousers pocket to actuate the raid.

The road grew less steep. He was at the top of the ridgeline, almost at the base camp. Moments later he saw the sparkle of a lantern and a campfire.

Quinn's heartbeat picked up until it was thumping hard in his chest. He remembered it was always this way before a bust of any kind—the adrenaline flow. His ulcer acted up again, churning acid in his gut. He reached deep into his pocket and pulled out the last Rolaids he had left and ate it.

He drove the van the last twenty meters to the barbed wire gate that was the only opening into the compound. It struck him odd that no one had stepped out into the road to inspect him when he got out of the van to open the gate before driving it across the cattle guard. He realized, gratefully, that the security post personnel must be asleep. Now he had a legitimate alibi for Dietrick's absence. Quinn got back into the van after closing the gate and drove into the compound.

He saw two lanterns, each one hanging on a cabin door. In between the cabins was a large fire with a half-dozen men standing around it, all cradling submachine guns in their arms. Grey was there. So was

Gunther. They watched him drive up. As Quinn drove the van the last few feet toward the fire, he saw one man, a blond-haired kid no more than twenty, break away from the group and walk down the ridgeline behind the cabins. Quinn supposed he was part of the night security element. He wondered if he was going to where the Rangers were being held. He'd have to identify where they were before calling in the raiding party. Maybe he could draw out the location from Grey as he talked to him.

Quinn pulled the van over by the fire and shut off the engine. Every man's eye was on him, and each one of them held his weapon at the ready. Grey was the only one smiling. He walked over as Quinn got out of the van.

"Good to see you, Larry!"

"Hey, Frank!" Quinn said. Grey came over and clapped him around the shoulders, squeezing him. Then he looked around.

"Where's Dietrick?"

A lone figure turned on his flashlight as he walked downhill through the brush and trees toward the contonement area. Jeb Hennessey mumbled to himself and swore as he punched through the inky darkness and tripped on the wait-a-minute vines, disoriented as he looked for the trail.

Jeb didn't like being put on the shit detail with the retard. It made him mad to think about it. After all, he reasoned, he didn't join his daddy's friend Grey's organization as a sniper just to be pulling a shit detail like this. He decided that he was being singled out since he was the youngest.

Jeb thought about how Grey had told him to go down and check up on Charley, who was guarding the pissants they had taken the night before. He was supposed to relieve Charley for the rest of the night, since he had been down there all day. Jeb knew someone had to do it, but why didn't they just leave the retard down there? All it was, was baby-sitting. There wasn't any way those Rangers could get loose, since they were handcuffed to trees.

He found the trail and walked downhill a little easier. He kept walking. Two minutes later he became uneasy, because he knew he had gone too far. Somehow, he had taken the wrong trail. He hadn't found Charley yet. Or the Rangers. Surely he would have found them by now. Snorting in disgust, he backtracked, climbing back uphill.

He ran his long, slender fingers through his blond hair, shooting the beam of his flashlight in several different directions. He must have taken the wrong turn. He thought about how the retard would probably get pissed and chew him out so he could feel important. He decided to go all the way back up to the camp—but not close enough to where the others could see him—and get a fresh start.

Then he heard a noise. The flesh on the back of Jeb's neck crawled. It sounded weird to him, like a baby crying, or a wounded deer. He aimed his flashlight at the sound but couldn't see anything. He quickened his pace, more than a little nervous.

Then he heard it again. It was a whimper, that much he could tell. Jeb turned toward the sound, swallowing.

"Who is it?" he whispered.

Jeb unlimbered the M14 sniper rifle he had slung around his shoulder and held it at the ready with one hand, aiming the flickering yellow beam of his flashlight toward the sound with the other. He took a step forward and walked downhill toward the sound, this time off the trail. Suddenly, he slipped on a pile of loose rocks and fell down on his hip, dropping both his flashlight and weapon. Shaken, he fumbled and clawed at the ground for his flashlight, found it, and peered into the small ravine he had almost fallen into.

He heard a groan no more than five feet to his front and down some. Jeb aimed his flashlight at the bushes hiding a false bottom to the ravine. Someone—or something—was in those bushes. He scraped toward the bushes on his rear end, knocking loose dirt and gravel that cascaded over his ankles and down into the ravine.

"Who—who is it?"

A bloody hand reached out of the bushes and grabbed him by the ankle.

Jeb Hennessey screamed.

"What kind of horseshit is this?" a voice whispered on the edge of the clearing between the tiny airstrip and the cabin. The sound came from a bush.

"Listen," another whisper replied from an adjacent bush. "I think I heard something."

"Bullshit. We're on another dry run, right?" the first voice said. The man shifted on his side to get at the canteen fastened on the left shoulder strap of his web gear. The movement betrayed the expert camouflage of what appeared to be a tiny clump of a bush no higher than the surrounding scrub at the edge of the clearing.

The other man reached out with his burlap-covered arm and gripped his partner's arm in a powerful squeeze.

"Stay underneath your Ghillie suit and keep still.

This ain't no dry run, Clement." He referred to their camouflaged suits made of burlap interlaced with fishnet and strips of tan and forest-green cloth. Sprigs of weeds and tiny pine boughs fleshed out the rest of the coverall suits designed to break up their patterns with the surrounding terrain. Every good FBI sniper made his own and practically lived in it whenever he was on a training mission. If made right, one could literally stumble over the sniper and mistake him for just another bush or vegetated log, and continue on.

The first man, Clement, gently replaced his canteen and resumed a good firing position with his weapon, a Marine Corps version of the Winchester Model 700. They were both equipped with the homely bolt-action rifle modified for sniping. An extra-heavy barrel embedded in the fiberglass stock and an AN/PVS-4 night vision sight mounted over the barrel enabled the snipers to pick off targets at night from distances of 500 meters with ease.

"Soltz," Clement whispered to his partner.

"What?"

"How much longer are we gonna watch that cabin?"

"Until we're told to move out."

"We've been here twenty-four hours already."

"And we'll stay here until—" Soltz broke off in mid-sentence and gripped his partner's arm again.

"Wha—?"

"*Shh!*"

One by one they crossed the road and formed back up into a security perimeter on the opposite side, ten meters inside the tree line. Once Levy, the last man, was across, they all picked up and followed

Christopher as he led them to the arms room. Fifty meters and ten high-crawling minutes later, every many in the Ranger patrol froze in place as Christopher stopped with his fist held up in the air. He then waved his hand down and moved it from side to side. Everybody behind him dispersed into a hasty perimeter, facing outward. On cue Levy walked up from the rear, meeting Christopher and Jakes in the center. The three of them bunched into a knot, and each took a knee, facing outward.

Jakes glanced back and forth between Christopher and Levy and exhaled softly. "How much farther?" he said in the quietest of whispers.

"We're almost on him now," Christopher replied. "I'm surprised he didn't hear us coming up."

"At the arms room?" Levy asked.

"Yeah. It's about fifty meters in front of us."

"Well, let's get on with it." Levy pulled out his Ka-Bar.

Christopher looked at his friend with concern, seeing that glaze in his eyes again. "Right." He focused his attention back on Jakes. "Me and Levy will move up front. You take the rest of the patrol and put them on line behind us in an overwatch facing the objective. Make damned sure they've got some decent cover." Christopher unslung the Mini-14 he had taken from Charley and gave it to country boy. "You keep us in sight the whole time." The other Ranger nodded. "And keep the Mini-14 trained on the guard. You'll see him when you move up front." Christopher looked up at the stars and the disappearing moonlight streaking through the forest canopy above them. Jakes followed his eyes. "Illumination's going," Christopher continued, looking back down. "But I think you can still see the guard easily enough. Their arms room is at the edge of an airstrip fifty meters to our right. He looks like he's sleeping. Me and Levy will sneak up on him and take him out. If he sees us first, you shoot him."

"What? They'll hear us!" Christopher didn't answer. Then Jakes understood. They either got the weapons they needed, or they didn't. "Okay," he said. "But don't let him hear you, for Christ's sake."

Levy grabbed Jakes by the shoulder and leaned into his face. "He won't hear a goddamned thing," he said.

Soltz lowered his M40 and turned toward Clement. "I counted eleven of them thirty meters to our right rear," he whispered, barely audibly. "Two broke off and moved farther to the right, following the tree line. The others are headed this way."

"Klan?"

"I don't think so. Remember that rumor?"

"Hostages?"

"Maybe. If so, then they've escaped somehow. Keep cool, here they come."

The two FBI snipers in the Ghillie suits became bushes again.

"Where's Dietrick?" Grey repeated to Quinn, this time frowning.

Quinn noticed how Gunther perked his ears up at mention of Dietrick. The neo-Nazi left the fire and walked toward them.

"Yeah, where's Dietrick?" he said.

"I let him out back at the gate," Quinn heard himself say, concentrating solely on lying with a poker face. He shoved his left hand in his pocket and knotted it into a fist, keeping his right hand free in case the worst happened. "He wanted to check out the perimeter. The gate guards were sleeping when we passed through." Quinn forced himself to chuckle. It came out as a high-pitched giggle. "He got a case of the ass and decided to check out the rest of the perimeter."

Gunther tilted his chin and gave Quinn a cold look. "Hood Dietrick's good at kicking ass," he said.

"Did you take care of them?" Grey broke in, also studying Quinn's face. "The two students?" he added.

"It was clean, real clean," Quinn replied, hoping he sounded convincing enough. "Hardly any mess at all. He took 'em both out with that little icepick he carries around in his boot. Drove it right through their ear canals. Real professional."

Quinn saw Gunther relax a little and knew he had him convinced. He was glad he had gotten Dietrick to boast about his little technique earlier.

"Good," Grey said, his relief obvious. "Have any problems hiding them?"

"Naw. We found a cave downslope from where we stopped and hid them in it. A bear will find them before any search party does." Quinn wrapped his arms around his sides and shivered in the mountain air. "Let's move over by the fire. It's kind of chilly."

Grey walked back to the rear of the van. "Hold on," he said. "Let's check out the goodies. C'mere, Gunther, and see what my buddy brought in."

Quinn thought about what would happen if Grey or Gunther discovered that the firing pins were filed down, rendering the guns useless. He stuck his right hand into his pocket and closed it around the mike as Grey grabbed the latch to the van's rear door.

"Grey!" a voice cried out from the distance. "Frank! Frank Grey!" Quinn spun around to the direction of a frantic voice shouting from behind the cabins. Grey and Gunther walked back to the fire to see who it was. The others shifted uneasily around the fire as they saw a man running toward them from the tree line.

"Jeb Hennessey," Quinn heard Grey say. "I sent him down to relieve Charley ten minutes ago."

Quinn saw a young man run up to Grey, recognizing him as the one he had seen earlier walking into the woods when he drove into camp.

The tow-headed kid tripped over a log as he ran up to Grey and plunged headlong toward the fire. Gunther grabbed him by the shoulders and held him steady.

"What's gotten into you, Hennessey?" Grey said, walking up to him. "What's the matter?"

"It's . . . it's Charley," he gasped, doubling over, trying to catch his breath.

Grey paled. He jerked the young man upright. "What about Charley?"

"Frank . . . he's been beat up bad. And those Rangers are *gone.*"

Clement's eyes bulged out of their sockets as he watched the jungle boot set itself down inches away from his nose. He hardly breathed, wondering how much longer it would be before one of the Rangers would trip over him or Soltz. He swallowed and looked at Soltz four feet away. The Ranger stood between them, pausing as he followed the rest of his patrol toward the cabin. When he finally moved away, both snipers softly exhaled sighs of relief. It was the ninth man, which meant that they were all across.

Seconds later Clement watched one of the Rangers move the patrol into a firing line thirty meters away from the cabin to their front and some to the right, barely out of his line of sight with the cabin and the guard asleep by the door. They were so close, Clement thought he could have picked up a pine cone and hit one of them on the head with an easy toss. He noiselessly resumed his firing position.

Soltz looked at Clement and nodded solemnly. He mouthed a single word.

Hostages.

Jakes held the butt plate of the Mini-14 in the hollow of his chest and lined up the muzzle on the guard's silhouette to his front as he would a pool cue. It was an odd technique, one not easily mastered. Jakes remembered how his squad leader back in the Ranger Battalion at Fort Stewart had spent the better part of the night and the early morning hours out on the rifle range with the rest of his squad, demonstrating how one could fire a twenty-round shot group the size of a grapefruit into a man's chest at twenty-five meters by using the technique. Jakes had been the only man in the squad to do it. The Ranger thought hard about shooting the guard dozing in the old cane chair in front of the arms room door. He had never killed a man before. The soft, glowing moonlight above provided just enough illumination for him to see his target, and he knew he could do it, but he hoped he didn't have to shoot.

The night was quiet. He heard only the hiss of air flowing in and out of his nostrils as he aimed the

Mini-14 at the guard. Every now and then Jakes shifted his eyes to the left and the right, checking on the rest of his patrol. After Levy and Christopher had moved out earlier, he, Keller, and the rest of them had crawled on their hands and knees to their present positions. Luckily, there were no hardwoods in the area, only ancient pines, which had provided them noiseless movement across the pine-needle-carpeted ground.

A twig snapped.

Darting his eyes toward the sound, Jakes saw a silhouette freeze in place fifteen meters to the right rear of the arms room. Jakes let his mouth open as his lungs demanded more oxygen from the adrenaline coursing through his circulatory system. He shifted his eyes back to the guard, who hadn't stirred. Jakes remembered how he always felt before pulling the trigger on the deer he had hunted growing up, how his breathing picked up, his heart hammering away, how the whole universe focused into a pinpoint where he trained his gunsight. Buck fever. He had it now.

One minute later the silhouette moved again, this time picking his feet up high and carefully setting them back down, toes first.

It was Levy. Jakes could see the knife in his hand. Another shadow emerged from a bush behind him. Christopher. They had picked a good route. They were approaching the cabin from the two o'clock position from Jakes's position at six o'clock. Should the guard wake up, Levy and Christopher would be out of his line of sight in case he had to shoot.

Jakes gripped the forward stock of the Mini-14 tighter with his hand and nestled the butt plate firmly in the center of his chest. Concentrating on breathing deeply and evenly, he then refocused the muzzle back on the guard.

Just like a pool cue, he thought.

Levy crept to the side of the arms room and pressed against the rough-hewn logs, feeling a splinter gouge his cheek. Christopher followed him in one fluid, quiet movement. Around the corner was the guard. He hoped it would be quiet.

Levy exchanged glances with Christopher. The black Ranger nodded, indicating he was ready. He held Levy's shotgun at buttstroke arms, intending to use it as a club rather than a buckshot launcher. His finger caressed the trigger-housing group nevertheless.

Levy turned back around. Suddenly, his bowels clutched, and he felt every muscle in his back quiver. He stood as still as he could, trying to gut it out. He trembled all over, and his cheeks and the back of his neck flushed as if he had a heat flash induced from a severe bout of flu.

Levy bowed his head and breathed deeply, trying to pull himself together. He felt a hand touch him on the shoulder. He turned his head and looked at Christopher, who motioned for him to hand over the knife. Levy shrank back and shook his head furiously. He swallowed and mopped the sweat away from his forehead with the back of his knife hand, then took another deep breath. He calmed down.

Then he took another step toward the corner of the cabin.

Arthur Wiley, a portly, balding, thirty-four-year-old father of three little girls who thought their daddy was crazy to go rompin' in the woods this weekend, jerked his head up suddenly, realizing he had dozed off again. He set the legs of his chair back down with a soft thud against the ground, swearing not to lean back against the cabin door and go to sleep again. He didn't know how in the hell he had let his boss at the tire factory persuade him that he needed "special training" every other weekend to learn how to kill niggers.

He needed to do something to stay awake. Like practicing his aim. He glanced around for an object to hit, and spotted a piece of quartz rock glowing in the night right next to the corner of the cabin four feet to his left. Leaning back in his chair and keeping a firm grip on the twelve-gauge in his lap, he worked the cud of Red Man in his mouth until he had the desired amount.

When he spit, he didn't hit the rock. He hit the toe of Levy's jungle boot. Wiley leaned forward, squinting, trying to understand what it was. Then, when Levy's boot moved, he understood.

Shouldering the shotgun, he leapt out of his seat. Levy jumped out from around the corner of the cabin just in time to see the immense bore of the guard's twelve-gauge staring him in the face.

"Let him go, Frank," Gunther said to Grey, who was still shaking a very frightened Jeb Hennessey. "The damage is done."

"Goddammit, they're gone!"

"And we're going to find them."

Grey released the kid. "Go find the assault element," he told him bitterly. "They went to the arms room thirty minutes ago."

Hennessey tripped over his own feet trying to get away from Grey, and dropped his weapon into the nearby campfire, sending a shower of embers and sparks into the air and on the men standing around it. A volley of curses and obscenities followed as it was kicked out of the fire.

"I'm sorry! I—"

"Goddamn your hide, Hennessey," Grey bellowed, "move your ass! And put your weapon on safe before you kill somebody!"

Quinn edged toward the van, realizing that things were rapidly getting out of control. Grey was close to the snapping point. If things got too bad, he'd need more firepower than the .45 holstered on his hip. Like the M16 he'd left by the front seat of the van.

It was time to initiate the attack. He shuffled closer to the passenger door of the van.

Gunther caught Quinn's movement out of the corner of his eye.

"Where are you going?"

"I left something in the van," Quinn replied, his stomach turning into acid.

Jeb Hennessey had hastily picked up his weapon and was fumbling with the safety.

"I said, move it, Hennessey!" Grey screamed. "You find Lucas Hainey and bring him here with the rest of the assault element. We're going on a search."

Hennessey scrambled for the trail leading toward the arms room, and then halted as a group of ten men emerged from the tree line.

"What's the problem?" one of them said. "You callin' for me, Frank?"

Grey looked at a tall, lanky man with a beaked nose and prominent chin walking toward him from the boulders.

"Yeah, I'm calling for you. Where the fuck have *you* been?"

"We just came back from the arms room. What's eating your ass?"

Grey straightened up and inhaled deeply, trying to calm down. Hennessey stood by the boulders, looking helplessly back and forth between the two, not knowing what to do.

"Okay, Jeb," Grey said to him not unkindly, "come on back to the fire. Everybody. C'mon in close. We've got problems."

Hainey brought in the remainder of his assault force, and they clustered in a knot by the fire. Grey stood near the center, where everyone else could see him.

Gunther jerked his head at Quinn, still standing by the van. "Let's go," he said menacingly, his eyes turning into slits. "Say—why do you look so upset?"

Quinn broke into an uneasy smile and wiped the perspiration away from his forehead with his sleeve. Spots darted before his eyes, and he thought he would pass out. "My gut's acting up again. I've always had this damned ulcer, you see, and—"

A shot blasted out from the direction of the arms room, immediately followed by a louder one.

Horrified, Jakes watched the guard he'd just shot spin around and blow off his shotgun next to Levy's face before dropping. Levy fell to the ground, holding his head. Jakes got up on one knee and stared at the cabin. Christopher yanked Levy to his feet. Then Levy stood on his own, still holding his hands over his ears.

Relieved, Jakes looked up and down his firing line at the others.

"Let's go!"

The Rangers leapt to their feet and sprinted for the cabin.

"What the hell was that?" Grey thundered, looking around in all directions at once. He broke out of the group and leapt on top of the closest boulder, listening to the shots echoing through the valley below. He acted like a bloodhound gone wild with scent.

"That came from the arms room," Hainey said, glancing back at the trail. "We left Wiley back there no more'n thirty minutes ago." The group of neo-Nazis and Klansmen muttered to one another, more than a few charging their weapons.

Quinn's stomach boiled over, and he moaned aloud as the acid inside him tore away at his stomach. He plunged his hand into his pocket and squeezed the beeper in rapid succession, doubling over in pain.

Gunther reached out and grabbed him beneath the armpits to keep him from falling. He froze for a second, then squeezed Quinn's armpits and rib cage harder.

"*You son of a bitch!*" he yelled. "*Frank!*" Gunther slammed Quinn against the side of the van and plucked his .45 out of its holster. He threw it on the ground and then started to frisk the agent, who was too weak to resist. Grey walked over to them, bewildered.

Gunther found the wires and the transmitter. Enraged, he ripped off Quinn's shirt, exposing the assembly.

"You son of a bitch!" he repeated, throwing a vicious punch to Quinn's kidneys. The agent collapsed to the ground.

"What are you doing?" Grey yelled, yanking Gunther back before he could hit Quinn again. "What in Christ's name are you doing?"

Gunther tore away from Grey and hauled Quinn up by the seat of his pants, shoving him upright against the side of the van. Grey's eyes widened in disbelief upon seeing the wire assembly. Gunther ripped the tape and the wires away from Quinn's body. He yanked the transmitter out of Quinn's pocket and wrapped the wires around his hands, turning the assembly into a garotte. He whipped it into a loop around Quinn's neck and pulled his hands apart, but not quite hard enough to strangle him. Yet.

"You see?" Gunther shouted. *"You see?* This goddamned *friend* of yours is some sort of fucking informer!" He pulled back on the garotte, making Quinn gag. He kicked Quinn's legs back, spread-eagling him against the side of the van. Red, raw marks where the tape had stuck to his back and chest gleamed wetly in the flickering firelight. The others gathered around the van, watching Gunther.

"I . . . don't . . . believe it," Grey muttered tonelessly, shaking his head. "Larry . . . why . . . how . . . ?"

"Where's Hood Dietrick?" Gunther demanded, jerking back on the garotte, whipping Quinn's head back.

Quinn made another choking sound, and his knees buckled. Gunther yanked him upright by his neck and then released the pressure so he could speak.

"You—you remember Donaldson, Frankie?" Quinn garbled. "Frankie, you remember how you—how you—"

"*Goddamn you!*" Gunther screamed, strangling Quinn with the garotte. *"Where's Hood?"* Quinn could do nothing but choke against the wire from his own transmitter, eyes bulging, face turning purple. His eyes rolled up into the back of his head, and he collapsed against the side of the van as Gunther pressed against him, trying to strangle the life out of him in rage.

Grey pulled his .45 out of his holster. He walked up to Gunther and violently shoved him aside. Then he shot Quinn in the back of his head, splattering blood and bone fragments and gray matter against the side of the van. The force of the blast bounced Quinn's face against the van, smearing a trail of blood on it from the exit wound as he fell down. He landed face up, his shoulders and legs jerking in death twitches. A bloody hole existed where his nose and eyes once were.

The group of men shrank back, stunned and silenced by the sudden execution. Gunther looked at Grey, himself surprised.

Grey turned and faced them, stepping over Quinn's body and holstering his .45.

"It's time to get back in control of this situation," he said calmly, yet his eyes flashed in a turmoil of hate and agony. "Obviously, we've been infiltrated. And something's gone wrong at the arms room." He turned his attention to Hainey. "Take your group back to the fire and get ready to move out with me to find those Rangers. We'll need them."

Hainey immediately gathered his force of twelve with him toward the fire, leaving eight more by the van. Grey looked at Gunther, who nodded back at him in silent approval.

"J.D.," he said, "you and your men stay here in case we get some unwanted company. I have a feeling something's about to blow."

"Roger that," Gunther replied. He glanced down at Quinn's body. "What about him?"

Before Grey could answer, a whirring sound penetrated through the air above. Both men locked eyes, immediately recognizing the sound.

"Choppers!" Grey yelled. "Blackhawks! Gunther, take charge here—I've got to get those Rangers. Get what you can use out of the van that Quinn brought up. You stand to and hold them off as long as you can!"

"Roger!" Gunther replied. He gathererd his men together and sent them out to their assigned perimeter positions.

"I'll meet you back here ASAP!" Grey shouted after him.

As Gunther took off, Grey yanked open the passenger door of the van and spotted Quinn's M16. He grabbed it, then ran back to the campfire, where Hainey and the others stood by. Already they had scattered the coals to keep it from signaling their position to the incoming helicopters.

"Let's go get 'em!" Grey yelled.

As they took off for the arms room, the first of the three Blackhawks screamed toward them and pulled to an abrupt and angry hover over the site. Two ropes were immediately thrown out from each side of the cabin.

And as the raiders from the FBI Hostage Rescue Team rappeled down the ropes, Gunther's men opened fire.

CHAPTER

· TWENTY-SIX ·

I will never leave a fallen comrade to fall into the hands of the enemy, and under no circumstances will I ever embarrass my country.

"*Levy!*" Christopher cried out, hauling the other Ranger to his feet. "You hit?"

Levy twisted away from Christopher, his hands clamped over his ears. "I'm okay," he said. He staggered over to the guard, who lay on the ground clutching at the bloody hole Jakes had shot into his belly. He was still alive, moaning in pain.

Jakes had shot the surprised guard just before he could kill Levy when the Ranger snuck up on him moments earlier. If it hadn't been for Jakes, the twelve-gauge the guard fired one split second after he had been hit would have blown straight into Levy's face. Instead, the lethal pellets passed over Levy's shoulder, missing his face by inches.

As Levy retrieved the guard's shotgun, Christopher ran for the door of the cabin and yanked on the padlock securing it.

"We'll have to shoot it off," he told Levy. Christopher looked back at Jakes and the rest of the patrol. "Jakes!" he yelled. "C'mon in!"

"Right behind you!" Jakes shouted back, materializing through the darkness with nine other silhouettes. "Where do you want everybody?"

"Form a security perimeter around the cabin. Wait a minute . . . give me that Mini-14." Christopher took Jakes's weapon and turned back to the padlock. "Everybody get down." Christopher shot the lock twice and yanked it apart. Then he kicked the door open. He ran inside and immediately came back out, holding the lantern he had seen the Klansmen use during his recon earlier. "Levy!"

"Yeah!" Levy ran back from the side of the cabin, where he had dragged the guard.

"Get this lantern fired up so I can see what I'm doing. I need someone else in here to help me. Then I want you and Jakes to set the patrol in a firing line facing back to the base camp."

Suddenly, a helicopter zoomed in from above and blasted across the treetops. The sound and suddenness of it all unnerved the Rangers, paralyzing them momentarily.

Levy acted first. He grabbed a Ranger by his arm, shoving him toward Christopher. It was Keller. "This is it!" he yelled. "That's the FBI. It's time to haul ass! Keller," he said, facing the other Ranger, "help Christopher with the lantern. As he gives you the weapons, you run 'em out to me and Jakes on the firing line we set up out front. Now, *move!*"

Keller leapt into action and within seconds had the lantern going. Christopher ran inside the arms room and came back out with weapons and magazines, literally throwing them at Keller. Simultaneously, Levy and Jakes set up a seven-man defensive firing line ten meters away in the direction of the base camp, positioning the other Rangers behind the rocks and deadfall and scattered trees surrounding the arms room. They were ready in two minutes, with each man positioned behind a rock or a tree and assigned left and right sectors of fire, so that each position covered another sector with interlocking fields of fire.

Levy ran back to the center of the defensive position and met Jakes there. "You stay here and control the element," he said. "I'll help Keller with the weapons detail." A hand pulled at Levy's shoulder from behind. Turning around, he saw it was Keller with an armload of M16s. "Way to go, Keller," he said appreciatively.

Jakes and Keller exchanged glances and held them for a moment, their minds going back to another conversation. Now there was no acrimony. There was no time for it, only the mutual necessity for survival. Jakes nodded his approval. Levy impatiently yanked at the M16s. "Go to it, guys. Move it!"

Jakes and Keller sprang to life and distributed the weapons down the firing line. Levy ran back to the cabin and burst inside, where he saw Christopher standing over a huge barrel loaded with magazines. He was busy setting thirty-round, loaded magazines out in groups of eleven for distribution.

Levy was speechless. Inside were racks of machine guns, grenade launchers, and night sights, along with scores of assault rifles of every make, and bins of ammunition. He spotted a case of grenades by the door and bent down and ripped off the top of the wooden crate.

"Man-oh-man," he muttered, looking at the rows of apple-size bombs.

Christopher looked at his Ranger buddy. "They had their shit wired, didn't they?"

"These guys are serious, man. This is the most lethal stuff I've ever seen in one place."

Christopher tossed a magazine to Levy. "Get it out ASAP."

Levy slung his M16 around his shoulder and scooped up an armful of magazines for the others, then ran back outside, hollering at Keller to grab the case of grenades from the arms room.

"The attack's a go, and this is really getting weird, Soltz," Clement told the other sniper. "You'd better notify headquarters and tell them about these Rangers by the arms room before the choppers zap them. That was the first bird that just passed by."

"Right," Soltz replied. He turned on a tiny transmitter to the whisper mike fastened to his collar.

Now comfortably out of earshot from the Rangers, the two had gingerly picked up and moved to an overwatching position thirty meters adjacent and to the left of the cabin. From that vantage point they could still face the direction of the base camp for the expected assault from the Klansmen and neo-Nazis. Unknown to the Rangers, they provided them with an incredible advantage in the additional, deadly accurate firepower with their M40s.

"Falcon-Sweep One, this is Falcon-Poach Two, over," Soltz muttered in his mike. He spoke to the command and control helicopter hovering in their position five kilometers to the south. They were the second sniper team guarding the most tactically logical escape route to south of the base camp. Another sniper team was set up on the false hilltop to the camp's north.

"Go ahead, Falcon-Poach Two," came the reply over the receiver, planted in Soltz's left ear like a hearing aid.

"Falcon-Sweep One, be advised there is an eleven-man element at the Klan arms room thirty meters to our right, over."

"Engage them now, Falcon-Poach Two! How copy?"

Soltz exchanged glances with his partner, and then said, "Falcon-Sweep One, we don't think they are the bad guys. They are hostages. Repeat, *hostages.*"

"Say again, over."

Soltz lost his composure. "Listen, goddammit, you fuckers didn't tell us about this! There are eleven hostages on site here. Ranger students. They've escaped somehow. The goddamned rumor's true, you *bastards!*"

Soltz grimaced as a sudden rush of static pierced his eardrum. The noise continued for a second, and then the reply from headquarters burst through with a squeal, broken and distorted.

". . . repeat, hold them down and we will . . ." More static broke through. "Airstrip, over."

"Say again, Falcon-Sweep," Soltz replied.

"This is Falcon-Sweep One. I say again: Hold them at the airstrip. Bird three will pick them up, over."

Firing burst from the tree line fifty meters to their front. Soltz and Clement immediately shouldered their M40s and scanned the perimeter with their night sights. A group of men from the base camp was assaulting the arms room and firing upon the Rangers. Already Soltz heard the loud stutter of an M60 machine gun already in place.

"You copy last transmission?" an angry voice crackled in Soltz's ear. "Acknowledge!"

Soltz swore and looked at Clement, who was already scoping his first shot at one of the Klansmen.

"We'll do the best we goddamn can!" Soltz yelled into the mike.

Furious at the lack of planning from his own headquarters, he lined up his M40 on a crouching silhouette in the tree line to his front, glowing green in his AN/PVS-4 night sight, and set the crosshairs on his chest.

"Get down, Keller!" Levy yelled, yanking him to the ground. He heard the crackle and pop of rounds whizzing overhead, immediately followed by a barrage of fire from the trees fifty meters to their front.

"They're firing!" Keller screamed, clutching at the ground. "They're firing at us!"

Levy crawled up to Keller and shoved him forward. "Keep moving for Jakes and the others," he shouted. "We gotta get them some more ammo." Keller shuddered but started crawling again. Within seconds they were on the firing line with Jakes, who grimly returned semiautomatic fire with his Mini-14. A burst of fire rattled on automatic at his left from one of the other Rangers.

"Keep it on semi!" Jakes cried. "Don't waste your ammo!"

A burst of machine-gun fire answered him, red tracers hissing overhead. Keller froze, looking at it. Levy knocked him down and pulled him to the right of the firing line.

"Let's go, Keller!" Keller numbly followed Levy, and they distributed the magazines of ammunition to the rest of the firing line.

Suddenly, explosions erupted on the same spot where Levy had seen the muzzle flash of the Klan's machine gun. He glanced back at the cabin. Christopher was pumping 40mm heat rounds into the tree line with an M203 grenade launcher he had taken from the arms room. For a moment the fire from the tree line abated, and Christopher's M203 gave the Rangers enough covering firepower to allow Levy and Keller time to get back to the cabin. Jakes took advantage of the lull by directing the other Rangers' fire toward the muzzle flashes he'd spotted in the tree line.

Levy and Keller high-crawled the thirty feet back to the cabin in seconds, adrenaline pumping and nerves strung out on high. Once there, Levy shoved Keller inside the door. "Get Christopher some more M203 rounds!" he shouted.

As Keller frantically searched the area for a case of rounds, Levy wrenched a machine gun from one of the racks and an armful of M60 ammunition in bandoliers of 100 rounds each. Then he crawled outside and set up the gun around the corner of the cabin next to Christopher, who was still thocking out rounds with the grenade launcher.

"Keller!" Levy screamed, searching for the other Ranger in a thickening haze of gun smoke.

"Here!" came the reply. Keller had crawled out of the cabin right behind Levy, dragging a box of M203 rounds for Christopher, and three more bandoliers of M60 ammo for Levy, who gladly accepted them.

"Help me out with this gun!"

Keller ripped open the top of a bandolier and crawled around to Levy's left, where he fed the belt of 7.62mm chain-linked ammunition into the chamber of the machine gun. Slapping down the feed tray cover, Levy switched the gun's safety to "fire" and sprayed a ten-round burst into the tree line ahead, careful not to shoot into the sector where he and Jakes had established their firing line.

"Christopher!" Levy yelled above the din.

"Yo!"

"Bring the rest of the patrol in from the firing line by buddy teams!"

"*What?*"

"We gotta break contact and shag ass!"

"*Roger that!* Keller, give me your weapon, and take this 203. Keep putting rounds inside that tree line."

The two Rangers traded weapons, and soon Keller was firing a steady supply of grenades into the tree line. The Klan's fire wavered. Christopher held Keller's M16 with his right hand and crouched low on the ground like a coiled spring as he prepared to leap up for a three-second rush toward Jakes.

"Okay," he shouted, "I'm moving. Cover me!"

Levy let the M60 loose with a sustained twenty-round burst as Keller fired out M203 rounds in rapid succession. A dense cloud of acrid smoke snaked around them. Christopher leapt up from their position and rushed toward Jakes and the firing line.

A second helicopter blasted overhead from the west, flying toward the base camp, and was immediately joined by a third, flying in from the east. From his position with Jakes, Christopher heard the chain-saw belch of a Gatling gun from the last bird as it spat out a solid stream of red tracers into the base camp.

Suddenly, another machine gun opened up on their right from the tree line, chewing up the ground immediately to their front with a steady burst of fire. Christopher pulled Jakes's ear to his mouth and screamed: "Break contact and pull back to the cabin! I'll crawl to the right of our firing line and get those guys. You get your guys on the left!"

"Okay!" Jakes yelled back, and he crawled away. Christopher gathered the three Rangers on his right and brought them in one at a time, setting them in an overwatch so each man could cover his buddy while they moved back. They continued to leapfrog each other back toward the cabin. Jakes did the same with the other Rangers on his side. Soon they had covered half the distance.

Abruptly, Levy's machine gun fell silent. Panicky, Christopher grabbed the nearest Ranger and shoved him toward the cabin in a low crawl. The Klan and Nazi machine guns increased their tempo, and soon rounds popped all around them as they were caught dead in the beaten zone of fire.

"Levy, return fire!" Christopher screamed. *"Levy!"*

Levy swore at his overheated weapon and took second-degree burns on his fingers as he fought to pull the jammed cartridges cammed inside the chamber out from underneath the feed-tray cover.

"Goddamn, but they're in good positions," Clement told Soltz. Both snipers were firing at the two Klan machine-gun positions in the tree line ahead, but most of their shots were smacking into the base of a tree or pinging off rocks right next to the guns, as they could not quite get to the gunner.

"Keep firing and keep those gunners pinned down!" Soltz yelled. "It looks like they're trying to flank those Rangers from our direction. When they move out, let 'em have it!"

Grey yelled triumphantly, and he slapped Hainey on the back.

"We've got 'em pinned down now."

"We can take those Rangers out by the arms room,"

Hainey replied. "I'll move a couple of guys around to the right and flank them."

"Go to it, hoss."

Hainey grabbed two of his men from behind the trunk of an oak tree and moved out to the right for fifteen meters, then bounded with them one by one around the tree line to the right of the arms room.

Grey watched them with glee and continued firing his M16 into the area where the Rangers were pinned down. Glancing at his right, he watched for Hainey's next bound with his team.

Nothing happened. He fired more rounds at the arms room and then looked for Hainey again. Finally, he saw a man leap up for a three-second rush, inwardly pleased that the man was doing it just as he himself had taught him months ago during their training sessions. Then Grey's jaw dropped as he watched the man's head pop in a spray of blood. The body flopped to the ground, contorted in death.

Grey's nerve weakened. How many casualties had he suffered? More choppers had flown over the area earlier, but in the excitement he had concentrated solely on taking out the Rangers at his arms room. Things suddenly weren't looking so good. If they were overtaken, the Feds would see what he had in the arms room, not to mention what he'd done to Quinn, and what Quinn had brought up in the van.

Grey's veins turned to icewater, and a cold sweat broke out on his forehead. He crawled to two of his men on his left.

"Who's left? Anybody else hit?"

One man looked at Grey with frightened eyes. "Alex Witherton's dead! Caught a round in his face. He was my best buddy, Frank!"

"Get a grip on it, Freddy," Grey yelled. "Who else?"

"Just Turner and Snodgrass on the machine gun over yonder!"

Grey turned purple. That meant he had only five men left, including himself. He'd either have to take the arms room, or break off now and get out of the AO.

He thought of Jerry. Hainey. Quinn. All of the death.

Then he thought of the Jew and the nigger.

"Rush around to the right and flank them!" he screamed. He grabbed the other man by the arm and looked at his frightened, pale face. It was Jeb Hennessey. They locked eyes for one second, and then Grey shoved him forward. *"Move it, goddammit!"*

Hennessey and his partner sprinted twenty meters to the right under the protective cover of the tree line. Grey followed close behind. While he high-crawled behind them, he fumbled at the ammo pouch on his web gear for the two grenades he had brought from the base camp. He pulled one out and gripped it in his right hand.

"How many?"

"Three," Soltz replied. "It was beautiful, man, they just came bouncing right out in front of us. Piece of cake."

"Keep your eye on those M60s they've got."

"No problem." Clement resumed firing at the machine guns ahead in the tree line.

"Whoa!" Soltz exclaimed, grabbing Clement by the arm. "Here comes another batch."

One by one, three figures rushed out of the tree line, heading straight for them as the others had done.

Soltz pulled his trigger and the first man went down.

* * *

Grey saw the muzzle flash this time, and he crawled forward on his belly.

"Freddy went down, Frank!"

"Move out!"

"But—"

"Move out, I said! I'll cover you!" Grey rolled over to a tree stump and emptied a full magazine into the bushes, where he had seen the muzzle flash.

Jeb Hennessey picked up and sprinted for a boulder, only to have his legs fly out from underneath him as if he had tripped over a rock. He lay very still.

Grey pulled the pin of his grenade.

"Speak to me, Clement!" Soltz screamed. He reached out and grabbed his buddy by the collar, only to find that he had caught a round just beneath his Adam's apple and was quite dead.

Soltz threw his bolt back and chambered another round, looking ahead. Before he could sight in on the running silhouette twenty meters to his direct front, the target plopped down to the ground and covered his head as if he had just thrown a grenade.

A hard, fist-sized metallic object glanced off his shoulder, sending a shock wave of pain down his arm and causing him to jerk his trigger back, throwing off his aim.

The M40 roared, and Soltz realized it *was* a grenade, and his target had thrown it. His feet drummed the earth as he tried to scramble away.

Then the ground erupted, and he was dead.

Gunther returned fire with his M16 at the Black hawk hovering above, only to be sent scurrying back inside the cabin door as the chopper's miniguns spat rounds at his feet. The other Blackhawk swarmed overhead at the other end of the camp, and more federal agents slipped down the ropes trailing from its cabin. He realized there must now be at least two dozen men in the compound, not to mention at least thirty or forty more in the tree line up the hill laying down a murderous base of fire.

Gunther counted the bodies he had left. *Five dead, and two more wounded,* he thought. *That leaves me and Struthers. Where the hell is Grey?*

A voice crackled to life over an amplified megaphone somewhere in the bowels of the Blackhawk above.

"You people in the cabin, you're surrounded. This is your last warning. Cease fire now and give yourselves up!"

"Give it up, J.D.!" an excited voice yelled in his ear. Gunther spun around and looked at Struthers. He was a good man, one of the few he had handpicked for this mission to Georgia. He and Dietrick were equally competent, and he had always especially trusted Struthers's steady judgment.

Gunther now glared into the eyes of a beaten man. "So what do you want to do, give in?"

The other man didn't reply. Instead, his eyes pleaded. Gunther hated him for it. "What do you think they'll do?" he shouted. "Send us to prison?" He didn't wait for a response. "Yeah, they'll do that," he snapped, thumping his forefinger into Struthers's chest. "Only as long as it takes to warm up the electric chair!" He pointed at Quinn's prostrate body splayed out by the van for emphasis. "Comprehend?"

Gunther shoved the man aside and crawled to the rear of the tiny cabin, where he threw up the mattress of a bunk bed. Struthers sank back against the cabin wall when he saw the yard-long cylindrical object Gunther brought back with him.

"No! You can't do that!" he screamed. "Not in here."

Gunther pulled out his .45 and backhanded it across Struthers's face, knocking him out.

"Oh, no?" he muttered as he snapped off the back cover of the M72A2 light antitank weapon and pulled it apart at both ends, expanding it into the locked position.

"We will commence firing with heat rounds in five seconds," the megaphone screamed from the hovering chopper. Like a giant, angry dragonfly, the Blackhawk swiveled its nose toward the cabin.

Gunther stared at the rocket pods aimed at him and swallowed, realizing that he'd either get it from the Gatling guns above or from the backblast of the 66mm rocket encased in his LAW, since he was firing it from an enclosed space. The shock from the contained backblast would probably kill him, or at least burn him severely.

He gathered his nerve and pulled the arming mechanism out, aiming the sight on the nose of the Blackhawk. A slow grin stretched and cracked over his crooked, uneven teeth.

"For the glory of the Aryan Covenant, you bastards! I'll see you in—"

Gunther pressed the trigger and burned in hell. The Blackhawk burst into a ball of flame, showering the entire base camp with burning metal and exploding rockets.

CHAPTER

· TWENTY-SEVEN ·

Readily will I display the intestinal fortitude required to fight on to the Ranger objective . . .

Levy felt the ground shake as the countryside rocked with the explosion, and he saw a fireball mushroom over the base camp. For a second the firing stopped. Then he slammed down his machine gun's feed-tray cover over the fresh belt of ammunition Keller fed to him and commenced firing at the Klan's gun position in the tree line to his front.

Christopher had lost hope and almost cried in relief when he heard Levy's machine gun crank back up. *"Jakes!"* he screamed at the top of his lungs. *"Move out!"*

Jakes immediately grabbed two Rangers by their shirts and hurled them forward, and they all sprinted for the arms room. Once there, he quickly set them into position, and soon they were returning fire with Levy and Keller at the last machine-gun position in the tree line.

Christopher glanced quickly around him. There

were only three other Rangers left. Incoming rounds popped all around them.

Suddenly, a helicopter screamed in from the direction of the base camp and belched thousands of rounds twenty meters to the left of the arms room. Christopher instinctively hugged the ground as the solid belt of red tracers erupted from the cabin of the Blackhawk, his eardrums nearly ruptured from the intensity and noise of the blast from a weapon that could take out the entire group of Rangers with one three-second pull of the weapon system's trigger. Instead, it hovered forty feet above Christopher. The prop blast from the chopper whipped and lashed at the Rangers below, whirling weeds, sticks, and pine needles high into the air. The chopper's spotlight beamed in on the Rangers at the arms room, blinding them with its piercing glare. Looking up, Christopher saw two 20mm gatling guns protruding from each side of the cabin, smoking from their lethal belch of destruction. The Blackhawk slowly turned and tilted its snout at the Rangers, who had by now ceased firing. Christopher's eyes widened in terror, thinking about the 20mm round ripping through his friend's ahead.

"No!" he screamed, getting to his knees. *"Don't do it!"*

A megaphone's squeal pierced through the din. *"Cease fire!"* it ordered. *"Cease fire now and lay down your weapons!"*

Levy and Keller and Jakes and all the rest immediately dropped their weapons to the ground. They put their hands on top of their heads to show the pilot they were no longer armed.

The machine gun in the tree line opened up at

them again, spraying rounds all around the Rangers.

The Blackhawk whipped its snout around and belched tracers into the tree line, cutting trees in half and slinging earth everywhere, a giant, invisible plow ripping the ground inside out. Small fires erupted all around the chewed-up area from the tracers, and soon the entire tree line was on fire. The helicopter scanned the left and right to see if anything else would shoot at it, and then it turned back around to the Rangers huddling at the arms room cabin.

Christopher wondered if it would blow them all into oblivion. The Blackhawk seemed to be deliberating just that.

"Assemble to the rear of the cabin!" the megaphone finally ordered. *"Leave your weapons on the ground and assemble to the rear of the cabin with your hands on top of your heads, or we will shoot!"*

Immensely relieved, Christopher held his hands up in the air with the other Rangers. He knew nothing in the tree line could have survived the onslaught of death from above he'd just witnessed. All that was left to do was join the rest of the patrol by the cabin and go home with the helicopters.

Two more helicopters whirled in. This time they were Hueys: Christopher recognized the thumpa-thumpa beat of their blades. He watched them touch down on the landing strip behind the cabin 100 meters away to his front. Six men from each helicopter, all armed with automatic weapons and dressed in black fatigues, jumped out and ran toward them, dispersing immediately into a wedge formation.

Christopher and the three other Rangers with him sprang to their feet and walked forward, joining the others at the cabin. Once there, they assembled on the side facing the landing strip as ordered.

"All personnel move away from the cabin in single file toward those helicopters," the Blackhawk's megaphone ordered, keeping the spotlight trained on them. *"Keep your hands on top of your heads."*

Levy and Jakes led the formation out toward the Hueys and the armed men coming to get them. Christopher brought up the rear of the single-file formation. The Blackhawk followed, keeping its guns trained on them. When they had covered half the distance, the megaphone told them, *"Hold it where you are. Remain in single file. Face to the rear."*

Everyone faced to the rear.

"Get down on both knees. Keep your hands on top of your heads."

They did as they were told. Then, the sound of running footsteps.

"Who's in charge here?"

"I am."

"I am."

Christopher turned around. He and Levy had spoken at once. The men from the Hueys had established a firing line, and were keeping all of them covered. The leader of the group stood in the center holding a PRC-68 radio with one hand and pointing an M16 at them with the other.

"You two that spoke, come over here by me."

Christopher moved toward the front of the formation with Levy, glad to see that his buddy was still in one piece. He looked at the haggard faces of everyone else in the patrol. They were walking dead. He felt something in himself go, and suddenly he was very weak and very tired. He stumbled up front with Levy, trying hard to keep his hands on top of his head. Then he was standing with Levy next to the man in charge. He was indistinguishable in his black facepaint and fatigues.

"Are you people the Ranger students from Camp Merrill?" he asked.

"Yeah," Christopher replied wearily. "We are. Oh, man, am I glad this is over."

"How many of you are there?"

"There's—twelve of us," Levy replied, looking at Christopher. "Another man is in the woods, guarding a neo-Nazi your man Quinn apprehended before he could kill us. His name is Prentiss, and he's guarding the neo-Nazi, and you'll find him about five miles back from here and—"

"Hold on, son, you're not making much sense. We'll debrief you soon enough. Meanwhile, all you people get in the choppers. We're going home." He brought the radio up to his mouth and said something in it neither Christopher nor Levy could hear. Then the Blackhawk above them banked to the left and took off for the base camp.

The Rangers whooped and slapped each other in relief. Christopher rounded them up. "You heard the man," he yelled above the din. "Get your act together and move out!" He started walking for the Hueys.

A hand grabbed him around the shoulder, and Christopher turned, looking into Levy's grinning face. Christopher grinned back at him.

He followed them, paralleling the Rangers' single-file formation from the tree line. Finally, he could go no farther, because they had stopped beside the helicopters. He got down in the prone behind a fallen tree.

One shot, he thought, *maybe two, before they see me. Which one first—the kike or the nigger? Fuckit. I'll get* both *the bastards.*

He yanked the bolt back from the M40 he had taken from the sniper team he had taken out and slammed a round in the chamber. At this range Grey decided he didn't really need the night sight.

They were at the helicopters now, and they had to shout to each other to be heard over the noise made by the whirring blades. The FBI element that had escorted them loaded up in the other bird as soon as most of the Rangers were in. The leader of the group and one other man remained behind with the Rangers' chopper.

Levy and Christopher stayed outside with the FBI element leader as they watched the others go inside one by one. Levy reached out and grabbed Jakes by the arm before he could get into the chopper.

"Got a dip?" he yelled above the noise.

The country boy broke into a huge grin and retrieved a filthy can of Copenhagen from his shirt pocket and gave it to Levy. The bottom cardboard portion had rotted and threatened to give way like a trapdoor. Levy snatched it from him.

Christopher laughed. "Still dippin' that nasty shit, Levy?"

This one's for Jerry.

It was the last thing Levy heard his friend say. He saw a flash from the tree line thirty feet behind Christopher, and then his Ranger buddy pitched forward with the cracking report of the rifle, grabbing him in a violent bear hug.

Shocked, Levy held Christopher tightly, blood seeping through his friend's uniform onto his own chest. Christopher's knees buckled and he collapsed to the ground, dragging Levy with him. Already Levy saw death in the whites of Christopher's eyes as the black Ranger stared up at him, clinging to his shirt.

"No!"

Jakes stood paralyzed in the door.

The FBI agent leapt out of the helicopter. Already his assault force had lifted up into the air and had taken off.

"Get in!" the agent yelled, flopping down to the ground and returning fire in the direction of the muzzle flash.

Levy shook his head and pried away from Christopher's grasp, deep in hurt and pain. *"Nooo!"* he yelled, looking disbelievingly at the massive exit wound in Christopher's chest. He pulled Christopher's hands off his shirt and shot his eyes at the tree line. He saw another flash, immediately hearing something crack by his left ear. The round smacked the chopper's fuselage. Levy fell to the ground for cover.

Grey cursed at the M40, which had jammed. Rounds zinged over his head and before him, kicking up clods of dirt and splintering the tree to his front he was using for cover. He flipped around, crawling for the safety of the tree line. Then he felt something punch inside his lower calf and burn its way up his right leg. He shrieked in pain, knowing it would get worse, much worse. He threw the M40 on the ground and limped into the tree line, crashing through the trees and brush, tripping and clawing through the tanglefoot, trying to escape.

"Goddamn you to hell!" Levy screamed, knowing it had to be Grey. Something inside him snapped, and acting on sheer instinct he planted his foot on the agent's shoulder and wrenched the M16 from his grasp, then sprinted for the tree line, where he had seen the muzzle flash. The agent automatically pulled out a .45 and aimed it at Levy, who was already halfway to the tree line.

"Stop!" he ordered.

Jakes leapt out of the helicopter and tackled the other agent, who was concentrating on Levy. He hit him on the head, stunning him, and took his M16, then trained it on both agents.

"Pick him up!" he told them, motioning toward Christopher. "Put him in the chopper, *now*!"

They did as they were told.

Five minutes later Jakes gave the weapon back. "I had to give him time to settle personal business," the Ranger told them. "That's all."

The two agents looked at Jakes disbelievingly. Then the man with the radio called the other chopper back.

CHAPTER

· TWENTY-EIGHT ·

. . . and complete the mission . . .

A lone figure lurched across the stream at the bottom of the mountainside and finally pitched forward onto the opposite bank. The direction of the slope abruptly changed, and soon he was stumbling uphill, fighting pine saplings and thick, tangled vines as he went.

Grey was limping more heavily than ever, and he knew he was losing blood at a rate faster than he could tolerate. He fell beside an oak tree and pulled his right trouser leg out of his boot, rolling it up to his knee.

It was worse than he'd thought. The bullet had hit him in the lower calf muscle, penetrating the fleshy side. It had then tumbled and spun up his leg at a forty-five-degree angle, ripping through tissue and severing many blood vessels in the process. Even though the bullet hadn't broken his shinbone or severed an artery, it had still caused considerable damage. Grey touched a hard lump in the hollow behind his knee and grimaced. The tiny lump of lead had finally lodged there.

Grey shook his head, trying to clear it, realizing he had to stop the bleeding before going into shock. He ripped off his belt and cinched it above the wound as tight as he could stand it. The bleeding slowed to a trickle.

As his labored breathing returned to normal, he realized how far off and distant the helicopters at the base camp sounded now. Above any other noise, he heard the pumping of blood in his ears. There had been so much noise during the battle. Only now—now that he was in the sanctuary of the dark woods, the woods he had played soldier in as a little boy, the woods in which he had hunted deer—had things finally quieted down. The helicopters no longer sounded like angry hornets spraying red-tracing death in shrieking passes; they were now far off and distant. No more rifle and machine-gun fire. No more grenade blasts. The only sound he really heard now was the blood pumping hard in his ears.

He had to give himself time to think. The last thing he had seen before running down the mountain was the Jew he had shot. A smirk creased his lips, thinking that regardless of what happened to him, at least he had taken care of the Jew and the nigger.

He had to get moving again. He had to contact his father somehow and then contact Gunther's organization so he could stay underground. He grabbed the huge oak roots beneath him as he would a gymnast's horse and did a one-legged squat press to his feet.

As he stood up, he heard someone running toward him from below. The noise of last autumn's leaves crunching and twigs snapping alerted him.

Grey pulled out his .45 from the holster fastened to his web gear, and leaned close to the tree, not wanting to expose his silhouette.

Levy had sprinted downhill the entire way, tearing through the brush and deadfall, wanting to gain distance on Grey before he had a chance to get away. He knew he wasn't acting rationally, but all he could really think about was the look on Christopher's face as his Ranger buddy had been blown forward into his arms.

And the shocked, hurt look on his Ranger buddy's face. The face with the squared, set jaw; a face with eyes that had always sparked with an intense, inimitable willpower. A face that now belonged to a dead man.

Levy's face and hands were cut from the vines and thorns and branches. Already he had sprained his ankle from a nasty trip over a log after reaching the tiny stream at the bottom of the ridgeline. How far had he gone? Three, four hundred meters? It had all passed by in a flash of milliseconds. He fought to get a grip on himself as he crossed the stream and slowed down when he reached the opposite tree line. He walked, then climbed. He stopped.

Levy looked at the M16 he held loosely in his right hand and felt nauseated, but automatically he straightened up a little and pulled back the bolt, checking the action. A bullet flew out of the chamber.

He realized how stupid he was just then for doing that, and bent down to pick it up. He should have removed the magazine before looking to see how many bullets he had left. The agent hadn't fired more than a dozen rounds before Levy ripped the rifle out of his hands in complete, utter rage. Levy got on one knee by a pine tree and shoved the magazine back into the weapon.

He was so tired. All the moving and the fighting and the killing had taken its toll. Christopher was dead. That was a certainty. He'd seen death in his friend's eyes as he . . .

Levy shook his head, trying to keep from remembering. A moan rumbled deep in his throat, and his eyes turned into slits as he allowed it to transform into a snarl of hate and vengeance.

"Grey, you *bastard!*" he shouted into the forest. "Where are you?"

No answer. But something in Levy's gut told him to keep it up.

"I know you're here . . . somewhere. What's the matter? You afraid to show yourself to a timid little Jew like me? Is that it, Grey? *Are you afraid?*"

Grey smiled, hearing Levy yell for him. So he didn't get him after all. It was dark, but not that dark. He had the advantage of knowing where Levy was, but what did the Jew have for firepower? His own .45 was only as good as far as you could throw a rock. He wondered.

Finally, he slithered down the tree and crawled back toward the stream, concentrating on Levy's voice.

"Hey, Grey," Levy cried out, laughing with no humor, "you picked on the wrong fucking *kike*, you know that? You may have even met my old man once, Grey . . . *where are you, you son of a bitch?* Now, there's a *real* kike! He actually connived a coupla Silver Stars and a Distinguished Service Cross outta his three tours in 'Nam. And he was just another worthless Jew like me! Dig it, Grey! *Are you afraid of me?*"

Grey moved in closer, creeping from one shadow to the next, his stomach muscles involuntarily contracting from the pain searing his leg. He pulled the hammer back on his .45.

Levy's voice grew louder. Grey moved toward the sound. Then he caught Levy's silhouette by the stream, but he didn't have enough of a shot at him. He *did* see Levy's M16, knowing he couldn't possibly take out the Jew with just a .45 unless he was in a much better position. And if he risked getting any closer, then the Jew would hear him and . . .

The odds weren't in his favor. He had to run, get out of the area, do something.

Then a better idea came to him. Much better.

He limped back up the slope.

Levy edged closer to the tree. He didn't know if he was wasting his time or if Grey was actually around somewhere listening to him. He did know he was tired of running.

"Where are you, Grey? Can you hear me? Sheenies like me are only good at talking. Making money, too. I got loads of it, Grey. I'm only doing the Army for *fun*, know what I mean?"

Nothing. He didn't know what else to say. He felt whatever remained of his energy drain slowly, inexorably away.

A rustling sound uphill. Levy's eyes followed the sound, but it was too dark to see. Well, if he couldn't taunt Grey into coming for him, he'd go find the bastard himself. His finger flipped the safety of his M16 to semiautomatic, and he stood up.

"Grey, you fuckin' douchebag. Where'd you go?"

Levy heard the rustling noise again, something moving in the bushes upslope about twenty meters. It *had* to be Grey.

Levy gritted his teeth together. "You didn't kill Christopher," he said, his eyes growing hot. "You hit him in the shoulder and fucked him over pretty bad, but you didn't kill him. You're a piss-poor shot, Grey, because you missed me, too. I don't *believe* you can't take out a nigger and a kike, Grey!"

Grey tried not to listen, sitting high up in the branches. He decided to get it over with. He threw the last rock he had brought with him in Levy's direction and held his .45 out with both hands.

"Over here, Jew-boy," he snarled. "I'm waiting."

Grey heard the sound of crackling leaves as Levy moved in closer. *Not much longer*, he thought, squeezing ever so slightly on the trigger. *Not much . . .*

The drone of the helicopters from the base camp picked up into a whine, and they took off.

Levy started at the sound of Grey's voice floating down from uphill. The Ranger hesitated, then walked up to the tree at his front, slipping on the sharp angle of the new ridge. He concentrated on staying in the pines, where he could walk exclusively on the pine needles instead of betraying his position in the rustle of hardwood leaves.

He heard the chopping sound of a Huey approaching him from behind. Looking down the valley where he had crossed the stream, Levy watched the two Hueys that had arrived with the Blackhawks earlier fly toward him at treetop level, beaming their penetrating spotlights into the forest below.

He was out of time.

"Grey," he bellowed, "you bastard! You fucking Communist! You . . . you . . ." Levy lurched uphill and crashed through the brush, holding his weapon at the ready, safety off, finger on the trigger, adrenaline at a hundred percent, ready to kill, ready to find and kill and . . .

A shot and a flash exploded, the round biting into a pine tree next to Levy's face. Levy dropped and rolled, looking in all directions at once, searching for the muzzle flash.

Then he felt the dirt erupt next to his neck as another shot cracked, and he rolled away from it wildly, scrambling to get behind a tree. Two more bullets followed him, smacking into the ground with the force and knockdown power of a sledgehammer.

The helicopters moved in closer, swinging their searchlights closer to them.

Grey knew he didn't have much longer. He had watched Levy charge uphill and couldn't believe his luck as he'd held the Ranger in his sights. Then at the last moment a muscle spasm had churned through his leg, and he jerked the trigger, his aim thrown. He wondered if Levy had pinpointed him.

Levy's heart raced as he tried to remember how many shots Grey had fired. Was it four? Only seven rounds to a clip. He'd have to draw out his fire and look for the muzzle flash. He poked his head out from around the tree.

"Out of ammo yet, Grey?" Levy flipped his selector switch to automatic as he steeled himself for the next move. "C'mon, Grey, shoot! *Shoot me, you son of a whore!*"

Bam! Another round planted itself with a thunk into the tree Levy was using for cover. He leapt out from it to a boulder five feet away, looking up where he thought he'd seen the muzzle flash from above.

Grey shot again and saw Levy spin around and crash behind a boulder, now hidden from view. The helicopters were almost upon him. Grey glanced up, and suddenly the searchlight washed him in its glare.

Levy's right arm hung useless and limp as he lay twisted and hurt in the leaves, and it felt for a moment as if the pain weren't even there, and then the hurt was incredibly there all at once like thunder in a baby's face where the round had broken and plowed through his upper arm.

Gathering all his will, he turned around, faint, weak, trying to get a purchase on the slippery mountainside with his feet. Levy bit his lip through trying to keep from crying out, and he crawled to the boulder where he had been knocked down by Grey's bullet. He raised his M16 up with his left arm and pointed it up, and as the helicopters approached with their searchlights, he saw Grey silhouetted in the trees above.

Levy pulled his lips back in a hoarse, voiceless scream as he pulled the trigger, emptying his magazine into the tree. The helicopter drowned with the prop wash anything he might have said.

A moment's hesitation.

Then Grey, tumbling from his perch and crashing through the branches. He smacked onto the ground below.

Levy walked toward him, dragging his M16 with

his good arm, eyes glassy with the kill. He remembered that Grey still possessed his Star of David, taken earlier in the Camp Merrill arms room. It was time to get it back.

But Grey wasn't dead. The RI struggled up to a sitting position and leaned against the tree trunk. Levy wasn't alarmed. Grey was hit bad. As the Ranger walked closer he saw where: in the arm, at least two places. Three rounds in his left thigh, at least one, maybe two in his chest cavity.

The helicopter hovering above trained its spotlight on him.

"Put your weapon down!" the megaphone squealed.

Levy grabbed his M16 by the muzzle, feeling the barrel burn into the palm of his hand, and threw it as hard as he could down the mountainside into the stream below. His knees buckled from the effort and the pain in his arm and loss of blood, but he stayed on his feet.

He looked up at the chopper as if to say *"Okay, that takes care of that,"* and stuck his middle finger at the crew chief aiming the chopter's minigun on him.

"Prepare to be lifted inside," the megaphone ordered.

A cable with a harness was tossed out of the cabin and then swung down toward Levy, winched out by the crew chief.

Levy ignored the command and walked toward Grey, who feebly picked at something inside his ammo pouch on his web gear.

"It's over, Grey," Levy heard himself say, his tongue thick and numb. "You pig."

Grey's eyes sparked back at Levy in reply, and he grinned. "Not bad, Jew—" He suddenly coughed up a great glob of blood, and it dribbled down his chin and formed a pool on his chest. Levy heard Grey making squeaking, whistling noises from his chest and knew he would die soon.

"You killed my friend, Grey," Levy said, pulling out his sheath knife. "And you've got something of mine." He edged closer to the broken RI, who was still grinning, even though Levy could see that the light had gone out behind his suddenly lifeless eyes, and that what he had been holding in his hand rolled slowly away, making a little pop and a hiss.

A piece of metal flew up and away from it.

A grenade.

Levy leapt out before it went off.

CHAPTER
· TWENTY-NINE ·

. . . though I be the lone survivor.

The smell. It was the first and last thing Levy remembered as he was wheeled into the hospital from the ambulance. He knew he was in a hospital from the smell and all the white, like he was being smothered in overt cleanliness, dying in sterile, surgical linen; it was the smell of incontinence in a nursing home. Before he passed out again he wondered if somehow it was all over—the killing, the pain, the endless running. Oh, God, he hurt.

He woke up the next day and immediately saw a doctor leaning over him, peering into his eyes with some type of scope.

"How are you feeling, Lieutenant?"
He's actually clean, Levy noticed.
He heard a bustling movement to his right. His parents were there, staring at him, worried. His father, the old colonel, was dressed in an immaculate business suit and holding his mother tightly around

her shoulders, visibly holding her back. Levy wondered why he was out of uniform. And then he remembered an entirely different world, a world of music and home life, a world of military drill and tactics in the infantry officer basic course. A world of parents and girlfriends, of dates and anything but Ranger School and killing and hunger and explosions. A world of peace. How it all clashed so violently with the events of the past three days.

"Like hell," he rasped, realizing he was back at Fort Benning's Martin Army Hospital. "Hi, Mom . . . Dad," he added, looking all round his Spartan-equipped room. It was *too* clean.

Levy glanced at his left arm, which was suspended by a pulley and encased in a plaster cast, bent at the elbow. He tried to take a deep breath and winced in pain. Levy's eyes went out of focus, aware of a nagging itch creeping along the left side of his rib cage and in spots on his left thigh and calf. His arm had a leaden, feverish ache in it, barely numbed by steady doses of Tylenol 3.

The doctor murmured something to his parents. He couldn't make out the words, numbed as he was by the anesthetic. Then, after his mother kissed him gently on his forehead, they left the room, the doctor following suit.

Three hours later he woke up in time for supper, this time feeling better and more alert. Prentiss was there with Jakes, and they were both watching the television with the volume turned down low.

"Hey, he's awake!"

"Fuckin' douchebag, that's all he does is sleep."

That prompted Levy to tell both of them to do perverted things to each other, earning him a hearty laugh.

Jakes chased the nurse down outside in the hallway to tell her Levy had woken up, then came back into the room. Two minutes later the same doctor Levy had seen earlier hustled into the room, flipped through his chart, asked him some questions, and then left.

An attractive brunette wheeled in a serving tray, and Levy was fed Motrin and soup for dinner. He chuckled, seeing Jakes ogle the nurse as she leaned over his bed to adjust the swinging arm platform for his soup bowl.

"Heard you got one hell of a zipper up your rib cage now, wild man," Prentiss said as soon as the nurse left. "Not to mention your arm."

Levy cracked his lips open to speak. They felt as if they had been glued together. "What happened?"

Jakes became serious. "Do you remember anything at all? What happened on that ridgeline between you and Grey?"

It all hit Levy in a rush. The chase. The shootout. Grey crashing through the trees. The spoon flying up and out from the grenade, and himself leaping into the darkness, clawing desperately at the air and then the ground trying to get away from it. *And Christopher. Ah, Christ, Christopher . . .*

Yeah, he remembered all right.

"The FBI told us about it later," Jakes continued. "They're holding our patrol here at Fort Benning until they wrap the entire investigation up. No telling how long that's gonna—"

"When can I leave this place?" Levy interrupted.

"I dunno," Jakes replied. "Doc says you'll be here at least another day or so. Your parents are staying at the Sheraton in Columbus. They should be back here pretty quick."

Levy thought of Christopher again and immediately shoved his bloody, lifeless image from his mind. He jerked his eyes toward Prentiss, who hadn't said much so far. "You missed out on all the fireworks," he said, forcing a smile.

Prentiss grinned and started to say something, but Jakes cut him off, clapping his arm around Prentiss's shoulder.

"Get this, Levy: Prentiss here—my man!—is an A-fucking-number-one hero, even if he did get shot in the ass." Jakes went on to tell Levy of Prentiss's ordeal with Dietrick, and how he had told federal agents of Levy's and the other Rangers' presence in the area just before they raided the camp. The last-minute information had saved the lives of the entire patrol from being indiscriminately fired upon by the FBI's assault force.

As Levy listened to the story, his attention wandered to the television, which was running the evening national news. He saw a burning white cross in the caption window behind the anchorman with a swastika emblazoned in the center.

"Turn it up!"

Jakes frowned, seeing Levy so upset. He turned around and watched the newscast switch from the anchorman with the swastikaed cross in flames to the reporter on the scene, with Camp Merrill's headquarters as a backdrop.

"*Turn up the goddamned TV!*"

Prentiss limped across the room and turned up the volume. "They're doing a story on us!"

". . . culminating in an assault yesterday by dozens of federal agents against their highly fortified compound sequestered along the mountainous Tennessee-Georgia border. According to FBI officials, all members of the fifteen-man assassination team were killed, fanatically holding on to their positions despite overwhelming odds during a two-hour gun battle with federal agents and students of the U.S. Army's Ranger School.

"Actually believing a race revolution was possible, leaders of the 'White People's Party' faction of the Ku Klux Klan headquartered in Dahlonega, Georgia, and a neo-Nazi organization known as the Aryan Covenant of True Christ Christians, headquartered in Helena, Montana, were arrested yesterday on charges of conspiracy to assassinate and murder black politicians and leaders at the Annual Black Leaders' Convention held every year in Atlanta.

"The assassination team was led by renegade Army Sergeant First Class Frank Wilson Grey, who was killed while making his escape. FBI officials report that unknown until the last minute, racists had killed the sergeant in charge of a twelve-man patrol of Army Ranger School students, and had imprisoned them for their future use as hostages, if necessary, after their planned massacre at the National Black Leaders' Convention held annually in Atlanta. After cleverly escaping their captors and upon their own initiative, the Rangers heroically assisted federal agents during the base camp assault by stealing weapons from the extremists' arms room and engaging the racists in open combat. The following gun battle lighted the midnight skies with explosions echoing through the mountains like a summer storm—"

Silas Grey slowly got up from his chair in Vernon Baggins's basement and turned off the TV. He had finally heard the rest of the story. His walk—once spry for an older man—had now lost all its energy. He sat back heavily into the chair. It had all happened too fast, and he was far too old to think clearly about contingencies and alternatives. Things were now up to Taylor, who had hastily departed two days before for his Montana sanctuary. He presumed Taylor had gone underground by now. Maybe someday Taylor could pick up the pieces.

But for now it had all been for nothing. Nothing. His son was dead. And it would only be a matter of time before the authorities tracked him down here at Baggins's house.

He had bristled at the reporter's words—*renegade Army Sergeant First Class Frank Wilson Grey*—and it had been all he could do to keep from shooting the television set with the .44 Magnum revolver *(Daddy, if you think you can handle it, you can keep it, you old coon. Happy sixty-ninth!)* resting on the magazine rack by the side of his easy chair.

He glanced at the weapon. Inside each chamber was a hollow-point. He thought of his wife back home. How could he face her now? How could he face her after causing their only son's death? He knew he needed to be with her now, to try to explain, to try to comfort her. But if he went back home, the Feds would surely apprehend him and take him away to face the slower death of a long trial, public embarrassment, and a terminal stay in prison. He didn't want her to see him that way.

Silas Grey picked up the .44 and awkwardly held it to his temple. The FBI could take care of their business here at Vernon's house.

Along with a body bag.

* * *

Levy had heard enough. The newscast and his friends had brought it all back: the pain, the hallucinations, the killings, the beatings. He dropped his chin to his chest and tried to blot everything out, and an intense pain seared all the way from the back of his head to his frontal lobes like thousands of barbed, poisonous needles.

Jakes, noticing, turned off the television and walked back to the bed. "We'd better get going," he said softly, nodding at Prentiss. "We'll come back tomorrow, Dan."

"Take it easy on yourself, buddy," Prentiss said. He and Jakes started for the door.

Levy jerked his head up. "Don't . . . don't go yet."

Jakes and Prentiss paused, glancing back at their Ranger buddy and seeing the silent tears that streaked down his face.

"Why did Christopher have to die?"

Jakes hung his head. Prentiss remained silent.

"Why did any of this have to happen at all?"

Jakes breathed deeply and replied, "Don't ask me, Dan. I'm only a country boy who likes to dip Copenhagen and raise pigs. I wanted to be a Ranger. To soldier with the best. I still do."

"As far as I'm concerned," Prentiss said, "I *have* soldiered with the best. *You* guys are the best."

"That's all Christopher wanted, Duane," Levy said, looking steadily at his Ranger buddy, who was swallowing and trying to smile at the same time. "He wanted it bad. He used to piss me off, he wanted it so bad. Remember how obnoxious he used to get?" Prentiss nodded his head but could say nothing. Levy looked back at Jakes, who was concentrating very hard on breathing deeply and evenly. "When's the funeral?"

"Tomorrow," Jakes replied, avoiding Levy's gaze. "At the main post chapel. His parents came in late last night. I think they linked up with yours at the Sheraton."

"What time?"

"Dan, you can't—"

"*What fucking time?*"

"The eulogy's at noon."

"Then bring me my class A uniform tomorrow at nine."

"But—"

"That's not a request, Corporal. You just do it."

Sneaking out of the hospital hadn't been easy, and technically, Second Lieutenant Daniel Levy was AWOL. Second Lieutenant Duane Prentiss and Corporal Luke Jakes were equal partners in aiding and abetting in the offense.

Already Levy could feel the stitches pull along his rib cage and leg as he walked stiffly out of the hospital's main entrance. His "zipper," as Jakes had put it. He was thankful for the Motrin. The painkiller had mercifully blocked out anything he might have felt in his arm, which was bound tightly to his chest.

Prentiss and Jakes helped Levy get into the back seat of the cab, whose driver they had bribed to wait outside for the thirty minutes it had taken to get Levy unhooked from the pully, dressed, and out of the hospital. Levy gripped the cast with his right hand and climbed awkwardly into the backseat.

"You sure you want to do this?" Jakes asked him, getting in the car after Levy.

Levy gritted his teeth together, popping out the muscles in his jaw. "Drive-on," he muttered.

Prentiss sat up front with the cabbie. "Main post chapel," he said.

The cab pulled slowly away from the hospital, and ten minutes later they drove up to the steepled, whitewashed Protestant chapel located under green-leafed hardwoods several blocks down from the bachelor officer quarters and surrounding major post command headquarters. The entire area looked like a college campus.

A small crowd had gathered in front, and Levy saw his parents there. They were talking quietly to a middle-aged black couple, the woman dressed in black and the man dressed in Class "A"s like his father, with as many combat tour hash marks on his right sleeve. Also on his sleeve were the chevrons, wreath, and star of a command sergeant-major. Levy knew they were Christopher's parents.

As Jakes helped Levy out of the car, a smaller crowd of soldiers dressed in their Class "A"s surrounded them. It was the rest of their patrol. A hand clasped Jakes's shoulder as he supported Levy's good arm, helping him on their way inside, and he turned and looked into the blue eyes of Juan Keller.

"You were right, you know. Back where they were holding us, handcuffed to the trees."

Jakes looked back at Keller, saying nothing.

"The definition of a nigger," Keller added. "I've done a lot of thinking the past couple of days about that. I'll always remember it. I want you to accept my apology." Keller shifted his eyes, staring at the ground in shame. Then he lifted his head and looked Jakes hard in the eyes. "For everything," he added.

Jakes switched arms with Levy and, after a moment's hesitation, held his right hand out to Keller. "I accepted it the minute you helped me pass out the rifles and ammo the other night," he said. They shook hands and looked at each other for a moment. Then, "C'mon guys," Jakes told the rest of the patrol. "We gotta get this ragbag Levy inside."

"What was that all about?" Levy asked, limping inside the chapel.

"I'll tell you about it some other time," the other Ranger replied, seeing a short, muscular colonel in his sixties approach them. "Looks like your old man wants to have a few words with you. Good morning, sir, please excuse me." Jakes took off to join the others.

"You are AWOL, Daniel."

"Yes, sir."

"Don't 'sir' me. I am your father."

"Dad—"

"The service for your friend is about to start." Eli Levy took his son gently by the arm and led him toward the patrol's pew. "There were many things I could not explain to you growing up, Daniel. Many things." They stopped by the pew. Eli Levy inhaled deeply and held his son's shoulders with both hands. "But now I am the one to have been spared a son's death." Levy saw his father's eyes mist over. "Do not worry about the hospital, Daniel; I will take care of your absence. Join your friends." He helped Levy sit down next to Jakes. Then, after resting his hand briefly on Levy's shoulders, he said, "I am proud of my son." He turned back to rejoin his wife.

As Levy watched the preacher making his way for

his pulpit, he suddenly remembered how once Christopher, while they pulled security on their first patrol together back at Camp Darby, had recited the entire Ranger creed quietly, reverently, saying it as if it were a prayer. He'd found out later on that Christopher's older brother, who had been killed in Vietnam, had taught it to him when he was in the third grade. Christopher had remembered it ever since.

Their pew was directly across from the Christophers'. Levy leaned forward and nodded at them as the minister started the eulogy. All eyes focused on the mahogany coffin up front.

"Let us pray," the ancient black Methodist minister said, and Levy pulled out his Star of David from beneath his collar and prayed with them.

They said the Lord's Prayer. The eulogy came and went. They walked by the coffin, and Levy saw his friend—his Ranger buddy—for the last time.

Then the service was almost over, and soon they would all be driving to the cemetery. The minister made his closing remarks.

"And now, may the power of the Father, the Son, and the Holy Ghost be with you in the name of Jesus Christ—"

"Wait a minute. Please."

Surprised, the congregation turned their attention toward one of the front pews and watched a skinny, bald-headed Ranger student with his arm in a cast and dressed in his Class "A"s struggle to his feet.

Wincing, Levy felt his stitches rip and his lacerations bleed through the gauze wrapped around his rib cage. Shocked into action, Jakes jumped up and helped Levy stand completely upright, keeping a steady hold on his good arm.

"Sergeant-Major, Mrs. Christopher," Dan Levy said, nodding at the couple, "if you don't mind, I'd like to add a few words."

"Go—go right on ahead, son," the sergeant-major stammered.

"As you can see," Levy told the congregation, "we here sitting together in this front pew were members of Sergeant Keith Christopher's patrol at the time of . . . his death.

"I want everyone to know what Keith was like on patrol. He was hardheaded and sometimes belligerent. But he was a *leader*." Levy paused, and his eyes twinkled. Then, "He was a chowhound, too, always trying to bum off the peanut butter out of my C-rations." Levy smiled, and some of the people in the congregation smiled with him. "But when the going got tough," he continued, "Keith kept us all together as a team. He led by example. He forgot about his own pain and put others' needs ahead of his own. He was a *Ranger*—" His voice suddenly broke, and he tried again. "He was a *Ranger*—"

Levy had to stop, feeling a hard lump stick in his throat, knowing his rambling was probably embarrassing the Christophers. The silence grew. He looked around and faced the rest of his patrol in the pew, who nodded back at him, knowing what he was trying to say.

Then he knew exactly what to say.

"I—I want all Rangers in the congregation to say something with me. You all should know it. It's not a prayer, but I know Sergeant Keith Christopher would want someone to say it, because Keith believed in it with all his might. He told me once that his brother taught it to him when he was a little boy.

"He *lived* by it."

Levy saw Jakes looking back at him with a curious expression on his face. Then he swung back around to the congregation and said:

"Recognizing that I volunteered as a Ranger, fully knowing the hazards of my chosen profession, I will always endeavor to uphold the prestige, honor, and esprit de corps of my Ranger Battalion."

Levy's voice was immediately joined by Jakes's and Prentiss's and the others in the patrol as every one of them sprang to their feet and assumed the position of attention, speaking the Ranger Creed.

"Acknowledging the fact that a Ranger is a more elite soldier who arrives at the cutting edge of battle by land, sea, or air, I accept the fact that as a Ranger, my country expects me to move farther, faster, and fight harder than any other soldier."

The voices were one now, as each Ranger spoke with vigor and pride. Glancing to his left, Levy saw Sergeant-Major Christopher's lips move with theirs as he tried to speak through his tears. Levy heard his father's voice boom out from the rear of the congregation as well.

"Never shall I fail my comrades," Levy continued, standing straighter and forgetting the pain in his arm and his side. "I will always keep myself mentally alert, physically strong, and morally straight, and I will shoulder more than my share of the task, whatever it may be. One hundred percent and then some.

"Gallantly will I show the world that I am a specially selected and well-trained soldier. My courtesy to superior officers, my neatness of dress, and care of equipment shall set the example for others to follow."

Levy felt good, feeling that what they were doing was right. Right and true.

He looked up just then at the white cross behind the preacher's pulpit. It was a cross with no flame and with no swastika to defile it. He thought of his good friend and smiled.

"Energetically will I meet the enemies of my country. I shall defeat them on the field of battle, for I am better trained and will fight with all my might. Surrender is not a Ranger word. I will never leave a fallen comrade to fall into the hands of the enemy, and under no circumstances will I ever embarrass my country.

"Readily will I display the intestinal fortitude required to fight on to the Ranger objective and complete the mission—though I be the lone survivor.

"Rangers lead the way!"

GLOSSARY

AN/PVS-4: a telescopic night sight that can be mounted on an M16, M60 machine gun, or any other weapon that has a mount for it. It operates by enhancing passive light shown on the ground by the stars and moon.

AO: area of operations

APL: assistant patrol leader, the second in command of a patrol

ART-1 Scope: a telescopic sight mounted on an M14 rifle for sniping

ASAP (pronounced *ay-sap*): as soon as possible

Azimuth: direction of travel, using map and compass

Beans and baby dicks: the beans and frankfurters C-ration

Blackhawk: current, state-of-the-art Army helicopter

Cammie stick: or camouflage stick; a metal-encased tube holding hardened camouflaged light green/dark green facepaint

Class A uniform: the Army's dress green uniform, on which all awards and decorations are worn

Claymore mine: a plastic-cased lightweight antipersonnel mine, detonated electrically. C-4 explosive blasts steel pellets in a fan pattern toward its front.

Commo shack: also known as the communications room; radios, field telephones, and all communications supplies are stored there.

Contonement area: a site where personnel and equipment can be secured, watched, and controlled

Cs: C-rations (plural)

DMZ: demilitarized zone. In this case, the DMZ is the border between North and South Korea.

Drone: to hallucinate from sleep deprivation; not pay attention

Force recon: an elite Marine unit, specializing in deep reconnaissance

40mm heat rounds: ammunition for the M203 grenade launcher; means high-explosive

Frag: Fragmentation grenade; also a term meaning to kill another soldier in combat, to make it look like the victim was a casualty

Front-leaning rest: the push-up position

Higher: higher headquarters; the element in overall command

Hundred-mile-an-hour tape: olive drab Army duct tape

HRT: hostage rescue team; an elite FBI organization, specially designed for hostage rescue operations

IOBC: infantry officers basic course, headquartered at Fort Benning, Georgia; course is designed to prepare new second lieutenants in basic company-level tactics and combat techniques prior to their initial assignment to a unit. Volunteers for Ranger training are encouraged after completion of this course.

Kalashnikov (AK-47): a Soviet Bloc–produced semi-automatic/automatic assault rifle that fires 7.62 millimeter rounds

Klick: kilometer, or one thousand meters, which is .62 miles

LAW: light, antitank weapon; official nomenclature—M72A2 LAW. A 66-millimeter rocket encased in a disposable firing tube, for usage against armor and bunkers

Meter/Kilometer: one meter is 39.37 inches, a little more than a yard; one hundred meters is approximately the size of a football field. One kilometer is one meter × 1000, or .62 miles. The military, when expressing distance, does so metrically.

Mikes: military phonetic term used for the letter M. Used as slang for minutes

M14: a semiautomatic rifle used by U.S. forces in the sixties. Was replaced by the M16, but is still retained for use as a sniper rifle.

M16: a shoulder-fired assault rifle used by U.S. soldiers, weighs 7.6 pounds, and fires 5.56 millimeter, or .223 caliber, rounds

M203 grenade launcher: a tube-shaped, breech-loading grenade launcher, fastened underneath the forearm grips of an M16. Fires 40 millimeter grenades with a maximum effective firing distance of 400 meters

M60 machine gun: U.S. medium machine gun; fires 7.62 millimeter rounds

NCO: noncommissioned officer, ranging in rank from corporal to command sergeant-major

OBJ: objective

OCS: officers candidate school, headquartered at Fort Benning, Georgia

OD: olive drab

OPORD(ER) (pronounced *op-ord* or *op-order*): operations order

ORP: objective rallying point

Patrol: a detachment of soldiers employed for reconnaissance, security, or combat. Combat patrols include the ambush and the raid.

Patrol base: a hidden, secure position off the patrol's route during which the patrol prepares for the next mission, maintains equipment, conducts personal hygiene, eats, and sleeps

PL: patrol leader. Commander in charge of a patrol

PRC-68 (pronounced *prick-68*): a small two-way radio, used by patrol and squad-sized elements

PRC-77: backpack-mounted FM radio; used for transmitting and receiving messages over long distances

Pre-Ranger: run by Ranger Battalion cadre, this course prepares all assigned personnel due to attend Ranger School in the basic skills necessary for successful completion

Prone: lying down, facing with weapon toward possible enemy contact in assigned sector

PT: physical training, usually in the form of a five-mile run, accompanied by an hour of vigorous calisthenics

Pucker factor: phrase used to describe sphincter-blowing fear

Rabbits: military jargon for targets, or persons to be surveilled or seized during a snatch operation

Ranger: The United States Army Rangers are the finest light airborne infantry known to man. A Ranger is a three-time volunteer; he has volunteered for the Army, airborne training, and Ranger training. Throughout history, and by using guerrilla tactics commonly employed by the American Indian, the American Ranger significantly contributed toward the outcome of our nation's conflicts by his daring, his stamina, and his astounding level of intestinal fortitude.

Ranger eyes: two inch-long strips of luminous tape sewn on the back of a patrol cap, side by side, resembling railroad track sections. They enable a Ranger to see his forward partner more easily during nightime cross-country movements.

Ranger instructor: often referred to as ''RI,'' the Ranger instructor is an officer or noncommissioned officer graduate of Ranger School, who generally has served within the Army's Ranger Regiment. These individuals are instructors and cadre of Ranger School.

Ranger School: The United States Army Ranger

School, headquartered at Fort Benning, Georgia, is the most demanding and realistic tactical leadership course in the Army. During the Korean War, the Department of the Army established an individual Ranger training course at Fort Benning in October 1951. Since then the Ranger Department cadre has turned out young officers and sergeants capable of leading patrols in highly stressful environments and on varying types of terrain. The mechanism for instruction during the sixty-eight-day course is driven by the students' leading combat and reconnaissance patrolling operations during periods of extreme mental, emotional, and physical duress. The patrols are conducted in all types of weather and terrain during four sequential phases of training in the forests surrounding Fort Benning, Georgia, the Blue Ridge Mountains of North Georgia, the desert of Dugway Proving Grounds in Utah, and in the swamps of Florida. Upon graduation from the course, the student is awarded the Coveted Black and Gold Ranger tab—a distinction that few soldiers in the Army possess.

RIP: the Ranger Indoctrination Program is a course taught by Ranger Battalion cadre which is designed to eliminate those personnel lacking the moral, mental, and physical discipline mandatory for those who serve throughout the elite Ranger Regiment.

ROTC: Reserve Officers Training Corps

Ruck: Army-issue nylon rucksack with an external frame; olive drab in color

SAS: the British Special Air Service, an elite commando unit whose specialty is combatting international terrorism

SF: United States Special Forces, aka "Green Berets"; an elite airborne special operations unit specializing in unconventional warfare

SOP: standard operating procedure

TAC (training assistance cadre): the term—the class TAC (pronounced *tack*)—refers to the head Ranger instructor, or "head RI," of the current Ranger class.

TOT: time-on-target

TOC (pronounced *tock*): tactical operations center; where the command, control, and communications headquarters sections of a battalion or larger unit controls their subunits out in the field

VC: Viet Cong

Wait-a-minute vine: slang for thorny vines characteristic of the woods and swamps of the Southeastern United States by their thick, tangled growth on most trees throughout undeveloped land. One inevitably gets caught up in them while on patrol, having to "wait a minute" before moving on while getting untangled.

Web gear: shoulder straps connected to a web belt; used for securing canteens, ammo pouches, first aid kit, and sundries

RANGER HISTORY

Early American colonists discovered that the best way to fight Indians and European invaders was to rid themselves of the European form of maneuver battle and employ tactics the Indians themselves used—guerrilla warfare. In the words of Major Robert Rogers, hero of the French and Indian War (1754–1763), here are two of the nineteen standard orders his outfit knew by heart: Rule No. 18: ''Don't stand up when the enemy's coming against you. Kneel down, lie down, hide behind a tree,'' and Rule No. 19: ''Let the enemy come till he's almost close enough to touch. Then let him have it and jump out and finish him up with your hatchet.''

The group of Rangers Major Rogers led during that war had developed raiding, reconnaissance, and ambush patrols to a degree that have been put to full use by other American Ranger units throughout our history.

Warfare's principles of surprise, objective, and

economy of force have always been put to full use by the American Ranger because he is oftentimes outnumbered and outgunned. But there is more to him than his supply trains will allow. The American Ranger is a tough, dependable individual who can be counted upon to pull through the most harrowing of situations to accomplish his mission. He is indeed the cutting edge of the infantry.

During the Revolutionary War, other Ranger units, led by the famous Francis Marion, the "swamp fox," outfought British units by sneaking in and out of the Carolina swamps. By raiding and ambushing British communications and supply lines, they greatly helped the American struggle for independence. Other Ranger forces included sniping and reconnaissance units, whose stealth and forest savvy aided them greatly in harassing the British throughout the war.

The Civil War saw Ranger units employed by both the Union and the Confederacy, the most famous of which was led by Confederate Colonel John S. Mosby. Operating behind Union lines, Mosby was a master at raiding, always picking on smaller, more isolated Union forces, and then annihilating them through aggressiveness and violence. His intimidation techniques compelled Union forces to deploy vast amounts of material and men to defend all portions of their lines.

American Rangers made their most significant contribution to American history during the Second World War. The 1st, 2nd, 3rd, 4th, and 5th Ranger Battalions fought in North Africa and Europe. The 6th Ranger Battalion operated in the Pacific theater. These volunteer battalions demonstrated the most heroic assaults employed by U.S. forces in history.

The 1st Ranger Battalion was organized and trained at Carrickfergus, Northern Ireland, in 1942 by Major William O. Darby. Darby's Rangers, as they were called, went on to seize footholds in North Africa by executing daring night attacks over austere, hazardous terrain. Darby also trained the 3rd and 4th Ranger Batallions in North Africa at the end of the Tunisian campaign, and they led the Allied assault into Sicily. From there they paved the way for Allied penetration into Italy's boot, fighting at the forefront of such battles as Salerno and Anzio.

During the D-Day invasion into Normandy on June 6, 1944, the 2nd and 5th Ranger Battalions cleared Omaha Beach, enabling Allied forces to break through Axis lines of defense and drive inland for continued operations. It was there that the Rangers adopted their motto: "Rangers lead the way!" Other Ranger units in the Pacific theater, the 6th Ranger Battalion and the 5307th Composite Unit (Provisional), operated in the Philippines and Burma respectively. There, these Rangers fought Japanese forces throughout many months of tough, desperate fighting in jungles, swamps, and mountains, seizing airfields, reconning and raiding deep behind Japanese lines, and disrupting enemy lines of supply and communications.

After a vast demobilization of American forces after World War II, American Rangers were once again called up to fight Communist aggression in Korea. During that conflict over eight handpicked 112-man airborne Ranger companies were formed out of the 82nd Airborne division. The first units to arrive in Korea were the 1st, 2nd, and 4th companies. Upon arrival, these airborne Ranger companies were assigned separately to the various Army divisions already in the fight. Throughout the first year of the war, they were attached to the front-line regiments, where they scouted out enemy weaknesses, raided enemy headquarters, and spearheaded assaults.

In the fall of 1951, these airborne Ranger companies were deactivated. Many veterans who stayed in the Army continued to serve in the 82nd Airborne division and were later the cadre foundation upon which the Army Special Forces were organized and trained. These men went on to fight in Vietnam as advisors to South Vietnamese Ranger companies and battalions as well as performing long-range reconnaissance missions in airborne Ranger companies assigned to division-level units.

It was decided by the Department of the Army in October 1951 to establish an individual Ranger training course at Fort Benning. Since then, the Ranger Department cadre has turned out young officers and sergeants capable of leading patrols in highly stressful environments and in varying types of terrain. The mechanism for instruction during Ranger School is driven by the students' leading combat and reconnaissance patrolling operations during periods of extreme mental, emotional, and physical duress. The patrols are conducted in all types of weather and terrain during four sequential phases of training in the forests surrounding Fort Benning, Georgia, the Blue Ridge Mountains of North Georgia, the desert of Dugway Proving Grounds, and in the swamps of Florida.

In 1974, the 1st and 2nd Ranger Battalions of the 75th Infantry were activated, and they served as the key combat units that spearheaded the Grenada rescue mission in 1983 during Operation "URGENT FURY." Parachuting onto the Point Salinas airfield, the Rangers rescued American medical students at the True Blue campus and then destroyed pockets of enemy resistance throughout the island during the following week of fighting.

As a result of the Ranger battalions' proven competence and professionalism, the Department of the Army increased the size of the American Ranger force into a regiment by establishing a regimental headquarters (the 75th Ranger Regiment) and activating the 3rd Ranger Battalion, stationed at Fort Benning, Georgia.

America now has over 2,100 fighting men serving as Rangers throughout the Ranger Regiment. They are a proud unit, a unit which has a long and colorful history. They employ the toughest standards by which it is necessary to maintain a fighting unit that simply cannot tolerate mediocrity. Every individual Ranger assigned to the regiment is a three-time volunteer: He volunteered to serve in the Army; he volunteered for airborne training; and he volunteered for service in the Ranger Regiment, which necessitates the successful completion of Ranger School. Indeed, Ranger training is the highest form of individual training in the Army today.

The American Ranger is a soldier who knows discipline and courage in the face of hunger, thirst, sleep deprivation, and fear. He can lead others when his leader is gone, or when faced with limited or an absence of guidance. He prevails regardless of the extremes he may face in all kinds of weather and climate. He is a soldier who can drive on when others will give up. He is mentally alert and intellectually a cut above his peers in other, more conventional forces. He can parachute out of an airplane with over a hundred pounds of weapons, ammunition, and equipment strapped to his body, link up with his unit on the ground, and then "hump" that equipment many kilometers across mountains, desert, and swamp en route to his Ranger objective, and then complete the mission, whatever it may be.

The United States Army Ranger is truly the finest light infantry fighting man deployed anywhere in the world today.

RANGER CREED[1]

Recognizing that I volunteered as a Ranger, fully knowing the hazards of my chosen profession, I will always endeavor to uphold the prestige, honor, and "esprit de corps" of my Ranger Battalion.

Acknowledging the fact that a Ranger is a more elite soldier who arrives at the cutting edge of battle by land, sea, or air, I accept the fact that as a Ranger, my country expects me to move farther, faster, and fight harder than any other soldier.

Never shall I fail my comrades. I will always keep myself mentally alert, physically strong, and morally straight, and I will shoulder more than my share of the task, whatever it may be. One hundred percent and then some.

Gallantly will I show the world that I am a spe-

[1]*Ranger Handbook*, ST 21–75–2, Ranger Department, United States Army Infantry School, Fort Benning, Georgia, October 1980.

cially selected and well-trained soldier. My courtesy to superior officers, my neatness of dress, and care of my equipment shall set the example for others to follow.

Energetically will I meet the enemies of my country. I shall defeat them on the field of battle, for I am better trained and will fight with all my might. Surrender is not a Ranger word. I will never leave a fallen comrade to fall into the hands of the enemy, and under no circumstances will I ever embarrass my country.

Readily will I display the intestinal fortitude required to fight on to the Ranger objective and complete the mission, though I be the lone survivor.

RANGERS LEAD THE WAY!